MW00466530

AMONG THE GRAY LORDS

A Tale of Indrajit & Fix

BAEN BOOKS by D.J. BUTLER

TALES OF INDRAJIT AND FIX
In the Palace of Shadow and Joy
Between Princesses and Other Jobs
Among the Gray Lords

THE WITCHY WAR SERIES
Witchy Eye
Witchy Winter
Witchy Kingdom
Serpent Daughter

THE CUNNING MAN SERIES
(with Aaron Michael Ritchey)
The Cunning Man
The Jupiter Knife

Abbott in Darkness

Time Trials
(with R.A. Rothman)

AMONG THE GRAY LORDS

A Tale of Indrajit & Fix

D.J. BUTLER

AMONG THE GRAY LORDS

This is a work of fiction. All the characters and events portrayed in this book are fictional, and any resemblance to real people or incidents is purely coincidental.

A Baen Books Original

Baen Publishing Enterprises
P.O. Box 1403
Riverdale, NY 10471
www.baen.com

ISBN: 978-1-9821-9313-3

Cover art by Kieran Yanner

First printing, January 2024

Distributed by Simon & Schuster
1230 Avenue of the Americas
New York, NY 10020

Library of Congress Cataloging-in-Publication Data

Names: Butler, D. J. (David John), 1973– author.
Title: Among the Gray Lords : a tale of Indrajit & Fix / D.J. Butler.
Identifiers: LCCN 2023040327 (print) | LCCN 2023040328 (ebook) | ISBN 9781982193133 (hardcover) | ISBN 9781625799456 (ebook)
Subjects: LCGFT: Science fiction. | Fantasy fiction. | Novels.
Classification: LCC PS3602.U8667 A86 2024 (print) | LCC PS3602.U8667 (ebook) | DDC 813/.6—dc23/eng/20230920
LC record available at https://lccn.loc.gov/2023040327
LC ebook record available at https://lccn.loc.gov/2023040328

Printed in the United States of America

10 9 8 7 6 5 4 3 2 1

For Eion Osiah and Yuto Harlee.

I wish you well with your Nigerian fortunes,
but I cannot wire you any money.

Instead, I've put you in this book.

Chapter One

"Watch your step," Fix said. "Some of the tiles are loose."

In the darkness, Indrajit's partner Fix, and the sole member of their jobber company who was not a partner, the dog-headed Kyone Munahim, both appeared as inky blotches. The blotch that was Munahim had two black antennae: the hilt of his long sword and the end of his long bow, both of which he carried bracketed to his back. Fix's melodic tenor voice sounded even more feminine when Indrajit couldn't see his stocky, broad-shouldered body.

"I noticed," Indrajit said. The tiles were of baked red clay and the rooftop was four stories above the street. Cool moisture from the sea drifted past on the night breeze. The three members of the jobber company called the Protagonists had come here by climbing an equally tall building two blocks away, endowed with trellises and a climbable exterior. Then they had carefully threaded their way over rooftops, jumping two alleyways. "And I would be very sad to have to sing the epic formulas of my own death by falling."

"You would be dead." Munahim's voice was a baritone rumble. "You wouldn't sing anything."

"Then I would be sad, as a ghost, to hear my successor Recital Thane of the Blaatshi Epic sing of my death."

"You have no successor," Fix said. "That's why you came to Kish in the first place. To look for an apprentice. If you fall, it's the end."

Indrajit ground his teeth. "And you both completely lack poetry in your souls, which is why I am still looking."

"True," Munahim said.

Kish lay spread beneath them, a constellation of torches and oil lamps that stretched uphill and over one city wall into the Crown, the quarter holding the decadent old capital's principal temples, its biggest banks, its greenest parks, the palaces of its great families, and its wealthiest institutions, such as the Hall of Guesses and the Hall of Charters. The Spike, the knob of rock at the peak where the five temples of Kish's ragged mixed pantheon crouched, was brilliant with light. About and below them, the quarter called the Lee spread out in thicker gloom, drifting out to other city walls to the south, east, and west, and beyond them the great flat trading ground called the Caravanserai. Beyond the Caravanserai and unseen lay the Necropolis, once part of an ancient layer of the city, but now home to the mostly silent dead—the dead and those that ate the dead, including Ghouls. The Lee was home to more popular institutions, such as the Racetrack, and families that were well off but not fabulously wealthy, and businesses that didn't need immediate access to the caravan roads or the sea.

Including this building, which was the home of a wholesaler of beans named Eion Osiah. The building vibrated with the sound of the party that rattled within its lower floors; the sounds of drums and flutes wafted up from open windows. Indrajit crouched close to a chimney, its heat warding off the chill of the evening.

"The line is secure," Munahim said.

The Kyone threw the unanchored end of the rope over the edge of the roof. The line made a slithering sound against the tiles as it bounced into place.

"I have the bag," Fix announced. "I'll go first."

He was simply repeating their previously agreed plan, but in the shadows of the rooftop, maybe being explicit was a good idea. Indrajit steadied himself against the chimney and waited. Fix appeared briefly at the edge of the rooftop, rope wrapped around his waist, yellow light from below limning his muscular frame, his chiseled face with its oversized, beak-like nose, and his short, black, bowl-shaped hair, and then he dropped out of sight.

"I could go instead of you," Munahim suggested. "If you prefer."

"You're so very good at being our backup," Indrajit said.

"You tell me that a lot."

"It's your bow," Indrajit said. "You can intervene to protect us in a fight from far away. And, of course, with that big sword, you can also jump into a brawl. I just have my blade, Vacho. And Fix has all his knives and his hatchet and sometimes a spear or a falchion, but even if he were to throw them, he couldn't throw very far."

"He could throw a spear."

"Not as far as you can shoot. And also, you're a natural tracker."

"I have a good sense of smell," Munahim admitted.

"So even if we end up in a chase, or going down under the city or something, you can follow us."

"I can't smell my way down a rope," Munahim said. "Or through a crowded ballroom. For that matter, I can't shoot my bow down through three stories of building."

Indrajit patted Munahim on the shoulder. Like Indrajit himself, Munahim was tall, with long muscles. They were lean and rangy, where Fix was blocky and powerful. "You'll do your best."

"I just want to help the pack." Munahim's voice had a faint whine in it.

"Company," Indrajit suggested. "'Pack' doesn't sound quite right."

Fix's whistle warbled up to the rooftop over a twittering of flutes.

"You're the bosses," Munahim said, surrendering.

"And you're a very fine jobber, and we're lucky to have you in the company. Remember the sign that we need backup?"

"Supposedly it's a whistle," Munahim said. "But my experience suggests that it's more likely to be screaming, yelling, and the clashing of swords."

"Good boy," Indrajit said.

He gripped the rope with both hands, wrapped it around his hips, and lowered himself down the side of the building.

Like many of the fortified homes of the wealthy in the Crown and Lee, Osiah's palace had no windows on the first or the second floor. On its third and fourth stories it had windows and even balconies, but their height off the ground deterred casual breaking and entering. Second-story men had to become third-story men, which required climbing equipment, extra-tall ladders, or descent from the rooftop.

He landed on the balcony beside a bead-filled doorway. The light bleeding through the beads was dim. Fix stood across the doorway from him, already wearing his toga over his kilt and tunic. Since the short Kishi hadn't removed the falchion, ax, or knives from his belt, or the empty bag hanging from his shoulder, he looked bulky around the waist, but the toga-wearing class of Kish tended toward plumpness, anyway. Fix handed Indrajit the second toga and Indrajit wrapped it around himself, over his own tunic and kilt, taking care that his leaf-bladed sword Vacho was thoroughly covered, but accessible.

The togas weren't really disguises. For one thing, even in a city that swarmed with all thousand races of man, Indrajit was distinctive. He was Blaatshi, with a long, bony nose, a subtle crest on his head, and eyes quite far apart. Also, the merchants of the Paper Sook—the market in Kish where companies themselves were bought and sold, along with currencies, commodities, risk, and other, even stranger and more abstract, investments—knew Indrajit and Fix. They were the Protagonists, a small jobber company that worked for Orem Thrush, the Lord Chamberlain. The Lord Chamberlain had the contract for overseeing the Paper Sook, and Indrajit and Fix spent a significant amount of their time investigating crimes among those traders. To the men and women dancing and drinking below, their faces were known, and not necessarily welcome.

But a toga might suggest that Indrajit and Fix had been invited, to other guests and especially to staff. And a merchant who had drunk enough might not notice their faces at all, and just see two more in a sea of togas.

If anyone looked, their worn sandals would give them away.

"She won't be down on the lower floors," Fix said, his voice low. "She'll be kept out of sight."

"She'll be under lock and key," Indrajit whispered. They had both said these things many times before; they were reminding each other.

Tonight, they weren't investigating a crime of risk-merchantry fraud or insider trading, much to Indrajit's relief. They were rescuing a princess.

Well, not really a princess. But a dancer named Sanara Chee, who was favored by the Lord Stargazer, Bolo Bit Sodani. The Lord Stargazer was, like the Lord Chamberlain, one of the seven Lords of Kish, heads of the city's great families, fortunate acceders into the Auction House and its many blessings, and rulers of Kish, at least by day. The Protagonists worked mostly, though not exclusively, for the Lord Chamberlain, and tonight they worked for Sodani. He had hired them because Sanara's clientele tended to be merchants of the Paper Sook. Three days of knocking on many doors and a few heads had led them to an assistant cook of the household of Eion Osiah, who could be bribed into admitting that the dancer in question was a prisoner in his master's house, though he couldn't be bribed into letting Indrajit and Fix into the building.

Indrajit didn't enjoy trying to puzzle his way through the strange language and stranger ideas of the Paper Sook merchants, and he liked feeling like a hero. Fix also had a fondness for rescuing women in difficulty; he was a warrior in unrequited love himself. As a young initiate, a Trivial, of Salish-Bozar the White, he'd fallen in love. He'd left the ashrama to try to win the woman's love, but had lost out to some merchant.

Indrajit pressed an eye to the bead curtain and pulled two strings aside. He saw small beds. "I think this is a nursery."

Fix slipped through the curtain and Indrajit followed. The room was a rectangle three times longer on one side than the other and was full of beds, only three or four cubits in length. Heaps of embers in fireplaces set into the two narrow walls warmed the room, and the bed occupants were covered with wool blankets.

Little red heads peeped out from beneath the coverings. Not red hair, red heads. Eion Osiah was of a race of man called the Haduri, who had skin the color of boiled lobsters and knobby horns on their heads.

"That's a lot of children," Fix murmured. "Maybe Osiah wants Chee because he has a harem."

"I don't know that a harem is much different from having a mistress," Indrajit said.

Fix shrugged.

"I don't care why he wants her," Indrajit said. "I'm here to rescue the princess."

"Yes, and if we have to negotiate to get the princess, it might be helpful to understand why Osiah wants her."

"There's an epithet about the Haduri," Indrajit said.

"What is it?" Fix asked.

"I'm trying to remember," Indrajit said. "It's one of the really obscure ones, in an optional side story."

Fix grunted and passed through the room, into the hallway

beyond. The building was rectangular, and the hallway, lit by oil lamps resting in mirrored niches every few paces, paralleled the outer walls. Indrajit and Fix crept down the carpeted hall, opening doors on the left and right to peer within. Indrajit saw a bedroom, a sitting room, a library, and then a blank stretch of wall before the next door. But that door opened to a bath.

"Fix," he whispered. "Secret room?"

Fix looked where Indrajit pointed him, and agreed there was space unaccounted for. They took a lamp from the hallway into the bathroom and probed the tiles, but found no hidden passages. The music from below echoed loudly in the bath, which made Indrajit feel as if he were being loud, and he caught himself holding his breath twice.

They carried out a similar search in the library. With distaste, Indrajit pulled at books and bookcases and tried manipulating the torch brackets, but they found nothing.

"A secret room could be accessible from below," Indrajit pointed out.

Fix nodded, his hawklike nose enormous and his brown skin ruddy in the lamplight. "But this is the most private floor, so an entrance is most likely to stay hidden up here. Let's not give up yet."

"What about the back, then?"

They followed the hallway around to the other side of the floor, ignoring the doors they passed. At the narrow end of the building, a staircase spiraled down. On the far side, where Indrajit judged they were opposite the blank stretch of wall, a door opened into an office. They let themselves in.

The office wasn't deep enough to reach the opposite hall, and it was also wide enough that surely, if there was a secret room, it had to be adjacent to this one. Indrajit closed the door behind them. The door had both a lock and a bar. Indrajit pointed them out.

"Private office." Fix turned the lock but left the bar alone.

They stood on a square of carpet and looked around. Two reclining couches lay beside a low table at the right end of the room. Two tables heavy with documents dominated the center of the room, and a desk occupied the left. Around the desk stood shelves stacked with scrolls and parchments, and on the back wall, opposite the door, hung a painting. It ran nearly floor to ceiling, and showed a Haduri man and woman, both wearing togas and smiling.

“Eion Osiah.” Indrajit set their lamp on one of the tables.

“And his wife?” Fix suggested. “One of the wives of his harem?”

“I know where I would hide a secret door.” Indrajit stepped forward and grabbed the heavy wooden frame of the painting. For a moment he feared he was pulling it forward and it would fall on top of him, but his intuition proved correct. The frame was hinged along one side, and the entire painting, frame and all, swung outward like a door.

Behind, beyond a narrow entrance, waited the secret room. On the floor lay the dancer Sanara Chee. She was bright yellow, with four eyes set in a rectangular pattern deep into her face, and a long, forked tail. She wore a green garment that was so tattered and torn that Indrajit wasn’t sure what article of clothing it had once been. A shackle on her ankle was attached by a short chain to an anchor in the wall, and two more shackles pinned her hands. A bottle of water stood beside her. A gag ran through her mouth.

Her four eyes all snapped open and she stared at them.

“Frozen hells,” Indrajit muttered.

“We’re here to rescue you,” Fix said softly. “I’m going to remove the gag and we’ll get you out of that shackle, but we need you to keep your voice to a whisper.”

Chee nodded.

“Find the key,” Fix said.

Indrajit searched the desk and its several drawers, finding loose coins, wax seals, an inkpot and quills and a ruling stick, a small pen knife, a wad of gum, and two ledger books, but no key. He checked the desk for secret drawers and found nothing. From the secret room, he heard the soft sobbing of Sanara Chee as Fix removed the gag from her mouth.

Then he heard laughter at the door. A woman’s voice.

“Shh,” a man shushed her.

Indrajit slipped out from behind the desk, gripping Vacho’s hilt inside his toga just to reassure himself that it was there.

A key scraped in the lock.

“Get in here!” Fix hissed.

Indrajit snatched up the lamp and sprang through the entrance into the secret room. He pulled the painting-door shut behind him, feeling it press snugly against the wall just as he heard the creak of the office door’s hinges.

Fix snuffed out the lamp.

"Shh," he whispered. Probably to Indrajit and the dancer both.

They pressed themselves to either side of the painting.

Whoever entered the office carried a lamp, and its light bled through the painting in patches. Indrajit turned to look and could make out Sanara Chee, crouching against the wall with a look of deep uncertainty on her face. Fix leaned toward the painting, cocking an ear toward the office and scowling.

"We must indulge in silent pleasures, my dear," the man's voice murmured. Indrajit recognized it; he and Fix looked at each other and nodded grimly. Eion Osiah. "My wife will not object, but your husband most certainly would, and the drummers can only play so loud."

The unseen woman laughed again. Her voice was musical, her laughter lilting.

Indrajit saw Fix stiffen.

"What is it?" he mouthed, barely vocalizing the words.

Fix said nothing, but his lips were twisted into a snarl.

Indrajit heard the lock being turned again, and then the bar being settled into place.

"Where shall I have my way with you, my tasty one?" Osiah moaned. "The desk? The table? The carpet? But we need not be imaginative, there are the couches."

"Who says I shall not have my way with *you*?" the woman purred.

Fix hurled the painting-door open and leaped through it.

"What?" Indrajit grabbed Vacho and struggled to draw it; the hilt was caught in his toga.

Eion Osiah spun about. He was short and sinewy, with long, pointed teeth, and he wore a vermilion-colored toga with indigo trim. A dagger jumped into his hand and he shoved his companion between himself and Fix.

She was taller than either of the men. She had a coppery red-brown complexion reminiscent of Fix's, and a willowy frame that was graceful rather than voluptuous, but her lips were full and her smile was seductive. She trained that smile on Fix, and then her eyes opened wide.

"Who are you?" Osiah demanded. "Wait . . . I *know* you."

Indrajit had a sinking feeling they'd be running for their lives at any moment. He grabbed Sanara Chee's chain and tried to yank it from the wall. It wouldn't budge.

"I know *you*, you filthy worm," Fix growled. "I know your evil."

"It isn't my *evil*." Osiah was trembling. "It's the way of my race. It's what we do."

"*Womb-hungry Hadur*," Indrajit recited, remembering the obscure epithet. "*From others, always stealing*." He left Chee in the secret room and Vacho in its sheath, but stood behind Fix, ready to act.

"We have to," Osiah said. "The other races of man are always trying to kill us. We have to reproduce in large numbers."

"Perhaps they're always trying to kill you because you act as if all women belong to you." Fix's voice was strained, as if he were trying to swallow a whole tamarind pod while speaking. His body was taut and trembling.

Indrajit had never seen Fix like this. Usually, his partner was calm and mild, until the moment when mayhem was necessary, and then he was brutal and direct.

What was bothering Fix?

"Hello, Fix," the woman said. "Are you disappointed in me?"

"It's not my business," Fix muttered.

"You're *acting* like it's your business." She smiled.

"You know him, Alea?" Osiah demanded.

"We're old friends," she said.

Fix emitted a strangled groan.

"I know you," Osiah said again. "Both of you. You're the Lord Chamberlain's men. The Portolans."

"The Protagonists," Indrajit said.

Alea. Was this the woman Fix had left the ashrama for? The woman who had married another man, and for whom Fix was still trying to make his fortune, so he could impress her? She was beautiful enough, but . . .

Indrajit felt disappointed.

"Alea." Indrajit stepped forward, taking his hand from Vacho's hilt and spreading his arms to show his harmless intentions. "We're not here for you. But we're going to take Sanara Chee with us now."

Alea looked past Indrajit into the secret room. Her face twisted into petulant fury and she turned to slap Osiah.

Osiah plunged the dagger into her belly.

She dropped to the carpet.

With a wordless howl, Fix headbutted the bean merchant. Osiah dropped his dagger and banged against the wall, and then Fix had his ax out of its loop on his belt, and raised overhead, ready to strike.

Chapter Two

"Wait!" Indrajit grabbed Fix by the wrist.

Fix pressed Osiah against the wall of his study with a hand on the red man's throat. Osiah was choking for air and Indrajit struggled mightily to prevent his cracking the bean merchant's head open with his ax.

"What for?" Fix grunted.

"Look to Alea!" Indrajit gasped.

Fix spun instantly, sliding out of Indrajit's grasp. Osiah grabbed for the lock to let himself out, and Indrajit hurled him to the floor and sat on him. Alea lay in a pool of blood and she wasn't breathing. Fix gathered her up in his arms and burst into tears.

Two floors down, stringed instruments joined the drums and flutes in a frenzied Xiba'albi dance.

"You invaded my home!" Osiah groaned.

"Shut up," Indrajit said, "or *I* will kill you."

"Don't leave me here," Sanara Chee pleaded.

"We won't," Indrajit assured her.

Fix stood. "He dies. He's a kidnapper and a rapist and a murderer."

"All true," Indrajit said. "But we need him to unlock the dancer."

Fix dropped to one knee over the bean merchant and raised his ax again. "Where's the key?"

"I don't have it."

"It's inside his belt," Chee said. "It's just one key for all three locks."

Fix ripped Osiah's toga away, revealing short pants and a soft leather belt. He tore the belt roughly from Osiah's body, nearly knocking Indrajit over. Inside the belt, he found several keys on a thin ring. With a moment's trial and error, he unlocked the shackles at the dancer's ankle and wrists.

She promptly kicked Eion Osiah in the head and then spat on him.

"We can't leave him." Fix trembled. Was it with rage? He still held his ax.

"Of course we can." Indrajit stood and dragged Osiah up with him. The red man squirmed, but Indrajit was much stronger, and held his prisoner off the floor, feet dangling. He carried Osiah through the painting-door, knocked him once against the wall to stun him, and then shackled him into place. Osiah resisted, but Indrajit tied the gag into place in his mouth, as well.

Chee spat on Osiah again.

"They'll find him," Fix said.

"Maybe." Indrajit shrugged. "But it won't be until after we're gone. And if they don't find him . . . well, justice is done."

Fix took a deep breath, then nodded.

"We need to take Alea with us," Indrajit said.

"We'll wrap her in our togas."

The blood, fortunately, was all on the carpet. The two men wrapped Alea's body in the toga sheets, knotting them together, and then tossed the bloody carpet into the secret room. The brick floor of the office was unmarked.

Fix set the manacle keys on the floor in the secret room, out of Osiah's reach. He shut the painting-door and Indrajit slung the sheet-wrapped corpse over his shoulder.

"Can you climb?" he asked Chee.

"Show me an open window," she said. "I'll jump."

"I admire your sense of the dramatic," he said. "But we'll help you climb."

They took both lights with them, replacing the one they had taken from the mirrored niche and leaving the other on the balcony by which they exited. The music continued below and the red-headed children all slept soundly.

Indrajit tied the rope around Sanara Chee and called softly. From the rooftop, Munahim hauled on the line and helped the dancer up the wall.

Indrajit nodded through the bead curtain toward the sleeping children. "Who are their mothers, do you think?"

Fix stared into space, his eyes narrow.

"Fix? I said, who do you think are their mothers?"

"We have to help her," Fix said.

"Sanara Chee? We'll take her to Bolo Bit Sodani, she can't get much more help than that, being under the wing of one of the Lords of Kish. And then we get paid, too."

"Alea."

Indrajit took a deep breath. "I don't know quite how to say this, but . . . you aren't her husband, my friend. She chose another man over you, and tonight we caught her cheating on that poor bastard. You owe this woman nothing."

Fix was silent.

"She's dead, in any case. We'll take her to her husband," Indrajit said. "I'm sorry."

Fix said nothing.

What was he thinking?

"Or, if you prefer," Indrajit continued, "we'll bury her ourselves. Buy a nice place in the Necropolis, bury her at sea, funeral pyre, whatever you like."

Fix still said nothing. Munahim tossed the rope back down to them.

"Say something," Indrajit pleaded. "What do you want, a postmortem wedding to her? A shrine? Whatever you want, we'll do it."

Fix handed Indrajit the rope.

Indrajit climbed up to the rooftop. Alea wasn't much burden when he walked, but climbing with her was awkward. He shook his head the entire time, trying to think of things to say to placate Fix. Then he waited in the shadow of the chimney with Munahim and the dancer while Fix climbed up.

Munahim re-coiled the rope.

"Alea was a wonderful woman," Indrajit said.

"We'll take her to be healed." Fix started marching across the rooftop toward their planned escape route, as if there was no more to discuss.

Indrajit followed. Fix didn't go the way they'd come, which

required jumping over two alleyways, but instead to where an adjacent palace was only two stories tall, so they could let themselves down by rope.

"Fix," Indrajit said, as gently as he could. "She's dead."

Munahim and Sanara Chee caught up. Munahim tied the rope to a chimney and let down the end. Fix went down first, and then the dancer.

"He's not listening to me," Indrajit said to Munahim.

The Kyone shrugged. "Neither one of you listens to *me*."

"That's an exaggeration."

"Not much of one."

Indrajit slid down the rope and rushed across the lower rooftop to catch up to his partner. This roof was peaked, so he had to place his feet carefully on the stone ledge above the lead gutter at the edge. When he caught Fix, Fix was tying a second rope—which they'd climbed up and left the night before—around a gargoyle.

"Okay," Indrajit said. "We'll take her to be healed. Where do you suggest, the Hall of Guesses?"

"The Vin Dalu."

"The Vin Dalu?" Indrajit's voice squeaked, and he cleared his throat. "What makes you think the Vin Dalu can . . . heal her?"

"The Vin Dalu healed me when I was a boy," Fix said. "My spine wasn't straight. It was so crooked, I could barely walk. The Selfless of Salish-Bozar brought me to the Vin Dalu, because the Vin Dalu are known to be masters of Druvash technology."

"The priests of the Dismembered One use Druvash sorcery to torture and maim," Indrajit said. "I'm glad they were also able to heal you when you were a boy, well done, your back is nice and straight now and you walk like a champion, but—"

"You don't have to come," Fix said.

"—they have an orphanage of young boys they torture and maim for their entertainment," Indrajit continued.

Fix took the rope in his hands and wrapped it around his hips. "Take the dancer to the Lord Stargazer. Then go back to the inn and sleep. I'll take Alea to the priests."

Fix went down the rope.

"Frozen hells!" Indrajit stamped his foot, nearly sending himself tumbling off the roof in his irritation. "What is he thinking?"

Munahim hesitated. “Shall I go next?”

Indrajit growled and slid down.

On the street below, two Rovers sat at a fire next to their wagon. A lavender-skinned Zalapting guard with a boiled leather helmet and breastplate leaned beside a door, dozing beneath a single torch. Fix paced back and forth.

“Fix,” Indrajit said. “Help me understand.”

Fix’s voice was strained. “In your precious Blaatshi Epic, is no one raised from the dead? Are there no miraculous healings?”

“Yes, of course,” Indrajit said. “Both things happen. But Alea is another—”

Fix pushed closer. “Miracles? Deeds of the gods?”

“Of course. Do you now believe—”

Closer. “And are there no extraordinary deeds for love?”

“The Epic abounds with extraordinary deeds undertaken for the sake of love. But—”

“But you would deny all these things to me?” Fix’s voice shook and so did his hands. “Then give me Alea, and I will go live my own epic.”

“But the Vin Dalu?” Indrajit asked weakly.

“You have been to the Hall of Guesses,” Fix said. “You have been entwined in the machinations of the Collegium Arcanum. Do you think the scholars of Kish can raise the dead? Do you believe that the wizards of the city have that power, or could be persuaded to exercise it if they did?”

Indrajit felt small. He was a head taller than his partner, but with Fix pushing into his chest and trembling with emotion, he felt he was looking up at Fix rather than the reverse.

“We’ll go to the Vin Dalu,” he agreed. “The Vin Dalu healed you as a boy. If anyone can heal Alea now, it’s the priests of the Dismembered One.”

“I want to carry her,” Fix said.

Indrajit handed over the body in its knotted sling. “We probably want to avoid getting stopped by the constables.”

Fix grunted. “Time may be of the essence. I’m going now.”

Sanara Chee alighted gracefully. Munahim was only a few moments behind. Across the street, the Rovers watched over their mugs of hot tea, so Indrajit kept his voice down.

"Munahim," he said. "You need to get Sanara food and water."

"I've given her food and water already," Munahim said. "I brought dried meat, biscuits, and a water bottle with me."

"Oh. Good." Indrajit cleared his throat. "Never mind. Let's deliver Sanara Chee to the Lord Stargazer. It's on the way."

"On the way to where?" Munahim asked, but Fix was already stomping resolutely up toward the Crown.

Indrajit caught up to his partner. "Gannon's Handlers have the gate contract into the Crown."

"They won't try to stop us. And they can make all the nasty faces they want, I don't care."

"I was going to suggest, let's emphasize that we're on the Lord Chamberlain's business. They know we work for Thrush."

"I'll kill them if they try anything."

This was not a side of his partner that Indrajit had ever seen. Fix was intense, but he was quietly intense.

"Noted. But let's try the persuasion first."

Indrajit struggled with clashing emotions as they walked. They had rescued the dancer, and he felt pride and delight in the accomplishment. On the other hand, he felt unbalanced and afraid at the urgency with which Fix now took every step and enunciated every word. And meeting Alea had been an unexpected and violent revelation. He and Fix had been partners for several months now. From the beginning, he had known that Fix was in love with a married woman, a woman who had turned him away from life as a Selfless, one of the scholar-priests of Salish-Bozar the White, and driven him to become a speculator, a businessman, and a rogue. In the space of a few heartbeats, Indrajit had met the woman, learned her name, and witnessed her violent death.

He felt uneasy, directionless, and nervous.

The half dozen Zalaptings and the powder priest of Thûl guarding the gate wore Mote Gannon's livery. "What's in the bloody sheets, Fix?" one of the Zalaptings asked. "Out of work, and reduced to eating offal again?"

"Kidnapping children is more like it!" A second Zalapting snickered.

"It's a bloody corpse!" Indrajit snapped. "It belongs to the Lord Chamberlain's Ears. Stand aside."

The Handlers and the Protagonists had clashed in the past, which had resulted in Handler casualties and an enforced truce. The Handlers stood aside.

"I'm reporting this!" the Zalapting snapped.

"We need to develop some reliable ways around the walls," Indrajit said. "Or through or under, I suppose." They had been into Underkish more than once; it had never really been convenient, and had often been violent.

Fix kept marching.

They took Sanara Chee to the Lord Stargazer's palace. It was an ordinary palace, not much bigger than the one belonging to Eion Osiah, but it fronted on two avenues in the Crown. These streets were lit with lamps, and were patrolled by armed men with torches—jobber companies that marched the lengths of the boulevards and wider streets under a constabulary contract, and fighters in the livery of the Lord Stargazer himself, who stood at the doors and the corners of the building.

"Ubandar Hakko," Indrajit said to the two men wrapped in bands of steel standing to each side of the palace's front door.

Fix growled, an impatient sound.

They knocked and whispered, and Hakko came forth.

Ubandar was the night steward of the Lord Stargazer's palace, and he'd had dealings with the Protagonists before. He was a pudgy man, dark red in color, with four long tusks in his mouth, and he appeared already in the act of bowing.

He moved more slowly than Indrajit was used to seeing, though. His limbs were thin and fleshless and his belly sagged. Had the man taken ill?

"Sanara Chee," he said, his voice a greasy smear on the air, "you don't know me, but I've been expecting you. Come in, come in, the Lord Stargazer is anxious for your welfare. I have a room and a bath and clothing and food and spiced wine."

Fix was already marching away. Indrajit accepted half a hug from the four-eyed, yellow-skinned dancer, and a purse from the lethargic night steward, and then he was racing to catch up, Munahim in his wake.

Was this a madman's quest they were on? Could the Vin Dalu raise the dead?

Did it matter?

"Why did you stop me from killing Eion Osiah?" Fix growled when Indrajit caught up. They were headed to a gate on the east side of the Crown, which led down into the Dregs. "He deserved it."

"He deserved it," Indrajit said. "And maybe he'll die in his secret little room, if they can't find him. But you don't deserve to have his blood on your hands."

"I want his blood on my hands."

"You want justice," Indrajit said. "You don't want to have killed someone in anger, in the moment. That's not the same thing at all. That would have been a *justifiable* reaction, but that's not the same thing as justice."

"This is a nuance I care very little about right now."

"I understand that." Indrajit shook his head. "But I think it's a nuance you would come to care a lot about, in time."

The gate into the Dregs was also guarded by Handlers—more Zalaptings, and a big blue Luzzazza with downturned ears. Indrajit looked closely, to try to determine whether this was the Luzzazza whose arm he had torn off, but he couldn't tell; a Luzzazza's lower pair of arms was invisible. That was their race's great magical talent.

The Luzzazza noticed him looking. "I am no longer on the path," he rumbled.

Had Indrajit knocked the man off his spiritual quest? "I'm sorry."

"For what?"

Indrajit had more questions, but Fix was already charging down the ramp into the Dregs. Indrajit gripped Vacho by the hilt and jogged to catch up.

Several quarters of Kish claimed to be the worst, as a badge of pride; the Dregs was the quarter where you could most easily get your throat slit. At the foot of the ramp, alleys spun away in every direction, flanked and crowded by leaning, ramshackle buildings. The streets were of earth, packed hard by feet and cold, and a whine of beggars immediately swarmed the Protagonists. Even the beggars seemed to threaten, their claws slashing at the air.

"I have never been to the temple of the Dismembered One," Munahim said. "Do we need to offer a sacrifice?"

"I don't think the Vin Dalu offer sacrifices like that," Indrajit said. "I think they torture certain classes of criminals for the city, and that's a kind of sacrifice. And they use the same skills to dissect corpses for the Hall of Guesses, and maybe that's a kind of sacrifice. Anyway, that's what I've heard. I have no personal experience."

"Maybe they can also heal, and that will be a kind of sacrifice," Munahim suggested.

"That would be the best outcome."

"What would be the second best?"

"That they don't allow us in at all."

Munahim considered. "And after that?"

"After that, my Kyone friend, all the possible outcomes are frightening."

Fix led them down three alleys, each at a dramatically different angle from the preceding ones, so that they zigged and zagged through the Dregs. At every junction, men snarled and showed the hilts of rusted swords or gaps in sharpened teeth. A pack of stray cats followed them, hissing and yowling. The Dregs seemed bigger to Indrajit than he had thought possible, and then the last alley opened into a courtyard. On two sagging poles jammed into a corner dozed a row of Kishi fowl, thin, scarred, and mean, chuckling in their sleep. Overhead, Indrajit thought he saw narrow windows looking down on the yard.

Were those cats in the windows?

And ahead, sitting cross-legged on the ground in front of a blank wall, was a figure in a black robe. The person leaned forward, so that its face was hidden within a deep cowl. Long hands emerged from the sleeves of its robe, and in the shadow, Indrajit thought perhaps he saw intertwining fingers. Two gnarled crutches leaned against the wall behind him.

Fix stood, swaying on his feet. Slung over his shoulder, the burden of Alea's body was enormous. Indrajit and Munahim hung back a step.

"I've come to ask a boon," Fix said. "A healing."

"The Dismembered One does not give boons." The voice coming from within the cowl was surprisingly youthful, and definitely male. Indrajit couldn't place the accent, but it wasn't Kishi. "Perhaps you intend to consult Saint Aileric. Or Sharazat the Kind, if death is the boon you seek."

"The boon I seek is life." Fix's voice was almost a shriek.

"You are alive. Go forth and live more, as long as you may."

"For her." Fix knelt and laid his burden gently on the ground.

The robed figure was silent for a few moments. When he spoke, his voice was gentle. "The Dismembered One does not give boons, O son of Kish. The Dismembered One gives, but also takes. All who have approached the Dismembered One come away dismembered themselves."

"The Dismembered One healed me when I was a child," Fix said. "By means of Druvash craft, I understood."

"I believe it."

"And yet I am not dismembered."

"That you know," the robed man said.

"You're warning me, but you're not refusing."

"I am not refusing."

"Then I would enter, guardian. And I would ask that the Dismembered One inflict upon me any cost he would impose."

"You may ask." The robed man stood. "And your friends?"

Fix turned. His hair was disheveled and blood stained his kilt. "You should stay here. I don't know what waits for me inside."

"I'm coming in," Indrajit said.

"It might be more dangerous out here," Munahim added.

Chapter Three

The robed man took the two crutches and hoisted himself to his feet. Then he hobbled into the wall. Indrajit scratched his head and Munahim emitted a low whine. Fix stepped forward and followed the man in robes.

"You don't want to keep being the backup," Indrajit said. "You're next."

Munahim sniffed at the wall and then walked through it. Finally, taking a deep breath, Indrajit pushed himself at the wall—

And passed right through. He stopped for a moment to look at the passage. What had appeared to be a wall was a taut piece of fabric, light and silky. It was solid black, but when Indrajit held his hand up against it on the outside, light projected across the back of his knuckles. Was the appearance of the wall only a projection, then, on a curtain?

He'd seen such illusions before. From magicians.

He shuddered.

He rushed to catch up, joining Munahim on the heels of Fix and the robed man. The robed man moved speedily, despite his crutches. They descended an alleyway between two brick walls: dim light came from bluish spheres set into the right-hand wall every ten paces, but above, Indrajit thought he saw stars. They ignored several turns. Warm, fetid air rose from one; another emitted a cool and steady breeze; from the third, Indrajit thought he heard the sound of running water.

"Are you of the Vin Dalu?" Fix asked.

"That is an excellent way to identify me."

"Vin Dalu . . . Rao?"

"If you please."

Indrajit wanted to argue that either the man was the Vin Dalu Rao or he wasn't, but he wasn't about to ruin Fix's chances of getting what he wanted, so he bit his tongue. They descended a stairway into darker gloom and the stars overhead disappeared.

"I don't know about the Dismembered One," Munahim said. "I come from the steppes, and we aren't familiar with this god. Is he one of the gods of the city?"

"The city has no gods of its own," the Vin Dalu said. "Black Reyiku has been here the longest, but even he, they say, was once a man. An emperor who gave so much justice in life that he couldn't stop, and continued to guarantee justice in death. Spilkar the Binder is a god of western merchants. Machak the Sea King is a sea god of the south, from Boné and Malik and Hith. Hort was also a sea god, but a sea god of the north, and when the two sea gods clashed, Hort became the Storm Rider. There's a little science parable there, if you will, on evaporation and on air pressure."

"I see," Indrajit said, though the man spoke nonsense.

"And Yispillilu?" Fix asked.

"Also once two gods," the Vin Dalu said. "Yespa and Lilu. A god of heralds and a god of librarians. But when they met, neither evaporated, and they became instead a single god of seers and lore. And the others: the Lady of the New Moon, Sharazat the Kind, Tlacepetl the Guide, they all come from somewhere else."

"I have never heard this manner of discourse about the gods," Munahim said. He seemed thoughtful. "Where does the Dismembered One come from, then?"

"Does he come from somewhere," the Vin Dalu countered, "or is he just here?"

"You're saying he is a native god of this place," Indrajit said. "Indigenous."

"Aboriginal," Fix added. "Autochthonous."

"I see why you're the bosses," Munahim muttered. "I don't know what you're talking about."

The stairs ended in a heavy wooden door under an arch. Here light came from a pipe that jutted from the wall beside the door and spit a constant blue flame. The Vin Dalu raised a brass knocker and clanged it solemnly against its plate, three times. "Is he the god of the place, or is he the place of the god?"

"What?" The word burped out of Indrajit without his intending it.

"Is he a dismembered . . . place?" Munahim was struggling.

"Or is he the dismemberer?"

"You remind me, Vin Dalu, that there were many reasons why I chose not to pursue life as a priest," Fix said. "But I will endure very large quantities of god-talk and obfuscation if that is the price I pay for you to heal Alea."

"You may address me . . . any of us . . . as Dalu. And no, that will not be the price."

The door swung open inward. A second person in a black robe pulled, though the work seemed effortless. Behind the door, the floor was an iron grill, the walls stone slabs, and green light shone up from beneath the floor.

Indrajit followed the others inside, and then the second robed person shut the door. Both men in robes lowered their hoods. Munahim gasped.

They had the same faces.

Or very nearly. They looked as similar as twins might look, but one appeared twenty years older. They might have been a father and his spitting-image son, except that the elder had gnarled limbs and digits, and the younger didn't.

"Dalu," the younger man said.

"Dalu," the elder replied.

"You're a family," Indrajit said.

"If you please," the younger man said.

"What pleases me," Fix said, "I beg you, is that you heal this woman."

The Vin Dalu gestured at an open archway. "Please. This is the domain of the Vin Dalu Nikhi."

Fix went first and the other Protagonists followed. Beyond lay a series of chambers and hallways, and Indrajit quickly lost track of the turns. He found himself standing in a room with steel walls studded with the handles of many cabinets and drawers. Bright white light blazed from tubes that ran along the tops of all four walls. In the center of the room was a flat white table, and above the table, a mirror on a jointed arm loomed, reflecting the white of the table back at itself.

"Please lay the woman on the table," the younger of the Vin Dalu said. "Let us examine her."

Fix stepped forward to hoist Alea's corpse, and staggered at the effort. Munahim and Indrajit helped, and when they had laid the woman's body out and cut away the sheet, Indrajit looked at his partner. He'd never seen Fix look so frail and so beaten. The enormous muscles across the man's shoulders and chest looked like weights dragging him down.

"Will the Vin Dalu Nikhi be joining us, then?" Indrajit asked.

The elder of the Vin Dalu smiled. He leaned his crutches against the wall and walked smoothly around the table, as if he had never needed the crutches at all, despite his twisted bones. "Perhaps he is already here." The two Vin Dalu closed over Alea's body and began probing it, at first with their fingers, and then with instruments they extracted from drawers in the walls.

Fix rested a hand on Indrajit's arm. "Don't get upset at the way they talk in circles. Just think of the great delight you will have in composing epic epithets for the Vin Dalu, when you describe this episode."

"I have to understand something before I can capture it in an epithet," Indrajit grumbled.

"Strange," Fix said. "I didn't think poetry suffered from that limitation."

As the Vin Dalu worked, they dragged the mirror in one direction and then the other, using it to examine Alea. At the touch of a control, the perimeter of the mirror began to glow. The mirror seemed to aggregate and direct the light, so that it cast an illuminated beam wherever it was pointed. Subtle controls touched in the sides of the table caused it to rise, sink, lean to one side, and glow. The Vin Dalu poured a caulk-like substance into the open wound in Alea's belly and then placed a patch over the slash. They dripped two different liquids between her lips and then turned to cabinets in the wall. The older of the two took two glowing green rods from one cabinet and laid them on the table alongside Alea, tucked one on each side between her arm and her flank. The younger of the Vin Dalu dragged a thick blanket made of a dull material that looked more like plaster than like fabric, and covered Alea with it entirely.

More magicianlike procedures.

Indrajit could like and let live with a wide range of men, but wizards made him uncomfortable.

"It's grown cold in this room," Munahim said.

It had, though Indrajit had been too fixed on the operations of the Vin Dalu to notice it.

"Come," the elder of the Vin Dalu said. He took his crutches again and led them from the room by a different door. As if a motivating spirit had left him, his motions again became awkward and ragged.

They entered a room with soft chairs and oil lamps. Had they come far enough that they were no longer underneath the Dregs? Indrajit had lost all sense of time and direction, and half imagined that he could open a window in this room and look directly out onto the Serpent Sea.

"Please," Fix said.

The elder of the two Vin Dalu sat and gestured at other empty seats. The younger of the Vin Dalu exited by another door.

Indrajit sat. "The Vin Dalu Nikhi?"

"We have done our part," the Vin Dalu said. "Wait, now, for the Vin Dalu Diesa."

"Do not ask the magician any more god-talk questions," Munahim said. "My people killed their gods, and I do not have a head for this."

"Are you magicians?" Indrajit asked. "Or are you priests?"

"We are keepers of an ancient lore," the Vin Dalu said. "It warps and wrecks us as it gives us power. We serve, and we propagate ourselves."

"When I was a boy," Fix said, "I was a Trivial of Salish-Bozar the White. I was brought here by the Selfless, and I was healed. The Selfless told me that the healing was performed by Druvash craft."

"You told me this before," the Vin Dalu said. "I believe all of it."

"Can you heal my love?" Fix's voice sounded raw.

"We've done the work of the Vin Dalu Nikhi for now," the Vin Dalu said. "The work of the Vin Dalu Diesa is about to commence."

"I could have stayed outside," Munahim said glumly.

"No, this is the clearest thing he's said yet," Indrajit said. "Nikhi and Diesa and . . . what's the other one, Rao? They're not men. They're roles."

"Functions." Fix seemed to come alive as his mind engaged. "Nikhi is the healer."

"Wait . . . the Vin Dalu Diesa isn't the torturer, is it?" Indrajit put his hand on Vacho's hilt, and then immediately regretted it.

The Vin Dalu smiled.

The younger of the Vin Dalu returned, and he brought a third man with him. The newcomer walked with slow, laborious steps, leaning forward heavily onto two crutches. One of his legs moved with a shuffling, dragging noise across the floor, and the other stamped with a wooden clack. His breathing was a thick, sawlike rasp. He was draped in a black cowled robe, and when he finally dropped himself into a chair, the cowl fell back to reveal a third iteration of the same face, only this one older still by a generation, scarred and mottled as if by burns, with one eye the color of milk.

"Dalu," Indrajit said. Fix and Munahim hastened to copy him.

The youngest of the three men in robes set about producing a pitcher of wine and cups, serving it first to his colleagues and then to the Protagonists.

"I am the Vin Dalu Diesa," the old man said. "You are unusual petitioners."

Indrajit didn't like the sound of that. "We're just a humble jobber company. Humble and poor."

"Perhaps." The oldest of the Vin Dalu chuckled. "But you are unafraid. Many are deterred from seeking us out, because we are in the Dregs, because we are hidden, because of the things we are said to do. And you are also curious. You ask questions and you think. That is more unusual behavior than you might imagine."

Indrajit shrugged.

"A Blaatshi poet," the old man said. "A dissatisfied Kyone."

"I'm not dissatisfied," Munahim said.

"And a man in love." The old man smiled. "If the situation were a little different, we would be inclined to heal this Alea and ask nothing in return. We favor selflessness. We understand commitment, you see, as well as tradition."

"I will pay what you ask," Fix said.

"It is not a matter of paying," the Vin Dalu Diesa said. "She is dead."

Silence. Indrajit rested a hand on Fix's shoulder. The shorter man was trembling.

"But your brothers treated her, Dalu," Munahim said.

"It is possible she may rise again." The Vin Dalu Diesa nodded. Even his nod was irregular, an off-centered lunge like the peck of a one-legged chicken. "My brothers have taken steps to preserve her as she is now so that we may raise her."

"Will she be crippled?" Fix asked. "Halt, as you are halt? Is it the Druvash craft that does that to your bodies?"

The Vin Dalu Diesa chuckled. "Are *you* crippled? Were you burned and disfigured as a boy, when your back was straightened?"

Fix put his face in his hands. He was shuddering. "I beg your forgiveness, Dalu. I thought perhaps—"

"You inferred that it is contact with our Druvash devices that scars us over our lifetimes of service," the Vin Dalu said. "Your inference is correct. And we cannot say what permanent marks your Alea may bear on her body after being raised. She may be scarred, or twisted, or burned, or bald, or discolored, or blinded, as I am. If so, these would be the prices the Dismembered One demanded."

"You ask whether I think *she* would pay the price," Fix said.

"No," the Vin Dalu said. "But it is a good question, and since *you* are asking it, what do you think the answer is?"

"I don't know." Fix paused. "I believe that Alea relished power over men. Perhaps she would mourn if she bore marks that reduced her power. Likely, she would be sad."

"Would it be more kind, then, to let her die?" the Vin Dalu asked.

Fix considered for a long time. "I don't know for certain. I think she would want to live. But I know something about myself. My friend saved me tonight from being the man who would kill in anger, and he did right. But I must be more than the man who wouldn't kill in anger—I must be the man who would sacrifice for love. So tell me what the price of your work is, and raise her. And if her beauty is marred by her return to life, and she loses her power over other men, then I can offer her this small consolation: she still has power over me, and she always will."

"My friend," Indrajit murmured, "I may be the poet, but you are the poem."

"You have answered your own question to my satisfaction," the Vin Dalu Diesa said. "But there remains a potent obstacle."

"We specialize in overcoming obstacles," Indrajit said.

"As I said, unusual petitioners." The Vin Dalu Diesa took a long and noisy slurp of his wine. The youngest of the three Vin Dalu sat now, the three magicians or priests or craftsmen side by side on a wide seat. "We know how to raise the dead, when the dead are recently passed and the body is whole. The Vin Dalu Nikhi have treated Alea's wounds and prepared her body so that it may receive this gift of the Dismembered One. But the . . . shall we say 'spell' . . . ? 'Prayer'?"

"Procedure, if you prefer," Fix said.

"*Most* unusual petitioners. The procedure is performed using a number of devices which we have in our possession, and one which we do not."

"Druvash devices," Fix said.

"We are not passive custodians of ancient lore," the Vin Dalu Diesa said. "We are slowly recovering lost technologies . . . crafts and procedures, as you say. And we offer our services to the great families and others to provide for ourselves protection, a space to breathe in as our brotherhood carries out its centuries-old task. We pore over old documents. We descend into the deep to find devices and manuals. We lean on the work of the Hall of Guesses—blindly though they fumble, arrogantly though they award themselves prizes for their terrible ignorance, yet sometimes those scholars open doors. Even the navel-gazers of Salish-Bozar from time to time generate key hints for our work. We learn to repair and operate what we discover, and to build that which we find only described. And our work is not complete. Indeed, it is only just beginning."

"What's the one device you require, Dalu?" Fix leaned forward on the edge of his seat, fists clenched.

"A girdle," the middle-aged of the three Vin Dalu said. "This girdle."

He handed over a sheet of paper. On it was drawn a picture of a woman. She might have been Kishi or Ildarian; her frame was neither noticeably stocky nor especially slender, and the picture was drawn in black ink. She was naked, but such details as belly button, nipples, and nails were omitted. She was, on the whole, a very sexless woman.

Characters were inked around the margins of the page, and lines connected chunks of text with parts of the woman's body, and parts of the girdle she wore.

Properly speaking, it was more of a vest. It consisted of rectangular pads connected by straps, the straps buckling around the woman's belly and waist and thighs. Strings emerged from various points of the girdle and seemed to attach to the woman's skin by means of coin-sized disks.

"Fortunately," Indrajit said, "Fix can read."

"I don't know this language," Fix said immediately.

"We can only decipher it partly ourselves," the Vin Dalu Diesa said. "The script is ancient. We give you this unblemished copy because completeness and perfect transmission are a key part of our ethic."

"What is the girdle's name?" Indrajit asked.

The middle-aged Vin Dalu rubbed his hands together. "In the manual from which we extracted this image, the girdle has a technical name. But in certain old tales told in Kish, it is referred to as the Girdle of Life."

"If we bring you the Girdle of Life, you will raise Alea," Fix said. "With no other price to pay?"

"We will raise her," the Vin Dalu Diesa said. "And we will charge you no price. We can guarantee nothing about her state when she is raised."

"Easy enough," Indrajit said, feeling that nothing about finding the Girdle of Life was going to be easy.

"You must bring us the Girdle within three days," the middle-aged Vin Dalu said. "This is not an ultimatum we impose, you understand. We do not work to deadlines of days, but to timelines of centuries and millennia. It is a limitation of our craft. In three days, Alea's body will be too far decomposed for us to raise her."

"Tell us where to find the Girdle," Fix said.

"Or where to pick up the trail," Munahim added.

"Please tell me it's not at the House of Guesses," Indrajit added. "Those guys are so tedious."

"We almost had it in our possession a few weeks ago," the Vin Dalu Diesa said. "A man claimed to have it, having recovered it from a chamber far beneath the city. An explorer of Underkish, he styled himself, and one of its lords. He offered to sell the device to us, but we could not meet his price, so he kept it."

"Perfect," Fix said. "Name the man."

"Arash Sehama," the Vin Dalu Diesa said. "The Gray Lord."

Chapter Four

"I don't understand why this is so distressing," Munahim said.

The Vin Dalu had hooded the three of them, led them through a long series of turns and steps, including stairs both up and down, and finally removed their hoods to reveal that they were in the Spill. In the Spill, a few steps from the Crooked Mile, and only a few more steps than that from the nameless inn where the three lived.

"Because the Gray Lords in general are not people to be trifled with," Indrajit explained.

"But we work for one of the Gray Lords," Munahim said. "Orem Thrush, the Lord Chamberlain. That makes *us* people not to be trifled with, doesn't it?"

Fix leaned against the stucco wall of a chandler's shop, bracing himself with both hands. In the shadows around them, Indrajit heard the slithering and tapping sounds of a small crowd of beggars, warily circling.

"Orem Thrush is a powerful man," Indrajit agreed. "But he's one of the Lords of Kish, head of one of the seven great families."

"Yes," Munahim said.

"I forget how new you are to the city," Indrajit said. "The Gray Lords are an entirely different group of men."

"Also said to be seven in number," Fix said. The muscles in his back were knotted as if he were trying to push the chandlery he leaned against to the ground.

"Perhaps coincidence," Indrajit said. "Perhaps deliberate mirroring of the city's official power structure. For legend-making purposes. Swagger."

"Propaganda," Fix added.

"The Lords of Kish bid for contracts in the Auction House, and then they carry out the contracts, administering the government of the city." Munahim said the words deliberately, as if the concepts were still somewhat abstract for him, despite the fact that he made a living fulfilling those very contracts for the Lord Chamberlain. "What do the Gray Lords do?"

"They carry out other contracts," Indrajit said. "Not the kind of contracts you win by bidding at the Auction House."

"Though it's said that they are sometimes hired by the Lords." Fix shook his head. "Welcome to Kish."

"Robbery," Indrajit said. "Extortion. Bribery. Arson. Kidnapping. Protection rackets. Risk-merchantry fraud."

"They are a thieves' guild." Munahim nodded. Constables marched past in thick leather armor, rapping the cobblestones of the Crooked Mile with the butts of their spears, and the beggars faded into an alley. "Ildarion has a thieves' guild."

"They are seven thieves' guilds," Indrajit said. "The seven Gray Houses. They divide the city among themselves, by quarter but also by industry. Arash Sehama is . . . a name we've heard before."

"He's the Gray Lord who rules the northern half of the Spill." Fix turned. Stray lamplight from a nearby tavern illuminated his face, which was taut. His mouth was flat, his eyebrows furrowed. "Including the Paper Sook."

"We police the Paper Sook on behalf of the Lord Chamberlain," Munahim murmured.

"'Police' is a strong word," Indrajit said. "But it's not wrong."

"So this is fortuitous," Munahim pointed out. "He must know who we are."

"On the other hand," Fix said, "I have a terrible uneasy feeling."

"Why is that?" the Kyone asked.

"*Because* he must know who we are." Fix marched off down the Crooked Mile, toward the Paper Sook.

Indrajit followed. Munahim shook off two beggars with rags for clothing and tentacles rather than arms, then came on Indrajit's heels.

"What's your plan?" Indrajit asked. He worried that Fix's ordinarily sharp, quick-thinking mind might be clouded by his emotions.

"Frodilo Choot," Fix said.

Choot was a risk-merchant. She had been involved in the scam that had originally brought Indrajit and Fix together, but, like them, she had been a victim. She had also posted the bond that had allowed them to form a registered jobber company. In a way—a way that Indrajit didn't fully understand or feel comfortable with—that made her a sort of partner of the Protagonists.

"She'll have a contact," Indrajit agreed.

"Or she'll know who's crooked, and is paying protection."

The sun was beginning to rise, sending exploratory tendrils of pink light down through the longest streets of the Spill, when they reached Choot's office. The shouting at the Paper Sook, a couple of blocks away, had not yet begun, and the smell of frying meats and bread tinged the smoke in the air.

Fix hammered on Choot's door.

"We may have to wait," Indrajit suggested. "You know, for her to feel out her contact, or to negotiate putting us in touch with Sehama."

"We have no time," Fix said.

The door opened. Choot's doorman, Yozak, who was enormous and covered in purple scales and had no visible eyes, stood on the other side. He stooped, and still stood too tall to walk through the door.

"The Punching Bags," Yozak rumbled.

"Today is not the right day to remind me that I owe you a beating," Fix growled. "Get Choot. Now."

Yozak snorted, slit nostrils opening in his fistlike face for the purpose. Then he turned and passed through a bead-filled doorway at the back.

"We're all friends here," Indrajit assured Munahim. "You know how men talk to each other when they're friends."

"I know how they talk when they're enemies, too," Munahim said. "Should I . . . watch the street? Be the backup?"

"No one's after us right now," Indrajit said. "Let's get inside and close the door."

They stepped inside and shut out the traffic that was just beginning to fill the street, flowing at this hour mostly toward the square where the Paper Sook merchants would shortly begin their daily feeding frenzy.

Frodilo Choot emerged promptly from the back room and

stepped up to her counter. She was a squarish women wrapped in rune-inscribed and green-dyed leather bands, and she held a glazed bowl containing a steaming hot liquid. Her tongue flickered between her lips to taste the air as she appeared.

"You better not be here to tell me I'm losing my bond," she said.

"Nothing that dire," Fix said. "Tell us how to get in touch with Arash Sehama."

Choot took a sip from her cup. "Funny. If I had woken up this morning with a strong urge to contact the Gray Lord of the Paper Sook, I would have reached out to you two to ask how."

Fix pounded the counter with a fist. "How can you not know?"

"How can *you* not know?" she shot back, calmly. "You've meddled enough in his business! He's behind half the frauds you've uncovered. I assumed that at this point you would know him personally."

"Maybe there is no Gray Lord," Munahim said.

"Shh," Indrajit told him.

"Has Sehama not tried to bribe or subvert you?" Fix demanded. "To approve a fraudulent claim, to overvalue some asset, to pay him a cut?"

"Yes," Choot said, "and I have told him no. And occasionally his goons have messed with me as a result. Broken things on which I owned the risk, to cause me to lose money."

"So how did you contact them?" Fix asked.

"I didn't. I don't. I never have. They have always contacted me."

Fix gave a strangled cry and banged his forehead on the counter.

"Do you know anyone who's working with Sehama?" Indrajit asked.

Choot took another sip. "Many people here. So if you go around and put the word out, and Arash Sehama wants to hear what you have to say, I'm sure you'll get an audience. You might not like it when you do, though."

"Or maybe we should stop another fraud," Indrajit suggested. "Something easy, like a falsified bell of loading."

"Bill of lading," Fix said.

"And then offer to let it go through," Indrajit said, "but only if the scoundrels introduce us to Arash Sehama first."

Fix threw open the door and left. Indrajit and Munahim rushed after him and overtook him prowling back and forth in the street.

"She's lying," Fix said.

"How do you know?" Munahim asked.

"She knows how to find him. They all do. They must. She's afraid."

"Maybe she'll pass him the message, then," Indrajit said.

"I can't wait and find out." Fix broke into a trot, heading toward the Paper Sook.

"I know that look," Indrajit said. "You have a plan. But if your plan is what I think it is, it's not a good plan."

"My plan is a great plan," Fix said.

"We don't really have the power to arrest anyone," Indrajit said. "Not without a warrant from the Lords, anyway. And interrogation always boils down to threats and beating people up and demanding information that you're not even sure they really have, so it's very… distasteful. Unreliable. Unsatisfying."

"I agree," Fix said.

They came to the edge of the Paper Sook proper. Men milled about in an unstructured mob, shouting. "Buying Ildarian River! Ildarian River, buying at seventeen! Seventeen! Seventeen and a quarter!" "Selling Wheel and Hook at twelve! Selling at twelve! Eleven and a half!" They flashed fingers in exotic combinations at one another and then jotted down notes with bits of charcoal on scraps of paper.

Indrajit stopped several paces from the crowd. He knew they were selling companies and things like companies to each other, but that was the limit of his understanding. Munahim stopped beside him, making a soft growling sound in his throat.

Fix waded in. "Buying contact to Arash Sehama, five! Buying a meeting with Arash Sehama, six! Buying at seven!"

Traders stared at him. Some kept up their own hurricane of shouts and finger flashes with each other, but others watched and fell silent. A few slunk away, or turned their backs on Fix to continue their business.

"You know me, damn your eyes!" Fix roared. "I'm good for it. Buying a meeting with Arash Sehama, eight!"

Indrajit was pretty sure that the numbers were prices stated in Imperials, the basic coin of Kish. Eight and rising was already a significant amount of money; perhaps he shouldn't have surrendered to Fix's insistence that he, Fix, should be the one to handle all their coin. At least Indrajit still had the purse that Ubandar Hakko had given them.

But Indrajit had always been much better at spending money than at making or saving it.

"Buying Arash Sehama, nine!" Fix yelled.

"Selling Arash Sehama, fifty!" roared a surprisingly tall Zalapting. Or maybe he wasn't a Zalapting after all, since his skin was closer to pink than to lavender, and his snout was half again as long as any Zalapting's Indrajit had ever seen.

"Fifty, you louse-ridden sack of ylakka fodder, you must be joking!" Fix was manic, waving his arms and jumping up and down. "Buying Arash Sehama, ten!"

Ten Imperials was a lot. They'd done jobs for less than ten Imperials.

"Selling Arash Sehama, fifty!" the tall Zalapting yelled.

Fix emitted a strangled cry. "Fifty?"

"Selling, fifty!" The Zalapting looked smug.

Fix pulled at his own hair. "You all know the bastard! Half of you must be on his payroll! Does no one else here want to make easy money? I don't mean him any harm, I just want a meeting!"

A copper-skinned Xiba'albi in a wool tunic raised his hand. "Selling Arash Sehama, forty-eight!"

A Fanchee woman, green-skinned and with a mass of tentacles covering her lower face, shouted, "Selling Arash Sehama, forty-five!"

"Buying Arash Sehama, eleven!" Fix howled.

Munahim leaned in to whisper in Indrajit's ear. "Sometimes, I fear I have come to live in an insane place."

Indrajit could only laugh.

"Buying, thirteen!" "Selling, forty!" The buying and selling of other things continued, but the knot of sellers around Fix captured Indrajit's attention. With their enthusiasm, they were yelling the loudest, and finally, the Xiba'albi seller shouted, "Selling Arash Sehama, twenty-three!" and Fix answered, "Buying, twenty-three!"

The Xiba'albi emerged from the crowd and Fix followed him. Fix was sweating and his arms shook.

"It's a good thing you didn't become a risk-merchant like you once intended," Indrajit told his partner. "I think the stress would kill you."

Fix ignored him and counted out coins to the Xiba'albi. "Take us."

"I honor all my contracts," the Xiba'albi said. "Come with me."

Indrajit cast an eye at the crowd of traders as they walked away. Most resumed their yelling of company and commodity names, but the tall Zalapting crept away, looking over his shoulder at Fix and the Xiba'albi.

The Xiba'albi led them down a single short alley to a tavern. The signboard overhead bore the chipped painted image of a standing Kishi fowl plunging a long talon into the heart of a prone bird. Through the doorway was a common room with broad flagstones comprising the floor and brick walls. Half a dozen tables filled the space and Indrajit smelled eggs frying in butter.

The man behind the counter had a swarthy Yuchak complexion and a beardless Yuchak face, but his sleeveless tunic and kilt were all Kishi, and he was a head taller than the average Yuchak tribesman. The Xiba'albi whispered something to him across the bar, passed him several coins, and left.

"Arash Sehama," Fix said.

"I'm Yuto Harlee, lowly proprietor of the Fighting Fowl." The barkeep smiled. "I'll take you to Sehama in just a minute. My job is to screen out any potential unwanted visitors."

"We're not here to harm him," Indrajit said. "We want to discuss business."

"We're here to make an offer," Fix added.

Harlee leaned forward, resting his elbows on the counter. "An offer . . . from the Lord Chamberlain?"

"He knows who we are," Munahim said.

"Shh," Indrajit told him.

"We know who you are," Harlee said. "The Protagonists. The most unlikely jobber company in Kish, and the one the Lord Chamberlain sends to watch the traders. Now including a dog."

"A Kyone," Munahim said.

"Shh," Indrajit said again. "This is why you are usually backup."

"I'm just correcting him."

"You don't need to say everything you think," Indrajit said. "Just say things that will actually help us."

"If you're here selling protection, I don't think Sehama is buying." Harlee smiled blandly. "Or maybe you want to buy some protection."

"He has something we want," Fix said. "We'll pay the fair price."

"Huh." Harlee reached below the bar and pulled up three eyeless hoods. "What is this marvelous thing which the servants of the Lord Chamberlain are unable to find on their own, driving them to turn to the notorious Arash Sehama?"

"It's an object." Fix pulled one of the hoods on. "It's of no value to him."

"That's clearly not true," Harlee said. "It's worth at least as much as you're willing to pay. And maybe more."

"Welcome to Kish?" Munahim said. "Is this where I say, 'Welcome to Kish'?"

"You can," Indrajit said, "but it's not especially helpful." He sighed. "And again, we go somewhere we must enter blind. Why is that?"

Munahim pulled on a hood, and then so did Indrajit.

"I expect it means you go to interesting places," Harlee said. "I'm going to press a line into your hands. Hold onto it, and we'll stick together."

Indrajit felt a knot in a length of rope pressed into his palm and he gripped it. When the cord tugged gently forward, he followed.

He heard a door creak, then stumbled awkwardly down steps. He learned that Munahim was in front of him when the Kyone, who was as tall as Indrajit, smacked his head into a low-hanging ceiling and grunted in pain. Sadly, the distance between them was short enough that Indrajit wasn't able to take advantage of the warning, and struck his face as well.

"Hey, there are tall men back here," he grumbled. "Give us a warning, Harlee."

"Watch out," Harlee said. "There are more low ceilings ahead."

Indrajit raised one hand before his face and slowed his pace. He tugged a little on the rope and slowed them down, but he was able to feel the other dangers coming and avoided being struck again.

They descended twice more. Kish was an old city, built on succeeding layers of ruins that dated back thousands of years, with no former incarnation of the city ever having been swept away. That meant that, wherever one traveled in Kish, one stood atop a many-leveled warren of ruins, caves, sewers, tunnels, and forgotten buildings. The whole was sometimes referred to as Underkish. In the Paper Sook in particular, Indrajit and Fix had more than once had occasion to use shortcuts through Underkish, or through the

Undersook, devised by the Sook merchants themselves, which cut across the uppermost of those buried levels. Those shortcuts, which allowed the traders to do business, visit banks, or escape annoying creditors quickly and secretly, connected many of the Sook's businesses at the basement level.

Indrajit hadn't counted the steps—which he regretted as soon as it occurred to him—but he thought they were roughly two levels below the basement level.

He heard running water. "Am I going to step into a pond?"

"Not if you walk straight forward," Harlee said.

He stopped when Munahim stopped, banging his nose against the back of the Kyone's head. Unseen hands patted him down and then took away Vacho.

"I'm letting them take my sword and bow," Munahim announced.

"We're cooperating," Indrajit agreed. "We're all friends."

They walked forward again, crossing a low arch that felt like a bridge. A damp, cold breeze blasted them briefly, and then they were standing still again. "Go ahead and remove the hoods," Harlee said.

They stood in a long, narrow hall. A brick arcade ran up each long side of the hall, to their left and right. Ahead of them, five steps on the left climbed up to a low brick platform. In the center of the platform, with a blazing multiarmed candlestick to either side, sat a heavy throne.

Behind him, Indrajit heard breathing and the shifting of feet. With his excellent peripheral vision, and turning his head only very slightly, he could see that the hall behind him was in shadow, and contained many men in cloaks, with their hoods up.

Sprawled on the throne was another cloaked and hooded figure. The skin of his hands and forearms, and the tip of a long snout poking out of the cloak's hood, were all that showed of the figure, and they were all bright yellow. The cloak, as well as the figure's tunic, trousers, and soft boots, were all a mousy gray color. A plain iron disk hung from an iron chain around the figure's neck.

"I'm Arash Sehama," the man on the throne said. "What do you want? More to the point, why shouldn't I save myself a lot of trouble and just kill you now?"

Chapter Five

"I'm Fix," Fix said.

"I didn't ask, because I know who you are already," Sehama said. "You're the Protagonists. You're the small and ineffectual jobber company that the Lord Chamberlain employs to engage in the charade of keeping order in the Paper Sook."

"Charade?" Indrajit harrumphed. "If we're small and ineffectual, why are you irritated with us? How would you even have noticed us?"

Sehama waved one hand in a desultory gesture of dismissal. "You aren't here to keep order, not really. You stop the odd fraud, you deliver the occasional scape-debt up to his creditors, and the Lord Chamberlain can say to his peers that he has done his work. That's your function."

"We also collect fees and fines," Indrajit pointed out.

"Don't misunderstand me." Sehama coughed weakly against the back of one hand. "No other part of the city is patrolled or policed with any more vigor than this one. It is all a charade and a shakedown and a swindle. You are merely the part of the swindle that relates to the Paper Sook."

"I didn't come to banter." Fix's voice had a hard edge to it.

"True order in the city is kept by the Gray Lords," Sehama said. "Only the Gray Lords understand the full size and scope of the city's economy. Only we truly know all the business that is done, and only we can impose true and accurate taxes. The city's merchants know that, if their shop is burned down, we're the only force truly able to exact justice, as an alliance with us is the only talisman truly able to ward off the arson in the first place. I myself am the cake of order, children. You are mere raisins."

The assembled thieves laughed.

Sehama was putting on a show. Was he demonstrating his greatness to his men? His ability to be cavalier with the servants of the Lord Chamberlain? And what else might he do to the Protagonists in order to impress his own men?

"What an unexpected metaphor," Indrajit said.

"Yes," Fix agreed. Indrajit could hear his teeth grind. "You are the true powers of the city. And we came because you have something in your possession that we want. You are rich. We are supplicants."

So Fix also understood the show.

"Are you asking on behalf of Orem Thrush, the Lord Chamberlain?" Sehama asked. "On behalf of the Lords of the Auction House?"

The men in cloaks seemed to be holding their breath. Indrajit thought he could hear drops of water trickling down the brick walls.

"No," Fix said.

"We're his men," Indrajit said. "We're under his protection." He wasn't actually sure that Thrush would do anything to avenge their deaths, but he certainly wanted Sehama's men to think he would.

"But we're here on our own errand," Fix said. "You have the Girdle of Life. You found it and chose not to sell it to the Vin Dalu."

"Very interesting, blah blah blah," Sehama said. A low chuckle ran through the assembled men in cloaks.

"We'll buy it from you," Fix said.

Sehama raised a hand palm out, dismissively.

"It can't be worth anything to you, except to sell it," Indrajit said. He wasn't sure that was true, but he thought it was unlikely that the Gray Lord was a master of Druvash sorcery. "So name a price."

"I won't discuss it with you," Sehama said.

"Would you discuss it with Orem Thrush?" Fix asked. His shoulders were twitching. Indrajit was glad his partner had been disarmed; otherwise, he might already have attacked the thieves' guild leader.

"Or his chief ear, Grit Wopal? Hmmm." Sehama shifted his posture from one slouched position to another. "Maybe. But that's not the world we're in. I would also discuss it with one of my own men."

"You mean Harlee or someone," Indrajit said.

"Anyone who was an initiated Sookwalker."

"What's a Sookwalker?" Munahim piped up.

Sehama said nothing. A buzzing murmur spread through the crowd.

"How does one become initiated?" Fix asked.

"The first step is to find one's way into the Undersook Palace," Sehama said. "You've done that."

"Everything is a palace here," Indrajit muttered.

"What next?" Fix pressed.

"Though you made rather more noise about it than I could have wished," Sehama griped.

"I didn't have a choice," Fix said. "I have no time. What do I have to do next to become a Sookwalker? Dues? A tattoo?"

"You have to show your commitment." Sehama sat up and leaned forward.

"What do you want?"

"He wants us to commit a crime," Munahim said.

"Ah, the dog is smarter than it looks." Sehama applauded gently.

"He's not a dog," Indrajit grumbled.

"It can't be that easy," Fix said. "I commit three crimes by breakfast, most days."

Which wasn't strictly true. But being a jobber, even in the service of the Lord Chamberlain, did involve a fair amount of stealth, trickery, breaking and entering, trespassing, and punching people.

"He wants us to commit a crime against one of the other Gray Lords," Munahim said.

"Good boy," Indrajit murmured. He hoped Munahim was right. The logical alternative was that Sehama would order them to commit a crime against the Lord Chamberlain.

"Is that right?" Fix asked.

"Every Sookwalker here has done it," Sehama said.

"I have no time," Fix said. "Tell me what you want done. It has to be now."

"It's no big deal," Sehama said. "We have a client named Marek Kotzin."

"'Client'?" Indrajit asked.

"He pays us for protection."

"I know him," Fix said. "He's a Wixit banker. Shipwrights Collective."

Sehama nodded. "An employee of his at the bank is blackmailing Kotzin. Threatening to tell depositors about the protection payments Kotzin makes to us, unless Kotzin pays the employee as well. Naturally, we must act, because this is the kind of thing Kotzin pays us to be protected against."

"That seems a little circular," Fix said. "But yes."

"And what is the involvement of the other Gray Lord?" Indrajit asked. "Is this blackmailer one of his . . . initiates?"

"That's correct."

"Which Gray Lord?"

"Does it matter?"

"I like to know my enemies," Indrajit said.

"Zac Betel," Sehama said. "He owns smiths, carpenters, and similar craftsmen. Specializes in arson, burglary, and blackmail."

"So we deal with the blackmailer," Fix said.

"Kill the blackmailer, and you're a Sookwalker. Then we can talk about this Belt of Death."

"Girdle of Life," Fix said.

"Ah, yes."

"I'll do this thing," Fix said. "But I warn you, Sehama, that I'm not a man to be trifled with."

"Nor am I, Fix." Sehama stood. "I know you're pressed for time. The blackmailer is a Fanchee named Toru Zing."

"Show us the way out," Fix said.

Sehama gestured to one of his men and the blinding hoods were dropped over the Protagonists' faces again.

Indrajit raised his hand to protect his head proactively this time as they were led out, clutching the same knotted rope. The path out wasn't the same as the path in, because they climbed only two flights of stairs before he could feel the cool morning sea breeze on his skin, and the tepid warmth of the winter sun. Once outside, still blindfolded, they were led a few hundred steps, including several turns, and then the hoods were removed.

They stood beneath an awning, among stacked pots and baskets. A stone's throw away, a city gate opened on the Shelf, one of the three fishing quarters. They were at the bottom of the Spill, ten minutes' brisk walk or more from the Paper Sook.

Yuto Harlee stood with them. He pocketed the hoods and then handed a large canvas sack to Munahim. "All your weapons are in the bag. I trust your business went well? Well enough that you emerged alive, at any rate." He grinned.

Munahim stared away past the basketseller's shop and the ropemaker's adjacent stall at the mouth of an alley, where a one-legged Kishi beggar sat on a ragged blanket, importuning passersby. His muzzle twitched slightly.

"No time to talk, Harlee," Fix said. "We're at the wrong end of the Spill for what we need to do."

He set out southward, uphill, toward the Crown, not waiting for his weapons. Indrajit and Munahim followed, leaving Yuto Harlee chuckling in their wake. As they walked, Indrajit and Munahim resheathed their swords. The Kyone held on to Fix's armory, still in the canvas bag.

Fix made a beeline for the Crown, which meant eschewing the gentle, zigzagging ascent of the Crooked Mile in favor of the narrow side streets, alleys, and stairs that climbed directly up the hollow, rotting hill on which Kish rested.

"That man Harlee," Munahim said as they fought their way past a string of camels emerging from a gap in a plastered wall. "He's not merely a tavernkeeper."

Fix charged ahead with purpose.

"Well, he must be a member of the Sookwalkers," Indrajit said. "At least, a gatekeeper of sorts. He blindfolded us and led us in. And I suppose he led us out as well."

"He led us in and out." Munahim nodded. "But there's more than that. The throne room . . . what did Sehama call it? The Undersook Palace? His smell was strong down there."

"What do you mean? Do you mean he was there?" Indrajit didn't quite follow Munahim's thinking.

"More than that. I mean, he must go there often. And . . . perhaps he lives down there. And . . . I can't be certain, but I think his scent was on the throne platform."

"But you can't be certain," Indrajit pressed.

"It didn't seem like a good time to go sniffing about the bricks," Munahim said. "But I think so."

The gate between the Spill and the Crown had a line of people, slowly passing through under the eyes of Gannon's Handlers. Fix bounced anxiously on the balls of his feet, but took back his weapons from Munahim and hung them on his belt. Indrajit continued to hold the canvas sack.

"We can't kill this guy Zing," Indrajit said.

Fix shook himself, like an animal shedding water.

"We've invested a lot in who we are," Indrajit said. "We're heroes. You're a hero, Fix, and you're not going to throw that away."

"I'm in love," Fix said. "I'm not going to throw that away, either."

"Why are we going to the Crown?" Munahim asked. "I thought the banks were in the Paper Sook."

"Many of them, yes," Fix said. "Many of them are located in the Crown, for the convenience of the great families, and the city's big institutions. The Hall of Guesses and the Palace of Shadow and Joy, for instance, want access to a bank without walking all the way down to the Paper Sook. Many banks have a filial in both places."

"And the Shippers Collection?" Munahim asked.

"The Shipwrights Collective," Fix said. "I know them. They started as ship owners, pooling their cash to merchant their shared risk. Then they used the surplus to start building ships, and they were so successful, they eventually had to go into banking, to have something to do with the money."

"And they're only on Bank Street?" Indrajit asked.

"They closed their Paper Sook filial years ago. I think to try to communicate that they were a strictly upper-class bank. No more work for mere merchants."

"They sound pleasant," Munahim said.

Fix shrugged. "They're bankers."

They reached the front of the line and were waved through by a pack of Zalaptings in Handler colors. Fix ignored them, but Indrajit gave them his best collegial nod.

Moisture struck him on the cheek. He paused, wiping his face.

"Did one of you just spit on me?" he asked.

The Zalaptings grinned and shrugged.

"Winter rains," one of them said. "Unpredictable."

"Welcome to Kish," said another.

They all cackled.

Indrajit rushed to catch his comrades.

"What's the plan?" Munahim asked. "If we're going to go in fighting, I think I should come along."

"We could light the bank on fire," Indrajit said. "When they all come running out, we grab the Fanchee."

"The bank is stone and won't easily light," Fix said. "And the guards will come running out, too. And what if it did catch fire? The Lord Chamberlain's palace is five minutes' walk from the bank. We might burn down the houses of some really important people."

"Also, it would be arson," Munahim said.

They turned on to Bank Street. Not all the buildings here were banks, but the banks were many, prominent, and large, with their names (Indrajit presumed) spelled out in banners at their front doors, or in metal lettering overhead.

"We don't need to break into the bank," Munahim said. "We don't want the vaults or the money, all we want is for one guy to come out . . . right?"

"Just one guy," Fix agreed.

"So what if we said we had a message from Zing's wife?" Indrajit said. "Or we said he had won a prize. What if we said we owed him money, and we'd come to pay?"

Fix shook his head. "These sound like ridiculous ruses. I don't believe anyone would fall for them. I suppose our backup plan is that we wait for the bank to close and follow him out. But we'll lose most of the day that way."

"Also, don't bankers go in and out of their banks through passages in Underkish, to avoid being mobbed at the doors?" Indrajit asked. "The filials down around the Paper Sook do that, at least. So we might wait here all day and then never see him. Or maybe he's not even at work today, and we wouldn't find that out until the day was over."

"We could tell the truth," Munahim said.

Indrajit and Fix looked at the Kyone.

"I don't mean to Zing, necessarily." Munahim cleared his throat, a low, growling sound. "But we can say to the bank that we're a jobber company with the contract to regulate the Paper Sook, including all the banks."

"Which is true," Indrajit said.

"Although Sehama is right," Fix said. "We're pretty lightly staffed to really regulate such much activity."

"Go on," Indrajit said.

"We also say to the bank that we're here to grab Toru Zing, who is a member of one of the Gray Houses," Munahim said. "He works for the Gray Lord Zac Betel, all of which is true."

"The bank might ask for a witness," Fix said, "or a written warrant, or proof."

"Then we'll have to bluff," Indrajit told him. "We know how. Maybe we involve Marek Kotzin at that point. Probably better if we don't have to."

Fix nodded, and stopped walking. They stood in front of a two-story stone building with an extremely steep rooftop suggesting a capacious attic floor. The walls were of gleaming, polished stone, and two horizontal flags flapped in the sea breeze, one to each side of the front door. Banner script marched in two rows down each side of each flag, and at the bottom of each was embroidered an image of a lateen-rigged ship over an immense anchor.

"Munahim," Indrajit said. "It's your plan, and it's a good one, and you deserve to be the one who goes in and implements it."

Munahim cocked his head to one side.

Indrajit cleared his throat. "However."

Munahim sighed. "The Fanchee might run."

"The Fanchee might run," Indrajit said, "and you have a bow."

"We don't want to kill Zing," Munahim said.

"Right," Indrajit said. "So if you see a Fanchee come running out of the bank, shoot him in the buttock."

Indrajit and Fix marched into the stone lobby of the bank. A line of customers stood waiting to take their turn with bank clerks sitting behind a thick glass wall. A pale Gund hulked in the corner, watching the lobby. Four of its six eyes were scratched out to prevent madness, which marked the Gund as civilized. It held a huge ax in one of its arms, and the mass of insectoid limbs sprouting from its shoulders flexed and rustled.

Fix approached the Gund. "We're the Protagonists, under contract with the Lord Chamberlain. We need to talk to whoever is in charge of this filial—the president, the manager, the head notary, the boss, whoever."

The Gund groaned, nodded, and shuffled back into the corner of the lobby. A pull-rope hung down from the ceiling there, and it tugged on the line, to no apparent effect.

"Wait," it growled.

They had only been waiting a minute when the door opened and a Wixit emerged. He was two cubits tall and covered with fur; going on all fours, he might be mistaken for an animal. He rubbed his knuckles and giggled.

"What's this about the Lord Chamberlain?" the Wixit asked.

Was this Marek Kotzin? Indrajit met Fix's eyes and they both nodded.

"We're the Protagonists," Fix said. "We have the contracts for banks and the Paper Sook under the Lord Chamberlain, and we're here investigating thieves' guild activity."

"Oh?" The Wixit's voice jumped an octave. "We're a clean bank, gentlemen."

This *was* Kotzin.

"I'm sure you are," Indrajit said. "One of your employees has been identified as a follower of the Gray Lord Zac Betel. We're here to take him into custody."

"And do what with him?" The Wixit's voice had taken on a manic tone.

"Torture, maybe," Fix said. "Certainly some beatings and interrogations. Eventually, maybe branding and release, maybe exile. It depends on what he's willing to tell us."

"Not killed?"

"Maybe," Indrajit said. "Maybe not."

"Who . . . what scoundrel, may I ask . . . would be so brazen as to follow a Gray Lord while working at a bank?" the Wixit asked.

"He's a Fanchee," Fix said. "Named Toru Zing."

"I know the fellow." The short manager seemed relieved. "Yes, of course, I'll go summon him." The Wixit disappeared back into his door, shutting it behind him.

"He seems cooperative," Indrajit said. "When he brings the Fanchee out here, we need to decide what to do with him. We're not going to kill him, right?"

"He does seem cooperative." Fix's eyes narrowed.

"We're not going to kill him, right?"

But Fix was lost in thought.

Indrajit snorted and took to pacing. He had been walking back and forth for only a minute or so when the Wixit returned. He had a look of alarm on his furry snout and he wrung his hands over and over.

"It seems that Zing has disappeared," the Wixit said.

"Was he here this morning?" Fix's voice cracked with sudden, barely restrained anger.

"Tell us where he lives," Indrajit said.

"Of course! I'll find that information right away, but I'm afraid if he realized you were coming for him, he might go elsewhere. Might he flee Kish altogether?" The banker sounded relieved at the thought. "I'll get you his street and number." He went back into his door.

"We don't have the time for this." Fix ground his teeth and clenched his fists.

"The time for what?" Munahim asked.

The Kyone stood in the bank door. He had a green-skinned, tentacle-faced man slung over one shoulder, and held his bow in his hand. The green man was whimpering and shuddering, and had a long arrow protruding from his buttock.

Chapter Six

Indrajit, Fix, and Munahim stood in the street a block away from the Shipwrights Collective. Munahim still held the Fanchee over one shoulder. Toru Zing moaned and wiggled, but didn't try to escape.

"Marek Kotzin lied to us," Indrajit said. "We were there to help him, and he lied to us. He warned Zing, his own blackmailer, so his blackmailer could escape."

"Welcome to Kish?" Munahim asked.

"Welcome to Kish." Fix looked up and down the street, clearly not focused on the conversation at hand.

"To be fair," Indrajit said, "we didn't tell him that we weren't after him, too. He might have thought we were investigating the bank, and when we interrogated Zing, Zing would throw Kotzin to us."

"So maybe even more honesty would have worked better," Munahim said.

"We couldn't very well say, 'We work for the Lord Chamberlain, oh, and now we're running an errand for one of the Gray Lords,'" Indrajit pointed out. "Our ability to be honest is sometimes constrained like that."

"Welcome to Kish," Munahim said.

"Maybe we shouldn't say so much in front of the prisoner," Indrajit suggested.

Zing stopped wiggling.

"If we're not going to kill Zing," Fix said, "we need to hide him somewhere. Somewhere he can't get out, at least for the next three days."

"If he gets out after that?" Indrajit probed.

"After three days, Alea is either safe, or gone forever. At that point, I don't care what happens. And I don't care if he hears that, either."

"I care a little," Indrajit said. "Let's put this little weasel somewhere he can't ever escape."

"That isn't our inn," Munahim said. "The inn is cheap and convenient, but not secure."

"The Lord Chamberlain's palace." Fix hadn't finished speaking before he was in motion, charging toward Thrush's residence.

As Grit Wopal had trained them, they didn't approach directly. They took several turns designed to let them detect anyone who might be following, and then finally walked to the back of the Lord Chamberlain's house.

They approached the secondary door of the palace, as they always had. The plain door with the iron peeping-panel was on a back street; where the front door of the palace was guarded by men in the livery of House Thrush, and a flag bearing the Horned Skull flew proudly, the tradesmen's entrance was nondescript, sturdy, and quiet.

Fix had knocked by the time Indrajit and Munahim caught up, and the panel opened. A pale face with a horizontal strip of four eyes peered out.

"Chosk, let us in," Fix said. "We need to talk to Wopal, if possible."

Chosk, whose official title was understeward, and whose job was to watch the back door and manage traffic in and out, let them in. Once inside, they could see his noseless and toothless face and his florid purple robes. Where he usually filled out those robes with ebullience, he sagged. His belly was still large, but his limbs were stick-thin.

"I'll summon Wopal. Do you need a physician?" the understeward asked.

"We could leave the arrow in," Fix said. "It would give us a handle if we need one." By way of demonstration, he grabbed the arrow and twisted it. The wounded Fanchee shrieked.

"Send a doctor," Indrajit said. "We'll be in one of the strong rooms."

The Protagonists didn't know their way around all of the Lord Chamberlain's palace, but they had briefly been prisoners in it, so they knew their way to the holding cells. Two of the heavy-doored rooms were barred from the outside, suggesting that they currently held prisoners, but the rest were open. Munahim draped their prisoner facedown on the floor and yanked out the arrow with a single quick motion.

Toru Zing wept.

"The truth," Indrajit said, "is that you're probably going to get off light. We just need to hold you in here for a while."

"I didn't want to do it," Zing whimpered. "They made me! They threatened my family!"

"Shut up!" Fix snapped.

A Zalapting with gauze and ointments came and treated Zing. The Zalapting was just leaving when Grit Wopal arrived.

Wopal habitually dressed like a cheap bazaar card-reader, in dirty yellow tunic and loincloth, with a faded purple turban. The look was effective as a disguise in part because Wopal was a Yifft, a race of man gifted with powerful spiritual vision when a Yifft opened the third eye situated in the center of his forehead. Wopal's third eye was now shut, and he looked irritated.

"I really prefer it if you wait until I contact you," the Yifft said. "I know you can't be out of cash, because Fix is managing the money."

"That's a little rude," Indrajit said.

"We need you to hold this guy," Fix said.

Wopal grunted. "Well, let's lock him in and go somewhere quiet so you can explain."

Once Zing's door was barred, Wopal took them to a room with high windows, puddles of warm sunlight on the floor and walls, and four reclining couches. They lay down, other than Fix, who sat on the edge of the couch and fidgeted as Wopal passed around a carafe of lightly alcoholic applejack.

"Tell me why I'm holding a prisoner." The Yifft's third eye opened. Its white was yellow and thick with mucus, its iris streaked red and gold.

"The woman I love is dead," Fix said. "To raise her to life, I need a Druvash artifact that is held by one of the Gray Lords. Before he will negotiate with me, I have to prove my good faith by killing this Fanchee, who is a blackmailer in the service of a rival Gray Lord. Rather than actually kill the man, we hope you will hide him."

"That is so succinct that it's difficult to follow," Wopal said. "But I can see you're upset and telling me the truth. So tell me a little more detail."

Fix gave Wopal the details. Grit Wopal was the Lord Chamberlain's spymaster, head of his so-called Ears, and in that capacity often hired Indrajit and Fix and gave them instructions. He was master of an immense amount of information about Kish and its various powers.

Wopal listened intently, nodding all the while.

"What an excellent opportunity," he said when Fix had finished.

"I swear by every god that Indrajit knows," Fix said, "if you wreck this for me with your plotting, I will kill you."

"I should advise you that I know a great many gods," Indrajit said.

Wopal smiled. "What a delight to work in a high-trust environment."

"You are a spy, after all," Indrajit said.

"And, as a spy, I must take all opportunities to gather information that come my way. What a tremendous opportunity this is to gather information about a quarter of the city that I don't know as well as I'd like. But we have a constraint: the Battle of Last Light is in two days."

"The winter holy day?" Indrajit asked. "Where actors dress in black to represent winter and white to represent summer and they battle each other across the city?"

"Yes, more or less."

"And throw candy to children?"

"The same."

"I find it strange that winter is represented by black costumes," Indrajit said. "But then, where I come from, it snows."

"That *is* strange," Munahim agreed.

"It's really about the sun," Fix explained. "It's light versus darkness. It's a holy and magical battle to bring back the sun."

"Welcome to Kish?"

"No, I don't think that's quite right." Indrajit shook his head. "You say 'Welcome to Kish' after a really cynical observation. Or bleak or defeatist. Throwing candy to represent the blessings of the sun isn't bleak enough."

"Eh."

"What does that have to do with us?" Fix asked. "I read that the Lord Farrier won that contract."

"So he provides security to sacred sites, yes." Wopal steepled his fingers in front of him. "And the actors are volunteers from various guilds and associations across the city, all doing their civic duty."

"I'm still waiting to hear why this matters." Fix buried his face in his hands, grinding at his eyes with the meat at the base of his thumbs. "You know we have limited time."

"There is a long tradition that the Lords of Kish participate in the battle," Wopal said. "Indeed, the formal theology posits that the rite will have no effect unless the Lords participate. Not all the Lords are believers, but those who are put considerable pressure on the rest to be present. Costumed, and all on the side of spring and the sun, of course."

"Does Orem Thrush want us to accompany him?" Indrajit leaped up from his couch. "I have a great deal of experience representing vigorous, manly battle during recitation."

"Still waiting," Fix said. "Time bleeds away by the second."

"The Lord Chamberlain needs two men to join him in the Dawn Priest Procession," Wopal said. "He wants you two, Indrajit and Fix. So, whether you solve your . . . problem or not, you are to meet him at dawn on Last Light Day, to march with him."

"Was that so hard?" Fix asked.

Wopal spread his hands.

"Fine," Indrajit said. "Two days is plenty of time. We basically have to be done by then, anyway, the Vin Dalu told us."

Fix growled.

"I'm sorry for the inconvenience of it," Wopal said. "I wish you success in raising your lady love, and will certainly hold this blackmailer as long as you want. But my first loyalty is to Orem Thrush, and we must protect him."

Fix stared at his clenched fists.

"Yes," Indrajit agreed.

"Fine," Fix said. "Is that it? You hold Zing indefinitely, for now, and we go back to Sehama. We negotiate for the Girdle of Life, having, at this point, about two and a half days before we run out of time. We also prepare to put on funny clothes, fight a mock battle, and throw candy at children, because those things are just as important as Alea's life and death."

"Those things *are* important," Wopal said, "and you'll be paid well for doing them."

Fix drained the last of his applejack and left.

"He's determined," Wopal said.

"We're men on a mission," Munahim said. He and Indrajit rushed down the hall after their friend.

Chosk let them out without a word, sagging in all his motions and smiling only weakly. Indrajit found himself working extra hard to stay caught up to the others with the big canvas bag under his arm.

Once they had reached the main avenue passing the Lord Chamberlain's palace, Indrajit swept his head right to left to be sure they weren't being followed. It wasn't hard, with his peripheral vision, just a slight jiggle of the skull. The boulevard was crowded with late morning traffic. Given the cool winter air, braziers of coals stood at the major corners, and the food-kiosk vendors focused on hot offerings: roasted nuts, skewered meats, and hot drinks.

"Alea first," he said in a low voice to his partner. "We go get the Girdle of Life right now, and take it to the Vin Dalu, and we can worry about the Dawn Priest Procession in due time."

Fix shook his head so fiercely that his shoulders shuddered. "We can't just laugh off that task, though. If we lose the Lord Chamberlain, we're back to square one—no patron, our biggest connection and protection and source of contracts gone."

"Of course. In due time. So we just need to help Alea . . . a little faster, that's all."

A young man in a pale green robe bounced into Indrajit's view. He clutched a scrap of parchment that seemed to be painted with a wheel of shifting colors, though the robed man juddered so dramatically that Indrajit couldn't get a clear look at the image. Behind him surged a mob of people in orange, yellow, and green robes, all with heads shaved but for a long forelock. They were flooding out of the open door of a low brick building—a shabby-looking, run-down structure, for the Crown.

"Did you know that you are already a god?" the man in green asked.

"Thank you," Indrajit said. "I'm a god in a hurry, so step aside."

He stepped sideways, but the man in green did, too, blocking his path. Fix struggled on ahead, into the crowd of robed initiates.

"No, really. If you haven't read the *Mirror Codex* of the great

Bonean philosopher Tassotolonga, you should start today. I can give you a copy—"

"Reading is a mistake," Indrajit said. "Flattery won't lure me into it. And, really, I have to go."

He shoved the man in green with his shoulder, but the preacher was surprisingly nimble. He kept his feet, staggered again into Indrajit's path, and raised the scrap of parchment. "That's okay, Tassotolonga teaches that not all gods are to be awakened by the written word. In fact, the greater number come to the realization that this world is the world of the gods by contemplation of the Great Wheel. You will see that my color is green. If you will let me ask you a few simple questions, we can determine what color you are, which will help me know how to enlighten you."

"Enlighten me?"

"Help you open your eyes to your own godly nature. So that you see that you are a god, living in the world of the gods, and that your actions reverberate across the cosmos into thousands of worlds of mortal men. Also, knowing your color will help us define what spiritual steps you need to take to ascend to the next color on the wheel."

"If I'm already a god, what ascent remains?" Indrajit struggled to get past the young man, but only succeeded in dragging the mystic with him, several steps along the avenue. Fortunately, Fix had run into a solid wall of acolytes, which was slowing him down.

"Ah, you see, here is an important question. That you would ask that particular question suggests that you are orange, my friend. I'll tell you that the answer is that ascent is a never-ending process, and it's for this that we are called Ascendants, but me telling you the answer is not the same thing as you truly learning it. Can I invite you to come inside with me, just for an hour or so?"

"Frozen hells, enough." Indrajit hooked his leg around behind the other man's. Indrajit's leg was longer, so he placed the long muscle of his calf behind the Ascendant's knee, and then he pushed the man in the chest.

The Ascendant sat down on the cobblestones, abruptly.

Behind Indrajit, Munahim started barking. Indrajit was used to hearing growls and the occasional yip or whine from the dog-headed Kyone, but this was a full-blown, explosive sonic aggression, and it was followed by the sound of sandals slapping the pavement as the Ascendants scattered.

Indrajit turned to congratulate Munahim, and saw the man with the blowgun.

The assailant stood on the far side of a wheeled metal cart where a vendor sold roasted camber nuts. Nuts hopped and skidded about on a flat iron plate over a large oil lamp, and the vendor, a brown-skinned Kishi in a red cape and trousers, pushed them back and forth with a wide, flat scoop. The assailant wore a blue faux-toga, the sort that snapped on for ease of wear and only imitated the true toga of the upper classes, plus a blue hood that hid his face. As Indrajit looked, the person was in the process of raising a long cane to his lips, hidden in the shadows of the hood.

The cane pointed at Fix.

Indrajit knew blowguns because the Blaatshi used them. They were no good for hunting fish, both because it wasn't wise to inject venom into food you intended to eat, and, more basically, because it was impossible to fire a blowgun dart into the water. But such darts could be used to kill predators that came from the land, or enemies. They were light and easy to carry in a boat, and the reeds to make them with grew abundantly in the inlets and bays where his people made their homes. Indrajit could craft a blowgun from such a reed, and make the darts to shoot with the gun. If a blowgun dart struck a man in the eye or behind the ear, it could seriously harm him.

And if it were dipped in venom, it could easily kill him.

Indrajit shouted a warning, but he knew Fix couldn't evade the dart. Fix wouldn't even have time to turn before he was struck.

Indrajit threw the canvas sack.

The man in blue fired his dart, and the dart and the sack intersected in midair.

"Protagonists!" Indrajit roared. He charged at the man in blue, but the would-be assassin was already turning and fading down an alley, and Indrajit found that the nut-seller's cart was in his way. Indrajit skittered around the man to his right and managed to get Vacho from its sheath.

He ran a few steps into the alley.

"I have an arrow to the string," Munahim growled behind him.

But Indrajit found no sign of the assailant. The alley quickly split into three, and Indrajit saw several means by which the man might have fled to the rooftops, as well: a trellis, a tall wagon beside a low building, a stack of crates.

"Can you smell the man?" Indrajit asked the Kyone. "The man in the blue false toga?"

"There are too many people here," Munahim said. "If I had his toga, I could learn his scent and then follow, but otherwise . . . there are a hundred trails here. A thousand. I do not know which to follow."

"It's probably a stupid question to ask who might want to kill us," Munahim said. "Or Fix in particular."

Fix laughed grimly.

"Welcome to Kish," Indrajit said. "Who doesn't want to kill us?"

"We've stopped thieves and kidnappers and spies and assassins," Fix said.

"Thwarted dark cults," Indrajit added. "Thwarted not-so-dark cults."

"Rival jobber companies," Fix continued. "Magicians. Demons. Aspiring academics."

"Not to mention the possibility that someone might attack us to make a name for himself," Indrajit suggested.

"A client might prefer not to pay a bill."

"So, lots of people." Munahim sighed. "I'm glad you have a head like a fish, Indrajit. Otherwise we never would have stopped that assassin."

Fix snickered. "Now you've got it."

"I'm glad you've got a head like a dog," Indrajit retorted.

Munahim nodded. "I do."

Chapter Seven

They passed under the sign of the Fighting Fowl. Yuto Harlee looked up from polishing the wooden countertop. "You've just missed the lunch rush. We do have fried tamarind and a little flatbread left, and I could dig up some berries."

Indrajit leaned over the bar. "Is there some sort of password we're supposed to say to let you know we want to be let into the Undersook Palace?"

"Yes," Harlee said. "And you don't know it because you're not Sookwalkers."

Fix rapped his knuckles on the wood. "You know what we want, Harlee."

Harlee produced the hoods and the knotted rope, disarmed them, and again led them into darkness. Indrajit had the presence of mind to protect his face from the beginning this time. Munahim must have done the same, because he chuckled several times as they walked. Indrajit walked over the same arch clutching the same knotted rope, heard the same flowing water, and then had his hood removed.

They weren't standing in the throne room, but in a much smaller chamber, furnished like an office. Two wide desks stood against two walls, perpendicular to each other and facing the center of the room, where the Protagonists stood. Arash Sehama sat at one desk, face still hidden in a hood, yellow tail flicking back and forth under his seat. Yuto Harlee, after plucking off the three cowls, sat at the other, setting a bag full of their weapons on the floor beside his feet. A candelabra stood in each corner of the room, and the single visible exit was a passage under a narrow arch, shut with a heavy curtain. Maps hung on all the walls—Indrajit recognized the city and its various quarters, but there were numerous lines and shapes inked over the top in various colors that meant nothing to him. The wide margins of all the maps were also full of written notations, which made him frown.

"You didn't bring the body," Sehama said.

"We're not idiots," Fix said. "Do you want that kind of attention?"

Harlee chuckled.

"No," Sehama said, his voice a dry rasp. "But I would like evidence. We're not idiots, after all."

"You've already had it," Indrajit guessed. "Either you followed us and your man saw us shoot Zing, or Kotzin came rushing right down here to tell you what we did, and demand to know what you were doing to protect him."

"Both, in fact," Sehama admitted.

"We got into the bank by announcing that we were on the Lord Chamberlain's business," Fix said. "When Kotzin came out, we couldn't very well reassure him that we were there as Sookwalkers."

"You're not Sookwalkers," Sehama said.

"No," Indrajit said. "If we were, we could have given him the secret handshake, and his mind would have been set at ease."

"My man who followed you couldn't see what you did with the body," Sehama said.

"We work for Orem Thrush," Indrajit said. "We have ways of disposing of corpses."

"Fire," Fix said. "Acid. Deep, deep wells."

"The Necropolis," Indrajit said. "The sea."

"Eat the flesh," Munahim said.

Everyone stared at him.

The Kyone shrugged. "It works."

"I'd feel a little better if you'd brought me . . . I don't know, fingers." The Gray Lord leaned his elbows on his desktop and spread his own eight fingers flat on the wood, as if illustrating what he meant.

"There are ten thousand Fanchee fingers in Kish," Fix said. "Do you want us to go collect some for you? It's time to deal, Sehama."

"You don't want to be initiated?" Harlee asked. "Secret handshake, passwords to the Undersook Palace, and so on?"

"We do," Indrajit said. "We think there are some interesting business possibilities."

"But we want the Girdle of Life first," Fix said. "We want it now."

"Initiation later," Indrajit said, to clarify.

Arash Sehama sighed. "Well, as prospective Sookwalkers, I can now let you in on a trade secret. I no longer have the Girdle of Life."

Fix's shoulders knotted instantly.

"You're not dealing in good faith," Indrajit said.

"You were outsiders before." Sehama shrugged. "You know what they say."

"They say, 'Welcome to Kish,'" Munahim said.

"Welcome to Kish," Sehama agreed.

"Where is the Girdle?" Fix's voice cracked.

"Strictly speaking, I can't tell you where the Girdle is," Sehama said. "Because I don't know. But I can tell you who I sold it to."

"Someone outbid the Vin Dalu," Fix said.

"The Vin Dalu offered us healing services." Sehama shrugged. "Apparently, they don't have a lot of cash. And, frankly, I'm usually just as happy to let my men die as to go to the expense of healing them."

Sehama and Harlee laughed.

"Don't say it," Indrajit warned Munahim. The Kyone nodded.

"Especially when your best sources of revenue have been shrinking because of the interference of the Lord Chamberlain's men," Fix said.

Sehama stopped laughing.

"Who bought the Girdle?" Fix pressed.

"Zac Betel," Harlee said.

Fix trembled.

"Okay," Indrajit said. "We'll go deal with Betel, and then we'll come back and finish our initiation. We still want to do business with you. Where do we find him? Does one of these maps show?"

Harlee pointed. "That map there. You see how the Spill is divided into red and green sections?"

Indrajit looked. The division was not a simple half-and-half split, but had lines and islands of green penetrating into red territory, and vice versa. Similar lines and islands splotched the map elsewhere, but if each color corresponded to one of the Gray Lords, then, roughly speaking, there was one Gray Lord each for the Lee and the Caravanserai, while a single Gray Lord ruled the East and West Flats as well as the Shelf, two Gray Lords divided the Crown between them, and Sehama and Betel split the Spill.

No one owned the Dregs.

"Jaxter Boom isn't one of your mob, I take it?" Indrajit asked.

Sehama snorted.

"Who's Boom?" Munahim asked.

"A gangster in the Dregs," Fix said. "No one to worry about."

"A gangster who probably doesn't remember us fondly," Indrajit said.

"Only one of us stabbed him in the eye," Fix pointed out.

"I'm not ashamed of that," Indrajit said.

"The Sookwalkers' territory is in green," Fix said, returning to the map. "But where do I find Betel?"

"The Sootfaces are the territory adjacent to our own," Harlee said. "And you can see the Silksteppers' domain up in the Crown, and so on. Betel does business openly in his territory, under his own name, as a blacksmith. You'll find his shop within a stone's throw of the western gate. There's a red blot on the spot where the building is."

Indrajit found the blot. "Take us out, then. Unless you just want us to find our way on our own."

"You don't want to do that." Sehama laughed. "There are much more dangerous things down here than Sookwalkers."

"Yes," Fix said. "*I'm* down here. Now let us out."

"You'll come back, though," Sehama said.

Fix ground his teeth.

"We will," Indrajit agreed. "We want to be allies."

They were hooded and led again, and once more when the hoods came off, they stood among baskets and pots near the gate to the Shelf. Harlee handed them their weapons.

"Cruel trick," Indrajit said to Harlee as he belted Vacho back on.

"You're dealing with a guild of thieves," Harlee said. "Are you really going to complain about tricks being played?"

"Increasingly," Munahim said, "I expect this sort of treatment from everyone in Kish." His gaze was distracted; he was looking at a one-legged beggar sitting in the mouth of a nearby alley on a ragged blanket.

Indrajit led the way, not waiting for Fix to finish buckling his falchion back into place.

"Don't worry," Munahim told him as they walked. "I have excellent hearing, and if a monster were to approach us in the Undersook, even if we were hooded at the time, I'd be able to hear it coming. And smell it, too."

"Or a person," Indrajit suggested.

"A monster or a person," Munahim agreed. "But I assumed we're more worried about Ghouls or a six-eyed Gund than an enthusiastic young man trying to make us read a book about colors and how we're all gods already."

"Sehama set us up," Fix said. "Deliberately. He's just using us to cause trouble for his rival."

"There's an obvious trade we can make here," Indrajit suggested. "We give Betel his man Zing back, in exchange for the Girdle."

"Except then we show Sehama that we didn't kill Zing."

"Which he suspects," Indrajit said.

"He suspects, but he doesn't know it." Fix snarled. "And he may be playing another trick on us with Betel, so we may need to go back to the Sookwalkers again. So we can't free Zing. And Betel might know that we've arrested his man."

"He might think we've killed his man," Indrajit said.

"Perhaps we should tell him we've done so up front," Munahim suggested.

Indrajit's head for written maps was not great, and when he got to the gate, he found himself floundering, trying to figure out which building corresponded to the tiny black square with the red blot he had seen. A line of beggars yelled taunts at him, and a pack of gray-skinned Visps circled, trilling eerily, shaking the feathers at their knees and their elbows.

"There." Munahim pointed down an alleyway. "I hear the hiss of water."

As they walked in the direction he indicated, Indrajit began to hear the clang of metal on metal. They marched down the alley to find a three-story-tall building of sturdy timbers. Two walls on the ground floor consisted of panels of folding shutters that were all open, leaving the work of the blacksmith within open to view. The smith was a Luzzazza, tall and muscular. With his two visible arms, he gripped a glowing iron bar against an anvil the size of a pony. Two hammers seemed to levitate in the air before him, dancing up and down and tapping on the red iron.

Like Arash Sehama, he wore an unmarked iron disk on a chain around his neck.

"Zac Betel," Fix said.

The smith plunged his iron into a tub of water, releasing a cloud of steam into the cool air. He turned to face the Protagonists, down-turned ears flopping as he moved. "I've seen you before," he said.

"My name is Fix," Fix said.

"No." The smith pointed at Indrajit. "You."

"My name is Indrajit Twang."

"You're a dancer or something. An actor, am I right?"

"A poet. The four hundred twenty-seventh Recital Thane of my people, as it happens. Here . . . well, my art is not much in demand."

"The Blaatshi. I thought your people were extinct. Finally swept up in the fishing nets of Ildarion."

"The Ildarians don't fish for us," Indrajit said.

"No, but they take the fish you want to eat, am I right?" Betel grinned, showing broad white teeth. "Leaving you less food. And there are so many of them, and they're fierce fighters, that it's hard to defend your territory. So you're driven back, year after year. You have fewer babies. You forget your old pride."

Indrajit snorted. "We remember all our pride. And we are as fierce in war as any Ildarian baron's men."

"Ah, good." The Luzzazza rubbed his knuckles. "I like to see some fire."

"We came to buy something from you," Fix said.

Zac Betel squinted at them. Did he know about Toru Zing? And how much did he value the blackmailer, if he did know?

"Horseshoes?" the smith asked. "A doorframe? A lamp? Pots and pans? Rims for a wagon wheel?" He lowered his voice. "Or did you want a building burned down?"

"None of those things," Fix said. "You've taken ownership of a Druvash artifact we want. It may have been identified to you as the Girdle of Life, but it's a chest harness. It attaches to a larger device, so you may have seen free-hanging straps."

"Ah." Betel pulled the iron from the barrel and examined it. "Well, I'm no collector. I'm a practical man. If I acquired such an item as you describe, I would have done so for a client. That client might already be in possession of the said item. And I couldn't betray a client by telling you his identity." He thrust the iron into a bed of hot coals. "For free."

Indrajit felt ill.

"We don't have time," Fix said. "What do you want?"

"You're Sookwalkers," Betel said.

"No," Indrajit said.

"Arash Sehama took you into his confidence, true or false." The Luzzazza frowned. "How else would you know I had the Girdle of Life from him?"

"He did tell us," Fix admitted. "We're not Sookwalkers, but we're dealing with him."

"Sehama has a map," Betel said. "It marks boundaries between the territories of the Gray Lords."

"We've seen such a chart," Indrajit admitted.

"If you were to get me that map," Betel said, "I would tell you who has the Girdle of Life."

Indrajit and Fix looked at each other. Betel couldn't possibly be ignorant of the territory of his own operations, so that meant that the map contained some other valuable information. But the map was in Arash Sehama's office, and Indrajit, at least, couldn't think of a way to break back into the Undersook Palace, find the office, and steal the map, without getting seen.

"Twenty Imperials," Fix said. "We'll just pay you."

"Twenty Imperials probably seems like a lot of money to you guys," Betel said. "For me, it's not very much."

"For a little information?" Fix pressed. "For a *name*? Twenty Imperials is a lot of money for anyone, just to say a name."

"A client's name." Betel shook his head. "A rich client, an important client."

"One of the Lords of Kish?" Indrajit suggested.

Betel laughed.

"Thirty," Fix offered.

"Get me the map," Betel insisted.

"Fifty."

"The map," Betel said. "Or else I will take it personally that you killed one of my men and didn't even apologize."

"Welcome to Kish," Munahim said.

There was a moment of silence.

Then Betel laughed again. "Welcome to Kish, indeed. Get me the map, and we have business to discuss. Otherwise, we're done."

"Okay," Indrajit agreed. "We'll get the map."

Betel nodded. "Give my regards to Arash Sehama. *And* to Orem Thrush."

The Protagonists returned to the western gate. Indrajit traded a few asimi for three flatbreads wrapped around roasted tamarind pods with a spiced yogurt sauce and handed one to each of the other men.

"We can go back and attack Betel," Fix suggested. "Hold that face in the coals by his big floppy ears until he tells us what we want to know."

"He's public," Indrajit said, "but I don't think he's alone. He has to have men watching him. A couple of goons in an upper window with a crossbow, and we'd regret it."

"If I don't save Alea, *I'll* regret it."

"We're going to end up with enemies," Munahim said, "no matter how this turns out."

"Again," Fix said, "not my biggest concern."

"We could try capturing one of Betel's men," Indrajit said. "Maybe watch the smithy until we figure out who they are. And interrogate that guy."

"Whoever we grab, he might not know anything about the Girdle of Life," Fix pointed out.

"What if we work it from the other end?" Indrajit suggested. "Maybe trying to do favors for the various Gray Houses isn't the right way to go about it at all. Let's ask ourselves instead, who possibly would want to buy the Girdle of Life?"

"The Vin Dalu," Fix said.

"The Hall of Guesses," Indrajit said.

"Anyone who buys art," Munahim said. "A rich merchant. One of the great houses. A temple."

"He's right," Fix said. "The list is practically endless. An ambassador, a guild, the Hall of Charters, the Auction House, the Racetrack. For all we know, some muleskinner bought it and it's already halfway down the Endless Road."

"We could get Grit Wopal down here," Indrajit suggested. "Read Betel's mind."

"Wopal doesn't read minds." Fix shook his head. "He's a good interrogator, but I think that would be a lot more involved than just a quick look into Zac Betel's brain. We'd ask a question like, 'So, did you sell it to the Hall of Charters,' and Wopal would tell us what Betel felt while he answered. It would take time and the right setting."

"So we arrest Betel and throw him into one of the holding rooms," Indrajit said. "And we really interrogate him, with Wopal's help."

"And the Lord Chamberlain has then declared open war on the Gray Lords. Not sure Orem Thrush is really ready for that."

"There's another option." Munahim took a large bite of the tamarind in yogurt.

Indrajit and Fix looked at him, waiting while he chewed.

"Yes?" Indrajit prompted the Kyone, once he'd swallowed.

"We go in and get the map," Munahim said.

"Sure," Indrajit said. "We just find our way in the darkness of Underkish, randomly feeling about until we find the Undersook Palace. Because one thing we can say for certain about us is that we are astonishingly lucky."

Fix chewed his lower lip. "Well, it's true that we know a little bit about where to find the palace. We know approximately where two entrances are. And we know that from the Fighting Fowl, we descend three flights of steps, whereas from the northern gate, we descend two."

"That knowledge is nothing," Indrajit said. "You seem to have completely forgotten our prior journeys beneath this stinking city, so let me remind you. It is a maze. It is a huge, slimy, rotting maze on multiple levels. It's a maze full of rapeworms and insane Gunds and pits and ghosts and Ghouls and rivers of sewage and worse, and we don't know our way through it. That's what you're proposing."

"There's probably a guard at the door," Munahim said. "We'd want to trick the guard out of position and then go in."

"Harlee," Fix said. "Excellent idea, Munahim! Good boy! We grab Harlee and he can show us the way."

"That's not my idea at all," Munahim said. "I don't like the idea of grabbing someone and forcing him. He might call for his friends, or lead us astray, or escape."

Fix frowned. "Well, what's your idea, then?"

"Easy." Munahim grinned. "I'll just smell our way back to the office."

Chapter Eight

The Protagonists lay on their bellies on the flat clay rooftop of a building just inside the city wall, looking down on a basket weaver's shop and a narrow alley. Indrajit held a hooded lantern. Once it was lit, he'd have the ability to darken the light or let it shine directionally, by opening or closing the shutters on any of its four sides. He also held a flask of spare oil, flint and steel, a thick cloth gag, and a black hood like the one that had been forced over his own head four times by the Sookwalkers. Fix carried two lengths of rope, one coiled over each shoulder.

"That beggar," Munahim whispered. "He was there both times. And the Zalapting standing just inside the doorway. Those were the two guards."

"To be fair, the beggar only has one leg," Indrajit said. "Maybe he was there both times because he doesn't move much."

"Better safe than sorry," Munahim said.

"Is the Zalapting alone now?" Fix asked.

The doorway was below them and several paces to one side, but Munahim raised his muzzle and sniffed. "I'm pretty sure he is."

A troupe of bawdy actors marched up the center of the street. "Performing now, outside the gate!" their crier shouted. He was a pudgy Kishi with a shaven head and an elaborately brocaded vest, which made him look vaguely like a eunuch. Two bang-harp players struck up an aggressive rhythm and an acrobat did cartwheels. "See the seven daughters of the Mad Duke get their just comeuppance! Saucy girls get what they have coming!" the crier shouted. Actors in masks swarmed the stalls. The crier stepped forward and addressed the beggar. "You, sir! Admission is free to all, do not worry, we operate purely on the basis of voluntary gratuities! Join us!"

All eyes turned to the troupe.

Which was why Indrajit had hired the performers.

"Now," he whispered.

The three men let themselves down the side of the wall, taking advantage of a broad windowsill and a rain barrel to get to the ground. Running on tiptoe, they charged through the beaded curtain into the exit from Underkish.

Fix went first, and knocked the Zalapting behind the beads to the ground. Indrajit leaped to avoid treading on his friend, and then dropped to all fours. Munahim skittered in crabwise behind them.

Fix held the Zalapting's muzzle shut with both hands; the lavender-skinned man kicked and punched Fix, but was pinned and unable to draw his sword.

Indrajit gagged the Zalapting and then yanked a black hood over his head. Fix quickly tied the small man up with one of his lengths of rope and then dragged him up onto his shoulder. The Zalapting squirmed until Fix pricked his thigh with a dagger, and then held still.

They were in a dirty room containing nothing but a broken, greasy reclining couch and stairs down into darkness. Indrajit lit his lamp, unshuttering one side, and drew Vacho. "Lead the way," he said to the Kyone.

Munahim sniffed several times and then went down the stairs. He descended at a fast trot, apparently confident that he was on the right trail and that no one lay in wait. Indrajit was hard pressed to stay at his shoulder, and Fix was soon huffing and puffing.

They were quickly in the maze of Underkish. Fix asked Munahim to identify a side passage that carried no traffic, and when Munahim did so, Fix disappeared down the passage alone for a minute. He returned without the Zalapting, and they continued.

Munahim ran bent over. He looked to Indrajit as if he were staring at the bricks, and Indrajit had to remind himself that he was smelling them. Indrajit learned to let Munahim get out in front, because he didn't need the light—in the deepest shadow, he never ran into a wall or fell into any of the gaping holes that yawned beneath their feet—and also because, from time to time, he would run a few paces down one passage or into an open vault, and then come back and choose another way.

Suddenly, Munahim stopped. He gave Indrajit the agreed signal for dousing the light, and Indrajit closed the shutter. A minute passed, maybe two. Then Indrajit heard a scuffling sound and a growl, and finally the whispered call, "Light!"

Indrajit and Fix rushed forward to join Munahim, who had disabled another sentry. He was sitting on the man, a Karthing or Ukeling by his pale skin and shaggy appearance, and pressing his face to the floor.

Fix tied the thief up, gagged him with rope, and lowered him into a pit.

"We're close," Munahim whispered. "But I hear and smell more people up ahead."

"Can you get us to the office?" Fix asked.

"Yes," the Kyone said without hesitation. "But I worry the lantern will be seen."

"We'll hold hands," Indrajit said. "I'll come last, so I can hold the lantern in my off-hand, but I'll shutter it. We'll go in darkness."

"You trust me?" Munahim asked.

"We always trusted you," Fix said. "When we leave you as the backup, it's because we trust you to shoot the running Fanchee in the buttock. When you lead us in darkness, it's because we trust your sense of smell."

"My hearing is sharp, too," Munahim said.

"You told us that." Indrajit nodded. "Let's go."

They held hands in darkness and Munahim led them. He kept them on sure footing. From time to time, breezes touched Indrajit's skin. The changing echoes around him suggested yawning pits and looming walls he couldn't see. In the distance, twice he thought he saw the glimmer of lamps, and once a dull green glow. He heard footsteps, and once a sustained metallic groan. And then Munahim was pulling them through a heavy curtain.

"We're here," the Kyone said.

Indrajit heard the curtain swish back into place and he unshuttered one side of the lantern. They stood in Arash Sehama's office, with its two tables, four candelabras, and maps. Indrajit pointed at the map in question, marking the territories of the Gray Lords. "It's that one, isn't it?"

Fix leaned in to inspect the map. "Can you brighten the light a little?"

Indrajit cautiously opened a second shutter. Together they pored over the seven colors of the map. "What do the words say?" Indrajit asked.

"I can't read most of them. I can see Sootfaces, Sookwalkers, Silksteppers, Sailmenders, Soulbinders, and so on. The rest might be in some kind of shorthand, a technical notation. Or it's a language I don't know."

"I am disappointed at the limits of your literacy."

Fix shook his head.

"Also, I find it peculiar that the thieves' guilds of Kish are so attached to assonance. Are they all named beginning with a sssuh sound?"

"We call that the letter ess," Fix said. "And yes, they appear to be. Perhaps they could use a lesson in creativity from you."

"We should take a copy of this map," Indrajit said.

"Do we need to know which Gray House rules where?" Munahim asked.

"Well, that is useful information," Indrajit said. "But also, if we make a copy, then we can keep it and try to figure out what these notations mean. Maybe they record something useful."

"Certainly, they record something useful," Fix said, "if we can learn to read them."

"We could also give the copy to Zac Betel," Munahim said, "and put this one back."

The two partners glared at him together. "Put it back?" Indrajit asked.

Munahim shrugged. "If we're worried that we're making too many enemies. We might be able to put this back with no one the wiser."

"Maybe." Fix removed the tacks that pinned the map to the wall and rolled the document up. "For now, we need to get out of here."

They joined hands again and Indrajit shuttered the light. Fix held the map in the same hand that gripped Indrajit's; the rustle of the paper was reassuring in the darkness. They retraced their steps down what Indrajit now identified as a hall, and then the echoes of their footsteps opened up in a wider space.

He heard running feet, and saw the glow of a lantern. Two glows, coming from opposite directions.

Munahim pulled the three of them unto a corner and they pressed against brick walls. The glows grew in brightness and distinctness until both lamps entered the space where the Protagonists were and Indrajit saw that it was the throne room. He and the other Protagonists were hunkered beneath one of the arches of the brick arcade, behind the throne room and near the corner of the hall. Two men with lanterns met, one coming from the opposite side of the hall, emerging beneath an arch, and the other coming from the far left.

The man coming from the left was Yuto Harlee. The other was a Zalapting in a brown tunic and kilt.

The Zalapting shouted something and Harlee shouted back, all in a language Indrajit didn't recognize. Then Harlee ran beneath one of the arches, and Indrajit guessed he must be going into Sehama's office. When he emerged, more shouting.

Then both men ran back the way the Zalapting had come, leaving the Protagonists in darkness again.

"I take it none of us speak that tongue," Indrajit whispered.

"It's a thieves' cant," Fix said. "Called Graykin. I recognize a few words."

"Such as what?"

"An alarm has been sounded. Something about a gate or a door."

"They realized that someone has broken in," Indrajit whispered, "which is to say, us."

"They probably realize that someone stole the map," Fix said. "Will they guess it was us?"

"Maybe they'll guess it was Betel," Munahim said. "Maybe they know there's something on that map that he wants."

"They still might guess he's sent us to get it." Indrajit felt tired. A missed night of sleep was no big deal, but they'd been moving nonstop, and the strain of hiding from enemies and trying to outguess opponents at every turn wore him down, too.

"We're going to have to fight our way out," Fix said.

The thought made Indrajit more tired still, but then he realized that Fix was wrong. "No, we won't. Munahim, can you lead us out through the Fighting Fowl? The way we came in, the first two times?"

"Yes," the Kyone said.

They set out. Indrajit soon felt beneath his feet the graceful rise and fall of the arch he had crossed twice before this same day. He took a deep breath and exhaled, realizing that his chest felt like a single tensed muscle. He heard the sound of flowing water, and then Munahim stopped.

"Someone's following us," the Kyone whispered.

Indrajit, last in line, looked about behind him. He saw no hints of light, not reflected lantern glow nor the weird luminescence he had seen more than once in creatures that glowed in their own bodies.

"Are you sure?" he asked.

"I can smell them," Munahim whispered. "They smell like rotting flesh."

"I smell nothing," Fix admitted.

"Listen," the Kyone urged them.

Indrajit cocked an ear and held his breath. He heard snuffling. Like the sound when Munahim sniffed at the air, but wetter, more phlegmy.

"Could it be Sookwalkers?" Fix asked.

"If so, it's some kind of Sookwalker that can travel in the dark," Indrajit said. "We can't defend ourselves like this. Arm yourselves."

He dropped Fix's hand, drew Vacho, and opened all the shutters of the lantern.

Five men charged him, running on all fours. They were naked, their mouths gaped wide and bristling with needlelike teeth. Their nails were long and green and sharp, like mold-encrusted talons. Their skin was white as sea-foam and thin tails lashed out behind them. Indrajit had barely noticed that one of them had two heads when the attackers were upon them and he was slashing the foremost through the throat with Vacho.

"Ghouls!" Munahim whispered.

Three of the creatures rushed past Indrajit, charging his friends. The last, the one with two heads, leaped at him. He was extended too far from his slash and he saw a momentary vision of his own throat opened by the Ghoul's ragged teeth, but he spun his shoulders back the other way and clobbered the Ghoul in one temple with the pommel of his sword.

He heard wet, meaty chopping sounds behind him. Hopefully, it meant that Munahim's big sword and some combination of Fix's weapons were at work, hacking up their attackers.

The two-headed Ghoul dropped, scrabbling at Indrajit's thigh and stretching its jaws wide to bite. Indrajit smashed the lantern onto the back of the creature's neck, right where it forked to bear the weight of two separate heads. The Ghoul screamed and lurched away, spinning in a circle. Flaming oil spilled around its neck and shoulders.

Indrajit moved to intercept the Ghoul. He got a glimpse, orange-cast and flickering, of Munahim running his hand and a half sword into the chest of a Ghoul up to the cross-guard. Fix had his back against a column of brick, one Ghoul still at his feet with an ax in its skull, the other shrieking and trying to get at Fix's throat.

The two-headed Ghoul lurched forward one more time. Indrajit stepped aside and grabbed it by its thrashing tail. The monster howled, but Indrajit was half again its size, so he took two steps, swung the Ghoul like a throwing hammer, and slammed it heads-first into a brick wall.

Then he stepped on the small of its back and ran it through the chest for good measure.

"Fix!" He turned and saw that Munahim and Fix were striking down the last Ghoul with simultaneous attacks, Munahim chopping off an arm with a single mighty swing and Fix impaling the creature through the belly.

The Ghoul shrieked, wailed, and flopped its arms. "Hungry!" it hissed, black bile pouring over its thin lips. "Only hungry!"

Then it fell still.

The whole battle had played out with almost no talking on the Protagonists' part, like a piece of shadow theater. Now Indrajit staggered in a short circle, stabbing each Ghoul one more time to be certain they were dead.

The fire on the two-headed Ghoul was dying. Indrajit quickly refilled his lantern and lit it, shutting off most of the light but leaving one panel open, mostly because he was nervous there might be other Ghouls approaching.

"Light-shunning corpse eaters, bane of brick and wall," he said, reciting the shorter epic epithet for Ghouls. He'd never seen one before; the Blaatshi Epic taught him that they were to be found in cities, and here indeed they were.

Fix scooped up the map, which had fallen on the floor; it appeared undamaged.

"Let's get out of here," Indrajit said. "Someone has to have heard that."

Munahim led them quickly through the darkness, hands linked. Indrajit listened intently, trying to notice snuffling or breathing sounds behind him. Despite the long nails on their feet and the tails dragging behind them, the Ghouls had padded in silence. He shuddered.

They walked, he thought, for five minutes.

"Shh," Munahim warned. "Light and feet coming."

The Kyone dragged them off their path. In the advancing glow of a lamp, Indrajit could see that they were hiding behind a crumbling brick wall. Slime trickled across the floor at their feet and a great patch of lichen engulfed and nearly entirely concealed a brick column.

Three men and two lanterns came toward them. They wore leather jerkins and skirts under gray capes; two were Zalaptings and the third a short, wiry Kishi. They wore short swords at their belts, and one Zalapting had a spear.

"I heard Ghouls," one Zalapting said.

The others snickered.

"Maybe that's the end of whoever broke in," the Kishi said. "Let's find the bones so I can get Harlee off my back."

They continued on, moving the way they had come. Their light faded.

"They'll find the dead Ghouls and know we're still at large," Fix said.

"And they'll know we came this direction," Munahim said. "They'll be back."

"Wait." Indrajit thought he saw a faint glimmer of light in a different direction. Not the yellow, greasy light of a lamp, but the bluish light of a winter day. "Those guys came from the Fighting Fowl, we can't go that way. What about over there . . . is that light?"

They joined hands again and Munahim led them. As they approached the light, the glimmer became a blur of white against gloomy red, and then a bright patch, and finally a shaft of light falling from the ceiling.

The floor was a foul trough whose contents oozed away across the brick in a trickle. A shaft twenty cubits high or more rose up to the unmistakable sign that this was a latrine: two circular, horizontal holes, through which light dropped in. If the shaft were a smooth chimney, built on purpose for the latrine, it would no doubt be slimy and unclimbable. Instead, it was a ragged, crumbling, rocky tunnel, whose sides leaned first one way and then the other as it rose. Indrajit saw shelves covered with green moss, and handholds that he thought looked dry.

"Can you carry the map in your kilt?" he asked Fix.

Fix answered by folding the map twice, tucking it into his pocket, and climbing. When he was halfway up and past the smoothest-looking parts of the ascent, Indrajit sent Munahim up next. "I'll be the backup."

As Fix pushed up the seat of the latrine and more light flooded in, Indrajit himself climbed. Chunks of dust and rock fell down, choking him; Fix had had to smash the latrine seat from the brick on which it sat. Then Fix was out, and he was helping Munahim exit.

Indrajit heard snuffling sounds below him.

His hands gripped holds at a ninety-degree angle from each other, and his sandals were wedged into cracks on opposite sides of the shaft. Looking down, he saw two Ghouls crouching, shielding their eyes from the light, and staring up.

One Ghoul had an extra arm on one side of its chest.

The Ghouls gripped themselves to the brick and began to climb.

Indrajit made himself move faster. "Any help you can give me would be appreciated," he called up the shaft. He made himself take risks for speed, grabbing handholds that looked less secure but were easier, reaching farther distances and pulling himself up without testing the stability of his holds.

"You're in the way!" Munahim called back.

Indrajit risked a look down and saw that the Ghouls were gaining. Their talons dug into the crumbling mortar or slimy dirt of the walls, affording them easy grips, and their tails seemed to help them balance. He pulled a rock from the wall and hurled it down. He struck a Ghoul in the shoulder but didn't manage to dislodge it.

He kept climbing. A depression in the wall above him might afford him a place to draw his sword and defend himself, if he could make it. Not finding a grip within reach of his fingers, he leaped across the chimney, grabbing and getting his fingers hooked onto a narrow brick ledge.

The Ghouls shrieked. A hand gripped his ankle, and he kicked. He kicked a second time and a third, finally planting the heel of his sandal into the Ghoul's face. It slid a cubit down the shaft but didn't fall.

He could feel hot breath on his calves. He scrambled, pulling himself up into the depression. He pivoted on his back, trying to get his hand on Vacho's hilt and discovering that he had pinned the scabbard beneath his own weight. He heard the scratching of the Ghouls' talons and one of them shrieked again, an awful, delighted sound. A Ghoul levered itself up into the mouth of the depression.

Then he heard the loud snap of Munahim's bow. The Ghoul howled and fell.

Another snap, instantly on the heels of the first, and then Indrajit heard two wet thuds as the Ghouls hit the floor below and lay still.

"Are you well?" Munahim called.

"Not a scratch," Indrajit said. "Give me a minute to catch my breath and then I'll be right up."

Chapter Nine

The Protagonists reseated the latrine board as best they could and emerged from an alley into the Paper Sook itself. At Indrajit's suggestion, they went to Frodilo Choot's office. Choot stood at her counter, copying one ledger into another; Yozak sat on a wooden block in the corner, scratching himself and making whistling noises, though Indrajit wasn't sure through which aperture he was forcing air.

Fix paced, rubbing his knuckles.

"You guys really drew some attention this morning," Choot said.

"I hope it wasn't too embarrassing." Indrajit smiled. "We didn't shout your name or anything."

"It was a little embarrassing. I did write your bond."

"You could have spared us that," Indrajit said. "Just as you can spare us from attracting attention now, by directing us to a forger."

"What attention?" Choot asked.

"You don't want to know," Indrajit said.

"*I* don't want to know," Munahim murmured.

"Danel Avchat," she suggested.

"The Bonean scribe?" Fix asked.

"I thought he was Pelthite." Choot shrugged. "He's been known to provide falsified documents, on occasion. Fake stockholder certificates, fake identities."

"Not to you, of course," Indrajit said.

Choot went back to her ledger.

Fix charged out the door and took a decisive turn.

"Why a forger?" Munahim asked. "Fix can read and write, can't he? Why don't we just make a copy? Or hire an ordinary scribe?"

"An ordinary scribe writes things down and reads things," Fix said.

"Which, as we all know," Indrajit added, "is a blot upon the races of man, and the reason why we were sundered into the thousand races."

"Reading and writing?" Fix asked. "Really, the Epic says that's why there are a thousand races of man?"

"No," Indrajit said, "but I kind of like the idea. I'm thinking maybe I'll compose a few lines to that effect and pass them on to my apprentice."

"But isn't that what we need?" Munahim pressed.

"A forger looks at an existing document," Fix continued, "or an existing type of document, and makes an *exact* copy. The stakes are high, because success means money, and failure means prison or mutilation. His copy has to pass scrutiny, sometimes the scrutiny of experts or of people familiar with the real document, who have to believe they're looking at the original."

"That's what we want," Indrajit said. "We want Betel thoroughly convinced we've given him the real thing. Or if we give him the real one and we give the forgery back, we want Sehama satisfied that he has his map back."

"But it has to be fast," Fix growled.

The sun was sinking in the west. The first of the three days was nearly past, and they still didn't even know where the Girdle of Life was.

Avchat's stall was a simple wooden box between and in front of a tailor and a fabric wholesaler, on a broad, curving and ascending street on the east end of the Spill. Behind the tailor and wholesaler, the city's wall rose up—beyond lay the Serpent Sea, or, if you preferred, the Bay of Ildar, lapping against the base of the wall in a deep stretch between the Shelf and the East Flats. Jobbers in livery Indrajit didn't recognize paced along the top of the wall and manned the nearby tower.

Avchat himself was an olive-skinned man with a long nose that swiped down at the tip, spreading into horizontal nostrils. His eyes never opened beyond halfway, so that he was perpetually looking through his thick lashes. He wore a sand-colored turban with a brass band across his forehead, the band stamped with characters that presumably announced that he was a scribe. His cheeks were rouged a dark red that matched his full lips, and his body was hidden by a false toga the same color as the turban. He sat on a cushion and held a writing board on his lap. To his left stood a low table covered with other writing implements: paper, a ruler, a wax tablet, a small knife, writing charcoal, ink, and pen. The front of his stall was open, but had a wall that could fold down to close it; the sides and back were hung with charts, letters, certificates, and drawings so layered and overlapping as to entirely hide the wood.

"Let me guess," the scribe said as Fix barged into his stall. "You want letters written to faraway sweethearts."

"We need a map copied," Fix said. "Very precisely. An exact copy. As exact a copy as you might make of, say, a stockholder's certificate or a risk-merchantry license."

"An exact copy of a document such as those would be a forgery." Avchat pursed his lips. "Unless created for academic purposes, of course."

"It *would* be," Fix agreed. "Of course, we just want a copy of a map. But we need it in one hour."

"An exact copy," Indrajit said.

"Let me see the map," Avchat asked.

Fix handed it to him, and the scribe carefully unfolded it and began to open it. He'd only seen a third of it when he shuddered, stopped, and rolled it back up.

"This is a very particular map," he said.

"Which is about to get an exquisite copy." Indrajit smiled.

"I could bring trouble on myself by copying such a map."

"You may not recognize us," Indrajit said. "We work for the Lord Chamberlain."

"Are you saying the Lord Chamberlain will protect me?"

"I'm saying that you have two choices: make the map and get paid; or don't make the map, and get dragged before the Lord Chamberlain as a forger."

"I've heard of you," Avchat said. "The fish-headed man who patrols the Paper Sook. And his dwarf companion."

"Dwarf?" Fix snarled.

"My name is Indrajit Twang. I'm Blaatshi, and I do not have the head of a fish. My dwarf companion is named Fix."

"Dwarf? I'm not even *short*!"

"It's because your shoulders are so broad," Indrajit said. "You *look* short."

"Thirty Imperials," Avchat said. "A perfect copy will take a week. I need to analyze the inks, match not only the colors but also the taste and smell of them. I need to select a piece of paper that can be made exactly to match this one, wrinkle for wrinkle, tear for tear."

"You have an hour," Fix said. "We'll stand here and watch you. Fifty Imperials."

"Perhaps this time I should handle the money," Indrajit murmured.

"An hour!" Avchat squeaked. "With the best of intentions, that's not possible. Give me six hours and let me go home to select appropriate paper and do the work with the shutters drawn. Sixty Imperials."

"Two hours," Fix growled, "seventy Imperials, you do it right here and now and you do your very best."

"I'll do it." Avchat sighed. "But I can't be seen working on this. We close the stall and I'll work inside—"

"Seventy Imperials!" Indrajit said. "We'll stand out here and wait."

Avchat nodded. "Try not to be too conspicuous." He lit a lamp and placed it in a glass cylinder, then selected a large rectangle of paper from a box in the corner. Removing the two long sticks that held the front of the stall open from their upper sockets, he closed the wall, disappearing entirely into the wooden box.

Two droggers, one a two-humped beast and the other endowed only with a single hump, slouched past, headed up the hill toward the Crown. Their drover, a man with eight limbs, six of which ended in hands, his entire body swathed in cloth like a powder priest of Thûl, cracked three short whips and shouted to keep the beasts moving. A string of chained men wearing loincloths passed the droggers in the other direction, heading down toward water, poked by three Kishi men with goads.

The Protagonists looked at each other.

"Can you sleep?" Indrajit asked Fix. "Pacing back and forth nervously is not going to help you, and the inn isn't far from here."

"Could *you* sleep?" Fix shot back.

"Maybe if I had a few drinks to relax me first." Indrajit shrugged. "I'm a little worked up."

"I'm a lot worked up," Fix said.

"There are enemies hunting us," Indrajit said. "Look, there's a tavern across the street. Let's get a table, slowly sip an ale, and place our backs to a wall for two hours."

"Watch out!" someone yelled. "Wagon loose!"

Indrajit heard the metallic rattle of rimmed wagon wheels on cobblestone as he turned toward the source of the shout. The wide back end of a freight wagon bounced in a straight line toward him and Fix and the tailor's shop. Crates jumped and slipped about in the wagon.

Indrajit grabbed Fix by the elbow and yanked him aside, in the nick of time.

The wagon crashed past them and smashed into the tailor's. The rear axle broke and the crates spilled backward, tumbling into a rough scree like the split rock at the base of a mountain. Yelling burst from the rubble-blocked doorway and the open window, and the three Protagonists found themselves on the edge of a wide-open stretch of street in front of Avchat's kiosk.

Where was the wagon's owner, where were its draft beasts? Indrajit turned to look up the avenue to find them, and saw a flash of blue out of his left eye.

Blue.

"Fix!" he yelled, but it was too late.

Fix staggered. A feathered dart had attached itself to his right arm.

On top of the tailor's shop, a figure in a blue toga and hood turned and ran downhill, leaping onto the next shop's rooftop.

Munahim raced to the wagon, nocking an arrow to his long bow as he ran, but before he could leap onto it and climb to the rooftop, two men stepped from the crowd. They were swarthy and wore fur caps and vests, which made them look Yuchak. Each had a scimitar and a round wooden shield, and they wore no livery.

Fix pulled out the dart and dropped it to the ground. "I feel woozy. I think I'm poisoned."

"Deal with them!" Indrajit shouted to Munahim. He lowered Fix to the ground. "Don't worry, the Blaatshi Epic tells me exactly what to do in this circumstance."

"Pray to the fish-mother?"

It was good that Fix was talking. It kept him conscious and distracted him. "Blaat is not the mother of fish. She is our mother. I will not stop you from praying to her, she may hear your plea. But no, there is a stock line in the Epic that says, '*venom of the serpent, venom of the coward's blade, sucked from the wound and kept from the heart.*'"

As he spoke, he drew one of Fix's belt knives and found the pinprick wound in Fix's arm where the dart had pierced his flesh. With the knife's sharp edge, he cut an X-shape centered on the wound. Blood oozed out.

His superior peripheral vision made it difficult to see what he was doing to the wound, this close up. On the other hand, it gave him an excellent view of what the Kyone was doing. Munahim backed away from the two attackers, quickly loosing two arrows over their heads. They ducked, but charged. He fired a third arrow, which sank into the center of an attacker's wooden shield, and then cast his bow aside, drawing his long sword just in time to accept their charge.

"Your translations of the Epic all have the same rhythm," Fix murmured.

"I try to approximate the cadence of the Epic when I am forced to translate," Indrajit said. "I cannot, of course, replicate the pervasive alliteration, assonance, rhyme, and word play."

"Word play? You mean puns?"

"A pun is word play as a joke. In the Epic, word play shows us sacred and essential truths. Meaningful connections between things in this world and things in other worlds."

Indrajit had already talked too much. He leaned forward and sucked blood from his friend's arm. He'd never done this before, but it wasn't purely an idea that came to him from the Epic. His uncle had done this to Indrajit once, when he'd been bitten by a venomous eel. Indrajit had lived, and hadn't lost his bitten leg, despite the dour prediction of his cousin.

Fix's blood tasted metallic and coppery. Was there another flavor as well? Something dark, bitter, and vegetable? Or was Indrajit imagining it, hoping that he was extracting the venom?

Munahim maneuvered sideways, putting the Yuchak with the arrow-pierced shield between himself and the third man. When the Yuchak swung his scimitar, Munahim parried once, twice, and then on the third parry he stepped inside and pushed the attacker's weapon back and up. At the same time, he gripped his own arrow, sunk deep into the wood of the shield, like a handle. He rushed into his foe, howling and slamming him into the second Yuchak. Munahim was taller and more heavily muscled than either of his attackers. The man in his grip fell to the ground and screamed as the bones of his forearm broke. The second staggered away off-balance.

Indrajit spat out the blood, then sucked and spat a second mouthful, then a third.

"I feel nauseated," Fix said. "And my mouth is dry."

Indrajit rolled his friend onto his side. "Throw up if you need to."

Munahim tossed the Yuchak with the broken arm aside and raised his sword into a defensive position. "Come, earn your pay with your death, assassin. Learn what it is to attack the Protagonists."

"Maybe you should take Munahim as your apprentice," Fix murmured.

"I don't think he has the head for all the memorization, to be honest," Indrajit said. "But I'm going to compose some lines about him, that's for sure."

"Anyway, he's good advertising." Fix vomited weakly.

The remaining attacker gamely moved forward. He and Munahim circled, the Yuchak probing with his scimitar for gaps in the Kyone's defenses. Indrajit worried that Munahim's movements were a little slow—he must be as tired as any of them, from lack of sleep as well as from exertion—but he had superior reach, both in arms and in his weapon. The Yuchak pushed in and was repulsed, pushed forward again and Munahim stepped back out of his reach.

Indrajit tore a strip off his tunic and bound Fix's arm.

"You're going to live," he ordered his partner.

"I plan on it." But Fix lay on the cobblestones, moaning.

The crowd around the fighters had grown. Why were there no constables? At this point, some jobber with the law-enforcement contract should have shown up. But there could be a thousand reasons why they hadn't. They might have been bribed or distracted. They might be lazy. They might be dealing with some other naturally occurring scuffle or riot elsewhere in the Spill.

The jobbers atop the wall were talking excitedly among

themselves and passing coins back and forth. They seemed to be taking bets.

Welcome to Kish.

Munahim's guard flagged, the tip of his sword sagging. The Yuchak batted the long sword aside with his shield and dove in for the kill. Munahim turned and brought his long sword up, catching the scimitar near the hilt of his weapon. Then he reached over with a boot that looked slow and inexorable, and kicked the Yuchak's feet out from under him. In the same instant in which the Yuchak hit the cobblestones with his shoulder blades, Munahim drove his sword down through the man's sternum.

Shouts of joy and disappointment both rained down from the wall.

Indrajit drew Fix to his feet. The shorter Protagonist wobbled, but stood.

"You could have helped!" Indrajit yelled to the jobbers on the battlement.

"Help who?" one shot back. "I was betting on the Yuchak!"

Indrajit joined Munahim, standing over the surviving Yuchak. His shield lay at a strange angle, strapped to his broken arm. Munahim had kicked his scimitar out of reach.

"Too bad your bow shots missed," Indrajit muttered. "You could have saved yourself a lot of work."

"I didn't miss," Munahin growled.

Indrajit looked downhill, trying to spot the Kyone's arrows. "Who did you shoot? Were there four Yuchaks at first? I was distracted trying to help Fix."

Munahim grinned. On his canine face, the expression was predatory and a little unnerving. "I shot the man in the blue toga. I believe the first arrow got tangled in the toga and didn't wound him. But with the second, I struck him in the approved target area."

Fix frowned. "The chest?"

"The buttock. I'll go see if I can find him on the rooftop. Perhaps you two would like to speak with this man."

Munahim recovered his bow from a pair of children who handed it up to him with a look of awe on their nut-brown faces. Then he pushed past the shouting tailor to scramble up the crates onto the rooftop.

"So." Indrajit kicked the Yuchak in the hip, lightly. "Now is the time you tell us who wants us dead."

"Joke's on you, fish-head." The Yuchak grinned. His yellow teeth were smeared with blood.

"That's not a very funny joke," Indrajit said.

"I know a funnier joke," Fix told their prisoner. "It involves us opening your belly and seeing how far we can stretch your intestine down the street, while you're still alive."

"He's a little on edge," Indrajit said. "But that doesn't mean he's lying."

"The joke is that I have no idea who wants you dead." The Yuchak laughed, a rasping noise. More blood bubbled from his lips.

"I think Munahim might have broken his ribs," Fix said.

"Dog-headed Kyone, breaker of rib bones."

"Does it rhyme in Blaatshi?"

"Yes." Indrajit returned his attention to the Yuchak. "Who paid you, moron?"

The Yuchak wiped blood from his mouth with the back of his hand. "The House of Knives."

Indrajit's heart sank. He very carefully said nothing to express his feeling of dismay. "We could kill this guy," he said to Fix, "but I vote we just take his weapons and his purse and leave him here. What do you think?"

Fix picked up the scimitar, took a knife from the Yuchak's belt, and cut away his purse. He poked a finger inside to look at the contents. "This won't cover the seventy, but it will make a nice dent in it."

"Don't forget the dead guy's money."

Fix lurched over to strip weapons and purse from the dead Yuchak, and Munahim returned, leaping nimbly down the avalanche of crates. "I didn't kill the man in the toga. But I definitely hit him, there's blood on the roof. And now I know for sure what he smells like."

"Is there a trail we can follow?" Fix asked.

Munahim nodded, grinning like a hungry wolf.

"Let's move Avchat," Indrajit said to Fix. "If we bring him to the inn, you can watch him. It will only take us a few minutes to get him over there, and then Munahim and I will go chase the assassin while the trail is still warm."

Fix nodded. "I wouldn't mind sitting for a little while."

They walked to the forger's stall. Indrajit rapped once on the wood. "Danel Avchat, it's Indrajit Twang. Don't be startled, I'm opening the stall."

He lifted the wall to step inside.

Avchat was gone. A panel in the back wall, previously hidden by a large nautical chart, opened onto an alley between the tailor's and the wholesaler's.

"Frozen hells," Indrajit said.

Chapter Ten

"How long a head start does he have?" Indrajit asked.

"How long were we standing out there?" Fix panted as he ran. "I wasn't completely lucid the whole time."

"I . . . I'm not sure. Not long. Twenty minutes?"

They followed Munahim, who ran with his nose to the ground.

"You know," Fix said, puffing, "if not for the assassins' attack, we'd have been standing around another two hours before we noticed Avchat was gone."

Munahim had led them to the back of the alley behind the forger's kiosk, and then turned a sharp right at the base of the city wall. He'd run uphill, then slowed and become more tentative as he picked his way across a busy street, weaving between two oxen pulling on a cart and a herd of long-necked sheep, and then broke into a run again, down a zigzagging flight of stairs.

"When we catch Avchat, I shall express my gratitude to the House of Knives in an invocation."

"Thanking . . . the fish mother."

"If you like." Indrajit turned on Munahim's heels, cutting across a triangular plaza toward a darkened arch.

Passing a well in the center of the plaza, Indrajit tossed the Yuchaks' scimitars in.

"He's headed to the Dregs," Fix said. "He must have gone immediately out the back door and run."

"Speaking of the House of Knives," Indrajit said, "who wants you dead?"

"Are you certain I'm the target?" Fix asked.

"Not certain, no. But doesn't it seem likely? Twice, this fellow with the blowgun has appeared, and both times fired on you. Now we find out he's with the House of Knives." They plunged into shadow, following Munahim up a roofed flight of stairs. Ahead, out the stairs' exit, he could see the gate into the Dregs. "Does the House of Knives count as one of the Gray Houses?"

"The way I heard it," Fix said, "the first Lord Knife was a servant of the last Emperor of Kish."

"You mean, along with the first Lord Chamberlain, the first Lord Archer, Lord Farrier, Lord Stargazer, and so on."

"Yes. Though I don't know what servant he was. 'Knife' isn't a servant. But maybe a bodyguard or something."

"So there's a Lord Knife today," Indrajit said. "And he's not one of the seven Lords of Kish, or one of the seven Gray Lords. He's number fifteen."

"Yes, counting like that. Though there are plenty of other people who call themselves Lord Something-or-Other."

"Priests and ambassadors."

"Scholars. Merchants."

"Really, the Lord Knife feels like the eighth Gray Lord, doesn't he?"

"I don't know." Fix was red in the face and breathing heavy. "The Lord Chamberlain sometimes acts to kill people without any warrant, and in secret. How is the Lord Knife different?"

"Because he takes money for it?"

"So does the Lord Chamberlain. Or the Lord Farrier, or whoever has the contract for constabulary. He takes money, and he hires jobbers to break heads and sometimes kill people."

"Okay, but the Lord Knife doesn't buy contracts through the Auction House." Indrajit chuckled, feeling he had finally put his finger on an important distinction.

"Yes . . ." Fix said slowly. "Yes, I think that's true."

"Is it possible," Indrajit asked, "that the tradition that the Lord Knife was originally one of the servants of the Emperor might mean that he was one of the original seven?"

Fix snorted like a horse in water. "One of the Lords of Kish, and also head of the assassins' guild? Doesn't that seem like a lot of power?"

"I'm not saying it's a good idea," Indrajit said. "I'm asking if it's possible."

Munahim crossed through the gate into the Dregs and soon turned down a narrow street into a small plaza. The air was thick with the bitter smoke of yip and the sweet, cake-like scent of blue loaf. The walls of the surrounding buildings all seemed to lean inward, as if the plaza were sinking into the earth and dragging the neighborhood with it. Yip smoke dripped from the windows and crawled up the walls and seemed to ooze from the very bark of the scraggly goblin-trees clinging to the cracks in the ancient pavement. Men stood in twos and threes at every exit from the plaza. Indrajit blinked.

The men were all cats, standing on their hind legs. Wearing kilts and tunics or breastplates, armed with long knives and occasionally crossbows, but cats. Several snarled as the Protagonists passed. One held a four-limbed creature impaled on a stick, uncooked, and tore at it with his teeth.

And growled at Indrajit.

Indrajit avoided looking too closely at what the creature was.

"Watch out," Fix said.

"You be careful, too."

"No, *Huachao*. That's the name of these people who look like cats. Huachao. I'd spell it for you, but what would be the point?"

"I'd stop listening as soon as you said 'the first letter is wuh.' I guess the Huachao live here?"

"This is the Armpit," Fix said. "Famous as a place to buy, sell, and consume narcotics and other drugs."

"I smell the yip."

"Also the blue loaf, a little." Fix nodded, his movements still slow. "You don't smell the yao or the yetzel leaf, but they are also undoubtedly here."

"And the Huachao?"

"As I understand it, they are one big clan. And they operate like a jobber company. So someone has them watching this place."

"Not subtle, as sentinels go. But fearsome."

Munahim stopped at the door of a narrow building of yellow clay bricks. Black mildew and unidentifiable green and blue blotches mottled the doorframe. Ironmongery suggested that a door had once hung here, but it was nowhere in evidence, and the hinges were all twisted and snapped. Within, glass shards lay on the floor. Two men crouched on the floor in the visible front room, one sucking smoke from a bowl and the other sipping from a clay bottle.

A white-furred Huachao with red-tipped ears and orange fur on his shoulders leaned against the wall beside the doorway. He wore a studded leather breastplate and skirt and had a curved sword belted to his waste. He peeled back his lips to reveal sharp, white teeth. Was that a smile? He eyed Munahim and Munahim glared back, showing his own teeth, neither backing down or moving a muscle.

"We're here to meet a friend," Indrajit said to the Huachao. "Just came in a few minutes ago."

"A few seconds ago," Munahim growled. "The pavement is warm from his sandal."

"Right." Indrajit took a handful of coins—sesterces and a chriso—and passed them to the Huachao. "We won't cause trouble."

The cat-man purred and looked away.

Within, a front entry room gave way to a narrow hall with an ascending staircase that doubled back on itself twice, rising to higher floors. "Upstairs," Munahim whispered.

Indrajit drew his sword and the others followed suit. Munahim led them up the steps to the second story, then up to the third story, and then to a closed door near the back of the building. He sniffed at the floor outside the door and at the door handle, then listened at the door, then finally held up three fingers.

Three men inside. Perfect.

Indrajit looked to Fix. Fix's color didn't seem right—he was too pale, and his face was sweating. But his jaw was set, he had a falchion in one hand and an ax in the other, and he nodded.

Indrajit kicked down the door.

Inside, Danel Avchat stood beside a table. The stolen map was spread across the table, and two men stood on the other side. One was a scaly, four-legged Shamb, who was counting out coins from a purse in his hand. The other was a tall but solid Ildarian; the left half of his face was a mask of burn scars, and his left eye was sealed shut with scar tissue. The Ildarian wore a scale hauberk, and he and the Shamb each had a sword.

Both wore bright silk scarves around their necks—the Ildarian's blue, the Shamb's a red that matched his skin.

Indrajit charged the table. He intended to slam it into the two strangers and pin them to the wall, but he had not reckoned with the size of the Shamb, or the Ildarian's strength. Indrajit roared and pushed the table, the Shamb didn't budge, and then the Shamb and the Ildarian pushed back, knocking Indrajit into the wall.

He dropped Vacho.

The map, dislodged by the violence of the sudden motion, rolled up and soared across the room at knee height like a low-flying sorcerer's carpet.

Coins scattered across the table and the floor. Avchat shrieked and dove for the money.

The Shamb groped across the table and grabbed Indrajit by the throat with both hands. His leverage wasn't good, but the Shamb's arm strength was proportional to the size of its body, which was overall twice the size of Indrajit. Indrajit gasped and choked.

Then Munahim rushed into the fight. He leaped and planted one booted foot on the Shamb's back, which stretched parallel to the floor, framed by legs at the four corners, a torso at one end and a long, lizardlike tail at the other. The Ildarian had his sword half out of its sheath, but he had been fighting his way forward to attack Indrajit, so he now abandoned the effort to arm himself and turned to catch Munahim's charge.

Munahim slammed the Ildarian in the face with a shoulder. His forward motion took both of them through a window, its glass long removed, and out of Indrajit's sight.

Indrajit heard a heavy *thud* through the window, and then the sounds of scraping feet and the meaty symphony of knuckles cracking into jaws and abdomens.

The Shamb cast a distracted look over its shoulder toward the noise, and Fix attacked. He crouched and came up under the table. The edge of the table knocked Indrajit's chin and hurled him against the wall again, but it also tore him free of the Shamb's grip. The table struck both the Shamb's elbows and the Shamb screamed in pain, a sound like the piping of a teakettle.

Avchat scooped up every coin he could as he staggered pell-mell across the room, finally snatching the map. The room spun about Indrajit's head. He saw Fix attacking the Shamb in his peripheral vision, but he staggered into the doorway.

He saw the head of a Huachao climbing the stairs at a rapid pace.

He slammed the door just before Avchat could get through. He had to grab twice, his vision was so disordered, but he finally got the forger by the neck and tore the map from his hands.

The Shamb was on the floor, dead.

"Huachao are coming," Indrajit said. "Help me block the door."

Fix turned the table over and jammed it sideways under the door handle with one-handed help from Indrajit. It would hold, but not for long. Avchat ran to the window, only to meet Munahim climbing back in.

"Where did the Ildarian go?" Indrajit asked.

"He ran," Munahim said. "I let him. Should I have shot him in the buttock?"

Avchat shrieked.

"Come with us." Indrajit dragged the forger out the window and down onto the roof of the adjacent, shorter building. From there they crossed to a second building, circling around a sagging patch of the rooftop and a second patch that had already collapsed. As they were dropping to a still lower rooftop, preparatory to lowering themselves to the ground, Indrajit looked back. Two Huachao glared at him from the window he'd left.

He thought he could hear them hissing, but it was probably his imagination.

"You're really going to regret this!" Avchat was trembling as they dragged him back into the Spill.

"Why is that?" Indrajit asked. "Because you outnumber us one to three? Or because your cause is just? Are you giving us fair warning that the gods will avenge you? You stole our map fair and square, so we have no right to take it back from you? Or are you going to tell on us to someone?"

"Those men were buying the map from me," Avchat said.

"You were selling them our map, which you stole," Indrajit said again.

"Which *you* stole in the first place!"

"What makes you think that?" Fix asked.

"The Graykin written all over it," the forger said. "The fact that the borders outlined on this map mark the territories of the seven Gray Lords."

Indrajit shrugged. "You were trying to sell our map," he said again.

"To Uthnar Roberts's men," Avchat said.

Indrajit stared at him. "Who is that?"

"Uthnar Roberts. The Silksteppers. Gray Lord of half the Crown."

"I let his man go," Munahim said. "He should appreciate the act of mercy."

"You let his brother go," Avchat said. "Tully Roberts. But you killed his Shamb, and now they know you have this map."

"So what?" Fix said. "This is ridiculous. Why would they be interested? Why would anyone chase after this map? Surely the Gray Lords all know their own boundaries."

Avchat stared at Fix and then laughed, a reedy, frightened sound. "You don't know, do you?"

"I am deprived of sleep, under a deadline, and fearful for the life of the woman I love," Fix said. "Also, I have been poisoned. Is that the right word? Injected with venom. This is not a good way to talk to me today, forger."

Avchat stared at the cobblestones. "I will make your copies. And I'll show you what you don't know about this map. For seventy Imperials."

"Twenty," Indrajit said, before Fix could agree. "And we let you live."

They returned to the wooden kiosk to retrieve paper and inks, but Avchat was afraid Roberts's men would come looking for him there and wanted to do the work somewhere else. Fix found an inn at the back of a winding alley two streets away, where the Grokonk Third at the front desk was willing to rent them a room for six hours.

The room contained a wooden chair, a table with lit lamp, pitcher, and bowl, and a sagging bed. It also had metal rings bracketed to the wall; the scraping pattern on the lower half of the rings suggested that sometimes, someone was chained to them.

They sat Avchat at the table. Munahim stood at the door and Indrajit watched from beside the single window, from which he could see the table clearly. Outside, the long winter night had come. Torches and lamps still lit the larger streets, but the alleyways had become black, frozen chasms cutting through an urban tundra.

"First," Indrajit said, "what are we missing? What's so special about this map?"

"I am going to hold the lamp near the map," Avchat said. "I will not burn the map."

"You die if you do," Fix said calmly.

Avchat held the lamp up to the map. Where the lamp was close to the paper and warmed it, new lines appeared, overlaying the old. They showed an irregular lattice, a demented spiderweb, every place he heated the map. Alongside the pattern of lines were additional characters of the same sort as visibly graced the page.

"How did you know that was there?" Fix asked.

"When you showed me the map," Avchat said, "I . . . invited you to give me some privacy."

"Tricked us into leaving you alone," Indrajit translated.

"And I tried a couple of standard tests to see if there were invisible inks on the map," Avchat continued. "Which, as you can see, there are. You have to admit, it's a map made by one of the Gray Lords. The invisible ink seems a little obvious."

It didn't seem at all obvious to Indrajit. He exchanged baffled glances with Munahim.

Fix sighed. "It's a map of the Undersook."

"I can't read all the characters," Avchat said, "but the map is bigger than the Undersook. I think it's a guide to getting around Underkish. Not a complete map, a complete map of the ruins beneath this city would run to many, many pages and require vertical cross-sections. It would be a book. But I think, with this map, you could get around. Travel underground basically from anywhere in the city to anywhere else."

The Protagonists sat in stunned silence for a minute.

"The Sookwalkers must be especially knowledgeable about the underground passages," Indrajit said.

"We already knew that the merchants of the Paper Sook used some of those passages to move around unseen," Fix continued. "It stands to reason that the thieves who prey on those merchants would have a strong incentive to get to know the passages even better."

"So Zac Betel wants this map because he would like to know the tunnels like the Sookwalkers do," Indrajit said. "And now the . . . Silksteppers? Roberts's men. They know we have it, too. Dare we hope they will leave us alone?"

"They were going to pay me two hundred Imperials," Avchat said.

"So let's assume no, they will not leave us alone." Indrajit sighed. "And have we perhaps angered the Huachao by causing a disturbance after we said we wouldn't?"

"We can avoid the Armpit," Munahim said. "Avoid the Dregs."

"Good idea," Fix said.

"And, of course," Indrajit said, "there's the House of Knives. Have I left anyone out? Have we angered the Selfless of Salish-Bozar the White without my noticing? Has the Collegium Arcanum decided that we're a threat to the city?"

"It sounds like the complete list to me," Munahim said. "For today. We have older enemies, of course."

"Frozen hells, Fix," Indrajit said. "Is she worth it?"

Fix sat on the bed and buried his face in his hands. "As a real person?" he asked. "As a woman, as a flesh-and-blood lover? I don't know. But love is worth it, isn't it?"

"Yes," Indrajit said at once. "Love is worth it."

"You two sleep," Munahim said. "I'll watch the forger."

"You can call me the 'scribe,'" Avchat said.

"We'll take turns sleeping," Indrajit said. "Fix first. Avchat, do you have the materials here to make invisible ink? I want to give Zac Betel his money's worth."

"I do if you can get me drogger's milk," Avchat said. "Or camel's will do, in a pinch."

Chapter Eleven

They debated briefly whether they should deliberately make the forgery wrong, and decided that such mischief could clearly get them into trouble. At the same time, it was hard to see what advantage could come from it, in the absence of a specific plan to deceive one of the Gray Houses.

In the end, they instructed Avchat to make the most accurate copy he could.

Fix and Munahim slept first, then Munahim woke up and spelled off Indrajit.

The winter nights of Kish were long. When he awoke, Indrajit estimated on the basis of the amount of lamp oil and wick consumed, that half the night, six hours, had passed. Avchat had produced a second map.

It was not a forgery; Indrajit could easily tell them apart. The inks were very slightly different colors and the paper of the copy was heavier and less tattered at the edges. But the point was not to fool Arash Sehama, the point was to fool Zac Betel, and Betel surely must not know the map as well. The shapes all looked the same, both the lines marking the streets and walls of Kish and the characters that even Fix admitted he couldn't fully read as well as the lines and characters that showed up under lamplight.

And "fool" wasn't quite the right word anyway, since they were giving Betel the information he was asking for. They were just keeping a copy for themselves, for now.

When Indrajit awoke, Fix leaned on the wall beside the window and Munahim rested against the door. Avchat fidgeted nervously in the chair at the table, sucking the calluses of his fingertips.

"We need to keep the forger under wraps," Fix said.

"Is this where we debate the choice of throwing him to the Ghouls," Indrajit said, "or drugging him and stowing him in the hold of a ship bound for Togu?"

"You have such a romantic imagination," Fix said. "A knife would be cheaper and faster."

"I won't say anything," Avchat said.

"We like to extend trust," Indrajit told the scribe, "but the stakes are really high right now." He turned to his partner. "What if we gave him to Wopal to hold?"

"We'd have to walk him up there and back," Fix said. "That's a lot of delay, and a long time of us exposed to enemies potentially seeing us." He nodded at the foot of the bed, and Indrajit now saw a coil of rope. "I say we just tie him up here, pay for two days' rent, and leave him."

"What if you die?" Avchat asked.

Fix shrugged. "Then you get out in two days, when the innkeeper rents the room to someone new."

"Do we leave the money with him?" Munahim asked. "He might get robbed. By the innkeeper, if not by someone else in the meantime."

"Good point," Indrajit said. "We're going to hold the twenty Imperials, Avchat. Don't worry, they're yours when this is over. Unless, of course, you go around telling more people about our map or our business."

"What if you die?" Avchat asked again.

"In that case," Indrajit said, "I think you're out the twenty Imperials."

Indrajit knew knots, and quickly tied the scribe to the two rings in the wall. Fix improvised a gag from a strip of the bedsheet, and then they set out for Zac Betel's smithy.

Dawn was still four or five hours away. None of them quite felt rested, but they each drank a ladleful of water from a safe well on the Crooked Mile and they chewed strips of dried beef that Indrajit bought at a dried goods store, open late in a plaza filled with torchlight where two separate caravans were loading up beasts of burden for a journey, and they felt somewhat recovered.

Fix held the forgery, rolled in his hand. The original map was carefully folded and hidden in Indrajit's tunic.

They cycled forward and back as they walked, taking turns moving out ahead and then standing and watching for pursuit as the other two caught up. There were too many people who might be following to even think through the possibilities all at once, but Indrajit didn't see any tails, including anyone shadowing them on the rooftops adjacent to the Crooked Mile. The other Protagonists confirmed that they, too, saw nothing, and they soon reached Betel's shop.

Betel was no longer at his anvil, but the fire still burned and three men in leather aprons stood watching the surrounding streets, apparently idle. Two were Kishi and the third was a Wixit. Indrajit noticed that each man had a smudge of soot in the same place alongside his nose, the Wixit's hard to tell from a streak of sandy-colored fur. Behind them, in the yawning shadowy gullet of an open doorway, he thought he saw the bottom two steps of a staircase leading up to the two stories above the smithy.

"We're here for Zac Betel," Fix said.

"He's asleep," the Wixit said. "Come back at dawn. Better still, an hour after dawn."

"This is urgent," Indrajit said. "Who runs the Sootfaces when he's not around?"

"He's around," the Wixit said. "He's asleep."

"He has to have a minister . . . seneschal . . . aide . . . someone," Fix said. "If something big happens and he's asleep, do you just wait until dawn?"

"You think you're something big happening, do you?" The Wixit chuckled.

The two Kishi chuckled, too. They were lightly armed, each wearing a falchion at his belt and studded leather bracers on his legs and forearms. They looked a little like gladiators dressed to fight in the Racetrack on a Pit Day.

"We stole something he urgently wants," Fix said. "And I urgently need what he promised to give us in return."

"That's a lot of urgents," the Wixit agreed. "Come back at dawn."

Indrajit took a deep breath, mustering his most persuasive arguments.

"Here's what's going to happen," Fix said. "I will count to three. Then I will kill both your men here, and then I will pick you up by the scruff and carry you upstairs, yelling Zac Betel's name until he comes out. He'll be pretty angry with one of us, I expect, and I'm quite willing to wager it will be with you."

"You don't want to pick a fight with Zac Betel," the Wixit said.

"I think he might be okay with it," Indrajit said.

"One."

"You know he's a Gray Lord, right? The great families are afraid of him."

"We're not afraid of him." Indrajit shrugged. "We have a deal with your boss."

"Two."

"Are you insane?" The Wixit's voice jumped an octave in pitch. "The Lord Marshal personally pisses his boots when he hears Zac Betel's name. What could possibly be this important?"

"Love," Munahim said.

"Three." Fix drew his falchion.

Metal hissed all around as the two Kishi drew their swords, and Munahim and Indrajit did the same.

"Whoa, whoa, stop," the Wixit said. "Okay. I'll go in and get Yammilku. He's the night warden."

"At last, we understand each other." Fix smiled. "We'll go in together."

The Wixit appeared to be about to object, but then he looked around at all the naked steel. "We'll go together. Dag, Hober, you two, stay here. Everyone . . . calm down, put the swords back."

Indrajit sheathed his sword cautiously, in time with the others, but he kept a hand on the hilt.

Fix loomed over the Wixit and for a moment Indrajit thought he might make good on his threat to snatch the small man up by the scruff of his neck. He didn't, but he pressed close, as if to communicate his sense of urgency by leaning over the little thief. The Wixit led them into the open doorway, up a single dark flight of steps, to a door. Light leaked out underneath, and the Wixit knocked a soft, complex pattern of raps. Then he opened it.

A man sat beside a table. The table was heavy with papers, weighted under old horseshoes, but the man wasn't reading papers.

He leaned away, over a bucket, and ran a whetstone along the blades of a long, straight sword. He wore a kilt, a chest harness of leather straps and buckles, and knee-high leather boots. His head looked like that of a hawk, with a piercing yellow eye, a bright yellow beak, and golden-brown feathers shooting straight back from the top of his skull to give him a crest. The golden-brown feathers gave way to smooth skin of a very similar shade, taut over rippling muscles. A smudge of black soot ran along one side of his beak. An oil lamp burned on a stand in the corner. The room had no windows.

"Yammilku, the Night Warden," the Wixit said.

"Indrajit and Fix," Yammilku said. "And their one hireling."

"We're famous." Indrajit nodded.

"We only need one hireling because he's so mighty," Fix added.

"You're Heru," Indrajit suggested. "*Bright-eyed Heru, longing for the upper sun, keen of eye, sharp of beak, no winds avail them.*"

"You may leave," Yammilku said. The Wixit bowed and stepped out, closing the door behind him.

"This is interesting," Indrajit said. "The Sookwalkers had a very definite look to them. Gray cloaks. You do, as well, but it's sort of..."

"You look like gladiators," Munahim said.

Yammilku laughed, a piercing sonic attack. "You would fit in."

"My face is too clean," Munahim said.

"We can change that."

"Do all the Gray Lords have uniforms for their men?" Indrajit asked.

"It's not crazy," Fix said. "Jobber companies do."

"The great houses do," Munahim said. "And the temples."

"Yeah, but... thieves," Indrajit said. "Don't the Gray Houses want to be sneaky?"

"Sometimes," Yammilku said. "Sometimes we just want to hire someone to be sneaky for us."

"Ah-ha," Indrajit said. "So Betel did leave someone in charge who knew about our deal."

"He expected you to come back." The hawk-headed man wiped oil off his blade with a rag and sheathed it in a scabbard lying across the desk. "Show me the map."

Fix handed over the forgery. The Heru unrolled it on the table and gazed at it. "Do you know what this map is?"

"We do," Fix said. "Tell us who you sold the Girdle of Life to."

"You'll understand if I check the authenticity of the map first."

Fix and Indrajit nodded. Indrajit resisted the urge to touch the real map, folded up in his kilt pocket.

Yammilku took the lamp from the stand in the corner. Holding the map up with one hand, he passed the lamp close to it. When the drogger-milk ink lines appeared, he sighed, a rumbling sound with a hint of a sharp squeak in it.

He replaced the lamp and map. "Zac Betel instructs me as follows," he said. "He sold the thing you seek to Philastes Larch. Philastes is the Archegos Minor of the diplomatic mission of the Paper Sultanates. He lives in the Sultanates' embassy."

"On the Street of Fallen Stars," Fix said. "With the walled garden containing a grove of duckfoot trees and thamber oaks."

"Just so," the Heru said.

"What does a diplomat want with a Druvash artifact?" Indrajit asked.

"You called it the 'Girdle of Life.'" Yammilku shrugged. "Who doesn't want life?"

They left Betel's smithy and climbed the Spill again, south, toward the peak of the city.

"We could keep the map," Indrajit said. "Learn to read it. It would be useful, don't you think? To be able to move freely beneath the city? Or at least, more freely than we do now. It could be worth a lot to be able to move from one quarter to another without having to pass through a gate."

"I thought we'd give the original back," Fix said. "To placate Arash Sehama. I don't really want to have more enemies than I absolutely have to."

"I agree." Indrajit nodded. "We could buy another copy from Avchat and then give Sehama the original."

"Of course," Fix said, "since we've given away the secrets of underground travel to the Sootfaces already, giving back the physical map might not be enough to assuage Sehama's irritation with us."

"Think positive," Munahim said. "We're on our way to get the Girdle of Life, and heal your lady love."

Fix grunted. "I've thought twice in the last twenty-four hours that I was going to get the Girdle. At this point, I will believe it when I see it."

"So if the map marks secret roads," Indrajit said, "think of them as underground highways connecting one quarter to another . . . then yes, we've just added traffic to those roads by giving a copy of the map to Zac Betel. But just having us three also using the roads, that's not a lot of traffic. No one should notice or care."

"It might not just be highways," Fix said.

"What else it is?" Indrajit asked.

"What if the map marks treasure caches?" Fix suggested. "Or secret entrances into the Sookwalkers' territory? Or entrances into good targets, like, say, banks. We might have given the Sootfaces ways to attack or undermine the Sookwalkers that we can't even imagine."

"We really should give the map back as soon as we can," Indrajit said. "At least the Sootfaces should be happy with us. Speaking of not wanting to have too many enemies, that is."

"You'd think so," Fix said. "On the other hand, what if Yammilku or Betel decided that it was a good idea to kill us, so we couldn't tell the Sookwalkers that we'd made a copy of their map?"

"This is why we need to keep a copy ourselves," Indrajit said. "Because right now, I would like to be walking on secret roads and out of sight."

"Except that the enemies we're talking about both have access to those same secret roads," Munahim said glumly.

"Right." Indrajit grabbed Vacho's hilt. "Keep an eye on the rooftops for that blowgun-wielding bastard."

"Or gray cloaks," Fix said.

"Or gladiators," Munahim added. "Or cats."

"Or silk scarves?" Indrajit asked.

"Silk scarves," Munahim suggested.

"Well, we're going into Silkstepper territory now," Fix said, "so watch out for anyone tailing us or setting an ambush. Whether they're wearing silk scarves or not."

Gannon's Handlers had the gate. A trio of Zalaptings hissed in staccato unison as if they were laughing, but the rival jobbers waved Indrajit and his companions through.

Once they were past, the Handlers blew raspberries and jeered.

The Street of Fallen Stars was not the longest street in the Crown, nor the widest. It was thought to be one of the oldest, which was a distinction in a city that was, as far as Indrajit could tell, thousands of years old. Maybe more than that, tens of thousands. Maybe millions. In the Epic, Kish appeared in a famous episode after many generations of Blaatshi history, but as a city that already existed and was an Imperial capital.

The Street of Fallen Stars did not have the aggressive, breathless fashionableness of, say, the Boulevard of Poses, which housed theaters and dance halls a few minutes' walk from the Fallen Stars. It had an air of controlled decay, its sprawling manors had enclosed gardens and fountains behind their gates, and were inhabited by old money—not old power, such as the Lords possessed, but mere wealth, that now wanted to shut itself away from the noise and filth of the rest of the city and spend its money in easy living for generations. As time gnawed its way inexorably through the institutions of Kish and wealthy families fell one by one into poverty, their manors were purchased by others, and the mansions on the Street of Fallen Stars were often bought by foreign embassies.

Many of the families had their own guards and all of the embassies did. Some of those guards wore family or national livery and some were hired jobbers, but the street crawled with armed men at all hours.

Therefore, Indrajit, Fix, and Munahim made their way down the street by stealth. At the corner of Fallen Stars and Bank Street they found a rickshaw pulled by a one-hump drogger, in turn led by a scaly purple man with no visible eyes. He was whatever race of man had also spawned Yozak, Frodilo Choot's doorman, but Indrajit didn't know what the race was. The rickshaw was wide enough for the three of them, being designed as a pleasure model. They burrowed beneath three slightly tattered blankets, Munahim ruminating gloomily on the likelihood of insect infestation in either the cab of the rickshaw or in the blankets. Then they pretended to be sleepers, or possibly entwined lovers, with their faces concealed beneath rucked-up hoods made from the edges of the blankets.

Indrajit watched his side of the street, whispering observations about men on watch as he saw them. When Fix called that they were in front of the Sultanates' embassy and was it a good time to jump, he told his companions, "Wait . . . wait . . . now," and while the Gund in house livery across the street turned and looked back through the gate he was watching, they slipped from the rickshaw and onto the cobblestones.

A thamber oak rose from the street in front of an iron fence, punctuated by stone pillars. Fix raced up the twisted and interlacing branches of the oak. Indrajit crouched between the oak's bole and the wall, trying to stay in the shadow cast by the many intersecting rivers of lamplight streaming sluggishly from the gardens and the porches and the poles all along the street. Once Munahim called down that he was positioned, Indrajit dragged himself up the tree as well.

"When we eventually get around to making a list of all the requirements necessary for joining the Protagonists," Indrajit said, "we must include strong climbing ability."

"Where would we embody such a list?" Fix asked.

"Why must we embody it?" Indrajit asked. "What kind of list has a body?"

"I mean, how shall we make sure we don't forget it?"

"I have a strong memory," Indrajit said. "How about you? Are you worried that your memory isn't strong enough to remember, 'Must be able to climb'?"

"I'm only saying that there are other ways to capture the list, in addition to just using our memories."

"Not good ones," Indrajit said.

They surveyed the embassy.

Chapter Twelve

Kish in general gave the impression that it strained to rise. Buildings were vertical, and became more vertical in wealthier quarters. The wealthiest quarter, the Crown, stood atop a literal hill, comprised of the ruins of centuries of successive cities, heaped atop one another. The walls separating the quarters from each other bounded them, forcing Kish's development to be vertical. The palaces—both those long subdivided into apartments and those still owned by wealthy individuals, such as the Lord Chamberlain—occupied city blocks and climbed into the sky.

Within the wall surrounding the Sultanates' Embassy, that general impression was reversed. The old mansion spread to fill its grounds, throwing out side buildings, a fountain, a pool, two groves, and a garden.

"We could knock on the front door and ask for the Girdle of Life," Munahim said.

"Yes," Fix said. "How do you think that would go?"

"We just need to borrow it," Indrajit said.

"Do you know that for sure?" Fix asked.

"No," Indrajit admitted. "Probably, Archegos Minor Philastes Larch would deny that he had purchased any such thing from the Gray Lord Zac Betel. And he wouldn't lend it to us, or sell it to us, or rent it to us, even if he did admit it. Should we try first, though?"

"If I had a week," Fix said, "or no time constraints at all, maybe. If I thought I could have an open negotiation that wouldn't render my backup plan impossible, maybe."

"Your backup plan of burglary," Indrajit said.

"Yes. But since neither of those things is true, my backup plan is going to be my main plan. Are you with me, or am I doing this alone?"

"We're with you," Indrajit said. "We just needed to think out loud for a minute."

Munahim nodded.

"It's a big manor," Fix said. "The Girdle could be anywhere."

"Our best bet is that Larch knows where it is," Indrajit said. "There will be servants awake. We grab one, ask if he happens to know where the Girdle of Life is. Probably he doesn't, so then fine, tell us where to find Philastes Larch, and the buyer himself gives us the answer."

"If we'd thought this out a little more, maybe we could have brought rope," Munahim said.

"We should hire another Protagonist to carry supplies around for us," Indrajit said. "Rope and lamps and things like that. Food. It's hard to plan for everything in advance."

"That would need to be someone big," Munahim said. "A Gund, a Luzzazza, a Grokonk."

"A female Grokonk," Indrajit said. "They're the big ones."

"We borrow the Girdle of Life," Fix said. "If we can. We plan to give it back."

"If the Girdle can be returned," Indrajit pointed, "and also assuming that the Vin Dalu let us give it back. So let's just accept that we're committing a crime, we know we're committing a crime, but we're doing it because we can't think of a better option."

"More than one crime," Munahim said. "Burglary and assault and maybe kidnapping."

"For love," Fix said.

"Too much talking," Indrajit said. He shimmied out along the heavy branch he sat on, then let himself down on the other side of the fence.

Fix and Munahim followed.

They crouched low and tried to stay in the shadows. The outbuildings and the groves helped, creating great swathes of the thick green grass that were cloaked in darkness. They pushed into a cluster of thamber oaks and cut through it in nearly a straight line toward the main house. The space between the oaks was groomed of weeds and planted with a carpet of grass. The garden gave the impression of wild disorder from far away, but close up, it was clear that it was the product of art.

They crouched at the edge of the thamber oaks. The wind bore moisture on it, and in the distance, thunder rumbled. The main building was a short sprint away, but a large oil lamp burned in a raised niche at the corner of the house, throwing light across the entire space. To their right, by contrast, a single-story building lay in darkness. Curtains bouncing in the windows suggested that they weren't shielded by glass, and that the Protagonists could step inside those darkened rooms and use them to make their way forward to a point where the two buildings nearly touched.

Fix went first, stepping from the shadow of a thamber oak through a low, wide, open window and then pressing himself against the wall, disappearing. Munahim followed and Indrajit came last, scanning for any sign that they were detected or followed.

Two men with spears and shields marched around the inside of the fence a stone's throw away, but their regular pace and the soft buzz of their shared conversation suggested that they hadn't seen anything.

"What is that smell?" Munahim wrinkled his face in disgust.

They stood in a room like a veranda, running the length of the outbuilding. Multiple doorways led deeper into the structure, and at the far end, an arch opened into a shadowed space between this building and the main house.

Indrajit shrugged. "I don't smell anything."

"I don't either," Fix said. "You tell us, Munahim."

The Kyone walked in a small circle, sniffing. "It's coming from underground. There's rot, but something else, too. A dry smell. Something . . . something is much bigger than it should be. Much bigger than the ones I've seen before. Something smells *wrong*."

He shook his head, as if confused.

"Well, rot is a pretty normal smell to be coming from Underkish," Indrajit said. "Sewage?"

"Corpses," Munahim said.

Without meaning to, Indrajit drew his sword. The map in his kilt pocket rustled as he did so. "Under this building specifically?"

"Under this building," Munahim said. "Maybe not only under this building."

"We're not here to investigate the smell of corpses," Fix said.

"Also, something else," Munahim said.

"Understood," Fix acknowledged. "We're here looking for the Archegos and the Druvash girdle he bought."

"But a big pile of corpses might mean there's something in here that threatens us," Indrajit said.

"We'll tell Grit Wopal about it, and maybe come back later." Fix turned to lead them toward the main house.

"Let's at least look at the map," Indrajit said. "If it maps Underkish, you yourself said it might show more than just passages. You said treasure rooms and banks, but maybe the map shows where there's a big pile of corpses. Maybe the map explains why."

"We can't read the map without heating it up. Do you want to light a lamp here and now?" Fix wasn't waiting. He had reached the archway and was pressing himself into it, examining the shadowed space beyond.

Indrajit felt like a fool. He said nothing, and he and Munahim followed Fix into the shadow.

They stood in a small courtyard. Pressing their backs to the main building, they could look right and see onto the main lawn, bounded by the thamber oak grove and the corner lamp and the fence. Looking left, they saw a portico before a door. Dim light leaked from the door, and two men with spears and shields stood in the portico.

Indrajit looked up. A second story rose over just a portion of the main building, and it was near them. Directly over their heads, red clay tiles covering a narrow strip of rooftop peeped down at them.

"A trellis right here would have been convenient," Indrajit said.

"But architecturally strange," Fix pointed out. "You don't grow vines in a stone courtyard. Push me up."

Indrajit put away his sword. He and Munahim together easily hoisted Fix into the air, each lifting him by one leg. Fix disappeared from view, and then, moments later, whispered down to them, "Come up."

"You next," Munahim said. "I can jump."

He crouched, and Indrajit stepped off his back, raising himself onto the rooftop. A few paces away across the red tiles lay a balcony with a stone balustrade. A door with curtains blowing from it opened upon dark spaces within.

The rooftop was nearly flat. Indrajit lay on his belly and extended an arm. Munahim stepped back and then ran at the wall. He was surprisingly silent as he leaped, kicked against the plaster with his sandaled foot, and pushed himself into the air. He caught Indrajit's arm with one hand and the lip of the rooftop with the other, and within moments, he lay on the red tiles beside Indrajit.

Lightning flashed north of the city, over the sea, and cold rain began to fall. The three men took shelter on the balcony, which was protected by a narrow slip of tiled roof. Indrajit took one of the flapping curtains in his fingers.

"Is this . . . made of paper?" he asked.

"The strange smell is here," Munahim said.

"I'd be more inclined to worry about that if you could tell me something about the smell beyond its being 'strange,'" Fix said.

"I don't know," Indrajit said. "I feel pretty unsettled."

"It's . . . parched," Munahim said.

Fix shook his head and passed through the door. Indrajit followed, with Munahim on his heels. They entered a room that was shaped wrong. The building's exterior had tall, straight walls and slightly sloped terra-cotta roofs, but the room was a misshapen sphere. Dim light from deeper within the building showed a knobby path at their feet and they moved forward.

"My sandals are sticking," Munahim said.

"Look for a servant," Fix said. "Really, any person."

"I have a flask of oil," Indrajit reminded them. "If we find even an empty lamp, we can light it."

They passed through paper curtains into a second room. It was similarly roughly rounded, and Munahim sniffed repeatedly.

"When you have a specific observation, feel free to make it," Fix said.

Munahim said nothing.

One exit led into darkness; the space beyond the other was gray-brown with distant light. They moved toward the light, and Indrajit kicked something with his foot.

"It's a stick," he murmured. "We could wrap some of the hanging paper around one end and make a torch."

He stooped to pick the stick up, and found that it was no stick at all.

It was a man's thigh bone, or something very like one.

"Stop," Munahim said. "Is that . . . ?"

Indrajit squinted to see clearly in the gloom, and his eyes took a moment to adjust. Bones lay scattered about the floor. The bones of men: skulls, rib cages, arms and legs. The skeletons were of different sizes, and of many different races of man, and they were all jumbled together in a heap.

"Is this an embassy?" Munahim asked.

"We can make explanations for this," Indrajit said, "but I'd rather just get what we came for and get out."

He lay the bone gently on the floor.

They took careful, quiet steps.

They passed next into a length of hall. At its end, Indrajit saw stairs descending, and beside the top of the stairs, a burning lamp in a niche. Before the stairs and to the right stood an arch that probably led into an adjoining room, but was blocked with paper. By the light of the lamp, Indrajit got his first good glimpse of the paper itself and was puzzled.

"Fix," he murmured. "Doesn't this paper look strange? It's . . . rough. It's flaking. You're the paper expert. What do you make of it?"

"I write on paper," Fix said softly. "I don't make the stuff. But this seems very crude. Maybe it's cheap paper?"

"The smell is strong here," Munahim said.

"Help . . . me . . ."

The three men froze.

"You heard that," Munahim said.

Fix drew his falchion. "It came from the other side of the paper."

Indrajit drew Vacho. "You sure this isn't distracting us from finding the Girdle?"

"We don't know who the person on the other side of this paper is," Fix said. "But it's probably someone who knows the embassy, and can help us find Philastes Larch."

"Good enough for me." Indrajit sliced a great vertical slash through the paper, and then a second, and then a horizontal slash above the level of his head. He pressed with his foot, and a door-sized panel of paper curled away and inward, opening an entrance. Indrajit stepped inside, sword in a defensive position and senses focused.

Fix took the lamp and followed.

"I think I smell it," Indrajit said. "It's musty and stale. Flat." He heard the roll of thunder outside the building. "Shine that light around, I don't see anything."

He heard rustling sounds, away in the darkness.

Fix raised the lamp. This room, too, was roughly spherical, and by the lamp's light, Indrajit could see that that was because paper filled the corners of the room. Layers of paper, affixed to the walls at the edges and layered. One shape covered by paper, standing on one side of the room, might have been a reclining couch. On the other side, a different, masked object might have been a covered table. A wide arch, wrapped in paper, led through the far wall into a room beyond. The far room was utterly dark.

From the ceiling, in this room, hung an oblong object.

"Help . . . me . . ."

"The voice is coming from that bundle." Munahim had his bow in his hands, an arrow on the string.

"It's coming from near the ceiling." Indrajit circled slowly, moving around to the other side of the hanging object while keeping it tightly in focus. He prodded the bundle with the tip of his sword, causing it to swing back and forth slightly.

"Kill . . . them . . . they will . . . kill . . . everyone . . ."

Indrajit stood in the corner of the room. He was loath to put his back squarely to the dark void of the next room, and even having it to his side and just slightly behind him made the skin on the back of his neck crawl. He kept an eye on the darkness with his peripheral vision and stared up at the hanging bundle.

He saw indeterminate movement, a writhing near the top.

It was a man's face.

"Help . . . me . . ."

"Fix," Indrajit said. "Watch the entrance and give me a knife. Munahim, keep an eye on the next room."

"Stop . . . murders . . ."

He took a knife from his partner and dragged the reclining couch across the floor, leaving it beneath the hanging man. He sliced into the paper wrapping the couch, freeing the flat surface of it to use as a step. The paper was dry as dust, but when he cut it a wave of trapped moisture and a sticky-sweet smell rose from the couch.

"Too . . . late . . ."

Munahim shifted from one foot to the other, growling.

Indrajit climbed onto the couch. The man hung from a thick cord of wrapped paper, almost like the stem of a pear. Indrajit wedged his body beneath the bundle, cut through the cord, and then brought the bundle down in a guided slide so that it came to rest on the couch.

The face at the top of the bundle trembled. It was emaciated, as if sucked dry of blood, and a thin paper film covered it. Indrajit peeled away the film, an uncomfortable tickling in his stomach.

"The parties . . ." The man groaned. "Everyone . . . will die."

"I'll get you out," Indrajit murmured.

"It may be . . . too late . . ." The man's voice cracked.

Indrajit sliced at the paper, peeling it away in scraps and sheets. The man wore only a loincloth, and when the paper was removed, his skin was covered in sticky patches. His ribs showed in the lamplight, and the bones of his wrists and shoulders. His belly was inflated; he looked as if he were starving.

Indrajit was deeply bothered. He felt the sensation that Munahim had been describing a few minutes earlier—something was wrong, badly wrong, and he couldn't put his finger on quite what it was.

Other than a man wrapped in paper, of course.

"Keep talking," he said.

"I'm the archegos minor . . . Lysander Frick."

"Ah, archegos." Indrajit pulled away the paper and tried to help the man stand. He was wobbly on his feet and could not balance without leaning on Indrajit. His sagging belly swayed left and right as if it had a mind of its own. "What is that, exactly?"

"A junior . . . member of the embassy." The archegos leaned forward on Indrajit's arm and retched, nothing coming up. "Below an archegos . . . major. And below the . . . hyperarchegoi."

"So you know Philastes Larch," Indrajit said, trying to keep his voice disinterested.

"My counterpart." The archegos retched drily again, and began to shudder. His entire body trembled. "Can you get me . . . to a healer?"

"What's wrong?" Fix asked, coming closer. "Why were you attached to the ceiling? Who bundled you up like this?"

"The . . . birthing," Frick said. "I don't want it . . . never wanted it. Can you . . . get me . . . a healer? I didn't know . . ."

"We can try," Indrajit said.

"We should burn this place to the ground right now," Munahim said.

"You must . . . stop them . . ."

"Stop who?" Indrajit asked. "Stop the healers?" That didn't feel right.

"Stop . . . the parties . . ."

The archegos lurched forward a third time, leaning heavily on Indrajit's arm. He retched, and this time as he retched, matter emerged from his mouth.

But it wasn't bile. An insect, wasplike, the length of Indrajit's hand, wet, and lacking wings, fell from his lips to the floor.

He retched again, and another wingless wasp dropped.

Munahim growled and Fix gasped. Indrajit scooted back to avoid the insects now crawling on the floor.

"No," Frick groaned. He clamped both hands over his mouth and tightened his jaw. He staggered away from Indrajit and threw himself against the wall. He stood alone, writhing.

A nodule of flesh the size of a pomegranate bulged out from his windpipe—and then burst.

In a shower of blood, another wasp fell to the floor.

Frick staggered away from the wall and sank to his knees. Two more nodules of flesh swelled up in his belly and then burst, and wasps crawled from the flesh.

"Kill them," Fix grunted. He stepped forward and smashed one insect, grinding it under his heel, and then a second.

Indrajit managed to smash two of the insects, and then the archegos minor's belly exploded, and more swarmed forth. Ten, a dozen, twenty?

Frick toppled forward and hit the floor.

"Fire!" Munahim spat.

Fix raised his hand to throw the lamp, but in the corner of his eye, Indrajit saw movement in the adjoining room. He caught Fix's wrist and they turned together, both men raising their swords.

Emerging from the darkness in the next room came two wasps the size of horses.

Chapter Thirteen

"Stop!"

Indrajit didn't immediately recognize that a voice had spoken. It was dry, and clicked, and the stops in it sounded too similar to each other, as if it were being made with a primitive mouth . . . or something that wasn't, in fact, a mouth at all.

It had come from the wasp.

"I'm not releasing my bow," Munahim muttered.

"Who are you?" Indrajit asked.

"And what have you done with the Girdle of Life?" Fix added.

The wasps retreated a step, cloaking themselves in the shadow of the adjacent room. They eased forward and backward, giving the impression that they rode a swing in and out of visibility.

"We are the hyperarchegoi," a wasp said. The smaller of the two wasps, Indrajit decided. "You are invading our home."

Indrajit released Fix's hand; Fix continued to hold the lamp ready to throw. "I don't understand. Does that mean you're the ambassadors?"

"From the Paper Sultanates, yes. Do not kill the archegos."

Indrajit looked down at Frick. He lay dead, his abdomen a gaping ruin. Wingless wasp nymphs swarmed over his flesh, plucking at it with tiny jaws, opening pockmarks on his face and legs and shoulders.

"I'm pretty certain he's already gone," Indrajit said.

"You are deceived by the veil of flesh," the smaller wasp said.

"What is this?" Fix muttered. "Does the Epic tell you nothing of these creatures?"

"Sailors from the Sultanates, stealing men and gold," Indrajit recited. "No, I have always understood them to be pirates. Frankly, I made something of a connection in my mind between the Paper Sultanates and the Paper Sook. I thought they were all piratical adventurers, named after paper because of the intrinsic evils of the material. Did you learn nothing of this as a young Mote of Salish-Bozar the White?"

"A Trivial, not a Mote," Fix said.

"Your language has so many synonyms."

"We sought to master and therefore preserve useless knowledge, for the sake of knowledge alone."

"For the beauty," Indrajit suggested.

"I know nothing of a race of insects in the islands of the north."

"We are men much as you are," the wasp said.

"You may be men," Indrajit said. "You are not men much as we are."

"That is true," the wasp said. "For instance, we would not murder the young of other men. And we would not break into their homes to commit such a murder."

"You haven't asked," Munahim pointed, "but I also know nothing of giant insect-men."

"Thank you," Indrajit said.

"And this, of course, is the strange smell I detected earlier."

"Yes, that seems clear. You might have told us that it smelled like insects."

"I didn't recognize that it smelled like wasps. The strength of the smell confused me."

The larger wasp surged forward two paces and crouched. The wasps had wings on their backs, but Indrajit saw now that they could walk on six legs, bellies parallel to the earth, or shuffle in a crouch on the rear two legs only. "You have already killed some of the Archegos Frick."

"You killed him." Indrajit kept Vacho between himself and the wasps, but tried not to look as if he was threatening them with it. He pointed at the mangled body. "There he is, right there, dead."

"There he is." The larger wasp inclined its head, and Indrajit realized that it was pointing with its antennae. "Right there, dead."

Indrajit shook his head. "What?"

"It's pointing at the smashed nymphs," Fix said.

"We are not sexless," the smaller wasp said. "Do we look like Gunds to you? Like Grokonk Thirds?"

"We are men," the larger wasp said. "I am Hyperarchegos Chach-shazzat and this is Hyperarchegos Kak-chandad. We are the envoys of the Paper Sultanates."

"I hear more feet," Munahim murmured. "Wasp feet. Big wasp feet. Many of them. I'm not sure which direction."

"You go in and . . . you have conversations with the Lords of Kish," Indrajit said. "About . . . fishing rights, or whatever."

"Of course not," Chach-shazzat said. "We send the hyparchegoi."

"Until the hyparchegoi, by their long service and personal merit, have earned the birthing." Kak-chandad crouched, rubbing his forelegs together. "Then they must be replaced in their menial labors."

"Sometimes they earn the birthing," Chach-shazzat clicked. "Sometimes, we run out of other options, and a lucky archegos is promoted in spite of himself."

"I don't understand why we're having this conversation," Munahim murmured.

"If you mean, why have we not killed you," Chach-shazzat said, "perhaps it is because we are civilized men, not given to casual murder."

"Or perhaps it is because you are armed," Kak-chandad added, "and pointing your weapons at us. Perhaps it is because you have killed some of the archegos, and we do not wish you to kill the rest of him."

"Frick told me he didn't want the birthing," Indrajit said.

"At the last minute, many grooms have feelings of reluctance," Chach-shazzat said. "Many mothers worry that they will not do a good job after they are already pregnant. This is natural, and the way of the world."

Indrajit felt ill. "You killed him. You implanted eggs into him and you killed him."

"We implanted eggs into him," Kak-chandad said, "and he has given birth. Now he is in many nymphs, and will live on in their lives."

"I look forward to welcoming him to adulthood," Chach-shazzat said. "Giving him names."

"So he'll be a hyperarchegos now," Indrajit said. "Or is the archegos major one of you?"

"The archegos major is a man such as you," Chach-shazzat said. "The hyparchegoi are the archegoi major and minor."

"So the archegos major hasn't merited the birthing yet," Indrajit said. "Does he know about it?"

The wasps were silent.

"He knows about it," Indrajit guessed. "He doesn't want it, so he hasn't earned it."

"An archegos major who deliberately shirked his duties would merit a different fate," Chach-shazzat said.

"What, you'd kill him?" Indrajit pointed at Frick's corpse. "That sort of sounds like the same fate."

"I remember my former life as a man with two legs," Chach-shazzat said. "I was a Yuchak tribesman. I hunted across the steppes. Hunted the dog-headed men, Kyones, such as your companion."

Munahim growled.

"I was enslaved by Ukelings," Chach-shazzat continued. "I pulled an oar for five years as we raided Karthing villages, and the monasteries and chapels of Ildarian saints. I killed two Ildarian soldiers with my chain, an act of valor which earned me my freedom from my Ukeling masters. I had grown fond of the life of a raider, so I did not return to my former home, but continued, no longer at the oar but now leaning against the gunwale and leaping into victims' ships or upon their wharves. Until one day we made the mistake of attacking another raider, a ship from the Sultanates. We were not expecting the beautiful horrors that climbed from belowdecks. We fought them as monsters. Many of us fell. I was defeated and became again a slave."

"This is more than I wanted to know," Indrajit said. "So you remember some of the life of the man in whose belly you hatched."

"I am that man," Chach-shazzat said. "I am transformed."

"And I am a Pelthite lochagos, who fell in battle against the soldiers of the Sultanates," Kak-chandad added. "As a boy—"

"Stop," Indrajit said.

"Sometimes," Fix murmured, "I wonder whether you should have more curiosity about such things. As your people's Recital Thane, I mean."

"I do not intend to add the life story of this wasp-man to my people's Epic," Indrajit said.

"You can see, surely, how the enhanced perspective of having had two lives enriches our understanding," Chach-shazzat said. "How it makes us wise in ways you cannot possibly understand."

"I don't need to have been a parasite in another man's belly to understand his life," Indrajit said. "I am guided by the Blaatshi Epic, which captures the wisdom of hundreds of generations of my ancestors, and not just one."

Chach-shazzat rubbed his forelegs together, looking at Indrajit. "So much wisdom. You would make an interesting archegos."

"He doesn't have the right temperament," Fix said.

Indrajit snorted. "What do you mean? I have an excellent temperament!"

"Oh, yes?" Fix said. "So you'd like to continue auditioning to replace Frick?"

Indrajit looked at the dead man and bit his tongue.

"You have the wisdom of hundreds of lives," Chach-shazzat said. Had he hunkered down, slightly?

"Yes," Indrajit said.

"That's nothing," Fix said. "You should try reading a book."

Indrajit snorted again.

"Do *you* have the wisdom of many lives?" Munahim asked the wasp-men.

They hesitated, drifting back slightly into shadow.

"That wouldn't make any sense," Fix said. "It's not cumulative. What do you think, the Yuchak hatched from the belly of a Karthing before him, bearing his memories?"

The hyperarchegoi said nothing.

Indrajit might need to add these wasp-men to the Epic, or prepare the epithets so that his successors could compose the incidents. Especially if he encountered them again in the future, and they became significant in the course of his own adventures. "Hyperarchegos is a title, isn't it? 'Elevated leader,' or something like that?"

"It is a title," Chach-shazzat agreed. "It doesn't come from our own language, but from the tongue of the men who lived on our islands before we did, the men we came to rule. They are a Pelthite people."

"Frick and Larch are from that stock," Indrajit said.

"Yes. A hyperarchegos is the head of something. We are heads of this diplomatic mission. Another hyperarchegos might be head of an army, or of a fleet, or of a trading caravan."

Indrajit nodded. The point of his sword had drooped, and he reminded himself that he was still talking with giant wasp-men, who might at any moment decide to kill him. He tried to be subtle about it, but he raised the tip again. "What do you call your own race?"

"We are Kattak," Kak-chandad said. "You have not heard of us because we prefer to remain in the shadows."

"Perhaps I *have* heard of you," Indrajit mused. "There is an epithet that goes, *'Hornets of the northern isles, eaters in waste places.'* But I think my people didn't understand that you were men. Or at least, the recital thanes before me didn't understand that you were men. So you are sung in the Epic as monsters."

Chach-shazzat hissed.

"That's neither here nor there, really," Fix said. "The question is, really, where do we go now?"

"You are intruders," Kak-chandad said. "We would be within our rights to kill you, even if you hadn't killed some of the archegos minor."

"Lysander Frick," Indrajit said, "but you'll rename his . . . the Kattak that came from him. They'll have Kattak names. Or will they all have the same name?"

"You will agree," Chach-shazzat said, "that we have been very civilized. We have treated with you, when we might have attacked."

"True," Fix said. "And you will agree that *we* have been very civilized. We have refrained from destroying the nymphs, once we learned what they were, and we have held discourse with you."

"Civilized trespassers," Kak-chandad said.

"I thought we were finding common ground," Indrajit said. "Why say such hurtful things?"

"We would forgive all trespass," Kak-chandad said, "if you gave us the Kyone."

"What?" Munahim took a step back and raised his bow.

"It would be valuable to us to incorporate his experience," Chach-shazzat said.

"We're not going to give him to you," Fix said.

"Then you must be preparing to leave." Chach-shazzat crept forward, rising onto his hind legs. "Our patience has already been tried."

"We came here to find Philastes Larch," Fix said. "The other archegos minor. You tell us where to find him, we'll have our conversation, and *then* we'll leave."

"We'll trade you Larch," Kak-chandad said.

"We won't give you the Kyone." Fix shook his head.

"We'll trade for the Blaatshi." Kak-chandad also rose onto his hind legs and shuffled forward. "We very much want to have the advantage of the wisdom of four hundred twenty-six generations."

Did the Kattak have stings? Indrajit studied their scythelike mandibles, glistening darkly in the lamplight, and peered past their bodies in the gloom, looking for sharp, stabbing points. How did they implant their eggs? Without meaning to, he tightened his stomach muscles and gritted his teeth.

"I'll come back and recite for you another time," Indrajit said. "Maybe out on the front lawn. At noon. With an audience. But I won't bear your eggs."

"You might not have a choice." Kak-chandad made a rattling sound. "Kishi? Kyone? What say you?"

Munahim growled.

Fix brandished his lamp. "If you lay eggs in my partner, I'll light him and you both on fire."

"We were having such a peaceful negotiation," Chach-shazzat said.

"Yes," Fix agreed. "Then you tried to buy my partners." He knelt and plucked a nymph off the dead archegos's body with a sucking sound. He held it up, revealing a row of wiggling legs and a moist underbelly. "I'll take this with me."

Indrajit quickly grabbed a second nymph. It felt like a roll of fat in his hand and it squirmed. He held its nutcracker-like pincers away from his own flesh. "Tell us where to find Philastes Larch," he said. "We'll have our conversation with the archegos minor and then we'll leave."

"I hear more feet," Munahim murmured again.

Chach-shazzat lowered himself onto his six legs and crept forward a pace. He stood in shadow, behind the mostly wrapped reclining couch and the paper husk that had held Lysander Frick. "You have taken hostages. You are kidnappers now."

"We didn't want to be," Indrajit said. "We just wanted to be trespassers, really. Maybe burglars, slightly. And only because we didn't think we had a choice. You're the ones who want to impregnate our Kyone."

"I don't want to be pregnant," Munahim said. "Especially not by a bug."

"The sooner you tell us where to find Larch," Fix said, "the sooner we get what we want from him, and leave you your lovely little baby Kattak, and go away."

"We could kill you," Chach-shazzat said.

"You kill me," Fix said, "I drop the lamp. In this room made of paper."

"The archegoi sleep in rooms beneath us," Kak-chandad said. "Larch is the younger man."

"You will leave the nymphs here," Chach-shazzat said.

"No," Fix said. "Munahim . . . Indrajit . . . let's go."

Indrajit needed no further urging. He ducked into the hall outside and headed for the stairs. The entrance by which they'd come into the building still showed darkness on the outside; how long until dawn? Surely, it must be imminent.

He waited until Munahim and Fix had both come out of the Kattaks' chamber before he headed down the stairs.

"Keep your eyes open." Fix drew his falchion. "I don't want to be surprised by the other Kattak Munahim keeps hearing."

"Still hearing them," Munahim said. "Not sure how many, not sure how far away."

"We also don't know what other stairways or passages there might be in this building," Indrajit pointed out. "Those same two Kattak might creep around and attack us from behind."

He kept his eyes open. At the bottom of the stairs was a square, high-ceilinged chamber with multiple exits. Most were open and a quick glance revealed where they led: to a kitchen, to storage rooms, to a lounge with reclining couches, to a greenhouse, to a passage leading to the front doors. A short hall was punctuated with four shut doors.

Paper covered everything. Pillars were wrapped in it. Walls were covered with it. Indrajit wasn't sure he was seeing all the doors, and he was nervous at each step that he might fall through paper into a concealed pit.

"The Pelthites of the Paper Sultanates," Fix wondered out loud. "What do they know about the Kattak?"

"Just keep the light high." Indrajit shuddered. "Remember that I have more oil, if you start to run low."

Listening for the crisp sounds of insect feet or mandibles, he began opening the doors. The first contained a bed, table, and shelves, but the bed was empty. This room was blessedly paper-free.

The second was a latrine.

The third contained a table and shelves, and a bed with a man in it, under a light sheet. "Watch the hall," Indrajit told his partners.

The man wore a long sleeping tunic. Indrajit sheathed his sword and grabbed him by the front of his garment with one hand, shaking him roughly. "Philastes Larch!"

The man jolted to a sitting position. He had the large nose and curly dark hair of a Pelthite. "Don't hurt me!"

"You're in no danger." Indrajit tried to sound calming and peaceful, but realized he was holding a squirming Kattak nymph in one hand. He checked the ceiling, looking for cracks or chimneys by which a Kattak might enter. "I'm looking for Philastes Larch. Is that you?"

The Pelthite shuddered and said nothing.

"Listen, Larch," Indrajit said. "I have no time. You bought something from Zac Betel, the Gray Lord. A girdle. Like a chest harness. I need that, and I need it now. I don't want to hurt you, and I won't take anything from you other than the Girdle."

"Are you carrying eggs?" Larch asked.

"What?"

"Kattak eggs?" Larch spun on sit on the edge of the bed. He shook visibly. "Are you bound for the birthing? Have you been to the . . . embassy parties?"

"No," Indrajit said. "We have a . . . Wait, why are you asking that?"

"Frick kept muttering about parties, too," Fix pointed out.

"Why do you want the Girdle?" Larch asked.

"Just tell me where it is," Indrajit said, "and we'll have no more trouble."

"I didn't get it for me," Larch said. "Or at least, I'm not the one wearing it now."

"The archegos major," Indrajit guessed. "He sent you to get it. What's his name?"

"Yes," Larch admitted. "Thomedes Tunk. He's next door." He pointed.

"Thanks." Indrajit turned to leave.

"But you'll take me with you?" Larch asked.

"Why do you want to leave?" Indrajit asked.

The Pelthite's eyes bulged and he trembled. "Why do you think?"

Chapter Fourteen

"Just hold on a minute," Indrajit said.

He emerged into the hall, hearing Larch's feet as the archegos minor leaped from the bed and came padding after him. Fix stood guard at the mouth of the hallway, lamp raised high. Munahim waited at the end of the hall, an arrow to the string.

Indrajit threw open the door to the next room. This was larger than Larch's, with a bigger bed, a dressing screen, and a divan. A completely bald man sat up in bed, sheet clutched around his chest. He wore a heavy dressing gown, and the lamplight over Indrajit's shoulder revealed chalky skin, pouting eyes, tiny ears, and delicate fingers.

"I have very little money," the bald man said.

"I'm not a robber," Indrajit said. "Thomedes Tunk?"

The bald man hesitated. "Yes. Are you here on an embassy matter?"

"Your underling Larch bought a Druvash artifact from one of the Gray Lords," Indrajit said. "I presume you know about that."

"What if I do? Who are you, and what business is it of yours?"

Indrajit shook his head. "I'm not introducing myself. Here's the deal. I need that harness. I can probably give it back, and if I can, I will. And I will pay for the rental."

"Are you . . . ?" Tunk's eyes narrowed. "Have you met the hyperarchegoi?"

"You mean the giant bugs? Yes. Despite not being invited to any of the good parties, apparently. Now where is the harness?" Indrajit rifled through the objects resting on the table: a book, candles, an unlit lamp, several pots containing various sorts of makeup.

"Are you . . . bound for the birthing?" Tunk asked.

Indrajit growled. "Larch asked the same thing. Frozen hells, why would you think that?"

Larch padded to the doorway. "It's just . . ."

"What do you want with the harness?" Tunk asked. "Do you know how to make it work?"

"Do *you* know how to make it work?" Indrajit asked. "How did you hear about it, anyway? You weren't walking along the Crooked Mile one day, and someone casually mentioned that a Druvash Girdle of Life had been found."

"I was at a party," Tunk said. "Eating cheese and drinking wine. And it was a Bonean prince, actually, who mentioned that a Druvash Girdle of Life had been found."

"This still doesn't sound right," Indrajit said. He poked around behind the dressing screen, finding a bar from which hung several tunics and robes.

"He was a minor scholar as well as a prince," Tunk said. "The Druvash were lords of Boné as well, you know."

"I did know," Indrajit said. "They were lords of the whole Serpent Sea and all its lands."

"But he had no money to buy the Girdle for his collection," Tunk said, "so he was complaining to me."

"Complaining to you?" Indrajit asked. "Or trying to borrow money?" He knocked cushions from the divan and then looked under it, but found nothing.

"Does it matter?" Tunk pouted.

"Not really," Indrajit admitted. "Are you trying to raise a dead person?"

"Dead person?" Tunk's jaw fell open.

"Okay, never mind. What are you planning to do with the Girdle?"

"Dead person?" Tunk asked again.

Suddenly, Indrajit understood. "You've been . . . impregnated."

"I'm a man!" Tunk snapped.

"You're bound for the birthing," Indrajit said. "Is this what happens at the parties? The embassy has elegant events. Come for dinner, dancing, and a little giant-wasp impregnation?"

Tunk shuddered, trembling in all his limbs. "I didn't ask for it."

"Of course you didn't ask for it," Indrajit snapped. He grunted, gnawed his lip, tried to think what to do. "You were promoted or punished, it looks the same to me. So the wasp-monsters came to the parties?"

"Behind the scenes," Tunk said. "They were the hosts. Something terrible is going to happen to the city."

"This is Kish," Indrajit said. "Many terrible things are going to happen to it. Which one did you have in mind?" He grew weary of holding the Kattak nymph, so he tossed it on the floor and ground it under his heel.

Tunk shuddered, staring at the pulped nymph. "I don't know. I just know . . . something terrible."

Indrajit nodded. "Look, I need the harness. I don't think you can make it work, anyway. It attaches to a larger device that makes it function. You have to have both. And I'm not sure that the harness will stop the birthing, in any case. Maybe it will, but, as far as I know, its purpose is to raise the dead. Or the nearly dead."

"Do you know Druvash craft?" Tunk asked. "I'll pay you!"

Indrajit snorted. "What good would that do, even if I did? If I . . . healed you, but left you here, they'd just do it to you again."

"I'll come with you!" Tunk gushed.

"So will I!" Larch said.

"I don't like it," Indrajit grumbled.

"I don't care, one way or the other," Fix called. "But we need to get out of here now."

"Give me the Girdle," Indrajit said. "I'll give you twenty crowns. And if I can't bring it back to you in a week, I'll give you another twenty crowns."

"You aren't listening to me," Tunk said. "I need to be treated. Do you know a Druvash sorcerer?"

The archegos major was lucid, but Indrajit now saw that his arms were gaunt, as Frick's had been.

"Yes," Indrajit said. "We know three of them. Twenty crowns, and I'll introduce you to them, too."

Tunk rose from his bed, sheet still wrapped around him. "I'm coming with you."

"I'm coming, too!" Larch said.

"No," Indrajit said.

"Hurry up," Fix urged.

"Yes," Tunk insisted.

He dropped the sheet. The robe he wore was of thick, layered silk, richly embroidered. It was also lumpy, as if he were wearing it over something else.

"Wait a minute," Indrajit said.

Tunk opened his robe, and beneath it, Indrajit saw black straps crossing the man's chest. Straps like those depicted in the picture of the Girdle of Life.

"Frozen hells," he muttered.

"Indrajit, now!" Fix snapped.

"We're coming," Indrajit said. He exited into the hall. Tunk and Larch followed him.

"We?" Fix shook his head, then saw Tunk's harness, then sighed. "Fine. You'll explain later. What's the fastest way out of here?"

Fix had also disposed of his nymph, which was now a smear on the floor.

Tunk shrugged. "However you came in. There are armed men surrounding the building."

"Secret exits?" Munahim asked. "Ways out, just in case?"

Indrajit moved from the hall into the square room. "There's the front door!" he cried. "Out the front door and we sprint for the fence!"

"Even if you make it to the fence," Tunk said, "there's the Fallen Stars Watch."

"What's that?" Fix raised the lamp, looking with suspicion at the stairs down which they'd come earlier.

Munahim wrinkled his nose.

"The guards of every house on the street are sworn to help each other," Tunk explained. "If you get past the embassy guards to the street, the guards next door and across the street and every guard all the way to Bank Street will try to stop you. They get paid a bonus if they succeed, out of a pot everyone pays into."

"I admire the civic self-organization," Fix muttered, "though I find it personally inconvenient."

"Besides," Larch said, "someone's at the door."

Indrajit looked, in time to see shadowy outlines of men through the glass of the front doors. Then a stone crashed through the window. One man with shield and spear rushed through, and Munahim loosed an arrow, dropping him to the floor.

The other outlines dropped out of sight as the men took cover.

"The map," Indrajit said.

"What map?" Tunk asked.

"You think there's an exit into the underworld here?" Fix asked.

Indrajit sheathed his sword and scrambled to open the map. "Just heat the Crown here and let's look."

Fix carefully unfolded the map. He held up the light and the hidden lines of the map of the lower city faded quickly into view. "Now, where are we?"

"Here," Indrajit said. "This is the Crown. There's the Spike. This must be the Street of Fallen Stars, more or less."

"The stairs!" Munahim raised his bow to loose an arrow, and the string snapped. "Ow!" His arrow flew sideways and skittered across the floor.

Indrajit and Fix turned to look at the stairs and saw one of the Kattak descending in a rush. Indrajit had no idea which of the two it was, or whether it might even be a third wasp-man. He drew his sword again, grunting in frustration.

Fix threw the lamp.

The clay lamp shattered against a paper-shrouded wall, scattering flaming oil against the wall, the floor beneath it, and the ceiling above. The Kattak made an angry clattering sound with its mandibles and Indrajit leaped forward to fight it.

He dropped the map. For a moment, he lost his sense of where he was, and where the fire was, and he feared that he or the map would be engulfed. Then Vacho crashed down on top of the Kattak's head, crunching into chitin. The Kattak shrieked and Indrajit snapped back into his own senses.

Munahim slammed into the wasp-man at his side, striking twice in quick succession with his enormous blade. The wasp-man shrieked and pulled back, plunging into a smooth paper wall and disappearing. In his wake, the wall was left a gaping hole, revealing a doorway Indrajit hadn't seen was there.

"We could follow the Kattak," Indrajit said. "He might be fleeing the fire. Or we could go back the way we came."

"No," Fix said. "Look, you were right. See this line?" He held up the map. Indrajit did not clearly see the line, because he kept swinging his head about, looking for more attackers. "This has to be very close to here. And this word here, of course, gives it away." He pointed at a glyph.

"Don't be smug," Indrajit said. "Gives what away?"

"It says 'spider.' And that one next to it says 'fire.'"

"First of all, I thought this was Graykin, and you couldn't read it."

"I can't read the other things on the map," Fix said. "The visible text. But the Graykin, the invisible text, I can puzzle out a bit. I was something of a notorious criminal before I met you."

"I remember," Indrajit said. "You were buying and selling risk without being registered. Pretty nefarious stuff."

"So I had a few dealings with gangsters, and I learned a glyph or two."

"Great," Indrajit said. "You have lit a fire, so now all we need to is to find spiders, and that will no doubt show us the way down into a good escape tunnel."

The fire engulfed the stairs now. Thunder rumbled. Through the broken front door, Indrajit heard rain crashing on the lawn and on the street. From the second story, he heard scratching and clicking sounds. Munahim had nearly finished restringing his bow, pulling the spare from his quiver.

"Men are trying to come in through the front door again," Munahim warned. He shot another arrow in that direction.

"There's a side door through the kitchen," Larch said. "Maybe no one will be watching it. Maybe in the rain, we can sneak out without being seen."

Indrajit rushed into the kitchen, dragging the others in his wake. The room was dark and cold, a long rectangle dominated by two long, narrow tables. Munahim wrinkled his nose as they entered the dark room, and Indrajit smelled rotting meat.

"Why aren't you wrapped in paper?" he asked Tunk as he groped for a light source. The fire in the square hall behind him threw erratic, dancing shadow around the kitchen. Meat hooks looked like hangman's nooses and the wide, tall windows like unfathomable abysses, with lightning flashing somewhere in their depths.

"You mean poor Frick." Tunk shook as he walked, and gripped

the edge of the table to lean on it. “Perhaps the harness is helping me.”

“What have you done to activate it?” Indrajit asked.

“Spells. Prayers. Wearing it, mostly.”

“The Girdle isn’t helping,” Fix said. “It isn’t powered, it might as well just be clothing.”

“You don’t know that,” Tunk said.

“We’re pretty sure,” Indrajit said.

“Then perhaps I’m just not as far along as Frick was.” Tunk’s voice was pained. “Or perhaps they needed me free, to continue to speak for them. I am, after all, archegos major. Or perhaps they would be wrapping me even now in paper, but for your arrival.”

“This door is locked,” Fix called from the corner. “Can we get a light?”

“Still looking for one.” Indrajit found knives, and the partly devoured carcass of a bird. And another Kattak nymph, crawling like a slug across the table. He picked it up and stared at its moving pincers.

“Please help me,” Tunk said.

Indrajit sighed. “We’re trying to help all of us.”

A clash of metal filled the room. Indrajit spun about and saw Munahim in the door by which they’d entered. He was a silhouette, and his long sword was a thrashing arm. Beyond him, yellow and clicking in the flame-scoured room they’d left, was one of the Kattak. Munahim yelled, slashed, and kicked, and Indrajit ran to help.

He pressed himself into one side of the doorway and together they erected a fence of sharpened steel. The Kattak didn’t give up, lunging to bite with its mandibles and scratch with its legs. Indrajit’s thighs grew bloody with small slash marks, and he feared they were being encircled, to be attacked from some other kitchen entrance. The Kattak’s sting, a long, sharp appendage the size of a spear, darted over its head, stabbing again and again and getting closer and closer.

Indrajit threw the nymph.

The Kattak spun about, lunging as if to catch the little sluglike creature. Indrajit dove after it, sinking Vacho into the wasp-man’s abdomen.

The Kattak shrieked wordlessly, and Munahim sliced off its sting in a single blow.

The Kattak scooped up the nymph and raced away toward the front doors. Indrajit heard the twang of bows or crossbows and he and Munahim ran back into the kitchen. Together, they overturned a table and shoved it against the door.

"I found one!" Larch raised a burning lamp, rescuing them from total darkness.

"Bring it over here," Fix ordered. Larch brought him the light and Fix worked at the lock on the doorway in the kitchen corner.

Tunk lay draped over the corner of the remaining table, breathing hard.

"How can you have been surprised by any of this?" Indrajit asked.

"Surprised by what?" Tunk's voice was weak, remote.

"You seem astonished and dismayed at Lysander Frick's death," Indrajit said. "But how can that be? Are these Kattak not the overlords of your people? Are they not your sultans? How do you not know how they reproduce?"

"They are few," Tunk grunted. "We are many. They are mostly hidden from view, inside the temples and their mountain chasms. Who can count how many priests go into a temple and how many emerge, especially when so many come from remote villages?"

"One of them said he . . . hatched from a Yuchak," Indrajit said.

"We always give them prisoners," Tunk said. "Our people are sailors and pirates, there are always prisoners to give to the sultan and his house. We knew they ate human flesh. We didn't know they laid eggs inside living human bodies. If anyone knows, perhaps it is a priestly secret. But here . . . prisoners are harder to come by."

Indrajit snorted. "Are you kidding? It's the easiest thing in the world to buy a slave."

"Welcome to Kish," Munahim said.

"A slave would not do." Tunk seemed to be pressing his face harder and harder against the wood. "Only a person of quality—a warrior, a scholar, a priest, someone of high value captured in a raid."

"A diplomat," Indrajit said. "A lord's servant."

"Help me," Tunk pleaded.

Munahim stood beside the fireplace, sniffing. It was an enormous brick cavern, large enough that an ox might easily be impaled and slung over flames inside it. Indrajit checked an open doorway in another corner, found only darkness and flapping paper, and then joined Munahim.

"What are you smelling? That moisture is rain, coming down the chimney, isn't it?"

"They don't use this fireplace," Munahim said. "Haven't used it for months."

Indrajit thought he heard a coughing sound. He kicked a chair against the wall beneath the high windows and then stepped onto it. He pressed his face against the glass. He could see bulky shadows.

Lightning flashed.

There was too much to absorb in one glance, but he saw the scarred face of Tully Roberts and his bright blue scarf. He saw more scarves, men in cloaks, and more.

He dropped down from the chair.

"Stop," he said.

Fix looked up from fiddling with the lock, a heavy iron rectangle adjoining the door's handle.

"There are men outside," Indrajit said, lowering his voice. "Shambs, men in scarves and cloaks, and something big. A Grokonk, a Luzzazza, a Gund, I'm not sure."

"The embassy guards?" Fix whispered.

Tunk groaned. "We do not employ Shambs or a Gund."

"I saw cloaks," Indrajit said. "But I also saw bright scarves."

Indrajit heard shouting elsewhere in the embassy. Fix pointed at the open doorway into darkness.

"Wait," Indrajit said. "What did you tell me you read on the map?"

"'Spider' and 'fire,'" Fix said.

Indrajit pointed at the fireplace. "There's a descending shaft here. Is it possible the words on the map say 'fireplace' and 'wasp'?"

Tunk burst into tears.

"Please, help me," he said.

"Do we risk it?" Fix asked.

Indrajit took the lamp from Larch's hand. He stepped into the dark open doorway and touched the lamp to the paper adhering to the walls. Flame exploded upward immediately, showing a nightmare landscape of paper-wrapped furniture and warped, irregular tunnels beyond.

The shadowy form of a Kattak scurried away into darkness beyond the reach of the flames.

"Munahim first," Indrajit said. "You may be able to smell things coming. Fix next. I'll bring up the rear with these two. Time to see if this map is worth all the fuss."

Chapter Fifteen

Once Munahim confirmed that the shaft in the chimney opened into Underkish, Indrajit smashed up the legs of a second table. The lamp had gone down with Munahim, but the fire in one connecting hallway that burned around the edges of the table, blocking the entrance to the square chamber, gave Indrajit light to help Fix and then the two archegoi, first major and then minor, into the crack. They had to climb upward first, over a crumbling brick wall into a slot that was nearly impossible to see in the shadow of the chimney, and detected only because of Munahim's keen sense of smell, and then down through that slot into a parallel chimney that descended.

Thudding sounds and the shaking of the door to the outside showed that the Silksteppers had realized that the Protagonists were not coming out, and set about trying to make their way in. Indrajit also heard yelling elsewhere in the building.

Once everyone else was in the chimney and well on their way down, Indrajit began to make his way. He piled the smashed table in the fireplace and climbed up into the slot. Splashing half of his flask of lantern oil on the stacked wood and on a last piece he held back for himself, he then set fire to the fragment, and tossed it on the pile.

Fire whooshed up into the chimney and Indrajit scrambled down the shaft.

If the Silksteppers had anyone positioned at a high point outside the kitchen, they might simply have watched Indrajit set the fire. And if anyone in the embassy knew about the shaft down, they might realize that the fire in the fireplace was a screen to hide the

Protagonists' flight. But if neither of those things was true, then maybe Indrajit had bought himself and his friends some time.

The interior of the shaft was initially rocky and irregular, but then become a smoothly structured wall resembling vertical steps or a ladder. Alternating rows of bricks jutted out or were set back deeper into the wall, giving very comfortable hand- and footholds for descent or ascent.

Which was good, because Indrajit judged the descent to be a chain or maybe a chain and a half in length. At the bottom end, it landed inside a three-walled niche in the corner of a wedge-shaped brick chamber with a trickle of black sludge flowing across the floor.

Indrajit pointed at the sludge. "It's good to know that all Kish's neighborhoods have the same grimy underside."

Fix held the lamp to the map. "I think there's more here than written thieves' cant," he said. "I think there are symbols that have meaning, but there's no legend."

"Like, 'water here'?" Indrajit suggested. "'Do not drink the sludge'?"

"Probably," Fix agreed. "But also, I suspect that these five hashmarks are meant to give an indication of the height of the climb we just did. And the warning that there's fire at the upper end would be necessary for a map user coming from below, to burgle the palace. You'd see the fire icon and you'd bring something to extinguish it with, or you'd fireproof yourself somehow."

"You're saying that the fire glyph wasn't put there to tell someone how to find the entrance," Indrajit said. "It was put there to warn a burglar so he could avoid burning his sandals."

"I think so."

"Well, take us home by the straightest road you can find," Indrajit suggested.

"I'm taking us to the Dregs." Fix tilted the map and looked at a different section of it. "Where there's some writing I can't read, but it just might be a connection to the Vin Dalu's complex."

"Faster," Thomedes Tunk pleaded. He leaned against a wall, spitting trickles of dark saliva onto the brick floor.

Larch tugged at Indrajit's elbow. "I worry about the archegos major."

"Yes," Indrajit said. "He's full of wasps."

"I worry that moving him will make the birthing faster."

Indrajit sighed. "Of course it will."

"We're not alone," Munahim said.

"Ghouls?" Indrajit asked. "Kattak?"

Munahim hesitated. "They've been here, but no. Men."

"How many?" Indrajit asked.

"Not many."

"Could they be beggars, sheltering from the rain?" Indrajit asked. "Or a servant sneaking home from an unapproved romantic liaison?"

"I can't tell that," Munahim said. "But I can smell men and weapon oil."

Indrajit and Fix unsheathed their swords simultaneously. "We'll go fast," Fix said. "This way."

They stepped over the trickle of sludge and entered a narrow crack between sagging walls. Tunk didn't move at first, so Indrajit grabbed him by the back of the Girdle of Life, gripping the Druvash device where two straps crossed and snapped together under the shoulder blades. At the crack, Indrajit spun the senior diplomat sideways and shoved him through, one hand on his shoulder and one on his hip.

Was he fatter? That wasn't right, his shoulder felt downright bony. But his belly seemed to be swelling before Indrajit's very eyes.

Beyond the crack, a void opened to their right, floor dropping away and ceiling rising out of sight as brick gave way to natural stone walls. Great walls of paper slanted down at multiple angles, quickly concealing all from view.

"I smell Kattak," Munahim said.

"I smell decay," Indrajit countered.

Tunk vomited.

Fix tore a strip from the hem of his kilt. He soaked the end of the cloth in lamp oil and then lit it. He tossed the upside-down fabric taper into the pit and they watched its sphere of yellow light draft down into the abyss.

It came to rest on the rotting bodies of men.

"We fed them slaves and prisoners," Larch said. "They pushed the bodies through a hole in the floor of the guest house."

"How many?" Indrajit asked.

"Many," Larch said. "In recent days, more. This is not what I aspired to as a young man. This is not what I thought I would do, entering the diplomatic service. My world has become a horror."

"Welcome to Kish," Munahim said.

The paper rattled. Shadows of beasts concealed within flitted across the surface.

"Not good enough to house their eggs, but not so bad they couldn't be eaten, eh?" Indrajit took deep breaths to fight off the urge to vomit and continued after Fix, who was already shuffling away.

Fix led them through a series of sharp turns. They walked along a perfectly preserved marble stoa, its pillars carved in the shape of gods and demons Indrajit couldn't identify at all, down a narrow staircase, around a torrent of dirty rainwater crashing down into a bowl of shattered red gravel, and across a needlelike arching bridge that leaped over echoing darkness. At each turn, and every fifty or so paces otherwise, Fix stopped to consult the map, muttering, turning it this way and that, and pressing the lamp or his face close to it to get a good look at particular glyphs and lines.

Tunk was no longer able to stand, and Indrajit dragged him by main force, holding onto the Girdle of Life. Larch stared at Tunk and shuddered.

Fix stopped and stared at a column.

"What is it?" Indrajit hoisted Tunk close under his arm to prop him up. "Are we lost?"

"Look at this pillar," Fix said. "What do you see?"

"White stone," Indrajit said.

"It's bone," Munahim said. And it was. And a series of curving columns just like it ran leftward from where they stood. Beyond and facing them ran a parallel row of columns, both rows curving inward and nearly meeting at the top, where they supported a roof of packed clay.

"It's a rib cage," Indrajit said.

"This is your chance, Fix," Indrajit said. He jested more to relieve his own fatigue than to actually tease his friend. "Take this to the Hall of Guesses and become a scholar. Or take it to the ashrama of Salish-Bozar. They'll probably let you weigh up each bone, measure it, calculate the angles, and you can probably draw a thousand pieces of useless information out of this skeleton right here. Maybe two. Really get you a strong start toward becoming a Selfless."

Fix chuckled gamely. “Except this skeleton is supremely useful.”

“It holds the roof up, for starters,” Munahim pointed out.

“And it’s a landmark.” Fix held up the map. “This glyph definitely reads ‘bones.’ We go left.” He raised the lamp and looked along the skeleton. “If I’m not mistaken, our next step is to climb through that eyehole over there.”

Munahim wrinkled his nose. “I think we’re about to hit a real river of sewage.”

“Yeah.” Fix held up the map. “There’s a thick line just beyond the eyehole. I won’t read you what the glyph says.”

Fix went first, raising the lamp and holding the map in his other hand. The ribs floated past him right and left like the pillars of the long nave of a temple. At the far end, as if a giant animal had once punched its head through a wall and then died on the spot, brick and stone sealed up one eye cavity and stopped forward progress to either side of the skull, but the lamp shone on empty space through the second eye socket.

Fix climbed through and stood examining the footing as the others joined him. “It’s not a river, it’s a pool,” he called. “There are stepping stones that cross the pool, but the level is rising fast. Probably the rain. We need to go now, or it will get foul.”

He put the map into his kilt and leaped to the first stone, just as Indrajit stepped through the eye. Indrajit stood on a shelf of wet stone. Water seeped through a stone ceiling above and flowed down over the giant skull and trickled under his sandals.

Fix had leaped out onto a second stone, and Munahim now followed his path, jumping from the shelf to the first stone. The gaps weren’t great, maybe four cubits for each leap, and the stones were large and flat and more or less dry. But Larch teetered at the edge, breath coming faster and faster as he stared at the rising sludge at his feet.

“You can do this,” Indrajit said. “It’s easy, one small jump at a time. Just let the others get ahead of you and then go. And if you miss the jump, you just get a little dirty. Small price to pay.”

“There could be rapeworms down there,” Larch said.

“There could be worse things than that,” Indrajit suggested.

Fix leaped ahead another stone, and then another. “I can see the other side,” he called.

Munahim followed him.

"Go," Indrajit said.

Larch jumped, and missed. He fell with a heavy splash into the grimy waters, screaming and thrashing with all limbs, and knocking himself farther from the foothold.

"Try to stand up!" Indrajit called. "It might not be that deep!"

"Help!" Larch squeaked.

"Frozen hells." Indrajit sighed, steeling himself to jump into the slime.

Thwack!

With the meaty sound of metal striking flesh, Tunk shuddered and fell back. Indrajit lost his grip on the Girdle of Life. Looking down for one brief instant, he saw a thin cable passing right before his own chest, a cable that ended in an iron harpoon, the harpoon sunk into Tunk's ribs. Looking along the line in the other direction, he saw it disappear into darkness.

Then the line was violently tugged, and Thomedes Tunk flew off the shelf and into the sewer.

The two archegoi moved in opposite directions, Larch thrashing his way away from Indrajit to the right and Tunk speeding like a captured whale to the left. Tunk floated on his back, moaning, his belly a white mound bobbing on black waves.

Indrajit leaped into the slime to go after Larch. To his enormous relief, his feet touched bottom and his head didn't go under, despite the wave of black, coagulating sludge he threw up. "Fix!" he yelled.

With his excellent peripheral vision, he saw Fix leap first onto the stone where Munahim stood, pressing something into the Kyone's hands. Then he leaped into the slimy flood. He was shorter than Indrajit, and maybe not as lucky, and he disappeared into the black goo briefly before emerging, striking out toward the harpooned archegos major.

Indrajit grabbed Larch by the hair. The archegos minor screamed and punched Indrajit in the jaw, prompting Indrajit to punch him back. "Stop!" he roared, when he had regained his balance and composure. "Hold still, I have you!"

Larch didn't stop shrieking and he stiffened like a log, but he quit thrashing about and he didn't hit Indrajit again. Indrajit grabbed him and dragged him back toward the shelf.

Munahim had dropped to one knee on his rock and was loosing arrows into the darkness. Fix's lamp still shone, sitting on the stone at the farthest point to which Fix had advanced before turning back. Screams came out of the darkness in response, and then crossbow bolts whizzed back. Munahim took a bolt in his left arm and grunted in pain.

"Help . . . me . . ." Tunk cried, weakly spitting out black ooze, his face bobbing alternately above and below the dark water.

Fix grabbed Tunk by an arm and was pulled along, toward the edge of the light. At the same time, the pulling party pulled itself forward, so just before Fix disappeared completely, a large flatboat emerged from the shadow. Ten men crouched in it, and two more lay flat with arrows in them. Four of them were pulling to drag the archegos major aboard their boat, five were reloading crossbows, and the last stood with a long, barbed spear, aimed as if he were about to thrust it into Fix's face.

It was the Heru, the hawk-headed lieutenant of Zac Betel, Yammilku.

"I will kill you if I must!" the Heru cried.

"I will die for her!" Fix snarled.

At that moment, Thomedes Tunk's belly burst open.

Kattak nymphs swarmed from the hole up onto the archegos major's face as he screamed one last wet, choking time. Others spilled down along his belly. Two raced along Tunk's arm and onto Fix, and then the arm ripped off. Other nymphs crawled up the harpoon; the men in the boat hesitated, but then, as Fix fell away, holding a torn-off arm, they dragged the ruins of the corpse into the boat.

"Take the harness!" Yammilku shrieked.

Fix pushed off the bottom and swung the severed arm like a club. He struck Yammilku in the chest, spattering the Heru with blood, but gore was also spouting in a fountain from the ruined chest of Thomedes Tunk.

"Fix!" Munahim shouted.

Indrajit saw what the Kyone saw: that the thieves with crossbows were raising them to fire again. Indrajit dragged himself and the archegos minor behind the nearest stepping stone. The waters were rising, but he could still stand with his face above the surface, and he could shelter from the bolts behind the rock.

Munahim dropped his bow and dove. He tackled Fix, dragging the shortest Protagonist down into the water again just as the crossbows twanged.

Indrajit heard the snap of several bolts striking the stone behind his head. He dragged Larch up to the rock. "Hold on here," he urged the archegos minor. "Grip the rock, stay above water, and just wait."

Then he slipped around the stone. He moved on the far side of the stone from the lamp that still lit the scene, keeping his head in shadow. Two men in the flatboat were reloading crossbows again, but the rest had picked up poles and were pushing themselves into the darkness.

"We'll give you back the harness, Fix," Yammilku called from the shadow, even as he was disappearing. "We need you to come perform a small job for us."

"Damn you!" Fix was howling. Even in the dim light, he looked as if he had turned bright red. Munahim held him up above the rising waters, and might also be holding him back. "Give it to me now!"

"Meet me at the Petting Zoo," Yammilku called, now completely shrouded in the gloom. "By the mernache grove. At dawn. That gives you two hours to clean up."

Fix roared. When the sound of rage and injury had finally echoed to nothing, the swish of the flatboat moving across the water was gone as well.

Fix stared in the direction the boat had gone. Munahim dragged him to the nearest stepping stone and pulled him out of the flood. Indrajit fished Larch out onto another stone.

Munahim collected his bow and the map. He handed the latter to Fix, but then held onto it when Fix continued to stare into darkness without responding. Indrajit hopped to the next stone to collect the lamp.

He ached, but he knew Fix hurt in ways he did not.

"Fix," he said gently. "The Petting Zoo . . . that has another name, doesn't it? Isn't that the same as . . ."

"Yovila's Gardens," Fix said.

"I didn't know Kish had a zoo," Munahim said. He was scraping gobbets of mud and worse from his skin with his belt knife. "And you can pet the animals?"

"It's not a zoo like that," Indrajit said. "It's a park. People go there to, uh, pet each other, I suppose you would say."

"It's in the Lee," Fix murmured.

"That's right," Indrajit said. "Kind of in the shadow of the Racetrack. Obviously, Fix, we need to head that way. We should probably clean up."

Fix stared.

"It's still raining," Munahim said. "That won't be hard."

"We got the Girdle once," Indrajit said. "We'll get it again. We need you to focus. For one thing, look at the map and find us an exit."

Fix suddenly hunched over, tensing all the muscles of his chest and stomach and curling his arms. He looked like a wrestler, warped into a tight knot and ready to spring, and he emitted a deep, echoing bellow.

Then he took a deep breath and slowly exhaled. "Give me the lamp and the map."

Fix ran the flame near the map and then pointed. "Some of the ink is running, but I can still read this. Back the way we came. I think there's a passage that will take us under the city walls and into the Lee."

They hopped back to the stone shelf and stepped through the giant skeleton's eye socket. Indrajit and Munahim both went out of their way to crush the several Kattak nymphs on the shelf, grinding them under their sandaled heels. When they reached the cascade of water pouring from the ceiling, they stepped into it and rinsed off, forcing Larch to do the same. Eventually, after folding the map and putting it away, Fix brought them up in a heap of rubble, the remains of a large building that had formerly stood just inside the wall of the Lee.

"Where can you go?" Indrajit asked Larch.

"With you." Larch trembled as he spoke.

"Do you need money?" Indrajit asked.

"I'm going with you," the archegos minor said again. "I'm not safe alone."

"You're not safe with us," Fix pointed out, but Larch only shivered and said nothing.

In the blue light preceding the dawn, Indrajit bought a strip of cloth and herbs identified as potent for healing in the Epic. Together, the Protagonists pulled the bolt from Munahim's arm and bound his wound. Then they bought four wool cloaks at a caravan supplier and walked toward Yovila's Gardens.

"Who are we meeting in this park?" Munahim wondered out loud. "And why in the Lee? This isn't Zac Betel's territory."

Indrajit looked at the lightening sky in the east. "We'll find out soon."

Chapter Sixteen

Yovila's Gardens were a maze. Even Fix, prodded to opine on the subject, had no idea who Yovila was, or had been, but her gardens were a tangle of stone walls, benches, and reflecting pools, which together formed a labyrinth. Over the top of the stone maze, and sometimes apparently in utter disregard of it, grew a second tangle of shrubbery, thick trees, vines, raised flower beds, and cane, constituting in itself a second labyrinth. The overlaid labyrinths were puzzling indeed, to first-time visitors like Indrajit, and constituted a large city block in their own right.

The Protagonists stood at the north end of the Petting Zoo, which was slightly higher than the south end, where Kish sloped away toward the Caravanserai, the Necropolis, and the Endless Road. They were looking for mernache trees. The rain was letting up, fading into a soft drizzle, and cold dawn was near.

"I see why this park is favored for assignations," Indrajit said. "There must be ten thousand hiding places in here, and half of those contain a solid bench or a comfortable bed of grass."

"My lady Elissa!" Two Zalaptings in an unfamiliar uniform passed, only a few paces into the park. They poked into and parted thickets with long sticks. "Lady Elissa, you're due at home!"

"Not only romantic assignations," Larch said.

"What do you mean?" Indrajit asked.

"I'm not sure," Larch said. "But I know Archegos Major Tunk came here for meetings from time to time."

"With other diplomats, you mean?" Indrajit asked.

"Meetings at night."

Indrajit grunted, and then realized what Larch meant. "Secret papers delivered, unrecorded payoffs, rumors bought and sold, that sort of thing."

"That sort of thing." Larch shrugged. "I want to be useful."

"Well, it does paint a picture," Indrajit agreed.

"There's only one mernache grove." Fix pointed.

The mernache was a tree that was very nearly a vine. Its boles were thin, flexible, and gnarled, its bark rough enough to cut skin. Its leaves were dark green and glossy, and stayed through Kish's cool winter, sheltering clusters of white berries in the spring. Its roots shot out, it was said, for leagues if nothing stopped them, throwing up a new tree trunk every few paces. The trunks of the mernache tangled together, so it could be used alone as a hedge that would stop large creatures, like droggers or ylakka, or with smaller, thornier plants to create a truly impervious wall. Within the grove, myriad small, sheltered corners played hosts to birds, animals, and, in this particular park, lovers.

The park's mernache grove filled a depression that might once have been a pond, it looked so regularly oval in shape. The mernaches were crowded between taller thamber oaks at one end and a heap of stones containing an artificial grotto at the other. A single path cut through from the oaks to the hill, spreading into a tiny clearing, only a few paces across, in the middle.

"If we're first, let's pick our ground," Indrajit said.

"If I had a dozen men with swords, I'd hide them in the oak trees," Fix said. "If I had one Kyone with a bow and an uncertain left arm, I'd want him on top of the grotto."

"My left arm is fine," Munahim growled.

"And I certainly don't want ten Sootfaces with crossbows on top of the grotto," Fix continued, "shooting at me when this discussion breaks down."

"It won't break down," Indrajit said. "They want something. If they just wanted to kill us, they'd have killed us in the sewer."

He didn't like saying the word "sewer." It made him think about the fact that he hadn't really cleared all the crud from behind his ears and between his toes, and he smelled sour.

"Yes," Fix agreed. "They want something from us. And since we own nothing, what can that be?"

"They want us to do something," Munahim said.

"Right. They want us to do something." Fix nodded. "They have a whole thieves' guild full of men, and they want *us* to do some task."

"They know how good we are," Indrajit said. "We're brave, and dashing. We have a poetic sensibility."

"Not one of the Gray Lords gives a rotten egg for your poetic sensibility," Fix said. "Not one thief in all the Gray Houses together does."

"You don't know that for sure." Indrajit harrumphed.

"They want something from us that their men can't do," Fix said. "We're going to find out that they want us to betray Orem Thrush. Or kidnap Grit Wopal. Or maybe protect them as they conduct some Paper Sook fraud."

"And some of those things we could do," Indrajit said. "Wopal might even help us do some of them. So let's hear these guys out, get back the Girdle of Life, and get over to the Vin Dalu. We have a day and a half."

"The Battle of Last Light is tomorrow," Fix said.

"I haven't forgotten. We can work around that, if we must."

Munahim made his way around the mernache to the grotto, taking Larch with him. Larch had no missile weapon, and it wasn't clear that he would even know how to use one if he had it, but Fix agreed with Indrajit that it was best to keep the archegos minor as far away as possible from any fighting.

Once Munahim was halfway up the slope, he crouched down among the rocks. He laid down his bow, within reach but out of sight, so he could quickly shoot down into the grove, but his own exposure to attack was limited.

Indrajit and Fix walked down the path to the clearing.

A thylacodon chewing on an old boot halfway along the trail grinned and bared its teeth at them, but didn't bother moving. Kishi fowl chased each other through the ground creepers and yellow grass around the ankles of the mernache, and other things, unseen, rustled where the ground cover was thick.

"We're going to save her," Indrajit said.

"Like we saved Thomedes Tunk this morning?" Fix asked.

"No, we'll succeed this time."

"Like we succeeded in protecting the opera singer Ilsa Without Peer," Fix suggested. Ilsa had been in their protection, though she had also been manipulating them, but she had been killed by her criminal coconspirators.

"To be fair," Indrajit said, "there's an argument that Ilsa got what she had coming. Ilsa might have been part victim, but she was more than a little bit villain."

"I'm just saying, let's not be overconfident. There was that priestess of the Nameless One, too."

She had been a client. She had been trying to trick them and sacrifice them to her goddess, but she had been forced. And she had died badly, when they'd tried to rescue her.

Indrajit was starting to feel depressed.

"There's Larch," he pointed out. "We got him away from the wasp-men."

"The day is young," Fix said. "He might still drown, or fall into a hole, or get shot by a crossbow."

They had been standing in the clearing only for a few seconds when three men came down the opposite path to meet them. Indrajit squinted at the thamber oaks and the mernaches near them, looking for men with crossbows. Or blowguns, now that he was thinking of it. Or even swords. He didn't see any.

"We know these guys," Fix murmured.

Yuto Harlee came first, the tavernkeeper doorman of the Sookwalkers. After him came Tully Roberts with his scarf, whom Munahim had released on a rooftop over the Armpit. And finally, Yammilku, the hawk-headed night warden of the Sootfaces.

Indrajit looked around and realized that the clearing was visible from both ends, but was concealed from most of Yovila's Gardens, and certainly from the buildings around it.

"I guess no introductions are needed," Fix said, when the thieves arrived. "You know I want that harness. You know I want it immediately. What will it take for you to give it back to me?"

"A couple hours' work." Yammilku handed Fix a rolled-up paper.

Fix unrolled it a few fingers to take a look. "I gave this to you last night. You told me where to find the harness."

He was avoiding saying "the Girdle of Life." Was he trying not to show how much he wanted it?

"Yes," Yammilku said. "But Zac Betel doesn't know that you brought the map back."

"The men on guard know," Indrajit said. "The Wixit. The other two fellows, Dag and Hober."

"You have a good memory," Yammilku said.

"I'm a poet." Indrajit shrugged. He was in no mood to explain his theater of memory.

"Those men are loyal," Yammilku said. "They haven't said anything about last night and they won't say anything. You're going to come back to the smithy with this map."

"It's not your map," Harlee growled.

"We'll sort that out later," Yammilku said. "You're going to come back to the smithy with this map, as Zac Betel asked, so that he will tell you where the harness is."

"Because Betel has no idea that his own men grabbed the harness from us in the middle of the night." Fix frowned. "You're trying to put one over on Betel. What do you want us to do, rob him? Change the deal, and ask for something else, some piece of information you want? What are you playing at?"

Yammilku chuckled. His laughter was a piercing rattle in the back of his throat. "You're very clever."

"You want us to kill him." Indrajit looked at the three men. "A bunch of his men are already loyal to you, and now you want him dead. You want us to kill Betel, so that you can take over the Sootfaces."

The thought of getting more deeply involved in the strife between the Gray Lords made him uncomfortable. On the other hand, he'd been half expecting that Yammilku would demand the assassination of Orem Thrush, or worse, and part of him now felt relieved.

"What's the rest of the deal?" Fix asked. "Do you then turn around and help Harlee get rid of Arash Sehama next? Tully, are you planning on killing your brother?"

"See, the problem with cleverness," Harlee said, "is that too much cleverness is bad for your health. You need to stop asking questions right now."

Indrajit took a deep breath. "You set us up, Yammilku."

"There we go again," Harlee said, "crying about tricks."

"You can't blame me for taking advantages of the opportunities that come my way," the Heru said. "That's just ordinary prudence."

"What's to stop our Kyone sharpshooter from killing you right now?" Fix asked.

"Our six men concealed in the mernache just below his feet," Harlee said. "He'd shoot one of us, and that would be the last thing he did."

Indrajit wanted to turn around and look, but managed to control himself. "What's the plan? Do we attack him, and then you come to our aid? Do you hide weapons for us in his office?"

"His office is the smithy," Yammilku said. "The plan is you walk up and attack him by surprise."

"He'll have men there," Fix pointed out. "He wasn't alone."

"You'll have surprise on your side," Yammilku said again. "And your Kyone sharpshooter. Are you telling me that the mighty Protagonists can't kill one simple Luzzazza?"

"We'll kill him," Fix said. "When do you give us the harness?"

"On the spot," Yammilku said. "It's already been taken to the smithy."

That had to be a lie.

Indrajit and Fix looked at each other. Indrajit had half a mind to draw his sword and attack. Maybe they were bluffing about crossbowmen ready to shoot Munahim, and maybe not. Munahim had a great sense of smell and a strong sense of hearing, and if there were men waiting in ambush a few paces from him, he probably knew it. Also, he was a very fast shot.

And two-to-three odds weren't great, but they weren't the worst odds the Protagonists had ever overcome.

But the men didn't have the Girdle of Life with them. If Indrajit and Fix overpowered them here and now, there was no guarantee that the men had the harness within easy reach, or even that they knew where it was.

Indrajit found himself nodding slow acquiescence, and Fix nodded, too.

"As fast as you can walk over there," the Heru said, "you can get the harness and go do whatever Druvash magic it is you want to work."

Indrajit and Fix turned and walked back up the path. Indrajit now imagined every rustle among the mernaches to be a concealed Sootface or Sookwalker or Silkstepper marksman. Munahim watched from his perch, and when Indrajit and Fix came close, he climbed down to meet them, bringing Larch with him. Indrajit signaled for silence, not trusting the hedges and walls around them, until they had walked out of Yovila's Gardens and stood on an adjacent street. Wagons heaped high with dried goods and barrels of alcohol trundled up and down the street past them. Shops were beginning to open, the streets before them to be swept, awnings and carpet unrolled.

"You don't have the Girdle of Life," Munahim said.

"They've concealed it somewhere," Indrajit told him. "They're pretending it's in Zac Betel's smithy. They claimed they had six men hidden, waiting to ambush you."

"They had eight," Munahim said. "I was prepared to shoot them first, if I had to."

"I was ready to hit one with a rock." Larch grinned. His hands shook, but it appeared to be with excitement rather than fear.

"I've been thinking about the harness," Munahim said. "I should be able to follow it."

"By smell?" Fix asked.

"If you can use the map to find where they docked the flatboat." Munahim nodded. "Even with the stink. I think the smell of Thomedes Tunk's blood and the Kattak nymphs will be on the Girdle, and I should be able to track it. Easily. Even in the sewage stink."

"Although when the rain lets up, some of that stink might be less." Indrajit shrugged. "The rain should have flushed out some channels."

Fix's face was screwed into a thoughtful expression. "We have another problem. And we should begin to make our way back toward the Spill as we discuss it."

They turned uphill and made their way toward the Crown. The rain had stopped, but the streets of the Lee were pitted enough that they were now stepping around and over large puddles.

Indrajit summarized their conversation with the Gray Lords' lieutenants. "They say they'll give us the harness if we kill Betel."

"So we have to appear to be doing that," Fix said, "and expeditiously. If we dally, they might move the harness."

"On the other hand, even if we kill him," Indrajit said, "there's no guarantee they'll keep their promise."

"They will certainly not keep their promise," Fix said. "Think about it. Yammilku wants to take over, but there's no reason to think that all the Sootfaces hate Betel. In fact, that can't be the case. If they all hated Betel, Yammilku would kill Betel openly and be done with it. So there must be a group, maybe even the majority, that supports the current Gray Lord."

"So he wants us to do the dirty work," Indrajit said. "That seems obvious enough."

"Think it through one step further," Fix urged him. "Once we three have killed Betel—"

"Four," Larch said.

Fix looked at Larch in surprise, then nodded. "Once we four have killed Betel, how does Yammilku make sure he has the support of all the Sootfaces, including the ones who were big Betel loyalists?"

"He avenges his old boss's death," Indrajit said. "He kills us."

"Welcome to Kish," Munahim said.

"So we can't do that," Larch said.

"Larch," Indrajit said.

"Call me Philastes."

"Philastes," Indrajit tried again, "I don't want to seem rushed, but now is a good time to tell us what skills you have. Especially if you have any really useful magical powers. Can you translocate? Appear to be elsewhere than where you are? Launch heat rays from your fists? Kill with a glance?"

"I'm good with bureaucracy," Philastes said. "And negotiation. And ritual."

"Okay," Indrajit said. "Forget I asked."

"Can you climb?" Munahim asked. "That was on the list, wasn't it?"

"I'm a pretty good climber," Philastes said. "The Sultanates are rocky islands. I was a shepherd as a boy, so I can play the flute. I'm good with a sling, and with thrown rocks or javelins. I know herd animals, I can start fires. I speak many languages. Pelthite, of course, Kishi, but also Xiba'alban, Ildarian, and several others."

"Languages," Indrajit said. "Hmm."

They stopped talking briefly as they were ushered through the gate into the Crown.

"We should get you a sling," Fix said to Philastes. "And we need to at the same time track the harness. Obviously, that's a task for Munahim."

"And a task for you," Indrajit said. "You're the one who can read the map. At least, more or less."

"Which means that you and Philastes need to move slowly," Fix said, "while not *appearing* to act slowly, pretend to be preparing to attack Zac Betel. Buying as much time as you can, so we can find the harness and then hopefully rejoin you."

"There's only so much time I can buy," Indrajit said. "Eventually, I'm going to have to do something."

"I agree," Fix said. "And I don't know what that something is. But I don't think it should be attacking Betel."

"I'll improvise," Indrajit said.

"Oh, good," Fix said, "that always goes well."

"What if the thieves wonder where Fix and I am?" Munahim asked.

"I'll tell them you're getting in position to attack from a distance," Indrajit said. "They know you're a sharpshooter."

Fix took the original map, soiled and blurred but usable, and Indrajit held on to the copy. As they approached the northern wall of the Crown, Fix and Munahim turned down an alley and disappeared.

"I don't know where to buy a sling," Philastes confessed. "I always made my own. Can we just get a soft hide and a sharp stone?"

"No time for that," Indrajit said. They joined the line to pass through the gate into the Spill, and found themselves standing behind a drover with a string of droggers. Indrajit looked and saw that the man, swaddled in silks in the style of Togu or Hith, had a serviceable sling tucked into his belt. "Sir," he said, "this is an awkward conversation, but we could use a sling, and I see that you have one."

"Go to hell," the man said in an accent that came completely out of his nose.

"I'll give you five Imperials," Indrajit told him.

"Sold."

They made the exchange, and Philastes took the weapon.

Indrajit recognized a jobber company called the Veterans working the gate. They shuffled closer. He took a deep breath at the thought that the Handlers weren't going to spit on him or worse.

"Is it always this exciting, being a jobber?" Philastes asked.

"No, I'd say this day has been more exciting than average." Indrajit turned his head slightly, looking for pursuit. He didn't see anyone tailing them, but they must be there.

Or were the thieves taking a shortcut through Underkish? In which case, might they cross paths with Fix and Munahim?

Indrajit ground his teeth.

"This has been a lot more drama than I'm used to." Philastes smiled gamely. "I mean, I set out to be a minor diplomat. It's all become much tenser, recently."

"Well," Indrajit said, "just you wait."

Chapter Seventeen

The Veteran at the gate was an Ulotar. He looked like nothing so much as a pale green willow tree made entirely of rubber. He (it could have been a she, Indrajit reminded himself) had a band of a hundred constantly blinking eyes at about the level of Indrajit's face, encircling a six-cubit-tall trunk. Beneath the eyes was a crease that traveled all around the whole cylindrical body and appeared to be able to open as a mouth on any side, and even on more than one side at the same time. At the lower extremities, the trunk split into four legs. When the Ulotar stood still, the knees looked like warty protrusions on the trunk of a tree; when he moved, the knees all bent out, away from the trunk, so the Ulotar walked with a bobbing or skipping motion. Like the branches of a willow, limbs hung down on all sides from above the band of eyes. They looked like unruly hair, or an upside-down squid, were prehensile, and ended in sharp points like talons.

"Treelike Ulotar, leaping over fences," Indrajit said. *"Faster than a running man, swims like a stone."*

The Ulotar made an agitated sound at Indrajit and Philastes.

Philastes made a bellowing grunt in return. The Ulotar scuttled aside and tittered and Indrajit and Philastes passed.

"You speak Ulotar," Indrajit said.

"Only a little," Philastes said. "It's an easy language, though. I could teach you."

"Do you know Blaatshi at all?" Indrajit asked.

"No," Philastes said. "Do you know a good textbook?"

Indrajit growled. "So, have you met Zac Betel? You bought the Girdle of Life from him, didn't you?"

"Not that I realized," Philastes said. "I thought I was buying it from an antiquities dealer and . . . ah, fence, named Hutch Squilo."

"A fence for the Sootfaces, I suppose."

As they passed from the gate into the Spill, Indrajit caught a flash of blue in his right eye. Lowering his voice almost to inaudibility among the whooping of early morning drovers and food hawkers, he murmured, "Look casually to your right. Do you see a man in a bright blue toga, with a bright blue hood?"

Indrajit stopped at the folding wooden table of a Zalapting selling gourds. He picked one up, rapped it with his knuckles, and weighed it in his hands to give Philastes a chance to look. Philastes hefted another such gourd and peeped past it.

"Yes," Philastes said.

"What's he doing?"

"He's holding a cane. In front of him, as if it's nectargrass and he's going to drink from it. Who is that? Is he a follower of one of the Gray Lords?"

"We . . . don't actually know," Indrajit said. "The cane is a blowgun. If he raises it to his lips, he's attacking. If he's not raising it now, that confirms what we already thought . . . that his target is Fix, not me. For now, at least."

"And not me."

"That's a good gourd," the Zalapting said. "Very juicy, very sweet. The flesh makes a nice pie or stew. You can also dry it and it will keep for a long time."

"So he's probably wondering where Fix went."

"So he's not our problem," Philastes said.

"Also," the Zalapting added, "you can dry the empty shell, if you're careful when you're taking out the flesh, and it will hold water."

Indrajit considered. "We could ignore him. Or, we could try to catch him."

"Because he wants to kill our comrade in arms."

"Yes. I like that. To defend our comrade in arms. And also," Indrajit pointed out, "we need to delay, without looking like we're delaying, to buy Fix time. Besides, if this assassin succeeds in killing Fix, who's to say he won't be sent after me next? Or after you?"

"Are you going to buy that gourd or make love to it?" the Zalapting asked.

Indrajit shuffled some coins out of his purse, sesterces and asimi and one Imperial bit. "How many gourds is that?"

"Three," the Zalapting said.

Indrajit took a gourd and Philastes took two and they headed down the Crooked Mile. Indrajit casually turned his head, looking for any sign of Gray House footpads. He saw none. But surely, they had someone watching the Protagonists.

Unless they had all followed Fix instead.

"Why are assassins and thieves our enemies?" Philastes asked.

Indrajit took a deep breath and tried to explain. To his credit, Philastes took it all in stride.

"Why do the Gray Houses wear uniforms?" Philastes asked when it was all in the open.

"I don't know," Indrajit said. "This is my first real brush with them. I suppose for the same reason as jobbers: uniform helps morale. A uniform gives people something to be afraid of."

"But they're thieves," Philastes said. "Won't wearing a uniform get them hanged?"

Indrajit chuckled. "But all the uniforms are deniable. A cloak, a smudge of soot, a scarf. Recognizable, and totally deniable if they became a liability. And anyway, this is Kish."

"That seems to mean bad things. And does the House of Knives have a uniform, too?"

"I wouldn't have thought so," Indrajit said. "It seems like it would be a handicap."

"So that raises the question why the man with the blowgun dresses in this same persistent fashion . . . doesn't it?"

Indrajit considered, but had no answer. "We need a way to turn the chase back on the blowgun man," he said. "I suggest these steps to our left."

They turned between a luthier's shop and a leatherworker's, where two Yuchaks were unloading a stack of hides from the back of a mule, and the Wixit shopkeeper was measuring each and making notations on a wax board. Three steps in, the alley dove steeply down stairs, turning left and then right again, and then splitting. Steps continued down and to the left, soon turning again and disappearing entirely.

Another flight of stairs, difficult to see as it lay behind the corner of a brick tenement building, ascended sharply.

Indrajit pulled Philastes with him into the ascending slot. A heap of earth and moldering compost, barely retained by a net of twine, rose on one side of the chimney, while crumbling bricks walled off the other. Indrajit wished devoutly for a mirror, promised himself that someday he'd have a Protagonist carry around a mirror, along with lights, oil, fire starters, waterproof canvas, rope, and a hundred other things.

He didn't want another Protagonist so much as a mule, really. An intelligent, creative, very loyal mule, that would carry its own gear, and always be prepared. Maybe an ylakka?

They pressed themselves against the brick wall and raised the gourds over their heads. Indrajit calmed his own breathing and counted his heartbeats, waiting. A hundred beats went by, and he began to think he'd made a mistake. Or rather, Philastes had been wrong. There had been no man in a blue toga, there had been some innocent person, wearing a blue cape and holding a walking stick, perhaps.

He was about to ask Philastes how good his eyesight was when the man in the blue false toga trotted down the stairs before him.

"Stop!" Indrajit roared. He wanted the man in the toga to stop and turn, so Indrajit could see his face, in case he got away, and also so Indrajit could see his blowgun, and be certain they had the right man.

Instead, the man in the blue toga burst into a run, down the stairs and past them.

Indrajit hurled his gourd. He struck the assassin squarely in the back of the head. The gourd cracked and then fell to the stairs, shattering on the steps. The man staggered, but kept running. Philastes threw his first gourd and missed, and then Indrajit raced after the man in blue.

He hadn't thought about the steps as he'd descended them earlier, but now they seemed terribly narrow. His footing wobbled, his feet slid from one stair to the next, his ankles felt as if they might snap.

He thought he heard Philastes puffing along behind him, but he couldn't wait. His stride was longer than that of the man in blue, and he threw his weight forward, racing down the steps at a pace that would break his neck, if he missed his footing.

The man in the toga turned left into an alley. He was running so fast that he couldn't slow for the turn, and slammed into a wooden wall at the corner. A flowerpot hanging from the eaves above was dislodged by the impact and fell, shattering on the cobbles as Indrajit took the same turn. Dirt sprayed into his face and he scraped skin off his right shoulder, but he was nearly stepping on the assassin's sandaled heels now.

They were turning into a tiny plaza, the cobblestones ceding to packed gravel. At the far end, a crack barely a cubit wide squeezed between two buildings onto a busier street beyond. Indrajit saw oxen and a drogger and the assassin was running toward the crack.

Indrajit hurled himself forward. He shoved the man in the blue toga sideways and crashed to the gravel himself. The assassin stumbled, slid, and then smacked into the brick wall, two paces to the side of the crack.

Indrajit sprang to his feet and drew Vacho. "Time to give us some answers."

He grabbed the assassin by a shoulder and spun him about.

The assassin wasn't a man. She was a woman. A youngish woman, he guessed. Hard to tell, because her skin was bright red and she had no hair, just short, knobby horns on her head. Her skin was unlined, though, and her eyes had the stubborn, apprehensive look of the young. She gripped a cane in her hands, but it was now snapped in two, and Indrajit could see that it hadn't been hollowed out, and indeed was still green, oozing juice. An actual cane, not a blowgun. Maybe, in fact, nectargrass.

And she appeared to be armed only with a belt knife.

"You're not the assassin," Indrajit said. He'd been tricked. He leaped to the side, trying to throw himself into the crack of an alley that would take him to the street beyond.

He didn't make it. Searing pain stabbed him in the calf and he fell to the gravel. He hit, hearing a ringing in his ears. He turned his head, his own breath suddenly very loud in his ears, and saw the silhouette of a man standing on a rooftop above the courtyard. He wore a blue false toga and he held a heavy crossbow in his hands.

The crossbow string was perpendicular to the barrel of the weapon, and the man reached for a pouch of bolts strapped to his leg. The crossbow was large and had a crank, so it would take the attacker a little time to load and prepare his weapon.

Indrajit tried to stand and his calf wouldn't support him. He collapsed again to the gravel and stared down at his uncooperating leg dumbly.

He had a bolt in his leg.

Of course. He focused on the bolt and the pain, tried to clear his mind. A fog seemed to have settled over him. He lurched upright on his one good leg, clinging to the wall. The woman in blue was running, but Philastes kicked her feet out from under her and she fell.

"Run!" Indrajit called to Philastes, but the Pelthite ignored him. He scooped and picked up a loose cobblestone from the ground and snapped it into the pouch of his sling. Just as the shooter on the rooftop gripped the crank of his weapon and began pulling back the string, Philastes hit him in the cheek.

The man in blue went down.

"Let's go!" Indrajit croaked. He felt nauseated at the pain.

The woman in blue tried to get up again. Philastes grabbed the hood of her false toga and yanked it downward, blinding her and forcing her to her knees. Indrajit hopped to grab Philastes and pull him away.

The woman lurched forward, slashing at Indrajit's other leg with her knife. Philastes was too quick for her; he kicked her hand, sending the knife flying.

"Leave her!" Indrajit gasped.

"She's an accomplice!" Philastes snapped.

The Pelthite diplomat grabbed another stone and put it into his sling. Watching the roof, he gathered up additional rocks in his free hand.

Philastes was right. "Come on, then." Indrajit grabbed the woman by the elbow and pulled her to her feet. "This way."

As he lunged across the little plaza, the assassin on the rooftop raised his head again. Philastes cracked a stone into the man's forehead, and he cursed loudly.

The woman tried to wrench her hand free. "Let me go!"

"Not yet." Indrajit edged into the crack sword-first. The narrow alley, only ten paces long, suddenly seemed completely dark. "Larch!"

Philastes slung another stone at the rooftop and then retreated to Indrajit's side. He stepped in front of the woman, blocking any avenue she had of escape, ignoring a savage string of curses she unleashed on them. He put another sling in his stone and held it.

The man on top of the roof suddenly stood and ran. Philastes slung a stone and hit him in the hip, knocking his pace askew, but he jumped across the alley, dropping a full story but landing on his feet. Indrajit feared for a moment that the assassin was circling around to get a better shot at Indrajit, perhaps shooting straight down at him while he was trapped in this crack, but then he saw the men pursuing the assassin.

Yammilku the Heru was in the lead, and five men ran with him, blades in their hands and yelling.

The Sootfaces. The rebel Sootfaces, he reminded himself. The ones who were trying to force him and Fix to commit a murder.

They had stepped in to protect their plot.

"Faster!" Philastes urged.

The Pelthite was right. Now was their chance to get free of the thieves, and maybe seize the initiative. Indrajit leaned into his step and dragged the woman through the alley as if it were by a single motion of falling to the ground. He emerged off-balance, dodged an ox dragging a cart, and leaned on her to avoid dropping.

Philastes, who was a much smaller man, made it through more easily. "I don't know the Spill that well."

"I do." Indrajit staggered across the street, ducking under a drogger's feed bag, and plunged into an alley on the other side. Mercifully, it was all downhill from here to Betel's shop.

"You're bleeding," Philastes said as he caught up.

"Bleeding a 'you're going to die' amount?" Indrajit asked. He was afraid to look for himself. "Or bleeding a 'you're going to need to rest and drink a lot of wine' quantity?"

"The latter, I think," Philastes said. "If we pull out the bolt and bandage it soon enough."

"Good," Indrajit said. "I like wine."

He didn't mention to Philastes that the blowgun the man had previously used had been poisoned. But Indrajit was deeply relieved that he was conscious and felt lucid, if distracted and sickened by the sheer pain.

"Tell us who you are," he demanded of the young woman, trying to focus.

"I'm no one! Let me go!"

Indrajit cut between two rickshaws, then leaped over the tail of a blanket-covered ylakka. He meant to leap over it, anyway, but with his injured leg, he didn't quite manage. When he stepped on the giant lizard's tail, its head spun, jerked from its winter torpor. It hissed, showing a flickering tongue and bony yellow ridges in its mouth that were as sharp as teeth.

"Not a good answer," Indrajit said. They passed two braziers full of coals, a Rover wagon, and a Kishi selling cups of hot tea from a metal tank strapped to his back. The tank had candles on a small shelf beneath it to warm it, and several blankets insulated the vendor's back from the tin of the tank. Indrajit was tempted to stop and taste the tea, but there was no time. "You just helped in an attempted murder. That's probably a crime, but, as you can no doubt tell by now, I'm no notary."

"If you were, you would know this is kidnapping!" She twisted to try to yank her arm free and failed.

"As I said, no expertise." Indrajit shrugged. "I'm more of a man of action, and if you're not going to answer my questions, I'm inclined to throw you down a well. There's a nice deep one coming up in about fifty paces. It's called the Spithole, do you know it? Water seeps from a rock, and then there's a chasm."

"You're bluffing."

"It's pretty deep," Indrajit said. "And there are Ghouls down there."

"She's just some prostitute," Philastes said. "She's too dumb to know anything."

"I'm a student!" she snapped.

Oh, clever Philastes.

"A student?" Indrajit mused. "What does that mean? Are you a journeyman at some guild? Or you pay some artisan for training?"

"I study at the Hall of Guesses," she said.

"What do you guess about?" Indrajit asked. "Poetry, by any chance?"

"Healing," she said. "Herbs and compounds, anatomy."

"Ah, good," Indrajit said. They passed the Spithole, where a line of the quarter's residents waited to draw water from the mossy seep. "How are you at carrying burdens? Say, a mirror and a rope?"

"What?"

"Never mind. Why did you put on the blue toga and hold the cane and follow us?"

They were nearing Betel's smithy. Indrajit looked about for signs that they were followed, and saw none. This gave him little comfort, since he had seen none earlier, and then Yammilku and his men had burst onto the scene to attack the assassin. The Sootfaces, at least, seemed to be stealthier than Indrajit was perceptive. Still, he was moving as fast as he could, and in a straight line, and it was hard to imagine that they could have caught up yet.

Had they killed the assassin? Maybe they had captured him and could interrogate him?

Maybe, at the end of the day, if Indrajit were forced to murder Zac Betel, he could get Yammilku to tell him what he'd learned from the crossbowman.

Indrajit sighed.

"I was paid." She sounded angry. "I needed the money. It's so hard being a student. Everything is expensive and my family can't pay the Hall of Guesses, so I have to pay. And . . . I didn't want to make the money by working as a prostitute. I had no idea that that man would shoot at you." She hesitated. "My name is Illiot."

"I laud you for that decision," Indrajit said. "I don't know that murderer is a higher calling than whore, but I believe you that you didn't know what you were doing."

"I thought it was some sort of joke. He said he was playing a prank on an old comrade. I thought he was going to jump out and pull a bag over your head, or empty a chamber pot onto you from the second story."

"Yes, ha-ha, that would have been hilarious." They were only a hundred paces from the smithy, and Indrajit felt this well of information had turned out to be unfortunately shallow. "How did he hire you?"

"He stopped a group of us coming out of the Hall this morning," Illiot said. "He wanted to hire one of the men, but I was the one who took the offer." She shrugged. "I suppose I needed the money most."

"And did he say his name?" Philastes asked.

"He called himself Chode. He paid in advance."

"Okay," Indrajit said. "I'm letting you go." He hesitated a moment, then dug into his purse and produced five Imperials, handing her the coins. "Look, be more careful in the future."

She looked astonished, but took the money and ran.

"How's your leg?" Philastes asked.

"Hurts like ten devils." Indrajit crossed the street, circulating around the crowd that stood watching a low bawdy performance and then diving into Betel's alley. Ten devils didn't really feel like an adequate number to produce the grinding, stabbing pain in his calf.

Zac Betel himself stood in the open air of his smithy. Three of his men, all armed with swords, stood casually around him, watching the alleys on three sides. Betel worked iron again, his visible arms holding the long, heated bar while his unseen arms swung hammers.

Could the men with Betel now be trusted?

Indrajit drew his sword as he limped closer. He felt blood squishing in his sandal. With his left hand, he drew out the copy of the map. He held it up and shook it open as he approached. The three men—a Pelthite, a Yuchak, and a fat Karthing, all clad in studded leather—drew their swords. The Karthing whistled a very nonmusical series of notes.

"This is for you," Indrajit said. "As promised. And we want nothing for it."

Betel hesitated. "Why do approach with a blade in your hand, Blaatshi?"

"Because Yammilku wants you dead," Indrajit said. "And I don't know which of your men are loyal to you, and which are loyal to him."

The three thieves raised their swords and attacked Betel.

Chapter Eighteen

The Karthing was closest to Betel, and was also within Indrajit's reach. Indrajit hurled himself forward, slashing down, aiming for a quick kill by decapitation or by opening up a vein in the neck. The longer any fight went, the bigger liability the bolt in his leg would become.

The Karthing saw him coming and stumbled back. He canceled his attack against Betel and raised his own sword, deflecting three blows and eventually getting a heavy wooden table between himself and Indrajit.

Philanthes launched a sling stone into the face of the Yuchak. A gout of blood spurted from the suddenly smashed nose and the gaping wound in his face. The blood splattered onto the hot coals beside the anvil, sending up a foul stink.

The Pelthite slashed at Betel's head. Indrajit saw the attack coming from the corner of his eye and wanted to leap sideways to intercept it, but there was a table in the way, and ten paces of hard-packed earth. He found himself screaming, a shredded yodel that didn't quite sound like a war cry.

Betel spun about, surprisingly quick for a man his size. His downturned ears bounced and his visible arms raised the iron bar he was working on, heated to orange. The Pelthite's sword, a long, straight machaira with no stabbing tip, hit the bar. The heated iron flexed and bent, the descent of the machaira slowed and turned. The Luzzazza crime boss moved and the iron bar wrapped itself around the sword coming at him, and when the weapon finally reached where Betel's head had been, Betel had moved on.

The two iron hammers, appearing to float unaided in midair because Betel held them in his invisible arms, slammed together, crushing the Pelthite's skull like an egg.

The Karthing staggered backward, staring at his downed and dead comrades. He stopped attacking, parried only, and tried to run. Indrajit wouldn't let him. He pressed the assault, slashing fiercely, not exposing his own torso or thighs, and trying very hard not to strike self-consciously heroic poses. Finally, the Karthing threw his sword. Indrajit scooped the blade aside with his own, sending it flying into a brick wall.

The Karthing ran.

"Ha!" Indrajit cried. "Easy!"

More men poured from the building. They were armored in studded leather and they carried long swords and round shields, and they charged Betel.

The Gray Lord threw the iron bar, now dulling quickly to a gray color, with the machaira trapped inside it. The sizzling hot and also bladed conglomerate wobbled awkwardly as it flew and then struck a screaming Xiba'albi in the chest. He dropped, stinking of charred flesh and blood, his voice suddenly gone.

Betel swung his hammers. They were short-handled, which reduced his reach, but the difficulty of seeing his arms made them lethal, anyway; it was hard to parry them, even with a shield, and the men who attacked him focused on following the hammers, leaving them little attention with which to plan good attacks.

Indrajit couldn't see clearly how many men there were. He threw himself at the mass of flailing limbs yelling, "Protagonists!" He saw Philastes at work with the sling; the Pelthite wasn't as fast as Munahim with his bow, but he had the advantage of being able to pick projectiles up off the ground and launch them. After he left one thief bleeding from the head and still on the ground, and a second swinging his shield like a club because his right arm hung useless at his side, two Yuchaks ran out after him.

"Treachery!" Betel roared. "To me, Sootfaces!"

But precious few Sootfaces rallied to his side. A man in a green tunic with a long knife in each hand showed up and stood at the Gray Lord's left, and then a pair of Zalaptings with short spears took up position on his right. Indrajit hadn't meant to, but backing away from attacks, he found himself standing at the fourth side of a defensive square with the others.

The attack became frenetic. Indrajit could no longer see Betel, but he heard the crunching sound of the big hammers in action. The man with two knives took wound after wound, having the disadvantage of a shorter reach compared to the men with swords. But each time he took a slash to an arm or to his side, it left him with an avenue of attack. He slid under guards and behind shields, he disabled men by slicing them across the wrist or the thigh or the throat. The Zalaptings were a match for any single man, one Zalapting keeping an attacker at bay with his spear while the other looked for defensive weaknesses. When two Ildarians with ragged teeth rushed at the same time, Indrajit closed from the side, knocking one of them into the other and creating chaos; the Zalaptings moved in with their spears and made short work of the men.

Indrajit took a shield. He was dizzy and short of breath, but he no longer noticed any pain in his calf, so that was good. He beat down another Ildarian's defense with Vacho and then smashed the man's nose with his shield, and then he saw Philastes.

The Pelthite had his back to the wall in the alley. He had dropped the sling and held a knife; blood was spreading through his tunic from a grievous wound in his side. A dead Yuchak lay in the middle of the alley and a second Yuchak climbed over the corpse, swinging his sword back and forth and making taunting, chickenlike noises.

Indrajit had an opening. He dashed across the alley. The Yuchak heard him at the last second and turned but couldn't quite pivot around in time. Indrajit hit the man shoulder first and crushed him against the wall, hearing bones make a satisfying snap.

Then he found he couldn't hold himself upright, and sank to the ground. Philastes sank with him, leaving a dark smear on the wall.

Indrajit rolled over. His head kept rolling and spun three or four times before coming finally to a stable position. He saw more men swarming Betel, and now some seemed to be taking his side. The defensive circle had expanded to surround the anvil and the fire. Betel had a weapon in each hand and was laying out death left and right as only a fully armed Luzzazza can, roaring his demand that his Sootfaces join him.

How long could this continue before constables showed up to do something about it?

Welcome to Kish, Munahim would say.

Yammilku and a group of armed men appeared at the mouth of the alley.

"Sling." Indrajit pointed. "Hit that guy."

He gripped his sword and dragged himself back up the wall. His leg might have been on fire, it hurt so much. The pain lanced up his back and neck and into his skull, making his breath come in ragged gulps. He forced himself to step away from the wall, anyway.

"Yammilku!" he roared. Then he very deliberately took a pose, a stylized challenge stance that was used when performing the Blaatshi Epic. It communicated the invitation to a duel, limbs raised and tensed to show full commitment, jaw set to show resolve to conquer or die, chest thrust out to show indifference to wounding or even death. Not that Yammilku the Heru would have any experience of the Epic, but the stance communicated in and of itself.

In fact, it communicated far more than Indrajit could realistically deliver. He fought to keep his knees from trembling and his breath steady.

Yammilku's hawklike gaze was unreadable. He drew his long straight sword and stood looking at the scene. He gazed on Indrajit, and Indrajit had never felt more like a field mouse.

"To me, Sootfaces!" Zac Betel bellowed. Two Kishi pressed him on his left, and the hammer on the right side had disappeared. Had he lost the use of an arm?

Yammilku charged, and his men charged with him. To Indrajit's astonishment, they attacked those who were fighting Betel, rather than the Gray Lord himself. Yammilku flew, his sword slashing and stabbing with astounding speed despite the unruffled expression on his face. The men they attacked looked surprised and betrayed, and fell quickly, like dry wheat before a scythe. The fight ended, as abruptly as it had begun.

The men with the Heru were quick to stab their downed enemies in the throat, and thorough, not missing a single one.

Yammilku knelt before Betel and offered up his sword, hilt-first. "Gray Lord," he said, "I must explain."

Betel sank heavily onto a sturdy bench. Indrajit dragged himself across the alley, feeling more light-headed by the second. "Help," he murmured. Then he laughed, because he reminded himself of the two archegoi he'd seen die of... well, of childbirth. Then he stopped laughing, because that wasn't really very funny.

Betel grunted. "Insurrection requires no explanation. Tell me why I don't cut off your head right now."

"Because I did not rise against you." The Heru pointed at one of the corpses, a Karthing who had died with two spears through the chest. "I knew you had enemies. I did not know for certain who they were. But I knew I could lure them into the open."

Betel grunted again, without words.

Indrajit sat down in the middle of the alley. "Wine, at least?" he murmured. Someone passed him and busied themselves over Philastes. He hoped they were helping the Pelthite rather than, say, looting his body, but he didn't have the strength to turn and look.

Someone handed him sour wine in a leather skin. It was better than nothing.

"The Blaatshi comic," the Heru said. "I deceived him, and sent him to attack you. I knew he couldn't harm you if he did attack, and I thought he might try to warn you instead, and either way, I believed your enemies would come into the open."

"And you did this while you weren't here yourself," the Luzzazza observed. "Why?"

"I knew my absence would embolden your enemies."

"Why not root them out more directly?" Betel asked. "Knife them one by one in dark alleys, stuff their bodies into the sewers, as they deserve?"

"I wasn't sure who they all were," Yammilku said. "Now we know."

Indrajit finished the wine and felt stronger. "Can someone help me with the crossbow bolt in my leg?" he meant to ask, but the question came out more garbled than that. He tried to stand, and instead fell on his face.

"Why not come to me?" Betel pressed.

"I feared you were beset by evil counsellors, and watched by spying eyes." The Heru lowered his head humbly. Indrajit was impressed at how well he was playing the role.

"We're weakened now," Betel said in the darkness. "We've lost many men today."

"Traitors," Yammilku said.

"Not all of them. Did Harrek do this alone?"

Yammilku said nothing for a short time. Then, "I'm not certain."

"I don't believe he was capable of it," Betel said. "He was greedy and ambitious, yes, but he wasn't a planner. There must have been someone else behind him, don't you think . . . Yammilku?"

"Yes," Yammilku said immediately. "You must be right."

"Who could that have been?" Betel asked. He waited, but no answer was forthcoming. "Who could benefit from my death?"

"Another Gray Lord, perhaps," Yammilku suggested. "If you died, someone might take your territory. Take your businesses. Anyone who replaced you would be weak and on the defensive, and an easy target."

Indrajit had the sensation that someone was touching his legs. He was dragged, and then hands touched his leg that burned.

"The Silksteppers?" Betel asked. "The Sookwalkers?"

"Perhaps," the Heru said slowly. "But the Sailmenders would also be interested in many of your businesses. And what about the Soulbinders?"

Indrajit floated in darkness, and then was racked with sudden, agonizing pain. He screamed, then flopped onto his back. Someone was trying to hold him and wrap his leg. Someone else was trying to force more wine into him. He whimpered, and then acquiesced to both.

"We won't let them get away with this," Betel said.

"We strike tonight?" Yammilku suggested.

Indrajit's vision cleared. He stared up at a bright midday sky. "Philastes?" he asked. "The Pelthite?"

"The Pelthite lives," a rasping voice said.

"We don't strike," Betel said. "I call the Conclave."

"To do what?" Yammilku asked.

"To flush my enemies from hiding."

"And the Blaatshi? I can get rid of him. He's seen too much. He works for the Lord Chamberlain."

"He's a jobber," Betel said. "He works for anyone who pays, including the Lord Chamberlain."

"Not quite anyone," Indrajit mumbled, but no one responded.

"The jobbers acted with honor," Betel continued. "I find that refreshing. They stay with me."

A chalk-white Gund with four scratched-out eyes dragged Indrajit up and slung him onto a heavy bench. Indrajit managed to balance in a sitting position, leaning forward and swaying slightly. "My sword," he croaked.

"Well done," Yammilku said, inclining his head slightly.

Indrajit nodded. "I had a feeling you were playing a deep game, Heru." Hopefully his fatigue and pain masked the lie.

A Zalapting brought him Vacho, wiping mud from it with a rag. Other thieves carried over Philastes, who winced as he was plopped onto the bench beside Indrajit.

"Where are the others?" Yammilku asked. "Fix? And the Kyone?"

"They went back underground," Indrajit said.

"To come here?" the Heru pressed.

Indrajit hesitated. How much should he say? He didn't want to give Fix and Munahim away to Yammilku, whom he distrusted thoroughly. If he just waited, wouldn't his partners show up? But they might not. If anything had gone wrong, they could be in peril. They could be dead, or captives of Ghouls, and he had no way to find them.

Except that Fix and Munahim would be following the spoor left by Yammilku and his men. Which meant that Yammilku should be able to show Indrajit exactly where they had gone, and where they had left the harness. So if Fix and Munahim were indeed in trouble, Yammilku was his best bet as an ally to rescue them.

Which made him feel thoroughly uncomfortable.

"Was the Blaatshi hit on the head?" Betel asked.

"Sorry, yes," Indrajit said. "Fix and Munahim were to come here. But they were taking the trail beneath the city that Yammilku took. They were to pick up . . ." He remembered at the last second that Betel thought he was receiving the map just now, and the location of the Girdle of Life was still his secret. ". . . another item in Underkish. So if they're not here, then perhaps they've come to a bad end. Or been delayed."

Betel nodded. He gripped Indrajit's shoulder, shaking him slightly. "I want you at the Conclave tonight. But I want your partners also. I will go to summon the Gray Lords. You and your Pelthite here, gather up the rest of your company."

"I'll need Yammilku." Indrajit felt light-headed. "And . . . I worry. There are Ghouls. And other perils."

His vision had cleared and his stomach calmed, and he met the Luzzazza in the eye. Betel nodded, his face inscrutable.

"Yammilku," Betel said. "Take them, and recover their friends. Get them back here before the Conclave."

"Where will it be held?" Yammilku asked.

"I'll summon the Gray Lords to the False Palace. I want all the jobbers unharmed, understood?"

"Of course," Yammilku said.

"Manko." Betel turned on his heels, addressed the white Gund. "Go with Yammilku. Protect these two men at all costs."

The Gund roared. The insectlike legs sprouting from its shoulders quivered, rattling against each other.

Indrajit climbed to his feet, followed by Philastes.

"I'll take Cholo and—" Yammilku began.

"Manko will be enough," Betel said. "I'll need everyone else to prepare for the Conclave." He handed the map to Indrajit. It had a few sandal prints on it, but had survived the scuffle intact. "Perhaps you can use this to collect your company."

Indrajit tucked the map into his kilt pocket.

A Zalapting pressed a lamp into Indrajit's hands.

Yammilku nodded. To Indrajit he said, "I'll retrace my steps?"

"Munahim should have begun tracking you from the point you left the boat," Indrajit said.

"Come." Yammilku sheathed his sword and led them away. Indrajit followed, gaining strength with each step and each deep breath, and keeping an eye on Philastes.

The rain had let up, but the iron-gray sky overhead and the gusting winds suggested that the storm was merely holding its breath, preparing to blast them again.

The Pelthite turned to the Gund, shambling on his heels, and emitted a sonorous belch. Indrajit was about to take Philastes to task when the Gund belched back.

"You speak Gund, too?" Indrajit asked.

"It's also a pretty easy language." Philastes shrugged.

Indrajit wanted to communicate things to the Gund, but they were things he didn't want to say within earshot of Yammilku. Still, he smiled. It was reassuring that Philastes, at least, could talk to the monstrous thief. "Let him know we're happy he's along."

"Gund doesn't have a word for 'happy,'" Philastes said. "Shall I tell him that we're satiated with good food, or sexually aroused?"

"Can you tell him he's our friend?"

"I can call him a good pack-mate."

"Do that."

Indrajit caught up with Yammilku as Philastes and the Gund grunted and snickered at each other. "Do we have to come to an understanding?" he asked.

Yammilku headed along the edge of a Rûphat court. Ten sweaty, shrieking Zalaptings played a team of two Luzzazza and a Shamb. The Zalaptings swarmed the larger players and dominated the court, but had a hard time getting past the forest of extra limbs to actually score. The Luzzazza wore gloves on their invisible hands, to prove they weren't cheating, but invisible elbows still disconcertingly caused the ball to change angle sharply in midair on a regular basis. At the back of the court rose a knob of shattered rock, crowned with a knot of pipal and amalaki trees.

"I think we have an understanding," Yammilku said. "I fooled you, but it was to defend my master, Zac Betel. I hope you can forgive me."

"Think nothing of it," Indrajit said.

Yammilku was obviously lying.

"There's a crack in the stone at the base of the wall." Yammilku pointed. "We'll go underground there. The harness isn't far."

He began to climb.

Chapter Nineteen

Indrajit held the lamp in his left hand, keeping his right hand on Vacho's hilt. Ahead of him, pushing into the shadow at each step, walked Yammilku. The Heru's hands hung easily at his side and his shoulders looked relaxed. Indrajit didn't feel relaxed. He worried Yammilku might have allies—Silksteppers or Sookwalkers or other corrupt Sootfaces—waiting in ambush. He worried Yammilku had agreed to bring him down here to kill him. He worried something bad had already befallen Fix and Munahim. He worried...

He worried.

He wondered about Manko's loyalties, and what the Gund thought its instructions were.

And what, for that matter, was Philastes telling the Gund? They continued to chatter away, croaks and groans and ribbits, punctuated with rattling laughter.

The crack in the knoll, hidden among the pipal and amalaki trees, twisted down and into the bowels of the city in the shape of a corkscrew. Near the entrance, the butts of yip and tobacco cigarettes, fruit rinds, cracked cups, and ratty wool blankets suggested casual use, but with a minute's steep climbing, they stood on a brick floor. Ahead of them, a brick arch leaped right and left, a ribbon of orange-red suggesting a passageway beyond. To the right, shattered stairs descended.

Yammilku stopped. He looked down the stairs and along the passage.

"What's wrong?" Indrajit asked, but the Heru didn't answer him.

Manko groaned.

Yammilku whistled a series of notes that echoed off distant brick, returning tremulous and watery.

"You surely haven't forgotten your way," Indrajit murmured. "So something is wrong. Were you expecting to find someone here?"

"Shh." Yammilku shook his head. "One must always be careful in Underkish."

"I know," Indrajit said. "Ghouls, weird Druvash sorcery, and worse. There are thieves down there."

"This way." Yammilku turned and climbed down the stairs.

They picked their way carefully down the steps, then crossed a rubble-strewn chamber. Beneath the shattered rock, the floor was slanted. In puddles of light thrown by his raised lamp, Indrajit saw shingles and tar. Halfway across the chamber, he passed the top of a chimney.

Dim light leaked up through the chimney.

Behind the rubble-strewn cavern, they passed through a square doorway, then found themselves at the edge of an abyss. A wooden pole, thick as a solid tree trunk, but shaved down to a smooth cylinder like a ship's mast, lay on the brickwork at the edge of the chasm and stretched into darkness.

Indrajit leaned over the ravine and tried to look down into it, holding his lamp high. "I think I can see the bottom."

"No," Yammilku said. "That's a ledge."

"How do you know?"

"I've stood on it. But from there, the abyss drops further, and you can't see the floor."

"We're not climbing down, are we?" Indrajit asked.

"We're crossing." Yammilku pointed at the beam.

"There's not another road?" Indrajit wasn't especially nervous for his own balance, but he worried about the Gund. Not to mention the possibility that Yammilku would attack him as he crossed.

"There is," Yammilku said. "But the guard I left behind isn't there anymore, and that makes me nervous. So I'd rather go this way. Or we can get the map out and try to find another road. I don't know how long that will take."

Indrajit nodded. "After you."

Yammilku started across the beam. The pole didn't budge at all as the Heru stood on it, so Indrajit let him get a few paces ahead and then followed. He breathed deeply, maintained his calm, and didn't look down. Ten paces along the bridge, he was able to make out the other side, a ragged hole that looked like a natural cave. Twenty paces along, he heard squeaking sounds and something furry and flying swarmed past him in the air, buffeting his head and arms. He windmilled a little, but didn't lose his balance.

Thirty paces along, the Gund joined him on the pole, and he felt the wood sag beneath his feet.

Indrajit picked up his pace, dancing lightly forward and catching up to the Heru just as they both reached the other side. Manko dragged itself forward across the bridge. Despite its size, the Gund was flexible enough that it leaned forward and gripped the pole with two hands. Its feet, Indrajit saw as it drew closer, had long and prehensile toes, so the Gund clung to the log with all four limbs. At its point of maximum bowing, Indrajit feared the log would snap under the Gund's weight, dropping it into the chasm to its death, but the beam held, and Manko arrived at the far side with chortling and gurgling sounds.

Philastes crossed easily.

Twenty paces farther, the natural cavern gave way to glass. Yammilku walked onto a translucent greenish floor. When Indrajit followed, he looked down and saw multiple slabs of glass below, each reflecting the yellow lamp light in a series that seemed to curve slightly away in the distance.

Then Yammilku led them up stairs. The stairs climbed through a broad shaft of empty space, between waist-high metal walls with rubbery black bannisters. The steps were metal also, each step ribbed into dozens of tiny spines and interlocking with the steps above and below it via steel teeth. On his first step, the entire staircase seemed to slide, slightly, but then it held and Indrajit ascended.

He was beginning to calm down. Yammilku hadn't attacked him or led him into an ambush. The Gund seemed to be cheerfully chattering away with Philastes, every time Indrajit paid any attention to them. The absence of Yammilku's expected sentinel could only be a good thing, surely.

At the top of the stairs, they descended a ramp that was covered with tattered scraps of rug glued to cement beneath. Ahead, the ramp ended in a balcony overlooking a larger room.

"Shield the light," Yammilku murmured.

Indrajit cupped the flame with his free hand. Yammilku slowly drew his sword, and Indrajit stepped away from the Heru. "What do you fear?"

"The unknown," Yammilku said.

Indrajit kept a few steps from the Heru. They both hunkered into a crouching posture as they walked. Coming behind them, the Gund stooped forward and walked on all fours again. Its neck was flexible enough that its head pivoted forward when it moved in this fashion. The thicket of insectoid limbs on its shoulders hung over it like a skeletal parasol, rustling slightly.

Philastes walked beside Manko, sling out, its pocket filled with a stone.

Yammilku and Indrajit crept to the balustrade of the balcony at the same time. Indrajit raised his eyes over the polished metal rail and saw a room whose walls were covered in narrow metal doors. They looked like the drawers of a cabinet or dresser, but vertical rather than horizontal. They were painted a dull green. Some were smashed. One lay open.

Narrow wooden benches ran around the room, standing on metal rods bolted to the floor.

Bodies lay on the floor. They were fresh, and Indrajit wondered for a moment whether they were even dead. But they didn't move, and he heard no sound of breathing, and then he saw that they had wounds.

Puncture wounds, smallish, with little blood.

He stood cautiously, holding the lamp out, and saw that the skin around each wound he could see was purple and bloated.

"The Girdle of Life," he said. "It was here?"

Yammilku pointed at the open metal door. "It was hung there. These men were guarding it."

A metal ladder descended into the room. Yammilku went first and stood in the center of the room with his sword gripped in both hands, slowly pivoting and looking in all directions while Indrajit and the others joined him. Several passages exited from this chamber. Nothing stirred.

Manko lowered itself directly from the balcony. Philastes came last, and his legs were shaking.

"The dead men," Indrajit said. "I think I saw them on the boat with you."

"Yes," Yammilku said.

"Fellow Sootfaces?"

"They're Sookwalkers, mostly."

Indrajit poked at one of the dead men with a foot. He felt relief again, this time that Fix and Munahim were not among the dead. "The way their flesh is swollen and discolored . . . what does that suggest to you?"

"Venom," Yammilku said. "They were stabbed. You can see the puncture wounds."

"Were they betrayed?" Indrajit asked. "Are any of them missing? Maybe one of the men you left behind had a dagger with venom on the blade, and he surprised the others."

Yammilku counted. "They would have to be idiots for him to surprise them all, eight men, one at a time. In any case, no, this is all of them. Someone attacked them. Your friends, perhaps? The harness is missing."

"We don't use venom," Indrajit said. "And this delicate stab wound . . . that's not really our style. If Fix and Munahim had killed these men, we'd see wounds from a hatchet and a two-handed sword. Maybe arrows, but not whatever did . . . this." He pointed at one of the fatal injuries, a circular hole in the throat of a dead man, big enough to shove his thumb into.

"The Kattak," Philastes said.

Indrajit felt ill.

"What do you mean, the Kattak?" Yammilku asked.

"The giant wasps," Indrajit said. "The secret rulers of the Paper Sultanate. You're saying they can inflict lethal wounds like this."

"Yes," Philastes said.

"But then . . . are these men impregnated?" Indrajit asked. "Do we need to burn them now?"

"Impregnated?" Yammilku sounded shocked.

Manko groaned.

"They lay their eggs in living men," Philastes said. "These men are dead, but they're only dead."

Yammilku cursed and spat.

Indrajit's growing sense of peace had evaporated. "Which

direction did you come from?" he asked. "After you left the flatboat you attacked us in, and came here, how did you enter the room?"

By way of answer, Yammilku turned and strode to one of the exits. Beneath a square metal lintel opening onto a wide corridor, he stopped.

A sword lay at his feet. It was a long sword, long enough that it could be wielded with two hands. It was of good but simple workmanship, with a plain cross-guard, leather braided around the handle, and a simple iron ball for the pommel.

"Frozen hells," Indrajit said.

"This is your friend's?" Yammilku asked.

"The Kyone's," Indrajit confirmed. He now saw, scattered around the floor within a couple of paces of the sword, severed insectoid limbs. He saw spatters of black ichor, too, and blood.

"Your Kyone fought something here," Yammilku said.

"The Kattak," Indrajit confirmed. "But I see no bodies. Philastes, can you think of any reason why the Kattak would take away a living man, other than to impregnate him?"

"Yes," Philastes said. "They may also have taken them to eat later."

"This city reveals a new secret every day," Yammilku said. "Each more foul than the one before it."

"Where would they have gone, though?" Indrajit asked. "The Kattak won't be lurking in the burned ruins of the embassy."

"The cave beneath is where they eat," Philastes said. "We passed the edge of it when we fled. The pit full of bodies."

"Might they lurk there for a while?" Indrajit asked. "While they arrange other housing, say?"

"Potentially for a long while." Philastes nodded. "They have other servants—the archegoi only do the diplomacy and negotiation. There are clerks and scribes who can help them find a new building and get new archegoi. And yes, in the meantime, they might very well wait in the pit."

"We need to go to the pit," Indrajit said.

"*You* need to go to the pit," Yammilku told him. "*I* need to go back and tell Betel that we tried, but sadly, the mission failed. Looks like some monster from the deep—maybe it was something called a Kattak but who knows, really—got the jobbers. So sad."

Indrajit wanted to threaten the Heru. He wanted to say he'd reveal Yammilku's leadership in the attempt to overthrow Betel, but

Yammilku had already claimed that he had tricked Indrajit by pretending to lead a coup. He'd gotten one step ahead of Indrajit. Either Betel already knew that Yammilku was a snake in the grass, or he didn't, and Indrajit had nothing more to say, either way.

He wanted to draw his sword, but Yammilku was already armed, and if Indrajit took Vacho in hand, Yammilku might take that as an invitation to attack.

"Please," he said. "We need help."

"Goodbye." Yammilku turned back, walking toward an exit opposite the one where they'd found Munahim's sword.

Manko seized him. With one hand, the Gund grabbed the front of the Heru's tunic. At the same time, the insectlike limbs sprouting from its shoulders fell on Yammilku and gripped him about the shoulders, pinning his sword arm in place and holding him. Manko lifted its prisoner off the ground.

Philastes groaned, and Manko groaned back.

"Do you speak Gund?" Philastes's voice was polite, almost cheerful.

"Put me down!" Yammilku snapped.

"That must be a no. Manko says you are to obey the fish-head."

"Hey," Indrajit objected.

"I'm just repeating what Manko says." Philastes shrugged.

"You could . . . smooth it out a little bit. You *are* supposed to be a diplomat."

"I'm a junior diplomat. Not very experienced."

Manko groaned again.

"He says, 'Take the fish-head to the pit,'" Philastes said.

"Blaatshi," Indrajit said.

"There is no word for Blaatshi in Gund," Philastes said. "He's saying 'fish-head.'"

"I understand that," Indrajit said. "When he says 'fish-head,' you can translate it as 'Blaatshi.'"

"That would be twisting his words, we'd risk misunderstanding."

"Oh, I think we'd understand him just fine."

Yammilku reached with his left hand to grab his sword, and Manko took the sword away. He roared, scarred face a handspan from Yammilku's beak.

"He won't tell you again," Philastes said. "Help the . . . Blaatshi."

"That's better."

"It's foolish," Yammilku said. "Your friends are dead, or will be soon."

"Tunk believed that the Girdle of Life could help him, didn't he?" Indrajit asked Philastes.

"It didn't, though," Philastes pointed out.

"Because it wasn't attached to the device," Indrajit said.

"What device?" Yammilku asked.

"The Druvash sorcery device the Vin Dalu have. Never mind." Indrajit shook his head. "Look, maybe we can rescue my friends before they're injected with eggs or eaten. And if they are impregnated, maybe the Vin Dalu can help them, assuming we can get them the harness."

"Maybe, maybe, assuming," Yammilku said, mocking.

"You planned to throw away my life in your coup attempt," Indrajit said. "I owe you nothing but revenge. You help me get to the pit, and I will forgive you."

Yammilku sneered. "I don't work for forgiveness."

Indrajit shrugged. "If you refuse to help, I'll throw you down the next pit."

Manko growled and belched.

"I have no choice." Yammilku shook his head. "I'll do it."

"No sword for you, until you've earned it," Indrajit said.

Manko set Yammilku on his feet, but held on to the Heru's weapon.

"You take us back to the spot where you attacked us," Indrajit said. "I'll get us to the pit from there."

"You don't want to just use the map?" Yammilku suggested.

"Actually," Indrajit said, "I do not. Get going."

Indrajit resumed following Yammilku through the underworld of Kish. The trail from here was not nearly as strange, and there were no abysses to cross. They padded through galleries and caverns and chambers by the light of Indrajit's lamp. When they heard rustling sounds in the darkness, Manko bellowed, and the rustling became the slapping of fleeing feet. They climbed up stairs and down, and finally came to the river of sewage, and a flatboat floating in it.

"The water is an ell higher than when I passed this way," Yammilku said. "Look how close the boat is to the ceiling."

"Is the water still rising?" Philastes asked.

"We'll find out," Indrajit said. "Get in the boat."

Chapter Twenty

The poles lying in the bottom of the flatboat were barely long enough to permit them to pole. They scraped along, only an ell or so from the rough cavern ceiling, for ten minutes. They followed Yammilku's directions and his actions; he worked a pole and Manko sat reclining on top of his sword. The Gund also carried Munahim's sword and the lamp.

Then the ceiling rose above them and pillars appeared. They had moved from a sluggish current into a faster one, and had to pole manically for a short time to get beyond the water's insistent tug.

"Where does the water go?" Philastes asked.

"No one knows," Indrajit said. "The center of the world. Or the most ancient level of Kish, laid on its foundations at the very birth of mankind, still inhabited, ten leagues down. Or out the other side, since everyone knows that the Earth is a sphere. If you want more speculation, I expect you can get your fill at the Hall of Guesses."

"It returns to the ocean," Yammilku said. "It has to. Water flows like air."

"See?" Indrajit said. "Another guess."

"Hey," Philastes said. "Is that the skull we came through?"

Indrajit agreed that it was and they moored the flatboat, tying its rope through the bone of the skull's eye socket. The clotted waters of the underground river were just a palm short of spilling over through the socket and into the skull.

"This is where I found you," Yammilku said. "I'll leave you now."

"Attacked us," Indrajit said. "We may need the boat again, so I can't let you take it. And I can't trust you to just swim away and leave it, so I'm afraid you're still coming with us."

Yammilku grumbled, but Manko honked.

"Very well," Yammilku said. "What are these things we're going up against?"

"Kattak," Indrajit said. "I guess that's both the singular and the plural. They are wasp-men. Approximately the size of horses. Venomous, as you have seen. Intelligent. Do they fly, Philastes?"

"I believe so."

"We believe they fly." Indrajit smiled. "Is that enough information?"

"Sounds straightforward. Kill wasp-men, rescue jobbers. Easier with a sword in my hand."

"I'll lead from here." Indrajit cast his eyes about first, looking for Kattak nymphs. Thomedes Tunk had died here, exploding into infant wasp-men, but those infants were gone now.

Perhaps the Kattak had collected them.

Perhaps, having the memories of Thomedes Tunk, they had known their own way home.

Indrajit took the lamp back.

Indrajit retraced his steps from a few hours earlier. He hadn't tried to place them in his theater of memory, but the needlelike bridge, the stairs, the puddle of water that had been the bottom of a waterfall crashing down from the unseen ceiling, and the stoa were easy enough to recall.

At the end of the stoa, under the watching stone eyes of a dozen gods he could not name, Indrajit drew his sword. "A few sharp turns and we're there. Philastes, can you tell us any more about what we'll find?"

"Once I was initiated into the mysteries of the Kattak... I threw purchased slaves and prisoners down a hole in the guest house floor," Philastes said. "Their screams lasted for hours, so the fall didn't kill them. I've never seen the pit itself, except the glimpse of the edge that you and I both had, a few hours ago."

"We're looking for Fix and Munahim." Indrajit turned to the Gund. "Fix is a Kishi man, short, with dark hair. Munahim is a Kyone. Do you know Kyones?"

Manko groaned.

"It knows what a Kyone is," Philastes said.

"It occurs to me to wonder how Gunds have a word that means sexually aroused," Indrajit said. "I thought they were sexless."

"They're like mules." Philastes nodded. "That doesn't mean they don't understand how other men reproduce."

"How do they reproduce?" Indrajit asked.

Philastes made a chuckling noise deep in his throat, ending in a squeak. Manko groaned twice, in different pitches.

"Manko says you're too young," Philastes said. "Ask again when you're older."

Indrajit chuckled. "Speaking of young, the nymphs should still be too small to hurt us, right? So . . . how many mature Kattak do we expect?"

"I think the nymphs are probably too small," Philastes agreed. "I have no idea how many Kattak there are."

Yammilku cursed.

"I saw them rarely," Philastes said. "Tunk worked with them directly and he saw them more often."

"You never had a list of names?"

"No."

Indrajit considered. "Did you ever see more than two at a time?"

"I never saw more than one at a time," Philastes said. "But Tunk always referred to them in the plural."

"Wait . . . Pelthite has a dual form, doesn't it?"

"Oh, you know languages, too!"

Indrajit harrumphed. "Just a smattering. But that means that there are at least three of them. And there could be a thousand."

"I don't think we fed them enough prisoners for there to be a thousand Kattak," Philastes said.

"Three Kattak?"

"More."

"Ten?"

Philastes hesitated. "More. I think many more. And remember that Munahim heard Kattak moving while we were in the embassy."

"Frozen hells." Indrajit considered. "Okay. So we're rescuing our comrades, not trying to exterminate the Kattak. We don't need to worry about hunting down every last wasp-man, but we also should not assume we're safe from attack until we have our friends and are out on the surface again."

"Also, we want the harness," Philastes added.

"Also, we want the Girdle." Indrajit turned and led them through the series of turns.

He reached the length of passage where, previously, the right side of the tunnel had opened into a vast empty space, carpeted with the bodies of men. Now that empty space, on the left side as Indrajit retraced his former journey backward, was hidden behind a veil of paper. A faint breeze made the paper expand and contract. Ragged strips only loosely attached to the rest flapped with the movement, and the main membrane made a taut snapping sound like the beat of a drum.

The pit was entirely hidden.

"Why do this?" Indrajit whispered to Philastes.

Philastes shrugged. "I have only recently become initiated to the mysteries of the Kattak, and to my great shock and dismay."

Indrajit nodded slowly. He wished he had Munahim's sense of smell to confirm that his friends were behind the paper, but it seemed reasonably clear, and he saw only one possible course of action.

"Give the Heru his sword," he said to Manko. "Please."

Manko groaned, but handed the weapon over.

"You and I first," Indrajit said to Yammilku. With two long slashes of Vacho's blade, he cut loose a flap in the paper wall.

Once Yammilku had done the same, they jumped into the hole.

The sides of the pit were not as steep as they appeared from above. Nor, strictly speaking, was it really a pit. Indrajit slid down a steep, moist wall of rock, and was stopped when his sandal came to rest against a shattered rib cage. His lamp illuminated shapes that must be stalactites and stalagmites, all wrapped in paper. Other lumps, more or less shapeless, were mysterious to him.

"None of this paper was here before," he said.

Yammilku stuck close by Indrajit's side. They scanned the darkness for movement as Manko and Philastes clambered down behind them. "The wasp-men make the paper?"

"We broke into their . . . home, I suppose you'd say, last night," Indrajit explained. "The building was full of paper. Walls and ceilings covered. As if the Kattak live and breed inside nests of paper, and they had built the nest to fill out the convenient space of an old mansion on the Street of Fallen Stars."

"And now they have built their nest here," Yammilku said, "in a cave beneath the street. What does the paper do?"

Indrajit turned to Philastes. "Do you know?"

"I think it dries the moisture out of the air." Philastes shrugged. "All Kattak nesting sites are full of it, I've been told. Inside temples, caverns, and palaces."

Indrajit examined the space around him, finding tunnels, entrances to passages, and rounded chambers. "It also means the Kattak created this space and they know it well. Watch carefully for attacks."

"If we find your companions and they're already dead," Yammilku said, "then I'll light this nest on fire."

"I'll help," Indrajit said.

Indrajit led them down a passage that ended in a stubby chamber. They returned, and followed another paper tunnel that seemed to wind back on itself and deliver them to the spot from which they'd departed. They walked on paper, which was sometimes thick enough that it felt like wood, but at other times seemed to be a thin wrapping over the top of a heap of bodies. Indrajit felt ribs cracking under his weight, and slipped twice as he stepped on skulls and they rolled out from under him.

"Can we call to them?" Philastes asked. "Thomedes was able to talk, right to the end."

"So was Lysander," Indrajit said, shuddering at the memory. "They'd wrapped his entire body, but left his face free. To be able to breathe, I suppose."

"Your friends may be unconscious," Yammilku said. "The same venom that kills in large quantities may render comatose in small doses."

"Fix!" Indrajit called.

They listened.

"I think I heard him," Philastes said.

"I thought I did, too." Indrajit shook his head. "But where?"

He took another angle and passed into an adjoining spherical nodule of what he was beginning to think of as the main chamber. The floor here was covered with paper, but a complete ylakka skeleton sat atop the paper, unwrapped. Perhaps it was dry enough not to be a problem for the Kattak.

Who must not like water, he reflected. Fire burned the paper of their nests, but it was a risk they took, because the paper dried the water out of the air. Perhaps the Kattak needed that dryness.

Perhaps it was their young, the nymphs.

Perhaps the nymphs who had burst from the belly of Thomedes Tunk had all perished in the flood of sewage into which they'd been born. He hoped so.

This chamber had three exits. One dead-ended quickly. The other bored horizontally for ten paces and turned abruptly vertical. Staring up the length of the paper cylinder, Indrajit could make out nothing.

The third tunnel led them in an elevated loop that again dumped them where they had begun.

"Loops and loops," Yammilku said.

Manko groaned.

"Has anyone been watching the walls for concealed doors?" Philastes asked.

"How would you conceal a door in these walls?" Indrajit pressed him.

"I'm imagining something like a slit," the Pelthite said. "I'm just imagining, I've never seen one, but we seem to be in a sealed-off space. It serves no use."

"Maybe it absorbs water," Indrajit said.

"Maybe it absorbs water," Philastes conceded. "But also, if there were slits in the wall that a Kattak could detect, or maybe the Kattak know the location of the slits because they made them, and if the Kattak could press their way through, they'd work like doors."

"Secret passages," Yammilku said.

"I've seen no such slits." Indrajit looked at the tunnel exit they'd just emerged from. The tunnel formed a loop that rose and fell again, which would have left a central space enclosed within the loop. The previous circuitous tunnel had followed a similar loop, but lower down . . . presumably, below the elevated loop. Leaving the same internal space untouched.

Which could be a stalactite. Or solid rock. Or some ancient building, or heap of glass, or an abyss.

But it could also be a chamber.

"What are you thinking about?" Philastes asked.

"I'm going to make my own slit." Indrajit walked slowly into the lower loop, probing at the wall with Vacho's pommel. It was sturdy paper, but not the multiple layers that was so dense, it felt like wood. The paper had give to it; it wasn't plastered over a rock wall. It was also consistent; he found no slits, or stretches made of thinner paper. The others followed, watching. Indrajit handed the lamp to Philastes. "Be ready, just in case."

He slashed through the wall. Once, twice, three times, and then a triangle of heavy paper fell askew and to the side. Lamplight flickered into the space beyond, and Indrajit saw Munahim's snout and nose. The Kyone's body was wrapped to leave only his face visible, and he hung by a thick paper cord.

"Munahim!" Indrajit plunged into the triangle, sword-first. He immediately looked left and right, searching for ambush, but found none. He was in a low chamber with walls and ceiling of paper, and a second bundle hung from above, with Fix's face protruding from the top.

"Watch for Kattak!" he cried. "I'll cut them loose!"

He held Munahim with one arm while he hacked at the stem holding him, until he cut the Kyone down. As he laid him on the paper floor, he found a paper-wrapped bundle that clinked when touched. He palpated it with his fingers—by the shape and size, it probably contained Munahim's bow and some weapons. He thought he felt Fix's falchion and ax.

Holding Vacho halfsword-style, he cut a slit down the length of Munahim's paper cocoon and tore away the worst of the paper. Munahim stirred. "Too late," the Kyone murmured.

"I hear wings out here," Yammilku called. "Hurry up!"

Indrajit cut open the bundle. Munahim's bow and Fix's weapons were indeed inside, sticky but unharmed. "Munahim," Indrajit said. "Get up. We need to get out of here."

"It's too late," Munahim said. "You should leave us." The Kyone leaned over and vomited a thin string of black liquid.

Indrajit hacked Fix free and lowered him to the ground. Fix was mouthing something, and when Indrajit leaned close, he heard, "Alea. Alea."

"She's not good enough for you, brother," Indrajit said. Snatching one of Fix's own knives from the bundle, he slashed Fix's wrapping and pulled his partner out. In the process, Fix's eyes opened and he groaned.

Fix was wearing the Girdle of Life.

"They're here!" Philastes shrieked.

Indrajit kicked Munahim. "Get up!"

"It's too late." The Kyone rolled over onto all fours and stared at Indrajit. "Don't you understand? They did it to us already!"

"We'll worry about that once we're out of here." Indrajit stood, dragging Fix with him. "Pick up the weapons!"

In the tunnel outside this chamber, he heard shouting and the buzzing of enormous insectoid wings.

"They hate this city," Fix muttered. "They ruled once. They resent it."

"A lot of people hate this city," Indrajit said. "Welcome to Kish! Time to get out of here!"

But as he spoke, Philastes was backing into the chamber through the opening Indrajit had made. Manko and Yammilku fought in the shadows beyond. They stood back-to-back, the Gund punching with his fists and stabbing with his insect arm, and both men swinging swords. The Gund still had Munahim's blade, Indrajit remembered.

"Stand!" Indrajit shook Fix. "Pick up your gear, right now!"

"I can remember so much," Fix murmured. "I was at the embassy parties. Ambassadors. Bureaucrats. Highly placed servants of the Lords of Kish."

"We're getting you to the Vin Dalu, right now!" Indrajit slashed a hole in the chamber opposite the first. Then he grabbed the lamp from Philastes and a strip of loose, heavy paper, and stepped through.

He turned right, listening for the sound of more Kattak, and closing in on the Kattak fighting Manko. He saw the wings and arching back of the Kattak as it thrust its sting forward again and again. Manko dodged and blocked, but it looked as if he was wearing down. Indrajit took the oil flask from his pocket, twisted paper into a wick, and lit the paper on fire.

He wasn't sure it would work. But he threw the flask at the center of the wasp-man's body.

Oil splashed all over the Kattak's thorax and burst into flame. The Kattak spun about, shrieking dryly, and lunged toward Indrajit. The Gund behind caught it by the base of its stinger.

Then Manko snapped the stinger off with a single sharp movement.

Indrajit ducked and the flaming Kattak raced past him. He heard thuds and saw dull reflected glows as it slammed its way through the paper caverns, screaming.

The Gund turned. It had Munahim's sword in one hand and a raw Kattak stinger in the other, and it charged the second wasp-man. Yammilku cowered, shrugging away from the sudden thunder of the charge, but the Kattak sprang to the attack.

The wasp-man stabbed his stinger into the Gund's chest. At the same moment, the Gund plunged the stinger it held into the forehead of the Kattak. The stinger sank a full two cubits into the Kattak's head.

Then the Gund and the Kattak both collapsed, clutched together and still.

"No!" Philastes rushed back out into the tunnel. His shriek quickly became weeping as he checked Manko and found the Gund unmoving. Munahim and Fix emerged more slowly, attaching weapons to belts. Indrajit handed Munahim his sword.

"There may be others," Indrajit said. "We have to leave."

"Did Munahim tell you that we contain eggs?" Fix murmured.

"Yes," Indrajit said. "I see you found the Girdle of Life. We're going from here straight to the Vin Dalu."

"I need to return you to Zac Betel," Yammilku said. "For the Conclave."

"Sounds good," Indrajit said. "First, there's a little detour we're going to make. Just to make sure we don't lose this little device again." He sheathed Vacho and wrapped his fingers around the shoulder strap of the Girdle of Life.

Dragging Fix by main force, he headed for the exit from the Kattak nest.

Chapter Twenty-One

"The Kattak hate us," Fix grunted.

"Yes," Indrajit agreed. "They eat the flesh of other men and they plant their eggs in us."

They stumbled toward the nearest exit Indrajit knew of. He would have pushed them to move faster, but as it was, he ran so fast the lamp flickered and threatened to go out.

He turned toward a distant hint of daylight and jumped at the sight of a crowd of ghosts, moving together to his left. He looked closer and saw a panel of glass, rimmed with steel and crowded about with crumbling yellow brick and black earth. Beyond it lay a chamber whose walls and floors were of a smooth, ceramiclike substance, the color of drogger milk. On the far side of the small chamber, mirrors hung on the wall. Raising the lamp, Indrajit saw himself reflected in each of the mirrors, and again in the window.

"Black god's breath," Philastes groaned.

Indrajit turned to look at the Pelthite. His face was contorted by sorrow.

The Gund. Manko had been a groaning beast to Indrajit, but Philastes and Manko had been chatting away for a couple of hours.

"I'm sorry," Indrajit said. "Maybe the life of a jobber isn't for you."

"I grieve," Philastes told him. "Don't warriors grieve?"

"Warriors grieve," Indrajit agreed.

"Go faster," Munahim said.

Indrajit resumed his trot.

"Does it hurt?" he asked Munahim. "The . . . eggs?"

"Not yet," the Kyone said. "But I know how it ends. I'll take my own life before I let that happen to me. I'll immolate myself."

"They hate Kish in particular," Fix said.

"Everyone hates Kish," Indrajit said. "Especially the people who live here."

They had reached the source of the daylight. A crack far overhead let in light; squinting, Indrajit thought maybe there was an opening in the floor of an alleyway, or a chimney that climbed between building.

But the shaft was steep, the walls were smooth, and it was raining again.

"Consult the map," Yammilku said. "What's the next nearest exit it shows?"

Indrajit and Fix each pulled out a copy. Indrajit put his away, deferring to the Kishi's ability to actually read, and passed the lamp flame behind the map.

Fix grunted. "Forget about an exit. I think we can get to the Vin Dalu directly, without going aboveground."

"That would be convenient," Indrajit said, "as there are people on the surface who do not wish us well."

"As always," Fix pointed out.

"Welcome to Kish," Munahim said. "Hurry."

Fix led the group down a staircase made of a steel lattice. At the bottom, they entered a smooth pipe. Indrajit heard an echoing sound, seemingly from overhead.

"Do you hear a voice?" he asked. "It's echoing, but it's rhythmic. Maybe it's chanting something? Or counting? Philastes?"

"It's a voice," Philastes said. "I don't understand the words. I can't even guess at what language it might be."

"The Kattak used to rule here," Fix said.

"You read this in a book?" Indrajit asked.

"No," Munahim said. "I know it, too."

"How do you know it?" Indrajit wasn't sure he really wanted an answer.

"I feel it," Fix said.

"In my belly." Munahim's voice was mournful.

"You know it because the eggs inside you know it," Philastes said.

"If you know more about Kattak life cycle," Indrajit said, "now is a good time to tell us."

"I'm just guessing," the Pelthite said. "But the Kattak pass down memories. They have the memories of their parents and also the memories of the men in whom they incubate."

Indrajit felt ill. "This does not make me feel kindly toward them."

"Perhaps the men in whom they incubate share in the experience," Philastes said. "Perhaps Fix and Munahim will know more about the Kattak as a result of this experience."

"I dreamed strange dreams, wrapped in paper," Munahim said.

"My knowledge of the Kattak grows more definite with the passing of time," Fix said. "I remember the bacchanalia hosted by the embassy. The drugs, and when servants of the Lords of Kish, or ambassadors of other nations, or wealthy merchants, were lethargic or unconscious from blue loaf or yip or alcohol, I remember the implanting of eggs."

"It will be greatest right before you burst," Philastes suggested. "As the eggs develop into larvae and then into nymphs, they are becoming conscious. Their consciousness and knowledge are bleeding into you."

"Burst?" Yammilku sounded nauseated.

Indrajit *felt* nauseated. "On the plus side, Fix, you're gaining knowledge without having to read a book."

It was a jape, and Indrajit expected Fix to respond as to any other jest, with a jab at the Epic, or at the shape of Indrajit's head.

"It's a strange sensation," Fix said. "My knowledge grows, but I don't have the feeling of having learned. I don't have a memory of when I discovered new facts, or the image in my mind of a page I was looking at when I read a new idea. Instead, I just look into my mind and there is more there than there used to be."

"Disturbing," Indrajit said.

"When you say 'burst,'" Yammilku said, "do you mean that insects will come out of you? That eggs are growing inside you that will at some point hatch?"

"Yes," Munahim said. "Hatch and kill us. Welcome to Kish."

"Why do you keep saying 'Welcome to Kish'?" Yammilku asked.

"I'm practicing," Munahim said. "Trying to sound like a local. So I throw in the phrase after anyone says something cynical."

"Just keep your mouth shut and growl," Yammilku suggested. "You'll sound local enough."

"Welcome to Kish," Munahim said.

"And don't worry," Yammilku said. "I'll light you both on fire if you start hatching insects."

"Thank you," Munahim said.

"The Kattak used to rule Kish," Fix said.

"A lot of people used to rule Kish," Indrajit shot back. "It's the City from the Dawn of Time, the First City. The Druvash used to rule here, you don't see them being grumpy about it."

"Possibly because they're dead," Yammilku said.

"Before the Empire," Fix said.

"So hundreds of years ago," Indrajit said. "Maybe a thousand years. A thousand years ago, the Kattak had a big paper mound here somewhere. Are you telling me they hate Kish because they lost that mound? That they hated the Empire for centuries, and now Kish, because a thousand years ago, someone stole their land?"

Munahim groaned. "We're learning that they have long memories. Some Kattak may perceive these as events that happened during their lifetimes."

"That's what I'm saying." Fix stopped. They stood on a brick plain, with a ceiling so high above them that the lamplight didn't reach, and walls so far away that Indrajit couldn't see them. "We're close," he said. "There has to be a passage from here that leads us to the Vin Dalu."

"Wait," Indrajit said. "You brought us this direction without knowing for certain there was even an open path?"

"I had a high degree of confidence," Fix said. "And we could always retrace our steps."

"I can smell the Vin Dalu," Munahim said.

Indrajit wrinkled his nose. "I smell mold. And slime. And maybe the hint of something rotting."

"The Vin Dalu have walked this way recently," Munahim said. "The one in the middle."

"Maybe this is the way to the foundling house," Indrajit said. "Where they keep the orphaned children of their murdered enemies."

"They experiment on those children," Yammilku said.

"I don't think those stories are true," Fix said. "And if they are, I will smother my conscience, if the Vin Dalu can help Alea."

"And me," Munahim said.

"Yes," Indrajit agreed.

Munahim loped into the darkness, sniffing at the air and stooping to sniff at the ground. The others followed him.

"If the Kattak hate Kish so much, why do they have an embassy here?" Indrajit asked.

"Oh, that's easy," Philastes said. "It's especially important to have embassies at the capitals of powers you don't get along with. An ambassador to a friend is just a host of parties. Ah . . . you know, ordinary parties. Receptions after a theater performance or the opening of an art gallery, that sort of thing. An ambassador to an enemy has to be a negotiator, and someone who delivers ultimatums, and a manager of spies and even assassins."

"Really?" Indrajit asked.

"Absolutely," Philastes said. "I mean, I'm not a spy. I thought maybe one day I would be, but . . ."

"But you procured men to be eaten by the Kattak," Fix pointed out.

"Slaves and criminals," Philastes said.

Indrajit was baffled. "Why would any power accept the ambassadors of an enemy? Knowing that they are there to give cover to spies and assassins?"

"Far better to have the spies at an embassy," Philastes said. "Then you can keep an eye on them. If there's no embassy, the enemy will still send spies, but they'll be disguised as merchants, or as neutral third parties. Harder to find."

"Also, you still want to be able to talk to your enemies," Fix said.

"And if you don't accept his embassy full of spies," Yammilku said, "he won't accept your embassy full of spies."

"That makes the whole world sound as cynical as Kish," Munahim said.

"Fine," Indrajit said, "the Kattak hate Kish. If they can hold a grudge for a thousand years, then they probably hate a lot of people. So what?"

Fix shook his head. "I'm not sure. It feels . . . there's more . . . there's something . . ."

"Huh." Indrajit saw a shape bulking in the shadow ahead and raised his lamp higher. "Is that an entrance?"

Munahim reached the door as Indrajit asked the question. The portal was circular and had a circular wheel jutting from its center, like a ship's wheel mounted as a knob. Both wheel and door were of brushed steel, gleaming orange in the lamplight.

Munahim grabbed the wheel and tried to turn it, but it didn't budge. He dragged on the door and then pushed, and it wouldn't move.

Fix took the ax from his belt. He spun it backward and rapped hard on the steel with the blunt poll. The resulting clang reverberated in Indrajit's bones, across the chamber in which they stood, and back again from the far wall, returning as a crisp echo.

Yammilku took a step back.

Indrajit shifted his position to keep an eye on the Heru and placed his hand on Vacho's hilt.

They waited.

Fix raised the hatchet to knock a second time, but the door opened first. The wheel spun, as if on its own. The door moved straight outward with a hissing sound, then swung away from the wall, stopping at a ninety-degree angle.

The middle of the three Vin Dalu stood in the door. A strip of white light ran around the inside of the circular doorframe, illuminating his features. He smiled. "Fix," he said. "Munahim. Indrajit. But I don't know your companions."

"Philastes Larch," Philastes said.

"My name is not important," Yammilku grunted.

The Vin Dalu nodded. He gestured at the harness Fix wore. "You have found something that may be the Girdle. Well done."

"Alea?" Fix's voice caught.

"She's unchanged. Bring the harness inside, let's put it to the test."

"Give the sorcerer the Girdle," Yammilku said. "We can wait outside."

"No, we can't." Munahim staggered through the door.

"We're going in," Indrajit added. "Betel wants you to come with us. *I* want you to come with us. You're not scared of a little necromancy, are you?"

Yammilku made a short piercing cry in the back of his throat and passed through the door.

"So when you answer the door . . ." Fix said as the Vin Dalu closed the door, then touched illuminated tiles on the wall beside it. "Do you do that as the Vin Dalu Diesa?"

"Then, I am doing the work of the Vin Dalu Rao."

The Vin Dalu Rao led them back into the complex of the Vin Dalu, stamping on his walking sticks. Yammilku walked stiffly, his hand firmly on the hilt of his sword the entire time. Philastes stumbled with his mouth open and his eyes racing to take in every sight that passed.

"How long can Alea wait?" Munahim asked. "And can you . . . can you kill Kattak eggs?"

"Eggs?"

Fix sighed. "The Kyone and I have been implanted with Kattak eggs. They will hatch as nymphs within us."

"When?" the Vin Dalu asked.

"That's what we don't know. We do know that someone else who died as a result of such an implantation believed that the Girdle of Life would save him." Fix stared at his feet. "Munahim has been loyal, Dalu. Heal him first, if you must choose. Heal me last."

"We diagnose before we heal," the Vin Dalu said.

"Is that also part of your ethic?" Indrajit asked.

"Of course." The Vin Dalu inclined his head slightly. "But also, to do otherwise would be madness. Let us examine you."

The other two Vin Dalu met them in a room whose walls were all brushed steel. A bulky ceramic box with handles and switches on three sides squatted in the corner. The box had an arm at the top that reached to one side and dangled a black cable beneath it. Alea lay under her blanket on a table, pale face and feet jutting from the covering. A second table stood parallel to the first, its top bare.

"Give us a moment," the middle Vin Dalu said. He then addressed his brethren.

Again, the language was incomprehensible.

"What are they saying?" Indrajit murmured to Philastes.

Philastes's eyes narrowed. "I don't know. But I think they might be speaking *Druvash* to each other."

"That's possible." Indrajit nodded.

Fix paced in a tight circle, taking deep breaths.

"What is it?" Indrajit asked him.

"The Kattak," Fix said. "They don't just hate Kish."

"Like I said," Indrajit agreed, "they probably hate everyone."

Fix shook his head. "No. I mean they have plans."

The Vin Dalu turned to the group. "Fix, Munahim," the eldest said. "We must examine you urgently. Fix, lie on the table."

Fix opened his mouth to object, but then complied. He moved gingerly onto the table, wincing as he bent at the waist. From a shelf beneath the table, the Vin Dalu removed implements: a metal tablet, a glass wand, a large pair of spectacles. The youngest of the three slowly passed the wand over Fix's body and limbs while the middle examined him through the spectacles and the eldest stared at the tablet.

Yammilku's fidgeting became a twitch. He turned his head to look at Alea every few seconds and made a discomfited chirping sound.

"Munahim," the youngest Vin Dalu said, and they repeated the process with the Kyone.

When they had finished, the eldest rested his hand on Munahim's shoulder, keeping him lying on the table. "We see the eggs," the eldest said. "They are low in your bodies, in your bellies, around your spine."

"We know," Munahim groaned.

"We believe the Girdle of Life can be used to kill the eggs," the eldest said. "At which point, your bodies will slowly absorb the eggs over time. Or, failing that, we could eventually remove them by surgery."

"But it will take many hours to repair the Girdle," Indrajit said. "To attach the Girdle to the machine. Is that it there in the corner? It will take lots of time to prepare."

"No." The eldest of the Vin Dalu smiled. "The Girdle is robust. We will examine it, but we think we can immediately connect it to the machine, and the completed device will be ready to operate."

With no further prompting, Fix shrugged out of the harness and handed it to the middle of the Vin Dalu. He in turn limped to the machine in the corner and began hanging the Girdle from the machine's arm.

"But killing the eggs will take many hours," Indrajit predicted. "So if you heal Fix and Munahim first, you won't be able to help Alea."

"You've got a pessimistic streak," Philastes said.

"I just don't want to get my hopes up."

"We think it should take mere minutes to kill the eggs." The eldest of the Vin Dalu smiled.

"But there are side effects," Indrajit said. "Fix and Munahim will be sick for days. They will each have to give up an eye. They'll be emasculated."

"Don't sound so enthusiastic," Munahim muttered.

"They will feel slightly ill," the Vin Dalu said. "Later, they will lose some hair. But not much."

"That's it," Munahim said. "Do it. Do it now before Indrajit suggests any more reasons why it might be a bad idea to heal me."

"I'm just trying to be thoughtful," Indrajit said.

"Wait." Fix pressed his face into his palms. "How long until the eggs hatch and kill me?"

"A day, at least," the Vin Dalu said. "Maybe two days, maybe even three. Of course, we're extrapolating a growth rate based on what you've told us. If the growth rate accelerates for any reason, it could be sooner."

"How would I know when death was near?" Fix asked.

"Your belly will become distended as the eggs become larvae," the Vin Dalu said. "As they excrete, you will spew black bile from your orifices."

"Ugh," Indrajit said.

"Heal Munahim," Fix said. "Then Alea."

The eldest of the Vin Dalu frowned. "But not you?"

"Me, yes, eventually," Fix said. "But not quite yet."

"Why not?" Indrajit asked.

Fix shook his head. "Because the Kattak have something horrific planned. I think they're aiming to destroy the city. And the longer I wait, the more I know about the plan."

Chapter Twenty-Two

The Vin Dalu clustered around the Girdle of Life, inspecting it closely in a process that lasted several minutes. Then Munahim stood beneath the machine's arm and the three necromancers strapped him into the harness. The eldest pulled a lever on the machine and its arm slowly rose until it dragged Munahim off the floor.

He dangled like fruit. As he had dangled when wrapped in Kattak paper.

"You should step out now," the middle of the Vin Dalu said to Indrajit and the other observers. "Otherwise, you may also feel mild side effects."

Yammilku needed no urging, and promptly evacuated. The others followed, but Indrajit lingered a moment. Munahim's facial expression was one of apprehension and anxiety as he hung, slowly spinning. Indrajit crossed the room to clap the Kyone on the arm.

"Good boy," he said.

Munahim nodded and Indrajit left.

He and Yammilku and Fix and Philastes stood in a smooth-walled hall, lit by a glowing yellow sphere sunk into one wall. As Indrajit rejoined the others, he heard a low, throbbing hum behind him.

"I will light you on fire if I have to," Yammilku said to Fix.

"If it comes to that," Fix said, "I'll help you."

"What is the evil plan of the wasp-men?" Indrajit asked.

Fix looked down. "I don't know. But they intend something. If we go to the Conclave tonight, maybe by the time it's over I'll remember enough . . . I'll have learned enough from the larvae inside me . . .

whatever . . . to be able to say something specific. And if not, I'll come back here and just wait."

"Wait until you remember the plot?" Indrajit asked. "That sounds crazy."

"I know it does," Fix said. "But that's my plan, anyway. Wait until I remember, and then jump right into the Girdle of Life. Maybe I'll just hang in the device, wearing the Girdle, waiting for the knowledge to hit me, and then immediately undergo the process when I receive the knowledge I'm looking for."

"Have the spell cast," Indrajit said.

"You're imagining very compliant necromancers," Yammilku said.

Fix shrugged. "So far, of everyone we've encountered today, the necromancers have been the friendliest."

"I'm friendly," Philastes said.

"What if you never remember the plan?" Indrajit pressed. "What if the clarity of the . . . inherited memories is never that good, or what if you remember the plan exactly at the moment when your belly bursts open and you die?"

"Then I die," he said. "But Alea lives."

"You're going to die to save the city?" Yammilku asked.

"I'm going to try very hard to live and save the city," Fix said. "There's a risk I die in the attempt. That's true every day."

"You're not generally stuffed full of maturing wasp eggs," Indrajit pointed out. "The risk seems a little more colorful today."

"You're not from here," Fix said.

Indrajit was momentarily flummoxed. He didn't feel insulted, but he felt pushed away. "True."

"This is my city," Fix said. "It's my home. I don't have another one. It's a rotten old town, but it's my town. And it's Alea's, too."

"Okay," Indrajit agreed. "Let's save your town."

"You should each drink this elixir," the youngest of the Vin Dalu said from the room's entrance. He held three steel cylinders in his hand. The cylinders were spangled with color and arcane characters, along with painted abstract images. The top of each cylinder was notched open with a triangular slot, and Indrajit detected an odor that was acrid and fruity, as if a bucket of paint were mixed with smashed berries.

"Vin Dalu Rao, right?" Indrajit said.

"Correct."

"Is this a healing potion?" Indrajit asked.

Fix looked suspicious. "It won't kill the eggs, will it?"

"It will give strength to your limbs for a time," the Vin Dalu Rao said. "It will not harm the eggs. Too much of the liquid would eventually harm your heart, but one cylinder will refresh you with no attendant evil."

They drank. The fluid left a coating on the inside of Indrajit's mouth, and an aftertaste that made him pucker his lips.

The necromancer took back the drained cylinders.

They returned into the steel-walled room as the other Vin Dalu were unbelting Munahim. The Kyone stood on his feet, an uncertain expression on his face. They slipped his arms from the straps and he wobbled slightly.

"How do you feel?" Fix asked.

Munahim opened his mouth, then shut it. He took a deep breath, then closed his eyes.

Then he lurched into the corner of the room and vomited.

"Grab him," Indrajit said. "He might have a sudden urge to eat his own vomit off the floor."

"He's not *actually* a dog," Yammilku said.

"No," Indrajit said. "But kind of yes."

Fix shoved his shoulder under Munahim's arm to support the Kyone, and together they lurched back to the group.

Indrajit did feel a little more alert than he had.

"We will treat Alea next," the eldest of the Vin Dalu said. "It will take some time. Also, the settings we'll use on the machine are different, and it's not wise for you to stand in the room during the process."

Indrajit nodded. "We have another obligation."

"How long will it take, Dalu?" Fix asked.

"You brought her to us quickly," the eldest of the Vin Dalu said. "Her body had not yet begun to be consumed by its worms."

"I don't need the details." Fix's hands were shaking. "Tell me how long."

"By dawn, I think we will be able to remove her from the device."

The second Vin Dalu pressed another opened potion cylinder into Indrajit's hands. Without explanation, Indrajit poured it into the

Kyone. Munahim gagged at first, but then slurped the elixir with enthusiasm.

"And . . . what ill effects will she suffer? Will she be marked by death?" Fix asked.

"She'll lose her hair," the Vin Dalu said. "The literature warns of the possibility of madness. The likelihood is greater, the longer the patient has been dead, and Alea has been dead for many hours. There may be loss of strength or other lingering issues. But of course, we've never done this before."

Indrajit rested his hand on Fix's shoulder. "Fortunately, we don't believe in literature. We'll come back in the morning."

The youngest of the Vin Dalu came forward. "You've entered by two different doors," he said. "How do you wish to exit?"

"We need to get to the Crown for the Conclave," Yammilku said. "Do you know the False Palace?"

Indrajit chuckled. "All the palaces are false."

"I thought that was just a rumor," Fix said.

"It's real," the Heru said. "I would think it would be on the map."

"I don't know the way to the False Palace," the Vin Dalu said. "But I can show you a short road to the Crown. Perhaps from there your map will lead you to this palace."

"Vin Dalu Rao," Fix said.

He inclined his head. "Yes."

They followed the Vin Dalu Rao through a maze of bookshelves. Fix walked resolutely, but with a noticeable limp. Indrajit brought up the rear, to make certain that Fix and Munahim both stayed with the group. At the end of the maze, they emerged onto a balcony jutting into dark space, with wind blowing. A white glass sphere sunk into the wall gave dim light. At arm's length from the balcony, a brass pole descended from darkness above and dropped into darkness below.

Munahim laughed. "This is an exit only."

"Yes," the Vin Dalu said.

"How do you keep creatures from climbing up?" Indrajit asked. "Ghouls, thieves, jobbers?"

"The pole is greased," the Vin Dalu said. "Hold tightly so you don't fall too fast, but in any case, you will descend."

"We'll be back." Fix leaned out in the void, wrapped two arms around the pole, and then hopped out to grip it with his feet, as well. He slid quickly out of sight.

Indrajit waited until he heard a thud and then called down. "Are you okay?"

"I'm not dead," Fix called. "But it's quite dark down here."

Indrajit went next. The transit down the pole was shockingly fast and he struck rock at the bottom with a force that jarred his knees and ankles. He staggered away, wiping greasy hands on his kilt, and bumped into Fix.

"Light," Fix said.

Indrajit relit his lamp, noting that it was almost out of oil. "Can you see us?" he called up. The balcony was a brim of shadow beneath a pale white corona of light.

"Sending the Heru down," Munahim called. "Don't stand too close to the pole."

Yammilku and Munahim and Philastes slid down in quick succession.

Munahim paced at the edges of the lamp's light, sniffing and peering into the shadow as everyone checked weapons and gear.

"Ghouls?" Indrajit asked. "Kattak?"

"There's a faint scent of Ghouls everywhere beneath the city," Munahim said. "I don't smell or hear them close. And I don't detect the odor of Kattak."

"Something's bothering you, though."

"I can hear something," Munahim said. "Faint breathing. The padding of careful feet on stone. Sometimes even a dull metallic clink."

"But you smell nothing?"

"The sounds come from downwind."

Indrajit considered this. "That could mean that there is someone or something coincidentally downwind of us."

Munahim nodded slowly. "Or it could mean that something is stalking us, and it knows we have strong powers of smell. Perhaps our stalker is also a creature with a powerful nose."

"I don't like that possibility." Indrajit clapped Munahim on the shoulder. "But I'm glad we have a Kyone in the company. Good boy."

Munahim growled low. "My instinct is to give a warning bark.

That would let our stalkers know they're detected, and possibly chase them off."

"But if they're intelligent," Indrajit said, "they'll just change tactic, and next time, we might not smell them coming. Let's keep quiet. Keep me informed of what you detect, and let's look for an opportunity to lose our pursuers, or trap them."

"If we can maneuver so that we're downwind of them," Munahim suggested, "then we can be the stalkers."

Indrajit gave Fix the lamp and the map. The Kishi managed those two things, limping through the darkness. Everyone else drew weapons and made a loose circle around him.

They traversed a grove of white-furred columns and crawled over a pile of sand, ducking low to avoid awakening bats gripping the ceiling. Then they passed under an arch and stepped onto an iron grate. Just beneath the metal, Indrajit could hear water rushing; he felt light spray splashing up through the lattice onto his ankles and toes.

"The wind," Munahim said. "It blows left to right here. If we hide down the river to the right, the breeze will conceal our scent from our pursuers when they come through. We can get the jump on them, or at least see them."

"Our road is left," Fix said. "We don't want to get trapped in a cul-de-sac."

"We don't want to get stabbed in the back by secret assassins," Indrajit said. "Or shot with a poisoned dart."

Fix nodded his acquiescence and they turned right. The grid over the river continued on into darkness, the breeze and the water flowing in the same direction, but they only walked thirty paces before they stopped to take up positions. Munahim armed himself with his bow, an arrow on the string. Philastes had a pocketful of stones he'd gathered as they traveled through the darkness, with one in the pouch of his sling. The others held swords. Where they stood, they were downwind of the arch, with the arch in sight. The wind should be sweeping away their scent and the burbling of the river beneath them should be masking any faint sounds they made.

So if the stalkers really had keen senses of smell, they would realize that the Protagonists were not upwind. They would then either cross the river and pass into openings on the far side, or turn toward Indrajit and his friends, in which case the Protagonists could attack with the advantage of surprise.

Fix carefully put away his map and then doused the lamp.

They waited in darkness.

Who could possibly be stalking them? Indrajit feared the man in the false blue toga, but there were other possibilities. Arash Sehama might or might not know that they had stolen his map, and his Sookwalkers might be following the Protagonists to take the map back or exact revenge. Or perhaps the stalkers were Sootfaces, sent by Zac Betel to dispose of his mutinous lieutenant, the same Betel perhaps having decided that Indrajit and Fix were of no use to him, and inconvenient witnesses to be disposed of. Or perhaps the stalkers were the Kattak.

A light emerged from the arch. It was faint and green, and cast so little light around it that it gave no warning of its arrival. It bobbed above the ground, and was shaped in such an unexpected curling manner that it took Indrajit a moment to realize what he was looking at.

It was a glimmersnake. A glowing reptile, alive, in a glass case like a lantern, and slowly coiling around itself.

The man holding the snake's prison raised it and stared across the river. He turned left and then right slowly, and Indrajit could finally make out his features. He had to bite his tongue to keep from saying anything.

Huachao. The man with the light was one of the cat-men of the Dregs.

Why would the Huachao be tracking the Protagonists? They were a clan, but acted like a jobber company. Who had said that, Fix? So were they following Indrajit and his friends because of the disturbance the Protagonists had caused in the Dregs? Or had someone engaged them to follow the Protagonists? The Silksteppers, maybe? And to what end? Or, if they were jobbers, could they now be in league with any of their enemies?

Was it possible they were in Underkish by unrelated chance?

Indrajit snorted softly.

The lanternholder moved farther onto the grid. Behind him came two more Huachao. They stopped and leaned their heads together, as if in conversation.

Then they turned toward the Protagonists and started walking forward. Were they creeping, or was it their natural catlike posture that made it seem as if they were, hunching over, noses out front?

The Kyone, Indrajit knew, had a head like a dog's, but possessed other features like any common man, including fingers and toes, and knees that bent like Indrajit's and Fix's did. The Huachao were more catlike than the Kyone was doglike; they had dewclaws on their forearms, their fingers were thick and furred so their hands looked like paws, and their knees bent backward, their legs resembling the hind legs of a cat. Munahim wore boots, but the Huachao walked on bare paws. Over the soft chuckle of the river, they made no audible sound at all.

"Get ready," Indrajit murmured. "Make your first shot a warning shot."

Then he felt a sharp blade on the back of his neck. He heard sudden intakes of breath from Munahim and Fix at the same moment.

"This is your warning shot," a throaty voice growled.

"We've been outmaneuvered," Munahim rumbled.

A second light appeared, also a glimmersnake's glow, this one coming from behind them. Indrajit turned slowly and found five more Huachao, swords in their hands. They also had a sixth man with them, hands tied behind his back, mouth gagged with a thick swatch of cloth under his drooping olive nose. He still wore his sand-colored false toga, but his turban was gone, revealing a bulbous skull pitted with small scars and overgrown with gray stubble.

The forger, Danel Avchat.

"We've done you no harm," Philastes said. "We can be friends."

The Huachao holding his long, straight sword to Indrajit's neck was an orange color, with brown stripes showing where his fur wasn't hidden by undyed linothorax and a skirt of studded leather strips. "No one is going to harm anyone. We've come to extend an invitation to you."

"What are you doing with the scribe?" Indrajit asked.

"We've rescued him." The orange cat-man laughed, a rasping sound. "Bad men tied him up, after making him copy a secret map. Would you credit it? And they didn't even pay him."

"And I suppose you discovered he could reproduce the map," Fix said.

"He has a very good memory," the Huachao said.

"You're looking for us," Indrajit said, "but you didn't come to kill us. We have things to do, so maybe get to the point."

"Indrajit," the orange Huachao said. "Fix is the man who groans in pain with each step. The Heru belongs to Betel. And the other two?"

"Members of our jobber company," Fix said. "Identified by name on our bond schedule. On contract business. Protected by law."

"What's your name?" Indrajit asked.

The Huachao laughed, throwing his head back. "The less truth you tell, the more emphatic you must be. You're not on contract business. Or did the Auction House sell a contract to send you to the Conclave of the Gray Lords?"

Silence.

"I thought not," the Huachao said. "My name is Budhrriao. You also have the smell of Gund about you, but I think your Gund is dead."

"You have enough information," Indrajit said. "Tell us what you want now."

"We are on contract business," Budhrriao said. "As it happens, the contract is not originated by the Auction House. Our employer, who had hired us to keep security in the Armpit, has now hired us to find you and bring you to him."

"Who's your employer?" Fix asked.

"We're all still friends," Philastes said.

"Depends on who the employer is," Indrajit muttered.

"He has heard that a Conclave has been called." Budhrriao purred, a deep, saw-edged, contemplative sound. "He wishes to attend."

"The Conclave is a gathering of the seven Gray Lords," Yammilku said. "They bring attendants. No one else is invited."

"You've accurately described the problem," Budhrriao said. "It would be more helpful if you proposed solutions."

The Huachao's sword had gradually moved away from Indrajit's neck, but everyone still held weapons.

"Who do you serve?" Fix asked. "The Lord Knife? Are you allied with the assassin in the blue toga?"

"The Lord *Knife*?" Budhrriao yawned contemptuously. "Why would the king of Kish's assassins ask to join the league of thieves?

No, we've been hired by a man who is himself a successful crime lord. A man of great reach and enterprise. A man whose empire includes drug peddlers, thieves, fences, blackmailers, forgers, arsonists, throat-slitters, pimps, and whores. A man who rules the Dregs with such ferocity and justice that the Gray Lords themselves have not dared encroach on his realm."

"I have a terrible feeling I know who this is," Indrajit muttered.

"We will take you now to see the gang lord Jaxter Boom."

Chapter Twenty-Three

The Protagonists cooperated and were led from Underkish. The Huachao consulted neither a map nor their bound-and-gagged forger, but stooped to sniff at the ground from time to time.

"Are they smelling Jaxter Boom from here?" Indrajit mused out loud.

"I don't know what Jaxter Boom smells like," Munahim grumbled, "but I think they're retracing their steps. I smell frequent markings with cat urine on the path we've been walking."

"You don't do that," Indrajit pointed out.

Munahim was silent for a moment. "As you are not really a fish," he eventually said, "I am not really a dog."

"Should I stop saying 'good boy' to you?"

"I don't mind it," the Kyone said. "But maybe it's causing you to think about me in the wrong light."

"Okay," Indrajit agreed, "not a dog. A fierce swordsman, a rapid and accurate archer, and a man who happens to have extraordinarily sharp smell and hearing."

"A Kyone."

They emerged climbing narrow clay-brick stairs that ended in a ragged green curtain at the bottom of a long, narrow alley. Budhrriao urged Indrajit to lead the way; at the mouth of the alley stood two Huachao in linothorax and leather, one with two long-handled axes and the other holding a heavy mace.

Indrajit grinned and the Huachao growled.

Indrajit recognized that they were back in the Dregs. One

cramped plaza after another were strung in a line through this district, connected by tight alleys. All the buildings leaned forward, and the sky was reduced to a purple sliver.

The purple of evening. The Conclave was coming on, and in the morning, the Battle of Last Light. The wool cloaks they had purchased in the morning served well against the cool evening air.

"We know Jaxter," he said brightly. "His place is still around the corner from here, is it?"

"Work for him?" Budhrriao asked. "Or did you work against him?"

"In the event, it was more of the latter," Indrajit said. "He wanted to punish a thief. But her father had hired us to rescue her."

"How did it end?" the Huachao asked.

"As I recall," Indrajit said, "we had to swim home."

He left out the fact that he had personally stabbed Boom in the eye, as well as inflicted various wounds on Boom's men.

Budhrriao laughed.

"But the girl lived," Fix said. "That was a princess we rescued."

"Ah, I knew there had to be *one*," Indrajit said.

Budhrriao took them through a right-hand turn and down a short alley. Overhead hung drying pelts on thick cables, and a vicious odor choked the air. They exited onto a tiny plaza surrounded by tall buildings, and the purple sky was quickly turning black. At a broad, unmarked door stood a familiar figure. He wore a black cloak with a deep hood. From the hood emerged a long nose, curling like an elephant's proboscis, and surrounded by shaggy black hair. This was Boom's doorman, and the Protagonists had had more than one prior interaction with him.

"We've met," Indrajit said. "Remind me of your name."

"Hastin Gink." The doorman laughed, a long, shuddering sound. "My last sight of you was your sandal, kicking me in the face."

"To be fair," Indrajit said, "that was only because you were trying to stop me from rescuing the Lord Chamberlain's daughter."

"That doesn't mean I forgive you."

"I wasn't asking for forgiveness."

Gink chuckled. "Boom is waiting for you."

They descended steep stairs under a low ceiling into the reception chamber of Jaxter Boom. The room was wide, with arches on both sides. A tank of churning water faced them along the broad opposite wall, a pedestal standing outside the tank at each corner. A young man in a plain gray loincloth stood on each pedestal; the youths stared vacantly, as if drugged or brain-damaged. Indrajit knew that the truth was worse, and he looked away, bracing himself.

Men with cudgels and knives crowded in through the arches on either side of the room. They grumbled, and held each other back.

"The welcoming committee," Indrajit said.

"Some of us remember you," said a short man with long arms and scarred knuckles.

"And I remember some of you," Indrajit said, smiling pleasantly. "Not you in particular, as it happens. You're quite forgettable."

Then a mass of pink flesh pressed itself against the wall of the tank from the inside and a single massive blue eye opened. Tentacles snaked from the dark waters and lowered themselves, easing forward and then pressing into the backs of the skulls of the two young men.

The young men were the Voices of Jaxter Boom. To any god who might be listening, Indrajit prayed that their minds were gone and they felt no pain.

The two young men spoke in tandem. "Indrajit, Fix," the Voices of Jaxter Boom said, "and friends. Jobbers. Rescuers of princesses, poets, spies of the Lord Chamberlain."

"Jaxter Boom," Indrajit said. "Gangster lord. Puppeteer of helpless young people. Fence, leg breaker, extortionist, drug dealer, and general purveyor of misery. Octopuslike fellow whose eye appears, to my great delight, to have healed. What do you want?"

"What any other man wants," Boom said through the Voices. "Wealth and power."

"Oh, good," Indrajit said. "I was afraid you were going to say 'love.'"

The waters in the tank bubbled into sudden froth and the blue eye blinked repeatedly. The Voices engaged in a spastic rattling of knees and elbows, which looked like an interpretive dance trying to visually represent a manic laugh.

"This isn't disturbing at all," Philastes said.

"Hey, you're the guy who was working for wasp-men when we found you," Fix said.

"You want to talk about disturbing?" Indrajit nodded at the tank. "Fix and I once swam *through* that."

“You have obstructed my goals once or twice,” Boom’s Voices said. “And once or twice, I have obstructed yours.”

“Okay,” Indrajit said. “Do we get to be friends now? That will make our Pelthite happy. He really likes making friends.”

“Most recently, of course, you caused a little disturbance in one of my territories.”

“We recovered something that had been stolen from us,” Indrajit said.

“Avchat said you had in turn stolen it from someone else,” Budhrriao said.

“Him?” Indrajit jerked a thumb at the scribe, still bound and gagged and standing surrounded by Huachao at the foot of the stairs. “If he says such interesting things, why do you keep his mouth tied shut?”

“We didn’t want him to warn you.”

“He’s on my side now, is he?”

“I’m prepared to forgive,” the Voices said.

“Here it comes,” Fix murmured.

“Indeed,” Boom continued, “I’ll give you something of great value in addition.”

Indrajit sighed. “This has to do with the Conclave, right? You heard there’s a Conclave of the Gray Lords tonight, you heard a rumor that we’ve been invited, and you want us to get you in, too.”

“Unless the Conclave is aboard a ship,” the Voices said, “I shall of course be sending emissaries rather than attending in person.”

“These . . . ?” Indrajit gestured at the Voices. “These . . . people? Can they talk when you’re not inside them? Or will you . . . detach your . . . tentacles?”

“Hastin Gink,” Boom said, “and the Huachao pridechief.”

“Nice enough fellows,” Indrajit said. “That’s not really the problem.”

“You’re going to tell me that the problem is we’re not invited,” Boom said.

“For starters,” Indrajit said. “Also, I don’t have the power to invite anyone. I think maybe I’m invited as a witness.”

“Fine,” Boom said through the Voices. “Just tell us where it is and we’ll let ourselves in.”

“Not a good idea,” Indrajit said. “We have a tenuous relationship at best with all the Gray Lords, and I don't want to jeopardize that. And Yammilku here, he's Zac Betel's man. He's fiercely loyal, don't even suggest that he betray his leader. He'll get enraged."

"Yammilku has already betrayed his leader," the Voices said. "We all know it. What's going to happen at the Conclave tonight, Yammilku?"

"I don't know," the Heru said.

"Are you Zac Betel's man?" the Voices asked. "Or do you want to be a Gray Lord?"

"*You* want to be a Gray Lord," Yammilku said.

"I'm not sure I'm really part of this conversation," Indrajit said. "Maybe we should just leave."

"I *am* a Gray Lord," the Voices said. "I should be acknowledged as one."

"Why do you think I have any influence on the outcome of that question?" Yammilku asked.

"You would . . . if you were Gray Lord of the Sootfaces."

"What do you have in mind?" Yammilku asked.

Fix stood beside Indrajit. Indrajit couldn't remember whether he'd always been standing there, or had sneaked gradually to that spot during the conversation. "We're going to become unnecessary," Fix murmured. "Or maybe even highly inconvenient, but either way, disposable. Get in there."

"Why me?"

"You're the talker. You and the Pelthite, but he's in over his head."

Indrajit cleared his throat. "Listen. We'll get you an invitation. We'll ask Betel. We'll talk to the Conclave itself. What's the request, just that there should be eight Gray Lords, and your territory is, what, the Dregs?"

But Boom and Yammilku both ignored him.

"I assume you have allies," the Voices said. "Perhaps Betel expects them, perhaps he doesn't. Surely, he doesn't anticipate the involvement of me and my men."

"Perhaps Betel doesn't make it to the Conclave," Yammilku said. "Perhaps Hastin and I go instead."

Indrajit could see exactly where this conversation was heading, and he hated it. "Stop!" he yelled, thrusting himself between Yammilku and Boom.

Yammilku made an impatient chirp in the back of his throat. The Voices shuffled their feet.

"Look," Indrajit said, "I know you two are both feeling very excited. We're not really part of your plans, but we like you both."

"You've been a thorn in my side," Boom said.

"To be fair," Fix said, "you're a gangster."

"So are you," the Voices said. "Your gang is just smaller, and has purchased a license from the Lord Chamberlain. Who is the biggest gangster of all."

"I accept the criticism," Indrajit said. "Here's the thing: We'll happily help you, if you think that's valuable. If you need skills, or a couple of extra swords, or a copy of the map. But we must get on our way, because it turns out there's a city to save."

"This is true," Fix said.

The big blue eye focused on Yammilku. "What are they talking about, Gray Lord?"

Yammilku shrugged. "I don't know, and I don't think they know, either. The Kyone and the Kishi were both injected with Kattak eggs."

"Kattak eggs?" The muscles around the big eye contracted, giving the strange impression of a circular squint. "Kattak, from the Paper Sultanates?"

"Yes. The Kyone has been cured by the Vin Dalu, probably. The Kishi has not." Yammilku's voice had a hard edge to it. "They believe that bearing the eggs in their bellies gives them a shared mind with the wasp-men."

"Yes," Boom said. "Everyone knows that's how the Kattak pass down their memories. No books, like the degenerate Lords of Kish, no chanting like the shrinking poets of the sea. With elegant simplicity, they inherit the mind of all who went before them. Including those in whose bellies they rode. It is an admirable species."

"We're not shrinking," Indrajit said. "We're on the tall side."

"You dwindle, you diminish," Boom said. "If your entire race came to the Dregs, you are so few that no one would notice you. There are not enough of you to make a sizable Rover caravan. At the Racetrack, you would not fill a single section. In the Hall of Guesses, you could all attend the same lecture and be marked absent because you were so easy to miss."

"Now you're just hurting my feelings," Indrajit said.

"The Kishi says the Kattak are planning a great evil," Yammilku said.

The giant blue eye pivoted and came to rest on Fix. "What is the evil?"

Fix shook his head. "I don't know yet."

Boom was silent for the space of several long breaths. Jets of fine bubbles burst from two deep crevices in his pale flesh, above his eye, in gentle, alternating rhythm.

"You will need scapegoats," Boom said.

"Yes," Yammilku agreed.

Indrajit drew his sword but men were already tackling him. He staggered forward, feeling Huachao dewclaws across his back, and both hands of a short, squat Kishi gripping him by the wrist of his sword arm.

"Resist and die!" Budhrriao shrieked into his ear.

Indrajit leaped toward the glass and pivoted, moving forward and down. He slammed the Huachao pridechief into the glass of the tank right in front of the big blue eye. Then he fell to the floor, wrestling with the short Kishi for his sword.

He saw Munahim, sword out, cut down first a Huachao warrior and then a Shamb in a dirty yellow cloak. He saw Philastes picked up by two men half again his size and slammed repeatedly against the brick wall, as he shouted in various languages Indrajit didn't know.

Indrajit heard a thick whoosh of water. Out of the corner of his eye, he saw one of the tentacles pull away from the head of the Voice it inhabited. What remained behind was a puckered white opening like a badly healed wound, and then the young man crashed forward.

The other Voice hit the floor at the same moment.

Budhrriao bit Indrajit on the shoulder, and Indrajit slammed his head sideways, slapping the Huachao awkwardly on the top of his skull. He lurched to his feet but the Kishi came with him, and chortled as he got both his hands on Vacho's hilt.

Indrajit poked the man with four fingers split into his two eyes, and he screamed.

Philastes lay unmoving on the floor. Munahim had lost his sword and someone had wrapped a cape around his head, blinding him. He held an arrow in each hand and stabbed, fighting as if with two daggers. A Zalapting hit him in the back of his knee with a club, and Munahim fell.

Where was Fix?

Indrajit kicked himself back against the tank wall again, and this time Budhrriao let go. Vacho cleared its scabbard, singing its quavering song of war, and Indrajit leaped into the fray in earnest. He cut the arm off one Zalapting, slashed a one-eyed Xiba'albi across the stomach, stepped on a Shamb's tail, and punched Hastin Gink—or some man who looked just like him—in his hooded face.

Then he saw Fix. His partner lay on his belly. His face was red, which might be because Yammilku knelt with one knee on the back of his head and pressed his long straight sword against Fix's cheek. Also, he was vomiting black bile.

Indrajit leaped forward to knock Yammilku away, and something hard struck Indrajit in the throat.

He landed on his back on the floor, no wind in his lungs. Staring up, he saw Budhrriao holding the thick shaft of a spear. The Huachao stepped on Indrajit's chest, and another Huachao picked up Vacho.

"Do I kill him?" Yammilku asked. "Are the wasps birthing?"

Through wobbly vision, Indrajit saw Jaxter Boom swim back into view from the depths of his tank. Gink knelt over each Voice in turn, but they were still and unresponsive. Boom thrashed the water with his tentacles and then returned into darkness.

"Don't kill him," Indrajit gasped. "The Kattak nymphs aren't coming out yet."

Gink leaned low over Indrajit. Indrajit saw a faint glimmer deep in the hood—did Gink's eyes actually shine? The proboscis rested on Indrajit's neck, bouncing as Gink talked.

"How will we know when the wasps are being born?" Gink asked.

"His belly will be distended." Indrajit found tears stinging his eyes as he explained. "He'll vomit. Also, the men we've seen die this way . . . I think the pain must be very great. They beg for help in the end. Beg for death, even."

"That's very helpful." Gink rose. "Stand the three of them up and tie them. Carry the egg-bearer into a cell. Throw the forger in with him."

Indrajit, Munahim, and Philastes were pulled to their feet as Fix was dragged away under one of the arches. All three had their hands tied tightly behind their backs, and then they were dropped to the floor.

"Is Boom mute now?" Yammilku asked.

"I'm Hastin Gink," Gink said. "I am the Doorman and the Wandering Eye and the Voice that Thinks."

That all sounded priestly. Indrajit bit his tongue.

"Is now a good time for a private conversation?" Yammilku asked.

Gink raised his arm. "Everyone, out. You too, pridechief."

Jaxter Boom's thieves all slunk away through the arches.

"We got distracted by this evil-plan talk," Yammilku said, lowering his voice to a bare whisper. Indrajit lay on the floor, an arm's length away, and could just barely hear. "Boom was saying we'd need scapegoats."

Gink shrugged. "Obviously, if the Paper Sultanates have some sorcerous plan to overthrow the city, that concerns us all. We'll hold Fix and listen to him. If we can figure out what this great menace is, then we can decide what to do about it. Above all, business must continue."

"Scapegoats," Yammilku said again. "I assume the idea is that you and your men and I will kill Betel. Then we'll kill these three and leave their bodies on the scene. We'll tell the other Gray Lords that the Protagonists here killed Zac Betel and that you helped avenge Betel's death."

That was little more than a repeat of Yammilku's earlier plan, and Indrajit bit back a quip about the Heru's lack of imagination. Then he remembered that once again, he was intended to be the dead man blamed for the crime.

"Will that make you the next Gray Lord of the Sootfaces?" Gink asked.

"There'll be a vote. I have allies in the Conclave. I'll win it."

"And then you'll announce that you're in favor of Jaxter Boom becoming the eighth Gray Lord, invited to the Conclave." Gink's proboscis quivered with excitement.

"We'll win that vote, too." Yammilku's voice was hard.

Gink nodded. "Time to march these poor bastards out."

Chapter Twenty-Four

Ropes were tied about the prisoners' waists and they were hauled away. Emerging from Boom's lair into the plaza, they stumbled down a short alley and then were dragged down a stone-choked crevice into the underworld.

Budhrriao and Yammilku each held one of the maps and a lantern. They puzzled over the lines and glyphs, argued, and then came to joint conclusions by which they guided the party farther down. Gink kept his own counsel, humming irregular tunes of long drone notes and staring often at Indrajit.

One cat-man walked in front of Indrajit, holding the ropes. Beside him walked a second, carrying the sack that contained all the Protagonists' weapons. Presumably, after Indrajit and his colleagues were murdered, their weapons would be placed beside their corpses to show that they were the assassins. The rest of the Huachao came behind the prisoners. Turning his head slightly, Indrajit could make out weapons in their hands.

But with the lamps in front of him, his own hands were in shadow. Indrajit worked to free himself, squeezing his fingers together to try to slip them from their bonds. It failed. He tried picking at the fibers of the ropes with his nails, to no effect. He tried tearing the ropes apart by main strength and got nowhere.

"Can I get more light?" Munahim grumbled. "I can't see."

By way of answer, one of the Huachao struck him with a club.

The sack. Indrajit needed to get his hands on the sack.

Vacho and Munahim's sword were both sheathed, but not all the weapons were. Fix's ax, in particular, only ever hung on a loop on his belt. It had no sheath, and its blade was sharp as a razor. If Indrajit could somehow get his hands on the sack, he could cut his bonds.

They marched across a wide brick chamber. Snuffling sounds echoing faintly in the darkness made Indrajit think of Ghouls.

A diversion might do the trick, but it would have to be something big, something that really distracted the thieves. Like a fire.

Munahim stumbled and fell against Indrajit. He knocked Indrajit forward, onto his face on the brick, and landed on top of him.

Briefly, Munahim's face was in Indrajit's back. Indrajit felt the Kyone's hot, wet breath, and the scratch of his teeth on Indrajit's hands.

"Ouch," Indrajit grunted. He rolled, trying to get out from under his Kyone henchman.

"I can't see," Munahim complained again. Three Huachao dragged him to his feet and punched him in the belly.

Indrajit lurched to his knees, and with the movements of his body, he noticed that there was new give in the ropes on his wrists. Munahim had torn at them with his teeth.

He had also torn Indrajit's skin; his wrists were bleeding. But he could feel that the fibers of two loops had been shredded, and suddenly the rope had slack in it.

He pulled in the slack with his fingers to conceal it and stood. "I'm cooperating, easy," he said, as the Huachao grabbed him.

They pushed him forward and he walked with his head down.

"We need to emerge as close to the False Palace as we can," Yammilku said, jabbing a finger at his map. "It's one thing to walk a few paces in the Dregs with three men tied up, but dragging prisoners openly around in the Crown is another matter entirely."

"Look at this line," Budhrriao told him. "That must be an entrance into the False Palace, no?"

"It's about the right place," Yammilku conceded. "It doesn't match up with the Sootfaces' entrance, but it could be one of the others."

"Each Gray Lord has his own entrance?" Gink asked.

"And there are further doors beyond those," Yammilku said. "Many entrances mean many exits, so if something goes wrong, flight is easy."

Indrajit slipped his hands from the loose bonds, holding the rope to approximate the look of the bonds still being in place.

"Could we go aboveground here?" Budhrriao pointed. "Then how far would the walk be to the Sootfaces' entrance? I presume that's where we want to encounter Zac Betel."

"We just go through the center," Yammilku said. "We don't go aboveground at all."

The large gallery ended in a span of brick that arched across a void. In the lamplight, Indrajit could make out a dirt wall opposite, with a ragged hole where the span connected with it. Below, he could hear the sound of flowing water.

How far down was the water, and how deep was it?

But he didn't think he'd get another opportunity this good.

"Now!" he yelled.

He grabbed the sack of weapons. With a split second's hesitation, he also tore a map from Yammilku's hands and jumped off the span.

Indrajit leaped off to the right. The rope around his waist went suddenly taut as he plunged into shadow, and then yanked him back up and sideways, beneath the brick span. He banged into someone else, all flailing knees and elbows, and it took him a moment to register by the smell that he'd hit Munahim, bouncing against him from the other side.

A moment later, Philastes smacked into them as well.

They swung apart, spinning. Indrajit felt he might vomit, but he kept his grip on the sack of weapons.

"Tie them!" Gink shouted. His voice snapped against distant, unseen walls and echoed back beneath the bridge with a dark, muted timbre. "Hold the lines! Pull them up!"

"Jump down there!" Yammilku shouted, but the only response was a feline yowl.

Indrajit worked an arm into the sack and patted around until he got his hand on Vacho's hilt. He could see the other two Protagonists now, swinging back toward him in the darkness. Was Philastes rising? He was the smallest, and would be the easiest to pull back up to the bridge.

Indrajit slashed the rope over Philastes's head and the Pelthite fell into darkness.

The resulting splash seemed delayed and remote. How far had he fallen?

Munahim gripped Indrajit, wrapping his arms around his waist. Indrajit felt his own rope tugging upward and could see that Munahim's had gone slightly slack. Gink's yells rose to a high-pitched shriek.

Indrajit looped a fist into Munahim's rope and pulled it tight. With a few seconds' sawing, he cut through. He wanted to yell a warning to Philastes, but he didn't want the thieves to know what he was doing, and fundamentally, if the Pelthite wasn't smart enough to get out of the way after falling into the underground river, he was probably too stupid to be a Protagonist.

The thieves dragged him higher. The bridge loomed over their heads like a starless void. But it was a starless void that would snap his neck if he cracked into its underside.

"Are we going to fight them?" Munahim growled.

Indrajit hacked through the last rope and they fell.

He splashed into icy water, still in Munahim's grip. The chill shocked the air from his lungs and the sack in his hands pulled him under. His cloak also became an anchor, dragging him down with its sodden weight. The current was swift, but the water wasn't deep, so he rebounded off the stone bottom and then thrashed to the surface.

He was afraid he'd lose his grip on the sack, but arms quickly grabbed him and pulled him onto a brick shelf. The light was dim and remote, but he could make out the silhouettes of two men. One of them smelled like wet dog.

All three of them smelled like wet wool.

"Shhh," Philastes said.

"Jump down there!" Yammilku shouted. "Go get them!"

"No!" Budhrriao roared.

There followed a brief silence, pierced only by the sound of water pouring from their bodies and their cloaks. Indrajit half expected to see men come falling down from the brick span, but it didn't happen.

"The Huachao appear not to like the idea of getting wet," Philastes murmured.

Indrajit chuckled softly. "I grabbed a map," he whispered. "But I lost it in the jump."

"It will be soaked," Munahim said. "And maybe carried away by the river."

"We could burn the sack," Indrajit said, "once it dries. Does anyone have lamp oil? Or flammable liquor?"

They did not.

The shouting above had tapered into ill-tempered carping and debate.

"Can we follow the thieves out?" Indrajit asked. "By smell?"

"Only if we can get up to the bridge," Munahim said.

"Which means we need to find our way up now, while there's light." Indrajit stood and scanned his surroundings. He hoped for a ladder, or stairs, and found none. But of course, if there were a ladder, the Huachao would simply have climbed down after them. He looked for vines, or other exits that clearly led upward, and found nothing encouraging. The river flowed from darkness into darkness, and above them, a rough, rocky wall ascended toward the dim light of the thieves' lamps.

"We're going to have to climb," Munahim said.

"It's not sheer," Philastes pointed out. "It looks like easy climbing, really. But if we miss a handhold, we fall onto this brick."

"The other choice is to throw ourselves into the river and hope for the best," Indrajit said.

"I'll take the climb," Philastes said. "Look, I think it gets easier up and to the right. Isn't that a ledge?"

"You sound cheerful," Munahim said.

The Pelthite was studying the slope. "Even going blind down the underground river is better than being a living wasp womb."

Munahim grunted.

The light changed. Indrajit looked up and saw most of the party of thieves move forward in the darkness. Two Huachao remained, standing at the far end of the bridge with a lamp. They were blocked from direct view by the bulk of the brick span, but Indrajit could see their shadows thrown up against the wall.

They stood guard at the far end of the bridge.

"They're waiting to make sure we don't reappear," Philastes said.

"If we can get up this slope without being seen," Indrajit said, "we can attack them."

"They'll sound the alarm," Munahim said.

"Not if we shoot them instead," Philastes pointed out.

Indrajit distributed the other men's weapons back to them. Philastes tucked the sling into his belt. Munahim tested his bow string, pronounced it good, and then attached sword and quiver to his person again. Indrajit belted Vacho back into place and then tied the sack, now containing Fix's weapons, to his belt.

Indrajit climbed first. He was a confident climber, having grown up surrounded by the cliffs and rocks of the seashore, and he picked a cautious path. He was careful to select handholds and footholds that were close enough together to work for the shorter Pelthite, and rugged enough to support the Kyone's weight. The wet wool of his cloak weighed him down, but with the night just beginning, and him far underground and potentially lost, he decided to keep it.

Climbing into the greasy darkness, he worried about Fix. Would the thieves grab Fix and use him now as their scapegoat? But even if they didn't, how much longer did Fix have to live, anyway? How long until he burst into Kattak nymphs, dying a horrible, painful death, out of reach of the Girdle of Life? And how long until he was too far gone to be saved by the Druvash craft of the Vin Dalu?

Suddenly, he found himself on a fin in the rock. It wasn't quite the ledge Philastes had taken it for, but a spine between the steep slope behind him and an even steeper fall in front. But he turned left and crept along the spine, toward the bridge.

He could see the Huachao; could they see him? He was maybe eighty cubits distant, and separated by the chasm. The two cat-men leaned over the edge of the brick span, peering down into the water below and raising their lamp. They didn't see him because they weren't looking, so he was careful to move silently.

He noticed that the fin of rock he straddled was marked with loose pebbles here and there. He also noticed that ahead of him, the fin ended, not quite connecting with the base of the brick span. There was a leap of some six or seven cubits to get from one to the other.

Indrajit hunkered down behind a fist of stone and waited. Philastes climbed up onto the rock and then Munahim, and they joined him in the shadow.

"Are you close enough?" Indrajit whispered.

For answer, Philastes picked up a rock.

The Huachao turned and were looking over the other side of the bridge. They muttered to each other, shrugged, and set the lantern on a ledge in the rock behind them, resuming their sentinel positions.

The other two Protagonists conferred briefly about targets. Then Philastes spun a rock once over his head and released it and at the same moment Munahim launched an arrow. Water snapped from the string of the Kyone's bow, which had been briefly submerged, but his arrows had stayed dry, tucked into his watertight quiver.

The slingstone struck one Huachao fighter in the back of his skull. The arrow pierced the other's lung. Both fell silently onto the brick.

Indrajit jumped over the gap onto the bridge. Over his protests, Munahim then threw Philastes and Indrajit caught him. They picked up the lantern.

"We have to rescue Fix," Munahim said. "I don't care about Betel, he's not my problem."

"Agreed," Philastes said. "Also, Fix is the one with Kattak memories in his head. If there's something going on and we're to have any chance of stopping it, we need access to his memories."

"If we go back to Boom's lair," Indrajit said, "it's us against all of Boom's men. How many is that? Twenty?"

"Maybe we can negotiate with Boom," Philastes suggested.

"I agree," Indrajit said. "But we need something to trade."

Munahim frowned. "His becoming a Gray Lord?"

"We can't promise that. And if we promise to help him get it, he won't believe us, or care." Indrajit shook his head. "The life of his doorman. Hastin Gink. The Doorman and the Wandering Eye and the Voice that Stinks."

"Thinks," Philastes said.

"We have to douse the light," Munahim pointed out.

Indrajit looked at the bridge, lacking hand railing or curb. "Because otherwise Gink and Yammilku and the rest will see us coming." He sighed. "Okay, Munahim. But no funny business. No leading us into pits."

"I'll follow exactly where the Huachao went," Munahim said. "They stink and are easy to track. But I can't promise they won't go into any pits."

They locked hands and Indrajit snuffed out the lamp.

"Remember that we want to stay downwind, too, if possible," Indrajit said. "The Huachao are sniffers."

Munahim in front and Indrajit at the back each had a free hand, so each carried a weapon; Munahim his bow and Indrajit the Voice of Lightning, Vacho. Munahim led them forward into darkness, a faint snuffling sound that Indrajit tried to tune out as he listened for the sounds of Ghouls.

The journey in the dark seemed infinitely long. Sometimes, light gleamed above, suggesting they were near the surface, and even after sunset, some lamp or bonfire cast its illuminating grace down into the bowels of the city. Sometimes, water fell, crashing on stone or hard earth, or slipping quietly past to fall to lower levels. Was it raining again, then? They walked through echoing galleries, up and down stairs, and through a long passage only a cubit wide.

Munahim led them clambering over rectangular stone objects, slightly longer than the height of a man. Scooting awkwardly on knees and knuckles, Indrajit found stone scrollwork and beveled edges. For the first time, he broke his silence.

"Is this . . . ?" he asked.

"Coffins," Philastes whispered.

They emerged from the corridor choked with coffins into a trench. The dirt walls, four cubits apart, were visible in a shaft of orange light that sliced down from above. A damp breeze gusted into the trench obliquely, causing Indrajit to wonder what exactly was over his head. If the thieves had taken the path they intended, shouldn't they all be beneath the Crown now? The floor of the trench was of earth as well, and was strewn with bits of broken pottery. Indrajit was careful where he placed his steps, envying Munahim his boots.

"There." The Kyone pointed at a dim light at the end of the trench as he whispered. "They went through there."

"Shouldn't we follow them?" Indrajit asked.

"I smell other men," Munahim explained. "I'm not certain what direction the scent comes from."

Indrajit took a deep breath and sighed. He looked up at the orange light for guidance, but it told him nothing. "Okay. Surprise is still with us." He strode ahead of Munahim toward the light.

The light settled through an open doorway. Indrajit pressed himself against the brick around the doorway and sneaked a glance through.

On the other side, he saw a vast rectangular chamber. Its walls were built of large, regular bricks, and it had no windows. It had no ceiling, either, and rain crashed down from above. For a floor, it had only a metal grate. Dim light rose through the grate, but Indrajit couldn't make out the source or sources of light at all.

Peering across the grate, Indrajit could make out other gaps in the wall, all low, at the level of the iron floor. Squinting and counting, he found eight of them. Nine entrances in total.

"This is the False Palace," he murmured.

"I can't follow the scent across that rain," Munahim said, leaning over his shoulder. "I can go stick my head into every opening and sniff, I suppose."

"That sounds risky," Indrajit said.

"What is this place?" Philastes asked. He pressed forward at Indrajit's side, peering out into the rain.

"If this is the False Palace," Indrajit said, "then it has a façade like a real palace, on all four sides. But internally, it's just this. Hollow." He looked down. "Although I had never heard that it lacked a floor and ceiling."

"Gases."

The voice came from behind them.

Indrajit turned and found himself looking at multiple drawn swords, all pointed at him. The men holding the blades were tall and fair, and one raised a shuttered lantern, cracked to emit a single weak ray of light. Indrajit recognized the man who had spoken.

"Tully Roberts," he said. "Which means that this fellow next to you is your brother, Uthnar, the Gray Lord."

Chapter Twenty-Five

“You’re lost, poet,” Uthnar Roberts said. He looked like his brother Tully, but leaner, with a body that curved forward like a hungry wolf’s and only a scar running down the right side of his face from temple to chin, rather than the mass of scars Tully had. He wore an unadorned iron disk on a chain around his neck. “You’ve wandered into my path. But I might yet spare you, if you have a gift for me.”

Behind the Roberts brothers crowded six more Ildarians. They were all tall and muscular and wrapped in studded leather.

“This is no time to quibble about the map,” Indrajit said. “Listen, one of the entrances to the False Palace is Zac Betel’s, isn’t it?”

“I’ve no interest in explaining to you the constitution of our ancient and honorable society.” Uthnar bowed, almost ceremoniously, his eyes never leaving Indrajit’s. “I want the map.”

“Betel’s lieutenant Yammilku is setting an ambush over there right now,” Indrajit said. He knew Tully Roberts had been an ally of Yammilku’s in at least some of the Heru’s scheming. He hoped Tully had been acting without Uthnar’s knowledge, and that Uthnar might not approve of the plots.

Tully frowned. “To attack us?”

“To attack Betel,” Munahim said. “He has men in the service of Jaxter Boom as his allies. Huachao fighters.”

“You could come to Betel’s aid.” Philastes’s voice was bright with excitement. “You could assist him and no doubt he would be grateful in turn.”

“Or we could assist Yammilku,” Tully said thoughtfully.

"I wouldn't mind taking Boom's trade," Uthnar growled. "We could kill them all."

The Ildarians laughed.

"You want the map, though," Indrajit said.

"Not as much as I want control of the Sootfaces," Uthnar said. "You've changed the menu, poet."

Did Indrajit care? He was tired, as if his potion of energy had burned itself out in him. He felt as if he and his heart had both been batted back and forth for two days straight in a vicious game of Rûphat. None of the Gray Lords was his friend, really, but Betel had dealt squarely with him while Yammilku had betrayed him. Twice. On a personal level, he really wanted the Heru to fail. It wasn't only out of a desire that he get his comeuppance, it was also because Indrajit didn't want to deal with Yammilku as a Gray Lord in the future. And Tully seemed to be every bit the backstabbing conniver that Yammilku was. For that matter, Uthnar was now turning out to be cut from the same cloth, too.

But more important than any of that was rescuing Fix. And to bargain to get Fix back, he needed to capture Hastin Gink.

"We'll help you," he said.

"To do what?" Philastes murmured.

"I don't even care," Indrajit said. "Look, we'll help you do whatever you want here. But I need Hastin Gink as my prisoner when it's over. Alive, and my prisoner."

"What do you want with Old Tail-Nose?" Tully asked.

"I want to trade him for my partner, Fix, who's being held captive by Jaxter Boom. So if Gink dies, you swear to me that you and your men will help me break into Boom's lair and rescue my friend."

"Why do I need your help?" Uthnar peered at Indrajit's face by the lantern light.

"They outnumber you," Indrajit said. "Three more fighters will give you a strong advantage, especially if you take them by surprise. Or we can *help* you take them by surprise. We were their prisoners and escaped. If they saw us again, they might chase us. And you could be lying in wait."

"That feels like a device from low bawdy," Uthnar said, squinting.

"Well, it is," Indrajit agreed. "If you prefer a device from high epic,

I will happily enter the passage, strike a pose with sword raised over my head, and recite my genealogy."

"We attack," Uthnar purred to his men. "Take Yammilku and Betel and Gink alive, if you see any of them. The others die if they don't surrender."

Indrajit nodded. "How can we support you?"

"By going first, of course." Uthnar pointed to the False Palace. "It's the third opening on the right."

Indrajit led the way. Munahim slung his sword onto his back and took his bow in his hands and Philastes held his sling.

The sound of the crashing rain on the grid was tinny and high pitched. Indrajit meant to be moving silently, but he couldn't help muttering, "What in all the frozen hells is the False Palace for?"

"Sometimes I think madmen built this city," Philastes said.

"Madmen built every city," Munahim said. "The sane men live free on the steppes."

"You're here with us," Indrajit said.

"I noticed."

Indrajit counted three openings in the wall of the False Palace. At the third, he eased his head around the corner and peered carefully within.

For a moment, he saw nothing. Then a stray glint of light made it through the pouring rain and limned the feathers of Yammilku's head. Squinting, Indrajit could see that the Heru leaned against the wall just this side of a bottleneck, waiting and watching for anyone to come through. The Huachao and Hastin Gink and several cloaked henchmen of Jaxter Boom all hid themselves around the bottleneck similarly.

Indrajit looked back. The Ildarians stood ten paces distant, swords drawn, rain pouring down the wool hoods of their cloaks.

Indrajit held up fingers to try to communicate to the Protagonists how many men were inside and how they were arranged, but all he provoked was uncomprehending frowns. Finally, he sighed, stepped away from the wall, and charged into the tunnel.

"Protagonists!" he roared.

He slashed the first Huachao to turn around through his forearm, causing the man to drop his sword and shriek. Indrajit planted a sandaled foot in the man's chest and kicked, sending him flying through the tunnel's bottleneck and into darkness.

A second Huachao leaped up, a knife in each hand. Indrajit caught the tip of Vacho on the tunnel wall, which nearly ended in disaster by blunting his swing and leaving him open to attack. Staggering back, he narrowly managed to avoid being sliced open by three slashes with knives.

Arrows whooshed past Indrajit into the tunnel. A thief in a long cloak fell with feathers sprouting from his chest and a cat-man dropped with an arrow in the neck.

"Not Gink!" Indrajit cried.

Slingstones followed the arrows in.

When did the Ildarians plan to help?

Then Indrajit caught a fourth attack on Vacho's cross-guard. The Huachao warrior with two knives lost his balance and stumbled sideways, leaving himself exposed. Indrajit kicked his knee, knocking him to the stony floor of the tunnel, kicked him in the temple, and finally stomped on his right forearm, snapping the bones.

The Huachao yowled.

"Don't hurt Gink!"

The Huachao pridechief, Budhrriao, stood before the bottleneck. He held Gink in front of him, one hand gripping the doorman's proboscis like a handle and the other holding a long knife to Gink's throat.

"Don't hurt Gink!" Budhrriao called again. "Why is that, fish-man? Is Gink your secret ally?"

"No!" Gink honked, his voice muted by the fist gripping his nose.

"No," Indrajit said. "I want my partner back."

"And you think if you save Gink alive," the Huachao said, "you can trade him back to Boom for your friend. What makes you think this worm has any value?"

"Hey!" Gink honked.

"It's my only play," Indrajit said. "A wild guess. Let him go, and I'll let you go. No more deaths."

"No more deaths." Budhrriao chuckled. "I'll give you another play, Blaatshi. I'll fight you. One on one. If you kill me, you get Gink."

"Don't you have an opinion here?" Indrajit called to Uthnar.

"No," Uthnar said. "We're just watching. We'll decide what to do after you've worn each other down. I'll tell you what, though. We'll guarantee a fair fight. No cheating on either side."

He glared at Munahim, and Munahim lowered his bow.

Indrajit looked around at the other entrances to the False Palace. If agents of the other Gray Lords were watching, they were all lurking unseen in the darkness. He sighed.

"And if you kill me?" he asked the Huachao.

"Does it really matter what happens then?" Budhrriao sneered.

"If you kill me, Munahim and Philastes get Gink." Indrajit nodded to his companions. "Gink lives in either case and we try to ransom Fix."

Gink chuckled nervously.

Budhrriao shoved Gink to the floor in the tunnel. He switched his knife to his left hand and drew a scimitar in his right, and then stepped out into the rain.

Indrajit circled and backed away from the wall. He swung Vacho in demonstrative poses, communicating his courage and resolution. The Ildarians backed away, not quite retreating to their own corner.

Munahim stood watching, an arrow to the string. Philastes held his sling with a stone in the pouch, poised to throw.

"I know you, Blaatshi," Budhrriao rumbled. "You're an actor. You're all poses and no action."

"You've got me all wrong," Indrajit said. "I'm not an actor at all, I'm a poet. And I'm not *just* a poet."

Budhrriao made an experimental lunge and Indrajit deflected his blade. "No? What else are you, then?"

Indrajit charged, driving a series of slashing attacks straight at the cat-man's head. The Huachao dodged, but evading the blows brought him back three long steps.

"I'm an *epic* poet," Indrajit told him.

Budhrriao threw his knife. Indrajit whipped his sword up to knock the missile aside, but didn't hit it as directly as he intended. The tip of the knife blade sank into Indrajit's shoulder and he grunted in pain.

"Kill the fish!" Yammilku shouted.

Budhrriao rushed Indrajit. The cat-man roared, a sound deeper than anything Indrajit had previously heard from any of the cat-warriors. The war cry vibrated in Indrajit's bones and made his knees tremble, and then he was struggling to parry and dodge a hurricane of scimitar attacks.

Rain slickened the metal grid they stood on. Air blasted up through some corners of the iron lattice, cold in one place and hot in another. Light similarly leaked up through the metal hatching in various places, giving the impression that the slippery footing was also uneven. Indrajit slid and stumbled back, the point of the scimitar growing closer by the moment.

Until he gambled, and took a great leap back. He was no dancer, but he jumped backward and into a pose, the so-called Sharpened Tongue Position, used for pointed martial orations. He leaped back and landed with his feet apart, one forward and one back, and his sword extended to maximum reach in front of him.

His arm was longer than Budhrriao's, and so was his sword. Budhrriao had been closing, inside Indrajit's guard, and suddenly he was outside and at sword-point, thwarted by Indrajit's greater extension.

Budhrriao snarled and pulled up, to avoid impaling himself.

Indrajit yanked out the thrown knife and tossed it aside. Then he in turn pressed. He made more circumspect attacks now, stabbing at the Huachao's face and torso. Budhrriao protected his eyes and face, but Indrajit landed several blows on his upper arms and sank the tip of Vacho two fingers deep into the broad muscle of Budhrriao's chest.

Then Budhrriao locked Indrajit's blade between his own and his free hand. With a snap of both wrists, he ripped Vacho from Indrajit's hand and hurled it away into the rain.

While the Huachao's blade was to the side, Indrajit leaped. He struck the cat-warrior shoulder to shoulder and knocked him backward. The collision sent a juddering pain through the knife-wound he had suffered, and a trembling that ran all the way to his toes. He heard a metallic rattling somewhere far away—was that Vacho, hitting the metal grill? Was it Budhrriao's scimitar?

Then he and the cat crashed to the iron deck. He heard bones snap and felt pain in his chest. Budhrriao rolled as they struck, and lashed up with a foot. He struck Indrajit in the thigh, and Indrajit's own forward momentum, aided by the blow, threw him over Budhrriao's head.

Indrajit landed on his back, hard. He couldn't breathe: rain in his mouth? Air slammed from his lungs? Both?

Claws raked his face and he lurched away.

Indrajit struggled to get to his feet. He couldn't see, but when he felt claws on his face a second time, he punched. He felt his knuckles connect with bone and heard a cry. Then he staggered away sideways, sucking air into his lungs and pawing water and blood from his eyes.

"Finish him! Kill him!"

Indrajit couldn't tell who was shouting, or to whom.

He regained his vision and found he was standing over a sword. Not Vacho, it was the Huachao's scimitar. He scooped it up; its weight and balance were strange in his hand, so he swung it around experimentally several times.

Then he stalked toward Budhrriao.

The Huachao was struggling to rise. He coughed and spat; it was difficult to be certain in the darkness, but it looked as if he might be spitting blood.

"You can surrender," Indrajit said.

Indrajit heard a shriek behind him. He turned and saw Yammilku standing over the body of Hastin Gink, pulling his sword from the dead man's chest.

Munahim emitted a howl of surprise and rage. He sank an arrow into Yammilku's neck and then a second into the Heru's head before anyone else could move. Zac Betel's rebellious lieutenant stumbled forward out of the tunnel and crashed to the floor in the rain.

"*What about a fair fight?*" Indrajit shrieked. Fix would die. Fix would burst apart in Jaxter Boom's dungeon, and now Indrajit had no bargaining chips to get him out. He turned to Uthnar Roberts, feeling his blood hot in his face. "You said you would keep it fair!"

Uthnar looked at the two fresh corpses and nodded slowly. "That looks fair to me."

Budhrriao tackled Indrajit. Indrajit fell to the iron, his right eye pressed against the metal, full of water and pale green light at the same time. He pushed off with hands and knees, weary to the bone, but rolling over in an attempt to throw Budhrriao off.

He managed to flop onto his back, but Budhrriao now sat astride him. Blood trickled from the Huachao's muzzle and his breath came in crackling grunts, but he held his dagger in his hand.

Indrajit raised the scimitar to attack the cat-man and found his hand empty. He'd lost the weapon again.

Budhrriao plunged the dagger toward Indrajit's face. With his long arms, Indrajit grabbed the Huachao by both wrists, stopping the blade's descent. His chest ached. Someone was screaming, but he wasn't sure whether it was him or the Huachao pridechief.

"Stay out of this," he heard Uthnar Roberts say.

In his peripheral vision, Indrajit saw dull light glinting on drawn blades. His two companions were fenced in and helpless.

He pushed with his knee, trying to unseat his attacker, but the knife only descended inexorably toward him.

"Why?" Indrajit grunted. "Yammilku and Gink are dead. You gain nothing."

"I gain the kill, fish-man."

The Huachao's breath stank of murder and blood.

Indrajit slipped his left hand free, punching the cat-man in the kidney repeatedly, and then in the back of the neck. The Huachao only grinned and hissed, a maniacal sound, and the dagger descended closer still.

"Do you want to compose your death-poem," Budhrriao asked, "or shall I?"

Indrajit spat in the Huachao's face.

The cat-warrior cackled in glee. Then Indrajit heard a loud crack, and Budhrriao fell over sideways.

A man stood over Indrajit in the rain. He wore a kilt and tunic and he held a heavy timber in his hand as a club, but it took Indrajit a moment to recognize his silhouette in the darkness.

"Fix," he said.

"Hey!" Uthnar Roberts yelled. "Where did he come from?"

"From under the city," Fix said. "Just like you." His voice was shaky. His belly looked swollen.

"Fix," Indrajit asked, "how did you escape?"

He dragged himself to his knees, wincing from pain in his ribs. Behind Fix, barely visible in the rain, Indrajit saw the forger Danel Avchat.

"I extended my belly as much as I could." Fix spoke slowly, breathing deeply every few words. "Then I made myself vomit. When the guard rushed in to ask me what I knew about the Kattak plot, I killed him."

"I guaranteed a fair fight," Uthnar Roberts said. "You made me break my oath."

Indrajit stood, wobbling. "You let Yammilku kill Gink."

"That death has been balanced." Uthnar grimaced. "How will you balance this murder?"

"That's a perverted idea of fair," Indrajit said.

"I'll kill your brother Tully, if you like," Fix said quietly. "Will that balance your books?"

"I'll rip your throat out!" Tully snapped.

The Ildarians surged forward.

"Hold!"

The shout was deep and loud, and it came from the third tunnel. Indrajit turned his head slightly and saw Zac Betel emerging. Behind him came Kishi and Zalaptings, swords and hammers in their hands.

"You're late, Betel," Uthnar said.

"I thought I should let things play out without me for a little while," the Luzzazza Gray Lord said. "I see that I was right."

"You knew," Indrajit murmured. "You knew Yammilku was a traitor. You didn't believe his explanations at all."

"He was an obvious liar," Betel said. "I had the strong sensation that he had already given up the Girdle of Life, and was now trying to hide that fact from me. Why would an honest man do such a thing?"

"What's your interest in these men?" Roberts asked the Luzzazza.

"Don't touch the Blaatshi," Betel said. "Or his companions. They did me a service."

Uthnar hesitated, but then sheathed his sword. "Put away your weapons," he ordered.

His men obliged.

Other men had emerged. Small groups, two to five men each, stood around seven of the entrances to the False Palace.

A man in a gray cloak stepped forward. Indrajit recognized him as the tavernkeeper Yuto Harlee.

"You summoned the meeting," Harlee called out to Betel. "What are we here for?"

Chapter Twenty-Six

Fix's knees buckled and Indrajit caught him.

"Excuse me," Indrajit said. "We need to leave."

"You can go." Uthnar stood aside to permit their exit, and Avchat rushed to position himself among the Protagonists. At the last moment, he lurched sideways and stood beside Betel—one of the Luzzazza's invisible arms must have grabbed him.

"No," Betel said. "You can't."

"Is this a Conclave or not?" The man asking this question was Fanchee, green-skinned with a mass of tentacles hanging off the lower half of his face. He wore a Gray Lord's iron disk. He had stepped forward, as had several others, each man leaving behind his entourage and now forming a circle of seven, all wearing iron disks from chains around their necks, loosely standing around the Protagonists. Arash Sehama was one of them.

The Gray Lords.

In the gloom, Indrajit searched in vain beyond the Gray Lords to try to make out what the uniforms of their followers might be. He thought he saw a group holding sticks, but otherwise could discern nothing.

"No witnesses." This was from another of the seven, a Wixit.

The Fanchee were kelp farmers and seafarers. Did that suggest that the Fanchee Gray Lord was master of the thieves of the East and West Flats? And the Wixits he knew were often merchants—was the Wixit Gray Lord master of the Caravanserai, or the Lee? Indrajit shook his head, clearing out the useless questions.

The Huachao had picked up Budhrriao. The pridechief was moving sluggishly, so Fix hadn't killed him after all. The cat-men huddled in a ring, with their backs to the center, as if they expected to have to defend themselves.

"We're not witnesses," Indrajit said. "We were brought here as prisoners, and we just want to leave."

"You were brought here as prisoners by the servants of Jaxter Boom," Betel said.

One of the Huachao snarled. "We are not servants!"

"Yes, we were," Indrajit said.

"Along with my own disloyal agent, Yammilku the Heru." Betel adjusted his grip on his hammer as he spoke, as if the Heru's very name caused him to want to smash things.

"That's true." Indrajit's throat felt dry.

"What is this, Zac?" Uthnar Roberts asked.

"The time has come for the speaking of truths," Betel said. "Standing here in the False Palace, where the heat and gas of the warren below are released so that the city isn't harmed. We must now release the heat and gas of the untruths and the conspiracies."

The awkward metaphor made Indrajit grind his teeth, but he said nothing.

"Have you been party to some conspiracy, then?" the Wixit asked.

Betel pointed at Indrajit and Fix. "I directed these men to steal Arash Sehama's map of Underkish for me."

Sehama hissed.

"A violation," the Fanchee said. "We don't steal from each other."

"On the other hand," the Wixit said, "I'd like to get my paws on that map, myself."

"I admit the fault," Betel said. "It was my idea that I would take the information on the map and then return it, but that's no mitigation. The information is precisely what Sehema would wish to preserve secret. I had offered him money for it, and he'd refused. In his weakness, losing men right and left to the jobbers of the Lords of Kish, I had offered him my alliance for the secrets of the map, and still he'd said no."

"I see this is a Conclave after all," Sehama said. "My 'weakness,' indeed. That you would insult me so before my brethren! What do you offer to make good your faults? The theft and also the insults!"

Indrajit had the terrible feeling that he was about to be sold out. His limbs shook with fatigue and the cold.

"Wait," Betel said. "Others may wish to admit fault."

There followed a long and terrible pause.

"Indrajit Twang," Betel growled.

"Ah . . . I don't know what would constitute a fault," Indrajit said, "but we stole the map from Sehama."

"Good," Betel said.

"And in fact we hired this scribe here," Indrajit said.

"No need to say my name," Avchat said.

"That's Danel Avchat," Betel said. "He's not one of mine, but we know him. He's a forger."

"A copyist!" Avchat insisted.

"We hired this 'copyist' so we could give the map back," Indrajit said. "And still give the copy to Betel. No harm done."

"Except," Sehama hissed, "that as my colleague Zac Betel correctly points out, you would have stolen the information, which was the real point. My proprietary, secret lore, distributed to one of my enemies."

"Competitor," Betel said. "Not enemy."

"We're thieves," Sehama said, "not grocers."

"Still," Betel insisted, "there's a reason we divide territories among us. I would have been your loyal ally, Arash." He turned to Indrajit. "What then?"

Indrajit was shivering, and the night was only getting colder. "We returned to give you the map and Yammilku was in charge. Acting as the night warden. He took the map and he told us what we wanted to know . . ." He trailed off, uncertain how much of the story to share—Alea's death, the Vin Dalu, the Kattak?

"I was attacked by my own men," Betel said.

Indrajit heard a murmur of several voices, but in the rain and the darkness he couldn't see from where.

"Is this a confession," Uthnar asked, "or an accusation?"

"We were there," Indrajit said. "Philastes and I. Yammilku forced us to do it. He took from us the thing we had worked to retrieve—not the map, but something else. An artifact we needed to save a friend's life."

"The stupid Girdle," Sehama hissed.

Indrajit nodded. "Yes. Yammilku took it and demanded we approach you. He planned to attack and kill you, and take your place."

"What was your role?" Betel asked.

"I think we were to be the distraction," Indrajit said. "And I believe that he planned to kill us and say we were the assassins."

"Some of my men were his coconspirators," Betel rumbled. "But you warned me, and I defeated the uprising."

"Yes," Indrajit said. "And I see now that you realized Yammilku's guilt. At the time, I missed that."

"Did Yammilku alone put you up to this?" Betel asked.

Indrajit's far-apart eyes meant that he could see both Yuto Harlee and Tully Roberts. In the darkness, he couldn't see them very well. What he didn't know was whether those men had acted on their own, or at the orders of their Gray Lords. And if they had acted alone, how would the Gray Lords now react?

"He had a group of men," Indrajit said. "Yuto Harlee of the Sookwalkers was one. Tully Roberts of the Silksteppers was another."

"He's lying," Uthnar Roberts said.

Arash Sehama spun about to face the tavernkeeper Harlee. "What is this, Harlee?" he hissed.

Yuto Harlee had a long knife in his hand. In the rain and the shadows it had lain unseen alongside his thigh, but when Sehama turned, Harlee stepped forward. The knife blade flashed gray in the dim light, and then Harlee plunged it three times into Sehama's chest.

The Gray Lord of the Sookwalkers crumbled to the iron grate.

"He was a failure!" Harlee snatched the iron disk from Sehama's neck and raised the bloody knife over his head. "He'd lost territory and lost money and lost his precious map, the one thing that gave us any advantage. His time is past. I am Gray Lord of the Sookwalkers now!"

Behind him, a handful of men in gray cloaks emerged from the tunnel opening. They stood like bodyguards, ready to defend Harlee.

The Fanchee Gray Lord drew a saber, wheeled about, and stomped into the tunnel opening behind him. A short, piercing cry was cut short by a meaty thwack, and then the Fanchee reemerged.

Betel turned to Uthnar Roberts, making a dull clicking sound in his mouth. "So, Uthnar, you were in on this."

"I was in on nothing," Uthnar said, "and I owe you nothing."

"What was the deal?" Betel asked. "You would help kill me and Sehama and Zaal and then three brand-new Gray Lords would owe you favors. What were you to get? Money? A copy of Sehama's map? Territory? All of the above?"

"What would you do about it if it was true?" Uthnar's lips were twisted into a sneer and his jaw jutted upward.

"You counted three Gray Lords who would be new and your allies," Betel said. "Which would have meant that, if there were questions, it would have been four against three, with the four on your side. Not a perfectly safe outcome, but nothing is perfectly safe."

Indrajit saw Yuto Harlee edging backward toward the tunnel, his men edging backward with him.

"But count again," Betel said. "It's five to two against you."

Harlee turned and ran. Munahim slipped an arrow from his quiver, quick as lightning, and sank it into the back of Harlee's thigh. The tavernkeeper fell into the darkness of the tunnel, dragged by his men.

No one pursued them.

"One," Betel said. "You're alone."

"I've got my men," Uthnar growled.

"You don't want to fight," Betel said. "We'll take your contracts, your clients, your territory. We'll squeeze you from all sides until you're squashed to a pulp. You should clear the slate while you can."

"What do you want?" Uthnar took an uneasy step back. His hands hung near his sword and knife.

"Did Tully propose this plot to you?" Betel asked.

"I don't see why that matters," Uthnar said.

"Oh, yes, you do."

"I won't let you kill my brother." Uthnar's voice was strained.

"Of course not," Betel said. "*You're* going to do it."

Tully Roberts snorted. "That's ridiculous. This is all a misunderstanding. Yammilku told me that he was defending you from plotters in your ranks."

"Tully," Uthnar said softly.

"I was coming to your rescue, Betel," Tully insisted.

"Tully."

"Besides, why would you listen to anything this fish-headed jobber says, anyway?" Tully drew his sword.

Uthnar slapped the sword from his brother's hand. Tully turned, shock on his face, and Uthnar stabbed a dagger into his belly. Tully collapsed slowly into his brother's arms, shuddering and gasping, and Uthnar sank to the iron grid.

"Decisive," Betel said. "Committed to order, even over personal loyalty. Even over family. The sort of man who should be Gray Lord."

"Shut up," Uthnar whispered. "Just shut your mouth now."

Betel nodded. Turning, he faced the knot of Huachao warriors. "And you. You came here with Yammilku."

"Actually, they were sent by Jaxter Boom," Indrajit said.

"The squid lord of the Dregs?" Betel tut-tutted. "Boom and Yammilku allied against me?"

"The plan was to kill you," Indrajit said, "and make me and my comrades look like the assassins."

"Yammilku would replace me," Betel said. "And Boom?"

"Boom wanted to become a Gray Lord," Indrajit said. "I suppose he still does."

"Is it the worst idea?" the Fanchee Gray Lord asked. "He dominates the Dregs. If anything, bringing him into our councils might help control him."

"Eight Gray Lords would mean more deadlocks," Betel mused. "An odd number protects against that."

"If Harlee's out," the Wixit said, "we're at six. Boom would give us back an odd number."

Uthnar laughed hollowly. "Men are dead. You were nearly killed yourself, and what you two worry about is the balance of voting?"

"I worry about balance and about neutralizing Boom so that we can avoid future bloodshed." Betel sighed. "Or minimize it, at least. But I fear we cannot reward Jaxter Boom for his temerity. It would encourage more bad behavior. We shall have to punish him, as we consider giving him what he wants."

"Hastin Gink is dead," Indrajit said. "Might that not be punishment enough?"

Betel wheeled suddenly on Indrajit. "You have carried out your work here, and your participation is no longer needed. You will hand over all copies of the map, including the forger Avchat."

"Copyist," Avchat said. "But what if I don't want to be handed over?"

"You will be escorted from the False Palace with your eyes hooded," Betel said. "You live and you walk away. We shall meet again, no doubt, but when we do, you should not assume that we are friends."

"That sounds perfect," Indrajit said.

"No," Fix said.

The Luzzazza crimelord straightened and loomed over the Protagonists. "What do you mean, no?"

"No," Fix said. "We need your help. Kish needs your help. Kish might even need Jaxter Boom's help. Now, tonight, and tomorrow."

"No one needs Jaxter Boom's help," Betel said. "He's a crushed worm. And you have not earned the help of the Gray Lords."

"There is too much to explain," Fix said, "so I shall try to summarize. Wasp-men called Kattak have been infesting the good and the great of Kish with their eggs." He met Indrajit's gaze. Was the sky overhead beginning to lighten? The rain was definitely tapering off. "The Lord Chamberlain's understeward, Chosk. The Lord Stargazer's night steward, Ubandar Hakko. Merchants, ambassadors, princelings. Those eggs will hatch tomorrow morning, during the Battle of Last Light."

"What happens to the men when the eggs hatch?" the Fanchee Gray Lord asked.

"They die horribly," Indrajit said.

"Is this true?" Betel asked.

"Jaxter Boom believes it," Budhrriao said.

"They did it at the embassy events we arranged," Philastes said. His voice was wooden.

"The Kattak have been filling the pit beneath their embassy with more Kattak," Fix said. "Hence their need for more and more food over time. As the moment of their attack approached, they no longer needed their staff—hence Lysander and Thomedes. You would have been next."

Philastes shuddered.

Uthnar wiped his dagger on his brother's clothing and sheathed it, then stood. "So what? So some of the rich and some servants of the rich die. Die horribly, as you say. The poor die horribly every day. My brother died horribly, and so did Hastin and Yammilku."

"No," Indrajit said, "death by Kattak nymph is much more horrible."

"In a few hours," Fix said, "the Kattak eggs will begin to hatch. I don't understand how that will be triggered. Maybe it's just time that they all hatch. Maybe there's a device, or a song . . . I don't know. In the middle of the ritual, people of prominence will explode into gory, bloody death. At the same moment, Kattak will swarm from Underkish and attack. They are not mere bugs, they have the intelligence of men, and they have long—and strange—memories. We killed some, but most survive. They will murder the Lords of Kish."

"Leaving us in charge." Betel chuckled. "Do you think I care whether there is a Lord Stargazer? Do you think that I'm troubled if the Lord Stargazer is a man who looks like an insect?"

"They aim to kill every man in Kish who isn't a Kattak," Fix said. "They aren't here to rule, and they hold an old, old grudge. They'll slowly implant their eggs into every person they can, until Kish is a mound of rubble, wrapped in paper and swarming with Kattak. Defend Kish now or prepare to flee."

"Fix," Indrajit said. "You need to get back to the Vin Dalu, immediately."

"I have an hour or two yet," Fix said. "And this is more important. And if we stop the Kattak now, perhaps their signal to hatch the eggs won't be sent at all."

"If it's a signal," Philastes muttered.

"Or perhaps it has already been sent," Indrajit said, "and the only hope is to rush you down to the Dregs right away."

"If we do that, maybe I live." Fix shook his head. "But Chosk and Hakko die, and many others."

"What's your plan?" Betel asked.

"We attack the Kattak now," Fix said. "Hard, immediately. We break their ability to make this assault. Then we warn the city and the Lords and every jobber company we can get in front of."

"My men are in," Uthnar Roberts said.

"You don't need to prove yourself," Betel said. "You've atoned for your brother's crime."

"I'm not doing it to prove myself," Roberts said. "I'm doing it to survive. My men . . . my men have seen the wasps."

"I am also in," the Fanchee Gray Lord added. Others murmured agreement, including the Huachao pridechief and Zac Betel.

"It's a shame to lose the Sookwalkers," Betel rumbled.

"Send a messenger and invite them." Fix leaned forward onto his knees and spat a string of thick bile. In the dim light, Indrajit couldn't tell what color it was. "Send messengers to summon all your men and to gather resources. We march on the Kattak pit immediately."

"What resources do we need," Roberts asked, "other than our swords?"

"Fire," Fix said. "Bring oil and torches in abundance. Let me show you on the map where we need to bring them to. The Kattak build in paper, and their nest is highly flammable. We'll burn them out."

"That's an excellent plan," Indrajit said. "I have an idea for another kind of attack we might make. I mean, if we can look at the map together for a moment, together with these fellows who know Graykin better than you do."

"What are you thinking?" Betel asked.

"I'm wondering this," Indrajit said. "Do any of the markings on the map show us where we can find Ghouls?"

Chapter Twenty-Seven

"You'll know when to kill me," Fix said through gritted teeth.

"It won't come to that," Indrajit said. "We're going to burn out the Kattak, then get you to the Vin Dalu for treatment, end of story. You're the hero. We'll tell Alea, she'll leave her husband for you, you retire to wealth and fame."

The four Protagonists traveled with a gang of Sootfaces, Silksteppers, and Sailmenders. They moved in a wide line as if they were hunting ground birds, trying to flush the creatures out of the bushes to catch them for a festal meal.

Which maybe, in a way, they were.

They were all armed, and they held torches. Some had nets and ropes and poles, and the thieves had all armored up. Elsewhere, other thieves lay in wait to effect the assault plan. They passed through a massive chamber dotted with pillars. Up ahead, and close, there should be a chamber with a stream and a nest of Ghouls.

Avchat followed behind the line of thieves.

"I was believing you until that last bit," Fix said.

"Okay," Indrajit conceded. "No fame for you. Should I . . ." He hesitated. "Listen, if anything happens to you, do you want me to communicate something to Alea?"

"No," Fix said firmly. "Or rather, no little love poems or anything. Tell her I wished her happiness to the last breath."

"If I die," Indrajit said, "please tell her the same from me."

Fix laughed, gagged, and then spit up bile. "If this works, and we destroy the Kattak, you should take Munahim to meet the Lord Chamberlain."

"While you're being treated by the Vin Dalu."

"Yes. Yes, exactly."

The map was marked with glyphs that seemed to indicate the presence of Ghouls. Graykin apparently didn't have a name or an icon for *Ghoul*, but *corpse eaters* was plain enough. When Fix and Betel had puzzled this out together, Indrajit had managed to refrain from any cutting remark about literacy.

Fix had shot him a quizzical glance, and he had ignored it.

"Ghoul!" a thief on the far right yelled.

Indrajit saw the creature, pale, long-tailed, and hairless. It sprang from the shadow of a brick column and raced away to the right.

"Don't follow it!" Fix shouted. "It's trying to lead you away!"

Munahim and a thief with a crossbow both turned to follow the Ghoul, launching their missiles at him simultaneously. The Ghoul took a bolt in the neck and an arrow through the lungs and dropped dead instantly.

"Here we go!" Uthnar Roberts bellowed. "Steady, and don't let them touch you!"

The brick field ended in a shattered chaos of brick and stone mingled, and then the posse of thieves and Protagonists entered the nest.

Ghouls hurled themselves forward. Thieves held them back with poles or threw nets over them. They slashed at the Ghouls to push them back, wounding them freely but killing them only if necessary. The plan was not to kill the Ghouls.

The plan was to drive them.

Beyond the fighting Ghouls lay their nest, which looked like a village of wattle and daub huts built of driftwood and bones. The village lay along a trickle of black water. Indrajit wrinkled his nose at the smell.

More Ghouls slipped out a passage at the back of the cavern, visible in the flickering torchlight. The line of Ghouls fighting formed into a snarling, ragged wedge and charged, but thieves placed in the middle of the line blew trumpets.

The Ghouls howled and fell back.

"On their heels!" Betel roared.

Zaal Pisko, Fanchee Gray Lord of the Sailmenders, blew a horn and fought with a spear in his other hand. He ran after the Ghouls, pricking at their heels with his weapon.

As they passed, the thieves gave the torch to the huts, setting them ablaze. They didn't want the Ghouls to circle back and reoccupy their nest.

"I feel slightly ill at ease, burning these creatures out of their homes," Indrajit murmured to Fix as they jogged. "I'd have felt better if they slept in a heap in the mud, rather than building buildings."

Philastes Larch overheard the conversation and interjected himself. "The Ghouls are men, and they are also monsters. If they learned not to be monsters, then we could treat them like men."

Was he talking about Ghouls, or about the Kattak?

Was he, in some way, talking about himself?

"Well said," Munahim told him.

They chased the Ghouls along two avenues. The first was lined with mausolea and tombs, and reminded Indrajit of his own foray to the necropolis south of the city—he had been there only briefly, and had been fortunate enough to avoid Ghouls, but they must haunt the place. As Ghouls tried to veer off left and right, thieves touched flame to lines of oil poured out in advance, sending up walls of fire.

The avenue of bones ended at a crude junction of natural caverns and a stone bridge over a chasm. Here, thieves with poles and nets sprang up from the natural caverns to present a bristling, impassable wall. Ghouls that got past the poles were dragged to the ground under nets, and then released to follow their fellows across the stone arch.

The Protagonists and the thieves plodded determinedly in the Ghouls' wake. They crossed the bridge, and on the other side one last group of thieves, Southlookers and Stilejumpers, battered the wave of Ghouls aside.

The Ghouls ran shrieking and gibbering to the only exit left to them: a wall of paper, rent by several large holes. It was the pit beneath the Paper Sultanates' Embassy, and the Ghouls poured in.

The great deficit in his plan, Indrajit thought, was that he would like to have lit the Ghouls on fire before launching them into the pit.

"Is it dawn yet?" he asked.

Fix shook his head. "If it is, we're late."

Thieves and Protagonists hurled bottles of oil into the Kattak nest.

"Keep your distance!" Pisko bellowed. "This will be a furnace!"

They threw torches and fell back.

Fire raced into the depths of the pit like an explosion. It leaped upward, too, springing up the great sheets and twists and cones of Kattak-made paper toward the ceiling. Above them somewhere was the hole into which Philastes and his colleagues had thrown slaves and prisoners.

Some in whom the Kattak had laid their eggs.

Others whom they had eaten.

As the paper burned, it threw images in all direction like a demented, spinning shadow show. Indrajit saw the chaotic, multiform Ghouls hurl themselves in panic and fury on large wasps, and the wasps respond with fatal stinger attacks, all as shadow play on enormous paper screens. He tried counting the Kattak.

"There are way more than we thought," he murmured. "Dozens."

"A hundred," Fix answered. "More."

"Frozen hells," Indrajit continued. "Think of all the memories in that. The minds, or souls, or whatever, of all the men in whose bodies the Kattak incubated."

Fix vomited.

The Gray Lord of the Stilejumpers was named Bocho Bin Bagu. He was long legged and long armed and had a tiny body and head, and his skin was blue; Indrajit thought his race might be called the Iyatu. They came from Easha and lived under trees, or up in treetops, or something similar.

"Hold the line!" Bin Bagu shouted.

A half dozen Kattak flew directly toward the thieves. They cast no shadow as they came, but were easy to see, because they were on fire.

Munahim began launching arrows. Philastes planted the butt of the pole he held against a chunk of masonry bigger than himself, projecting the tip forward. Fix gasped for breath and leaned forward, and Indrajit moved to put himself between his friend and the oncoming wasp-men.

"Stay down," he muttered.

Two Kattak crashed through the paper, heading right for the Protagonists. The paper ripped from the ceiling and came with them like a veil, so they looked like two burning eyes in the face of a ghost. Philastes struck one right in the center of its face with his pole and held it at bay as it hummed angrily.

Munahim shot several arrows into the other and then Indrajit slashed it through its spherical head with Vacho. The Kattak veered right, twisting and crashing and carrying the paper with it. It struck the stone floor in a burst of flame and ichor just cubits from the forger Avchat, insectoid body spasming violently. Avchat shrieked and jumped back. Indrajit lashed the Kattak's head again with his sword.

As the paper jerked sideways, Philastes lost his grip on his pole. He yelled and jumped, falling into the pit in his effort to get out of the way. The Kattak, freed of impediment, dove on Fix with its stinger raised high. Fix struggled to raise his weapons in defense, but could barely move. Indrajit smelled a dry and dusty reek of roasting insect and saw the gleam of venom on the Kattak's sting. He turned and tried to get back in time to defend Fix, but he was in motion the other way and his balance was off; he wasn't going to make it. Munahim yelled and slapped his quiver, but found that he was out of arrows.

Zac Betel himself came to the rescue. A barrage of four hammers crashed into the side of the Kattak, and Indrajit heard a loud cracking sound as the Kattak's carapace gave way. The Kattak spun sideways abruptly, bumping into its flaming companion and then slipping to the edge of the pit. It pawed at the stone underfoot weakly, but its limbs seemed to have lost strength, and the weight of its thorax dragged it down.

Fix lurched to its side and dispatched it with an ax-blow to the head.

Fire hung in columns and curtains from the ceiling. The manlike shadows of Ghouls and the horse-sized wasp shadows of the Kattak still struggled down among the ashes, but slowly, as if they were all wounded or dying.

Philastes dragged himself from the pit.

The shadows of further Kattak slipped up and away through the ceiling.

"With me, Sailmenders!" Zaal Pisko marched into the pit to dispatch the Kattak there.

"The entrance to the embassy!" Betel barked. "The wasps are on the surface!"

"Take Fix and the scribe and go," Indrajit told Philastes.

Philastes nodded. He gathered up Avchat, who was gibbering and shaking; two Kishi Sootfaces accompanied them, and they set out on the path to the home of the Vin Dalu.

"Gods go with you!" Indrajit called to his partner's receding, limping form.

"The entrance," Betel growled. "We lose time."

Indrajit led the Sootfaces and Silksteppers up the shaft and through the chimney into the embassy of the Paper Sultanates. Munahim came just behind him, and Indrajit was prepared at any moment to die by wasp sting, or at least to leap into combat with one of the massive insect-men, but he got all the way up and into the kitchen without encountering them at all.

The room and the building were scorched, much of the paint peeled away and the wood reduced to ash or to charred, whittled timbers.

"Dawn is here," he murmured, seeing the gray light through the shattered kitchen windows.

"Not yet." Munahim clambered out of the hearth behind him. "Soon, but not yet."

They rushed out into the yard, not waiting for the thieves to catch up.

Kattak dead and dying littered the embassy compound. They were scorched, stabbed, slashed, and chopped, and they lay grappled in death with men in studded leather armor and gray cloaks and men fighting with short clubs.

Several knots of men in gray still fought Kattak, and Indrajit and Munahim charged to the aid of the nearest. A Kattak missing two legs hovered above the marshy ground, trying to land a stinger blow on a fighter with a shield and an ax. When the Kattak lunged to stab again, Munahim swung his long sword and severed the stinger.

Indrajit sank Vacho's blade into the Kattak's thorax, and then the man in the cloak jumped forward with his ax in motion. He chopped off another pair of arms and a wing, and finally sank his ax's blade into the wasp-man's head.

The Kattak fell still.

"Thank you," the cloaked man said. It was Yuto Harlee.

Indrajit felt uncomfortable. "You might be in trouble," he warned the tavernkeeper and usurper Gray Lord. "Betel and Roberts will be out any minute."

He saw, now that he could catch his breath, that the buildings of the embassy were all on fire. How far had Fix gotten?

"I might be in trouble," Harlee admitted, "but I've done my part to save Kish."

"Are the Kattak all dead?" Indrajit asked.

"I don't know how many died below," Harlee said, "but many emerged."

"And you killed them," Munahim said.

"Of the many, we killed a few." Harlee pointed at the nearest Kattak corpse. "Many still escaped us and are on the loose."

"Frozen hells."

"Where did they go?" Munahim asked.

Harlee made a wide gesture with his ax that might have encompassed half the city. "Some flew. Some crawled. Some climbed. One leaped onto the back of a two-humped drogger and stung the beast until it burst into a gallop. We tried."

"How did you know to come here?" Indrajit asked.

"I'm a Gray Lord, and full of guile." Harlee grinned. "We pretended to leave the False Palace and then spied on you."

"In order to help?"

"I don't wish war against the other Gray Lords," Harlee said. "I just want them to acknowledge me in my place."

"Good luck with that," Indrajit said. "My much simpler hope is to survive the day."

He and Munahim threw off the cloaks that would only slow them down now, turned toward the east, and ran.

"The Lord Chamberlain is acting the role of one of the Dawn Priests this year," Indrajit said, reminding himself of what Grit Wopal had told them earlier. "The Dawn Priests meet in the East Flats and proceed in solemn march until they reach the Dregs Gate, which for today only is called by its formal name, the Dawn Gate. At noon, the Dawn Priests break through that gate and the battle proper commences."

"We go to meet the Lord Chamberlain in the East Flats," Munahim said.

"At the Stink Sook, at dawn."

"I'm afraid to ask why it's called that," the Kyone said.

Indrajit chuckled. "Guess."

Without Philastes and Fix, the two long-legged Protagonists fairly raced across the Crown. Around them, Indrajit saw signs of the Battle of Last Light in its preliminaries. Men dressed in black from head to toe, who must be Dusk Priests, assembled at corners and in small plazas, beneath banners. He couldn't read any of the writing on the banners—neither could Munahim—but seals and images told him that these were battalions sponsored and mustered by various guilds and families.

Would Orem Thrush be marching under his own banner? Or under some other flag?

"Fertilizer," Munahim guessed.

"Ah, no, there is indeed such a market," Indrajit said. "But it's located in the Caravanserai, and it's called the Emperor's Paddock. For whatever reason. Maybe the Emperor once kept cattle there, in the days when Kish had an emperor."

"Sewage?" Munahim asked.

"Fish," Indrajit told him.

"That would have been my third guess."

They rounded a corner and found a dead drogger blocking the street. Constables with shields and spears formed a loose wedge at the base of a palace; looking up, Indrajit saw a Kattak perched on the edge of the building's roof.

"Fire," he advised the constables' captain as they passed. "And show no mercy."

"But there should be more of them, shouldn't there?" Munahim asked.

"Maybe they fled," Indrajit said. "Maybe they realized that their plan was defeated and they ran away."

"Is that how the Kattak strike you? Prone to fleeing?"

"No." Indrajit increased his pace.

The Dawn Gate was manned by Handlers. Indrajit found himself struck by a sudden inspiration, and searched the faces for Mote Gannon himself, head of the Handlers. He was disappointed—the Dawn Gate garrison consisted of a Luzzazza, a scab-eyed Gund, and six Zalaptings. Wearing ceremonial black, four Dusk Priests also stood in the gate and pantomimed defending it.

Indrajit stopped in the gate to address the Handlers. "Ah . . . I know we have some history."

The Luzzazza bellowed. Was this the very one who had lost an arm to Indrajit? Indrajit tried to look regretful.

"Listen, there are Kattak all over the city," Indrajit said. "Wasp-men, the size of horses."

The Zalaptings looked at each other. "We've seen one," one of them said.

"They came to destroy Kish," Indrajit said. "It may be that their plan has basically failed."

"If you see any men bursting open and spilling larval insects on the ground," Munahim said, "kill all the larvae. And the man."

"Yes," Indrajit said. "Also . . . look, if you can spare any men from your various gate contracts, you might think seriously about seeing to the defense of your patrons. Maybe the crisis is past, but . . . maybe it's about to get crazy."

"We don't take orders from you," the Luzzazza grumped.

"Just think about it." Indrajit and Munahim passed through the gate, Indrajit speaking over his shoulder. "And tell the guys on the walls. They're not Handlers, I know, but maybe they can be useful."

The Handlers stared as Indrajit and Munahim descended into the Dregs. There were neither Dawn Priests nor Dusk Priests mustering here, just the usual strung-out addicts who happened to be awake at the end of the night, staring at nothing or asking for alms.

Indrajit wanted to turn aside and run to the Vin Dalu, to ask if Fix had made it in time, if he was healed, and what price he had had to pay. But he had no time.

The Handlers at the easternmost gate jeered Indrajit and Munahim as they passed through. The sun cracked over the plains to the east just as the two Protagonists reached the Stink Sook.

Chapter Twenty-Eight

"I don't know why you would call this odor a 'stink,'" Munahim said.

"Because of the pungent reek," Indrajit said. "The general foulness of the scent, the way the air creeps into your pockets and sticks there like tar. Because if you jumped, the smell itself would catch you midair and slow your fall."

"It just smells like fish."

"Yes," Indrajit agreed.

"Aren't your people fishers?"

"Is this a cannibalism joke you're preparing?"

"No, I mean, of all the smells to dislike . . ."

"Yes, as it happens, I don't love fish. I don't love to eat it, I don't love the smell. Oh, the irony."

The East Flats rang with the sound of trumpets, drums, and bang harps. The ordinary activities of the quarter seemed to have been suspended, so the fishing boats sat beached and unengaged, and the nets hung unmended. The men mustering for the parade played their instruments and sang, a leaping melody that broke into recurring shouts, and the fishermen standing in their doorways sang along.

Men marshaled in groups of various sizes. Some units contained as few as three men, some as many as twenty. The Dawn Priests wore white tunics and leggings, and white cloaks, all made of linen. They wore white linen masks as well, like bags over their faces, with holes cut for the eyes and another cut for breathing. Their leather sandals were stained white. Some of the costumes were more elaborate than others, with gold trim, or with gold suns stitched into the linen. They marched under banners.

"This is the Stink Sook proper," Indrajit said as they turned into the choked and winding road that led down to the water. "Look for anyone we know, or any sign of the Lord Chamberlain's presence."

"I will go out on a limb and say that's them." Munahim pointed.

At the eastern end of the Stink Sook, six banners flapped in the breeze. They hung from crossbars lashed to poles and each was carried by a man in white and gold, masked. Each man wore on his chest the blazon of one of the great houses: the flaming eye of the Lord Usher, the hammer and sword of the Lord Farrier, the leafless tree of the Lord Gardener, the rearing horse of the Lord Marshal, the noonday sun of the Lord Stargazer, and the true compass of the Lord Archer. The man wearing the Lord Stargazer's sign and carrying his banner was thin and had transparent skin, showing the muscles of his hands and forearms; the man with the banner of the Lord Stargazer was tall and broad, with hands and forearms that were violet.

Each banner-bearing man was accompanied by two more men in Dawn Priest clothing.

"That's the Lord Stargazer," Indrajit muttered to Munahim. "And the Lord Archer."

"I remember the Lord Archer." Munahim frowned.

"But where is Orem Thrush?" Indrajit scanned the sky. Were there Kattak yet to attack? If so, how and where would they do it?

He felt a tugging at his elbow, and turned to find Grit Wopal. The Yifft was dressed, as always, like a bazaar fortune-teller. He clasped his hands in front of him and cleared his throat. "You're late."

"Barely," Indrajit said. "Where's the Lord Chamberlain?"

"Come with me." Wopal turned and led the two Protagonists into a sagging hut with stone walls and a roof of brambles in knotted bundles, squatting beside the sook. Within, a fully covered Dawn Priest waited; Wopal shut the door. In one corner, a banner with a horned skull leaned against the wall. In another, a table carried two bundles of white linen and three pouches. "Today, *you* will be the Lord Chamberlain."

"What?" Indrajit choked.

"If you'd come earlier, we would have explained at leisure." Wopal shook his head. "And Fix?"

"Being tended by a healer," Indrajit said. "That's a long story."

"The Kyone will do." Wopal took the two linen bundles, tossing one to each Protagonist. "The Lords must participate. But the Lords prefer not to be targets. So you will carry the banner and wear the blazon, Indrajit. The public will take you to be the Lord Chamberlain, and you will act accordingly."

"I don't know the ritual battle," Indrajit said.

"Follow the others," the Dawn Priest said. "Follow me. I know it."

Indrajit recognized the voice. "My lord."

"Good," Wopal said. "Every Lord has a double and also a second bodyguard. The Lord is present to see that the gods' will is done, but a mummer holds the banner. Munahim will accompany as the bodyguard."

"It's the first time I'll have been a priest," Munahim said.

"Our priority is to protect the Lord Chamberlain," Indrajit said.

"Obviously." Wopal shook his head. "But you should complete the rite, too. The city expects it, and most of the city will be participating. It ought to be easy."

"Except that we may be attacked," Indrajit said. "By giant flying wasps."

"I have many sources telling me of turmoil among the Gray Lords," Wopal said.

"Yes," Indrajit said. "The Sookwalkers have a new Gray Lord. I think. And . . . maybe there will be an eighth, but that doesn't really matter right now."

"Why do you expect giant wasps?" the Lord Chamberlain asked. "Is it an assassination plot?"

"Well, I think it's more like an assault plot," Indrajit said. "I don't know that it's targeted at you, but I think it *is* targeted at the Lords of Kish. There's a burning embassy on the Street of Fallen Stars this morning because the assault has started, and we pushed to thwart it. Whether we've managed to fully—"

"What is the assault?" Thrush demanded. "What wasps?"

"Kattak," Indrajit said. "Giant wasp-men. The rulers of the Paper Sultanates, it turns out."

"I am aware of the Kattak," Thrush said. "Have the Sultanates declared war?"

"I briefed him," Wopal added.

Indrajit nodded. "We burned their nest, but many escaped; we're not sure how many. They're loose in the city, and they hate the city. I don't know if they see it as war. Maybe they see it as revenge."

"Fix is being seen by a healer . . . ?" Wopal prompted.

"He was injected with Kattak eggs," Indrajit said. "That gave him access to their plan. Ah . . . because the eggs in his belly knew about the plan, I suppose, so he shared that awareness. It's because of him that we knew to rally the Gray Lords and go burn out the Kattak."

"We have to stop the Battle of Last Light," Wopal said.

"The people expect it," Thrush said. "The gods expect it."

"Then I will go as the third Dawn Priest for House Thrush," Wopal said. "You stay out of sight."

"You can deceive the people, perhaps," Thrush said, "but Spilkar the Binder will know that we did not fulfill our obligations."

Indrajit was at a loss for words. The Lord Chamberlain had religious scruples?

"My Lord Chamberlain—" Wopal tried again.

"I insist," Thrush said. "Get dressed, men."

Indrajit pulled on the Dawn Priest garb and took the banner. Munahim struggled to get into his linens, which would have fit Fix well, but eventually got them pulled on. He had to hand his bow to Grit Wopal first, and strap his long sword awkwardly around his waist. His limbs showed to the knees and elbows, and a band of black fur was visible beneath the edge of the mask.

Once they were dressed, the Lord Chamberlain took one of the three pouches and handed one to each of the Protagonists. "The most important part is throwing candy to the children."

The Lord Chamberlain had religious scruples, and he also felt strongly about throwing candy to children.

"What do we tell the other Lords?" Indrajit asked. "About the Kattak?"

"Leave that to me," Thrush said. "I'll warn them. You keep an eye out for Kattak."

Wopal opened the door and Indrajit angled the banner down to pass through as he led the way out. "We go up through the Dregs, don't we?" he murmured to the Lord Chamberlain.

"We walk the main thoroughfares until we get into the Crown," Thrush said. "Then we followed designated paths. You will appreciate this—the routes we take are supposed to invite the sun back, but they're believed to trace actual movements of an ancient Druvash battle that took place here."

"That is fascinating," Indrajit said. "I would also appreciate it if I could draw my sword without having to tear this robe off."

"Watch out for attackers," the Lord Chamberlain reminded him. "We begin the procession now."

The man mumming the Lord Stargazer was shooing away two Zalaptings as Indrajit approached. The Lord Chamberlain came behind him and Munahim followed in the rear. The other Lords' parties stood in formation; each banner-bearer was on the right, and Indrajit now saw, by looking at wrists and forearms, that the man in the center of each row matched the banner-bearer, while the man on the left might or might not.

He turned to glance at Orem Thrush's hands and found them tinted mahogany with a hint of green, to match Indrajit's complexion. The Lord Chamberlain was wary about appearing in public without a mask, because he was of a race of man that transmuted its appearance frequently. Indrajit had had only limited experience with the phenomenon—he and Fix mostly worked with Wopal—but Thrush seemed to metamorphose to resemble, at least somewhat, the person he stood nearest. Or perhaps it was the person he was concentrating on. Or, for that matter, perhaps it was a person he chose.

At this moment, he matched Indrajit.

"At the rear," the Lord Chamberlain muttered.

Indrajit followed his direction and put himself at the back of the line. "If I caused us a loss of face by being late, so we're in the back of the procession, I'm sorry. But I had an embassy to burn."

"It is an honor to us to be in this line at all," Thrush said. "We please the gods. I suspect we also please the gods when we burn embassies, I've never known any good to come out of them."

A horn blew and the procession rumbled forward. The songs and the drumming continued, and the Lords and their companions fell quickly into a cadence. Their steps were slow and set to a length that let everyone in the group keep pace.

"Stand straight up," Thrush said to Indrajit. "Everyone thinks you're me."

"I *do* stand straight up," Indrajit objected.

"Then stand more *heroically*. Assume one of your poses."

Indrajit considered, and entered the stance called Dagger Eyes. It was appropriate for moments in the Blaatshi Epic when a noble warrior rejected something unworthy of him, or refused to comply with a weak foe's demand for surrender. He threw his shoulders back and his chest forward, and he raised his knees slightly higher as he stepped. He focused on the banner in front of him, and matched his own standard to the same angle and height.

"Better." The Lord Chamberlain leaned forward. The man in front of him had to be Bolo Bit Sodani, the Lord Stargazer. Thrush murmured words Indrajit couldn't hear.

He looked for signs of the Kattak. Searching the crowd, he didn't see Kattak or their nymphs, but he started to spot faces he recognized. Grit Wopal was in the crowd, but so was Chosk, the Lord Chamberlain's understeward and keeper of his palace's back door. He thought he recognized Zalaptings from Thrush's household guard, too, though Zalaptings were difficult to tell apart. The Lords had surrounded themselves with their household people, on top of having a double impersonate each of them and a bodyguard companion. Thrush might speak cavalierly about pleasing the gods, but he had taken precautions.

Indrajit took a deep breath. He felt a little more at ease.

He saw little hands waving, and he threw candy at them.

Chosk. Indrajit looked again. The pale man with four eyes wore his ordinary vivid purple, but he also shook a brass rattle in each hand. He mumbled along with the song, but his eyes shut as if he were fighting off sleep, and his face was twisted into a mask of pain.

His arms looked thinner than they should, and his belly was distended.

"My Lord Chamberlain," Indrajit said, "I think your understeward has been implanted with Kattak eggs."

"With what end?" Thrush asked. "Is he doomed? Should we kill him now, out of mercy?"

"Maybe he can be saved," Indrajit said. "By the Vin Dalu. If we can get him there in time."

"Where is 'there'?"

Indrajit hesitated, then nodded at the city wall they were approaching. "In the Dregs, actually."

"We'll look for an opportunity," Thrush suggested. "Maybe Wopal can take him. I must walk this path, and you must impersonate me."

"Ironic, I suppose."

"Oh?" The Lord Chamberlain's voice was cold.

"Since you are impersonating me." Indrajit immediately felt he had said something impolite. "I mean, you and I look alike . . . at the moment. We look similar."

"How do we look similar, Blaatshi?" Thrush asked. "Have you become handsome?"

"We . . ." Indrajit coughed, trying not to disrupt his pose. He took the appearance of Fanchee children in leather kilts as an opportunity to interrupt the conversation, throw a fistful of candy, and catch his balance. "We are both Dawn Priests," he said.

"We are both Dawn Priests," Thrush agreed. "Only I am really a priest, as a Lord of Kish."

Indrajit decided not to bring up the fact that his calling as Recital Thane was of a priestly nature. "Yes," he said.

The gate drew near. The jobbers at the gate were probably still Gannon's Handlers, but they wore gray-dyed linen over their livery now. A line of them stood perpendicular to the gate, each holding a long-stemmed flower in his hand.

The sun was slowly climbing toward zenith, but that moment was still hours away.

"These men must be defeated," Thrush said.

"They only have flowers," Indrajit said.

"Ritual combat," Thrush reminded him. "By the time you reach the gate, only one will be standing. You will slap him in the face and shout, 'House Thrush'!"

"How hard?" Indrajit asked.

"You must make a noise the gods can hear," Thrush said. "Hard. Don't worry, they're part of the ritual, too, and they know it."

Indrajit watched the front of his procession pass the line of men and enter the gate. The first two banner-bearers slapped Zalaptings loudly, and the lavender-skinned men spun and dropped. Surely, their rotation was exaggerated—it was drama rather than the result of a truly violent blow.

Indrajit threw candy at a crowd of Zalaptings that he thought included children. He looked to the sky as he rained sweets on them. "Go home," he muttered. "Take the candy and go!"

He threw more their way to encourage them, but they just yelled louder.

The third man slapped was an Ildarian and the fourth a squinting, wind-burned Valkali. Indrajit hadn't realized the Handlers included a Lost Northerner, but the man took his slap and went down instantly. The fifth was another Zalapting, the sixth a Yuchak, and only at the last minute did Indrajit realize who stood at the end of the line to take his slap.

It was a hulking, blue-skinned Luzzazza.

The Luzzazza whose arm Indrajit had caused to be yanked from its socket? Surely not.

"House Ne'eku!" The Zalapting struck by the Lord Archer's surrogate spun three times on his heels and fell, to the cheer of the crowd. "House Sodani!" The Yuchak was smitten by the Lord Stargazer's double and dropped backward like a felled tree, not bending until he struck the cobbles. Indrajit shifted his banner into his left hand, preparing to make the slap.

"Indrajit Twang," the Luzzazza grunted.

Indrajit raised his hand almost as high as he could, and slapped the Luzzazza hard in the face.

The Luzzazza stood still.

Indrajit froze.

The front part of the procession kept moving, but the last three rows hesitated. The Lord Stargazer turned to see what had happened.

Thrush nudged Indrajit with an elbow.

"House Thrush!" Indrajit yelled.

The Luzzazza roared, real rage and humiliation in his voice. He stomped backward three steps, then sat down hard on the stone. The crowd cheered again.

Indrajit quickened his step to get through the gate.

The Dregs did not share the enthusiasm of the East Flats. Jobbers on the walls emitted perfunctory huzzahs, but the denizens of the Dregs seemed mostly to be ignoring the procession and its accompanying crowd. Jeers and catcalls cut through the ordinary hubbub of haggling and cursing to announce their arrival.

There were children here, too, in canvas smocks. They hefted balls of mud in their hands. "Give us candy!" they screamed.

"Well," the Lord Chamberlain muttered, "*most* of Kish is participating. Each in his own fashion."

Indrajit threw candy. One of the boys picked up sweets and then threw his mudball at Indrajit, anyway.

A whip cracked somewhere ahead of the procession. It cracked again twice more. Despite his height, Indrajit couldn't see over the men in front of him. He tried standing on his toes, and all he saw was a jostling crowd.

"Drogger!" someone yelled. "Drogger stampede!"

The crowd before Indrajit didn't part, it evaporated. Each person in the crowd took on energy and exploded, bouncing in random directions. The Dawn Priest Procession sagged to the right, onto a scrap of dirt that almost made a plaza in the angle where two alleys broke away from the street. A woman selling coal shrieked at them in rage and hurled several chunks of her wares; one struck Indrajit in the side of the head and he winced, but he stayed focused on the street ahead of him.

Three droggers came galumphing toward him. One had two humps, but they all had the long neck and the rubbery skin of their kind, and they all had panic in their eyes. One dragged a wagon, but its rear gate was open and casks fell, bouncing and cracking open on the gravel. The other two dragged shattered traces as if they too had borne loads, but they had shaken them off.

"Fire!" Indrajit heard. "Fire!"

Behind the droggers, flame and smoke licked around the corner into view. The flames were rushing toward them, drinking up the spilled liquid from the casks and growing taller and hotter.

The crowd around the procession screamed. Some fainted, others shivered where they stood, and many tried to flee. Curses and the sounds of fighting broke out at the gate.

"Do we have to walk it straight?" Indrajit asked Orem Thrush.

"What?" Thrush asked.

"Crossing the Dregs." The flames raced in their direction. One of the droggers fell, tangled in his traces, and the fire overtook him. His squeals of panic became bellows of pain. "Do we have to stick to the main street and walk straight across? For the Battle of Last Light, to please the gods."

Thrush shook his head. "We just have to get to the Dawn Gate." He looked up at the sky. "In about an hour."

"This way!" Indrajit waved his banner and headed to the nearest alley mouth.

Chapter Twenty-Nine

The procession followed him.

As he ran, Indrajit bounced the standard pole within the crook of his elbow, managing to keep it upright despite knocking it against brick walls right and left. That freed his right hand, and he managed to work it up under the skirts of his own linen robe, grab the hilt of Vacho, and rip the sword free.

Halfway down the alley, a small triangular plaza let in a little light, and Indrajit stopped to look back. Munahim had ripped off his skirts almost entirely, but held his sword free and upright before him; the Kyone turned to position himself between the Lord Chamberlain and the alley mouth. The rest crowded into the plaza. All the banners were upright, everyone still dressed in linen, but Indrajit had the sensation that some of the standards were being held by different hands.

Looking past the procession, he saw corpses in linen lying at the edge of the street. One was burned, one was crushed, as if trampled by droggers or run over by a wagon. The third . . . just lay still. Indrajit couldn't see what had killed the man.

Linen masks confronted him. "Who knows a way through the alleys?" he asked.

No one said anything. He looked for Grit Wopal and couldn't find him; had the Yifft been killed also, or separated from the procession when the droggers had run amok?

"No problem," Indrajit said, "because I do." He pointed. "I'm pretty sure if we go that way, we'll get onto the long corner, and that will take us right to the gate."

"Who put this idiot in charge?" a Dawn Priest snarled.

The Lord Archer's standard-bearer guffawed. "This is your creature, Orem. Are you going to restrain him, or shall I?"

But then Indrajit realized that there was only one large, violet-skinned man in the group. Which presumably meant that the Lord Archer's standard-bearer was dead, and this man was Arda Ne'eku himself.

"I'm in charge," Orem Thrush growled.

Indrajit heard a metallic ring as something struck Thrush in the chest. The Lord Chamberlain took a sudden step back, then patted around under his robe, and brought his hand out holding a dart.

So Thrush was wearing armor, at least. If all the Lords were, that might give them an important edge.

"It may be poisoned," Munahim said.

"This way!" Indrajit turned and charged down the alley. "Assassins! Run!"

Turning his head to the side, he could look with his widely spaced eyes at the edges of the rooftops. He saw the silhouette of a man in a short cape, running to keep pace with the procession. He held a long stick in his hand, which might be a rod . . . or a blowgun.

He heard a distant hum. Was it the sound of the fire, or of keening droggers in pain, distorted by the intervening city?

He wished for Munahim's bow. He wished that Philastes were present, with his sling and his ability to pick up a projectile off the ground anywhere he went. He wished that his own eyes were closer together so that he could use any kind of missile weapon with accuracy. But all his wishes were in vain and he knew it.

"Follow me closely!" he called.

He stuck close to the wall beneath the caped man. The eaves weren't wide, but they should be enough to protect him. He skinned his shoulder against the wall running, then held his breath as he darted across the street.

He heard the steely *clink* as a dart struck the cobbles near him.

The street widened. Ahead, Indrajit saw flames at the mouth of the alley. To his left, another alley opened.

Without giving a warning, Indrajit turned left and veered across the street. Laundry hanging on lines overhead gave him a little notional cover, but mostly, he wanted to force the assassin to backtrack or come down to ground level, to follow.

As the procession raced across the street to follow him, he picked up a stone and threw it. Embarrassingly, it struck the wall two ells beneath the caped man's feet. Still, he threw himself flat on the roof tiles, and the procession crossed unmolested.

They raced down the alley. A shadow crossed Indrajit as he ran; had the assassin caught up so quickly? Or did the man have confederates?

And who was it? He didn't think any of the Gray Lords would want to kill him anymore, but maybe he underestimated their anger or resentment toward him. The Handlers? The Lord Archer had been very dismissive of him. Who would be sending an assassin after Indrajit?

Although, previously, the killer had seemed to attack Fix in particular. Was this a murderer intent on killing Fix, and attacking Indrajit as a second-best? Or attacking Indrajit because he thought he could get to Fix that way?

The alley ended in a square plaza. A crumbling stone well squatted in the center of the muddy pen. Two doors opened onto the plaza, both shut, and three balconies with iron railings looked down from the second story, darkened doorways opening on each. Two more balconies peered down from the third story.

That was a lot of balconies to be staring down at a patch of mud.

Indrajit turned to look back up the alleyway by which they'd come, and saw the short-caped man raising his blowgun. Indrajit threw himself sideways, into the shelter of the corner of a building, and heard a dart whiz past him, disappearing into the mud.

Munahim hurled his bag of candy at the man with the blowgun, causing him to duck for cover.

Indrajit tried each door, and they were barred. He spun about to face the procession.

"We climb!" he called. "Munahim, help me—we hoist the Lords up onto that balcony there. Quickly now, before the sharpshooter can double back!"

"Which balcony?" Munahim held his sword up in a defensive position. "Indrajit?"

Indrajit turned his back to the alley to see what Munahim was looking at. A Kattak crept forward, emerging from the darkness of one doorway and then leaping to perch on the iron balustrade.

Indrajit saw more Kattak behind the first, and wished again for missile weapons. Or for a friendly Gund.

In the corner of his vision, he could see both of the other lower-level balconies. At the same moment, Kattak leaped from the shadows to perch on the rail.

"Arm yourselves!" Indrajit snapped to the procession. Most of the men drew swords or daggers. A few stood with empty hands, crouched uncertainly, or gripped standard poles. Orem Thrush drew a long knife, and also took the standard from Indrajit. To the Kattak, he called out, "Whatever you thought you would accomplish, it's over! Go home!"

"We *are* home," a Kattak hissed.

"What is over is your friend Fix," one of the Kattak called back. Indrajit thought he recognized the voice of Chach-shazzat. Though really, the voice was so inhuman, could it have any personal character at all? "He has given birth now, and he is one of us."

"He is *many* of us," another Kattak said.

The Kattak laughed. It was a hideous rattling sound, dusty and sharp at the same time.

"You don't know that," Indrajit said. To the Lords and their men, he barked, "Get into a circle. Use the banners like spears, to push them away. Don't let them attack us from above. Make them approach on the ground!"

"You don't know what we know," Chach-shazzat taunted Indrajit. "But you could. Wouldn't you like to?"

"This may have been your home once, but you can't take it back!" Was it possible that Fix was dead? It certainly was. Indrajit tried not to think too much about that idea. "There are too many men here! Too many thousands!"

"Every man a walking womb," Chach-shazzat called back. "We delight in Kish's abundance of men!"

Should he direct the Dawn Priests Procession to climb down the well? If they were lucky, there might be enough light down there to be able to navigate. Or, if they weren't pressured by the Kattak, Munahim was able to maneuver in the darkness of Underkish. If he wasn't following his own scent, maybe he wouldn't be able to navigate great distances, but there would be other scents he could follow. But if they went down into the darkness, and the Kattak followed, they might be pressed into a corner and unable to see the monsters that massacred them.

Indrajit found the latter possibility depressingly likely.

"We go into the well," he murmured to the Lord Chamberlain, "but only as a last resort."

"You are amusing," Chach-shazzat called. "We'll let you go, Blaatshi. You and the Kyone. You walk away, and we'll deal with these upstarts. We'll give Kish a lesson it will never forget, a lesson that will mark the beginning of a new era in Kish."

"You're stalling," Indrajit shot back. "Because you know you can't take us."

Chach-shazzat made a rapid clicking noise and hummed at the same time. His wings flapped rapidly, but he stayed gripped to the railing. "I *was* stalling, so that our reinforcements could arrive."

Indrajit looked up, and saw Kattak heads peep out on the edges of the rooftops, in ragged but quick succession, until the open sky above was entirely ringed with insectoid skulls.

The Kattak attacked.

They dropped without clear strategy from the sky, leaping over the muddy plaza and not even flapping their wings. Not without strategy, Indrajit realized. With a strategy that gave not one orichalk, not one sesterce, not one Imperial bit of value to the life of the individual. The swarm would throw away any number of individual Kattak lives to get what the Kattak collectively wanted.

If they all died, they could kill the Lords of Kish by crushing them with the weight of their corpses.

Indrajit fought with slashing strokes; now was no time to risk getting his sword stuck in a foeman's corpse. He sliced deep into the face of one Kattak, sending it swerving against the stone wall, where it hissed like a boiling kettle and ground itself in a tight, muddy circle. He stepped sideways and sliced through the thorax of a second wasp-man, amputating its stinger. When the Kattak landed beside him on the ground, shrieking in pain, Indrajit put a second swipe of his sword through its insectoid neck, severing its head.

Around him, the Lords and their men stabbed and slashed and poked. Kattak hit the mud, bounced, and lay still. Others winged away wildly, blinded or mad with pain.

Indrajit sliced into the abdomen of a Kattak, three times in quick succession, until it lay still. He stood surrounded by heaps of the dead, not because the corpses were so numerous, but because they were so large.

"The bodies!" he cried. "Shove them aside!"

"Into the pit!" the Lord Chamberlain barked.

The Lord Archer, who was the biggest man present, together with a burly northman of some sort, picked up a Kattak and heaved it into the well. Then each man separately grabbed a wasp-man and threw him in.

"They're big," Ne'eku yelled, "but they weigh little!"

Defenders fell. One man lost his thigh to Kattak mandibles and collapsed in gouts of blood, dark red against his muddy white linens. Another took a stinger through the chest—was that the Lord Farrier, or his double? A third was seized by two Kattak and lifted off the ground. He fought back fiercely, stabbing the belly of each Kattak as they rose, and forcing them to drop him. He landed across the stone lip of the well, a marionette without strings.

Two more men joined the crew removing bodies, but they couldn't move them fast enough. Horse-sized wasp corpses piled up.

Indrajit slashed Vacho through a Kattak's face, but found a second Kattak immediately behind. He couldn't get his arm out wide enough to slash again, so he did the only thing he could, and stabbed.

He pierced the Kattak through the abdomen. It died in a spasm and a burst of ichor, but it also landed on top of him. Ne'eku was right, the Kattak didn't weigh as much as a horse did—but it was still heavy, and it knocked Indrajit to the ground. He fell splayed on the mud, arms wide, sword pinned under the dead wasp-man.

With a high-pitched hiss, another Kattak fell toward him.

The severed stinger was within his grasp. Indrajit seized it with both hands, braced it against his chest, and pointed the sharp tip at the enemy.

The Kattak died impaled through the face and wailing.

Indrajit dragged himself from beneath the first Kattak with Orem Thrush's help. Munahim made it possible by shoving aside one of the bodies and then cracking another attacker's head with his sword. Indrajit picked up Vacho and shook off the worst of the mud.

Half the party lay dead, crushed, severed, impaled, mangled.

"The alley," Indrajit gasped. "We take the risk of the assassin."

"The alley is full of wasps." Thrush's voice was calm. "We die here, poet. We make a bold stand, such as will be remembered. Such as will inspire Kish to resist these monsters. Such as will be sung of in your Epic for ages to come."

"No one will sing the Epic for ages to come." Indrajit said it, and tears ran down his cheeks. "The Blaatshi Epic has been sung for the last time."

"Let's get against the wall." Munahim pointed to the wall facing the center of the Dregs. "By that door. We will have less sky to defend against. Better, given our smaller numbers."

Munahim's white linens were entirely gone. He bled from multiple wounds, but he gave no sign that he noticed them.

"To the wall!" Thrush bellowed. "Rally around the door!" He raised his banner and waved it back and forth.

The Lord Archer and the Lord Stargazer each shoved another Kattak into the well; so at least three Lords of Kish still lived. Indrajit smashed aside a dropping Kattak and turned to the door, but then saw movement at the well.

"Kattak!" he howled. It was a pointless thing to yell, since there were Kattak all around, living and dead. Ne'eku didn't respond at all, but slowly moved toward the door, rallying to the Lord Chamberlain's banner.

Behind him, three Kattak climbed out of the well.

Had they been thrown in as casualties, but not really been dead? Or were the Kattak swarming up through Underkish?

Did it matter?

Indrajit took advantage of a gap in the attack and strode toward the wall and the door. The door sat beneath a balcony, which would also give them a little shelter from attack. Not that it mattered. Thrush was right: they were doomed.

"Assassin!" Munahim barked.

Indrajit spun and found the man in the short cape. He stood on a balcony above the one swarming with Kattak, and he aimed his blowgun at Indrajit. Indrajit had no cover. He swung Vacho, hoping for a miracle, hoping that he could intercept the tiny dart midair.

"Protagonists!" someone yelled.

Someone who wasn't Munahim.

Across the plaza, across the two stories of separation, despite the air full of dropping wasps, Indrajit saw the assassin's cheeks puff. He swung Vacho again.

A Kattak, dropping to Indrajit's right, lurched sideways. It swerved across the space between Indrajit and the assassin, and behind it, Indrajit saw the Lord Chamberlain's banner. No dart touched Indrajit.

Orem Thrush had batted the Kattak with his standard, and knocked it into the path of the assassin's dart.

"Protagonists!" Thrush yelled.

"Protagonists!" Fix yelled in his high-pitched voice.

Fix?

Fix appeared on the balcony with the assassin. He attacked with ax and falchion both. The blowgun fell to the balcony floor, bounced, and then dropped into the plaza. The assassin dodged the first two attacks and then drew a slender scimitar.

Philastes was at Fix's side, sling spinning. He struck two Kattak quickly, and then the wasp-men regrouped, a portion of them swarming to attack the balcony where Fix and Philastes fought.

"Against the wall!" Thrush bellowed.

The surviving Lords of Kish and their servants complied, backing into a defensive semicircle against the brick. It was a pitifully shrunken remnant of the original Dawn Priests Procession. Ten men, maybe?

Indrajit wanted to rush up and help Fix and Philastes, but he could barely spare them a glance. Between the bodies of leaping Kattak and over the heads and wings of Kattak boiling out of the well, he saw flashes of color. A savage battle raged on the balcony—Fix and his foe slammed each other against walls and against the railing. Both men slashed, both bled. Philastes was busy with his sling, keeping attacking wasp-men from overwhelming all three of them.

Indrajit cut down a Kattak but a second leaped on him, grappling his two arms with its four. The insectoid face leaned in close, mandibles the size of short swords clacking repeatedly, a handsbreadth from Indrajit's own nose.

The Lord Archer came to his rescue. The big, lavender-skinned man grabbed the Kattak by its two mandibles and then tore them apart, ripping them entirely from the waspish face. Ichor poured onto Indrajit's chest. The Kattak spasmed, but Ne'eku grabbed its thorax and jammed it downward, sinking the stinger into the mud and trapping the wasp-man. Then with a single pivoting motion, he ripped off the Kattak's head and hurled it at the incoming enemies.

He bled from multiple wounds, too.

"It is a loss that no one will tell this story," Thrush said.

"Someone will make up a better one," Bolo Bit Sodani said. "Even a corrupt old pile of rot like this one needs heroes."

"Welcome to Kish," Munahim said.

Were there eight of them still standing? Seven?

Kattak from the rooftops sprang into the air en masse, darkening the sky in their descent.

Indrajit braced himself to receive the charge.

He heard the door behind him open.

Chapter Thirty

The darkness fell and fire broke it.

For long and confused seconds, Indrajit didn't know where the flame had come from. Did one of the survivors of the Dawn Priest Procession have a magical gift with fire? Or some sorcerous device? Had the fire in the streets—set by the Kattak, he thought—burned its way through the building?

The fire burned and he staggered aside. He expected to die, burned or crushed or impaled.

Instead, the fire rose into the sky and shattered the Kattak assault.

Wiping sweat from his eyes, he saw Gannon's Handlers. The Handlers, and the Huachao. They had torches, buckets of pitch, bows and arrows, and javelins. The first wave of flaming missiles they launched upward stopped the Kattak, sending several away on fire and dropping many dead into the candy-speckled mud. But then they continued, not in waves but in a ragged and constant barrage. Kattak hissed and shrieked and fled and died.

"There will be fires in the city," Bolo Bit Sodani said solemnly.

"There is a fire constabulary contract," Thrush said. "It was doubled for the festival, as always."

Indrajit's knees wobbled. "Thank you," he said, to no Handler in particular and to all of them.

A Luzzazza stalked up to him, mud sucking at his sandals.

"Thank you," Indrajit said.

The Luzzazza slapped him in the face, knocking him to his knees. "I am no longer on the path."

Indrajit stayed down. For one thing, he felt too tired to stand.

Also, he didn't want another fight, especially not with one of the jobbers who had just saved his life. "Sorry to hear that," he said.

"Fix," Munahim said, before plunging into the open door.

The Handlers and the Huachao continued to apply fire to the Kattak. Two Huachao hurled buckets of pitch down the well and then several others, including the pridechief Budhrriao, launched flaming arrows in after them.

Budhrriao snarled at Indrajit. It felt like a friendly greeting.

Indrajit followed Munahim.

They raced through an off-kilter warren of brick rooms. They smelled occupied, and filthy, but whoever slept on the cots and bedrolls and ate off the leaning tables had vacated, at least for the moment. Indrajit heard feet behind him and looked back to see one of the surviving Dawn Priests, or maybe a bodyguard—a man in white linen, holding a sword.

They wound their way through a tenement, and eventually found a door that was opening just as they arrived. Philastes let them in; he was bloodied and filthy and he held a stone in the pouch of his sling, ready to shoot, but he was grinning.

Indrajit looked at the man following him and saw a tall, lean fellow, with a Kishi complexion. He wore the true compass of the Lord Archer on his chest.

On the balcony, Fix knelt on the chest of the assassin. After all the struggle against this would-be killer, Indrajit was disappointed that in person, the man seemed weak and defeated. He breathed with difficulty and Fix gripped him by the hair. Ax, falchion, and scimitar all lay on the floor of a room that was otherwise full of crates and the smell of dirty straw.

"Tell me a name," Fix said.

"No." The assassin grinned, teeth bloody.

"Tell me a name and you live."

"You fool." The assassin laughed. "There's no chance I survive. I failed and I have been caught."

"I'll protect you."

"You can't protect me," the assassin said. "You don't even know who you'd be protecting me from."

"You're from the House of Knives," Fix said.

"I don't deny it."

"Sent by one of the Gray Lords?"

"Stop wasting your time," the assassin said. "I won't tell you."

"Hired by a rival jobber company?" Fix pressed. "What did I do to anger them?"

The assassin guffawed, choking.

"Some Paper Sook fraudster we stopped?" Indrajit asked. "Someone whose smuggled shipment we impounded?"

The assassin laughed.

"Eion Osiah?" Fix sat up, straddling the man. "Did Eion Osiah hire the House of Knives to kill me?"

That might explain why the assassin had seemed to want Fix's death more than Indrajit's.

The assassin hesitated, then opened his mouth.

"Chode!" The Lord Archer's bodyguard leaped forward. In one sudden motion, he sliced through the assassin's neck, severing his head from his body.

Fix sprang to his feet. "What do you think you're doing?"

The bodyguard, face still obscured with a linen mask, wiped blood off on his Dawn Priest robe. "The Lord Archer's bidding. This man and his guild will not trouble you again."

He sheathed his sword and walked out.

Fix stepped briskly to follow the bodyguard, but Indrajit moved into his way.

"That man knows something," Fix growled.

"He does," Indrajit said. "He clearly does. Chode was the name the assassin gave to Illiot. Also, he's the Lord Archer's bodyguard."

"Who is Illiot?"

Indrajit explained.

"But—"

"Let it go, Fix."

Grit Wopal had only one comment, after the Battle of Last Light was over and the Lord Chamberlain safe in his palace, and Wopal had ordered the Protagonists to recount the three preceding days in detail as he gazed upon them with his third eye.

"You Protagonists grow symmetrically," the Yifft said. "Two men with large noses, and two with animal heads."

Indrajit and Fix stood at Zac Betel's forge as the Gray Lord of the Sootfaces immersed an iron blade into water, then examined it, and set it aside.

"Eventful day, yesterday," Betel said. His men stood guard, but at a distance that granted the two Protagonists a measure of privacy. "A lot of fires."

"A lot of deaths," Fix added. "The Lord Chamberlain's understeward was saved, and the Lord Stargazer's night steward. Many others were lost."

"I'm composing an episode for the Epic now," Indrajit said. "To be fair, that's supposed to be the task of the Recital Thane who follows my successor, but at least I can hand down some notes for him to work on." He hesitated. "And, of course, there's no guarantee I'll have a successor."

"The best account is always that of an eyewitness," Betel said.

Indrajit nodded. "It's hard to make the lines about squishing Kattak nymphs underfoot scan. There are already lots of good lines to describe the fires, fortunately. And you're in it."

"Perhaps not wise," Betel suggested.

"Not by name," Indrajit said. "And not as a Gray Lord. As a noble blacksmith, from whose fires the resistance to the insect invaders arose. Not false."

"Not true, either," Betel said.

"Poetically true."

Betel harrumphed.

"Apparently, enough of the Dawn Priests emerged from the Dregs to finish the Battle of Last Light," Indrajit said. "To the priests' satisfaction, at least, which hopefully means that Spilkar and the other gods are also pleased."

"The city is saved, so they still exist." Betel shrugged. "How can they be *dis*pleased?"

Indrajit nodded. "The city is saved, so we all still exist."

"We're here to make sure that we're at peace with the Conclave," Fix said.

"You work for the Lord Chamberlain," Betel said. "Maybe I shouldn't say anything to you."

"We work for the Lord Chamberlain," Indrajit agreed. "Isn't it better that we know each other? Don't you want the Lord Chamberlain to keep the peace in Kish?"

"More or less," Betel agreed. "You shouldn't imagine that I'm in your debt."

"We don't," Indrajit said.

"Are the Sookwalkers in good standing?" Fix asked. "Yuto Harlee is part of the Conclave?"

"The Conclave has yet to gather since the meeting at which you participated," Betel said. "But it is the general view of the Gray Lords that Yuto Harlee should be made to feel uncomfortable, and then, without any official approbation, admitted into normal dealings with the rest of us."

Indrajit nodded.

"And Jaxter Boom?" Indrajit asked.

"He conspired against the Conclave," Betel said.

"He conspired to *enter* the Conclave," Indrajit said. "I'm not sure that's quite the same thing."

"Why do you care?" The Luzzazza Gray Lord of the Sootfaces folded his visible arms and squinted at Indrajit.

"At the end, his Huachao fighters were part of the group that rescued us," Indrajit said. "With Gannon's Handlers. Broke through to where we were pinned down and drove away the Kattak with fire. Saved most of the Lords of Kish, and us personally. Maybe saved the city, I suppose."

"They helped the Handlers find us there," Fix added. "They know the Dregs well."

"Did they do it at Boom's direction?" Betel asked.

"No idea," Indrajit said. "Budhrriao and his pride vanished as soon as the fight was over."

"We'll enter into negotiations with Jaxter Boom," Betel said. "We'll see how the negotiations go."

"And are we . . . marked men?" Fix asked.

Betel laughed, a deep rumble. "You enforce the law at the direction of the Lord Chamberlain. Are you asking me whether some of Kish's thieves, or even some of her Gray Lords, may hold a grudge against you? Or may seek to stop you in the future? I'd say that's fairly certain."

Indrajit nodded. "Fair enough."

"But." Betel raised a finger. "But, no one will take revenge on you for anything that's happened in the last three days. The Gray Lords have agreed it. Harlee will agree, if he wants to join us. So will Boom."

"Thank you," Indrajit said.

Betel inclined his head. "Thank *you*."

"Marek Kotzin?" Indrajit asked. "Toru Zing?"

"Beneath my notice," Betel said. "As they should be beneath yours."

"I have one last question," Fix said. "Do you know anything about a House of Knives assassin who was sent to try to murder us? And maybe specifically sent to murder *me*?"

"I didn't do that," Betel said. "I doubt any of the Gray Lords would do it. We have our own men, why tangle with the mysterious House of Knives?"

"I thought so." Fix sighed.

"What are you going to do about that?" Betel asked.

"We think we know who did it," Indrajit said. "We're going to pay him a visit."

The four Protagonists made their way across the rooftop of Eion Osiah's palace. Philastes was surefooted as well as a good climber, and didn't slow them down a bit. The night sky overhead was deep and cold, and Indrajit found it relaxing.

A nice change of pace from three manic days.

"I think I should go first," Indrajit said, when they lowered the rope. He had an additional length of rope this time, coiled over his shoulder.

"You're worried I'll kill him," Fix suggested.

"Should I not be worried? Our warrant is to grab Osiah and deliver him to the Lord Chamberlain to face trial."

"Okay, you can go first," Fix conceded.

"Maybe I should take Munahim with me, and you should stay up here on the rooftop with Philastes."

"Maybe you should get sliding down that rope."

Munahim and Philastes took up their positions with sling and bow, watching for uninvited guests. Munahim's bow was new and he had a quiver full of new arrows, and he had spent two hours in the afternoon shooting at straw targets in the courtyard of the Protagonists' inn. Indrajit slid down to the balcony where Osiah's children slept and checked the room inside; they breathed deeply. Fix followed close on his heels.

"Funny how the warrant is for kidnapping and assault," Indrajit said. "No mention of hiring an assassin to kill us. Or kill you, anyway."

"I think that's going to be quietly swept under the carpet," Fix said. "For reasons of state."

Indrajit snorted. "Don't you mean, for reasons of who exactly is the Lord Knife after all?"

"That's the same thing."

"What was being healed like?" Indrajit asked. "By the Vin Dalu, I mean?"

"I felt sick," Fix said. "I thought I was going to explode. I could feel my flesh being eaten from the inside. Then they put me in the Girdle of Life and activated the device."

"Cast their spell."

Fix shrugged. "I felt hot, and then intensely nauseated, and then both sensations passed. There was fire in the Dregs, so Philastes and I came running."

"Glad you did."

"I have passed dead Kattak nymphs in my stool," Fix said.

"I didn't need to know that," Indrajit said. "That's not going in the Epic. And I'm not going to tell Munahim, either. He's way too interested in that sort of thing."

"He had a similar experience."

"I didn't need to know that, either."

"Shh, let's go get Osiah."

They tiptoed across the children's room; the rhythmic breathing continued unchanged.

"It occurs to me that I lost track of Danel Avchat," Indrajit murmured, when they were in the bean merchant's hall. "Did he stay with the Vin Dalu?"

"He was terrified to leave," Fix said. "So I told Grit Wopal to take him into custody. For his own protection. No doubt Wopal is having him generate map after map of Underkish as we speak, for use by the Lord Chamberlain's Ears. Perhaps one of those will come back to us."

"And Alea?" Indrajit whispered. They had rescued her from a secret room on this very floor of this very building. Well, not rescued her. Collected her dead body.

"She's lost some hair and struggles to keep food down," Fix said. "She's weak and says she feels fragile."

"So she's with the Vin Dalu? Being treated? Recovering?"

"She returned home. To her husband."

"Will you see her again?" Indrajit asked.

They peeked into doorways by the light of a small lamp burning in the hallway niche. Indrajit remembered that there was a bedroom on this floor, but he didn't recall exactly where it was. Earlier in the evening, they had spent hours hidden inside a rented Rover wagon, watching until they saw Eion Osiah come home and go upstairs.

"I don't know."

"Does she know what you went through? To rescue her, I mean? You were injected with wasp eggs. You nearly died yourself."

"So did you." Fix hesitated. "I don't think she knows. I doubt she does. I certainly didn't tell her."

Indrajit shook his head. "You're being surprisingly cavalier about all this."

"Funny," Fix said, "I don't feel cavalier at all."

Indrajit pointed at the next door. "This is it. I'm pretty sure."

"Be ready with the rope," Fix whispered.

There was no knob, just a simple brass latch that could be lifted from either side. Fix raised the latch and opened the door a handsbreadth; they both listened.

Deep breathing sounds.

Fix nodded and swung the door open. Well oiled, it swung wide without a creak.

Within, a wide canopied bed filled the center of the room. Hallways led away to washrooms; Indrajit could see a washbasin through one opening and a bath through another. Against the walls stood vanities and cupboards of various sort. Mirrors hung in several corners. Niches the height of a man stood in every wall, with white statues of Haduri standing in them. Some looked like warriors, others like kings, others like farmers. Haduri gods? Indrajit gave them barely a glance, and focused on the bed.

Two long lumps under the cushions, and slow breathing.

Indrajit uncoiled his rope, prepared to tie Osiah up, and to tie up his wife, as well. Some servant would free her in the morning, but there was no point in letting her sound an alarm in the meantime.

Each Protagonist grabbed an edge of the thick winter blanket covering the bed. Counting down from three with gestures, they pulled the blanket back at the same time.

Beneath it lay a Haduri woman in a night dress. She continued to breathe deeply, and made no sign that she was awake. Beside her lay not Eion Osiah, but a collection of bolsters.

"Don't move, or I kill you."

The voice came from behind them and above. It was Osiah's voice.

"The Lord Chamberlain wants to talk to you," Fix said.

"I wager he does," Osiah said. "Drop the rope, hands up, and turn around slowly."

Indrajit turned to see that Haduri bean merchant standing in one of the wall niches. His skin was caked with some thick white concealer. He wore a sword at his side, and held a double-layered crossbow.

"You're just making trouble for yourself, Osiah," Fix said. "If we don't bring you in, another jobber company will come next. And if you kill us, the next jobbers will be bigger and meaner. Come along, stand trial, and your family can live unmolested."

"I wonder if the Lord Chamberlain would be interested in a trade," Osiah said.

"For us?" Fix shook his head. "No."

"Hey," Indrajit said, "I feel like I'm worth something."

"To Thrush?" Fix laughed.

"Hey."

"Walk." Osiah climbed down from his perch, stepping first onto a vanity and then a stool and then a chair, descending without ever removing his aim from the Protagonists. "You know where my special little room is. Let's go there."

"Is this your wife?" Fix asked. "Does she know what you're doing? Maybe she'd like you to cooperate?"

The Haduri chuckled. "That's my wife. She'll sleep until the morning like a corpse, thanks to the potions I slipped her. I'm an expert at knocking women unconscious."

"Of course," Indrajit said. "You Haduri are really charming."

"I am as the gods made me." Osiah shrugged. "Now go, or I shoot you and just keep the short one as a bargaining chip."

"I'm not short," Fix complained.

Indrajit and Fix exited the bedroom and turned, heading toward the office and the secret room. Indrajit whistled, but would Munahim really hear? Even with his keen ears?

"Shut up," Osiah snarled.

Indrajit reached the office door. He and Fix turned.

Osiah stood in the center of the hallway, facing them with his crossbow. "So, back where we started. I could take you to trade with. But I feel like I would really enjoy killing you. Or at least one of you."

As the Haduri spoke, a door behind him opened slowly and quietly. Munahim and Philastes crept through. Their feet were bare and their hands were empty.

"I think the trading option is a good idea," Indrajit said. "But if you really feel the need to shoot someone, let us help. We can find someone who deserves it."

Munahim tiptoed to stand directly behind Osiah. His nostrils flared. Philastes crouched at his side.

"Oh, believe me," Osiah said. "You deserve it."

Munahim reached his long arms around Osiah, grabbed the crossbow and yanked it upward, to point at the ceiling. The bolts both launched, cracking against the ceiling and then angling downward and down the hall. Munahim continued his motion, dragging the Haduri's hands up and falling backward, until he toppled over and landed on his back, Osiah clutched to his chest and squirming.

Philastes leaped astride Osiah and clamped his hands over the bean merchant's mouth.

"Get the rope," Munahim grunted.

Fix sneaked back for the rope.

"You guys didn't hear me whistle," Indrajit said.

"We did," Philastes told him. "But we were already down here."

"You didn't wait," Indrajit said.

"After the last three days," Philastes said, "it seemed like a good idea to stick close."

Fix returned with the rope.

"Let's tie this piece of garbage up and get him out of here," Indrajit said. He took the rope and began to bind the Haduri.

"You didn't stay where you were supposed to," Fix said. "If you're down here, who has our backs?"

"Obviously," Munahim told him, "*we* do."